TEARS
OF THE
MAELSTROM

TIMOTHY WOLFF

ISBN: 979-8-9867655-6-3 (Paperback)
ISBN: 979-8-9867655-5-6 (Hardcover)
ISBN: 979-8-9867655-4-9 (eBook)
ISBN: 979-8-9867655-7-0 (Audiobook)

Front cover image by Alejandro Colucci
Edited by Jonathan Oliver
World map by Chaim Holtjer
Title page image by Apex Infinity Games
Book design by Lorna Reid

First printing edition 2023.

TimWolffAuthor@gmail.com

MAP

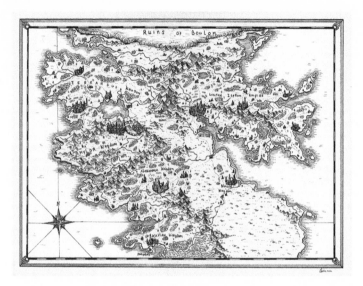

PLATINUM TINTED DARKNESS RECAP

With her home of Mylor under siege by the kingdom of Terrangus, Serenna Morgan breaks the Guardian Pact and involves herself in the battle, escalating the conflict into a year-long war. During the war she meets Zeen Parson, who she spares in a duel, and General Nyfe. In a later conflict, Nyfe's forces surround her, forcing her to accept the God of Death's offer of a temporarily influx of power. Drawn to Zeen's kindness, she resists the temptation to slay him, and collapses into his arms after relinquishing Death's power.

Zeen brings the unconscious Serenna to Terrangus, to the ire of veteran Guardians Melissa Euhno and David Williams. While David recruits Zeen to the Guardians, Terrangus Emperor Grayson Forsythe makes his intentions known to execute Serenna. These plans are interrupted by a Harbinger of Fear manifesting in the middle of Terrangus. Pyith Claw the lizard-woman (zephum) and Francis Haide the elemental sorcerer join the rest of the Guardians to battle the Harbinger. The demon is defeated, but David hears whispers from the Goddess of Fear. After the battle, Serenna is to be executed for her crimes while Francis ignores them and follows the God of Wisdom to Serenity, where they discuss freewill.

To save Serenna, David and Zeen align themselves with Nyfe and a woman named Mary Walker, accepting a mission in the ruins of Boulom. Sardonyx Claw, Warlord of Vaynex, joins them to defeat a demon, then demands they accompany him to his empire and meet his son, Tempest Claw. As they travel back, Melissa is murdered by Grayson. The loss causes Serenna to contemplate accepting Death's power forever, but she refuses. After Vaynex—David, Zeen, and Mary return to the southern capital of Alanammus, reuniting with Francis. Once David learns of Melissa's death, he has an emotional breakdown, banishing the other Guardians and choosing a self-inflicted end by jumping off the tower. His fall is stopped by the Goddess of Fear, who makes him her champion for a chance at vengeance. Nyfe takes advantage of David's chaos in Terrangus to crown himself emperor after Grayson falls.

With Nyfe as emperor, the kingdom leaders and Guardians make an alliance to bring him down. The war is successful; Nyfe is captured for a trial and Terrangus is occupied by the Southern forces, led by Julius Cavare, Francis, and Tempest. Nyfe finally accepts the God of Death's offer to become a Harbinger in the Terrangus dungeon. He breaks free, killing Julius while Francis and Tempest flee.

The Guardians reunite in Mylor to discuss the final battle. David convinces Zeen to admit his feelings for Serenna, who returns them. Francis and Mary have a one-night stand. With that out of the way, they battle Harbinger Nyfe in Terrangus. Before they're about to win, Zeen hesitates, feeling pity for Nyfe, which leads to a blade in his neck. Zeen awakes in the Great Plains in the Sky, the afterlife for zephum and their loved ones. The God of Strength agrees to sacrifice himself to bring Zeen back to life, who defeats Nyfe upon his return, then falls unconscious.

With Terrangus saved, Francis ponders why he is never the

hero. The God of Wisdom reveals himself to be the first Harbinger, the one who destroyed Boulom. His true title is the God of Arrogance. Francis accepts his staff and uses the power to make himself emperor. As he looks over his subjects, he wonders, how much can a person be damaged before they are considered broken?

Two months later, Serenna returns to Terrangus to check on the unconscious Zeen. She pulls up a chair and reads him his favorite story: *Tales of Terrangus – Rinso the Blue*.

The pain of family is unique, like water flowing down the stream of a river. We crash into the rocks, jagged fragments of earth, molding us into a storm of lost dreams and expectations. Our loved ones know where to strike, where the pain lies, for they knew us when we were children—when we were too young to hide our weaknesses away into the shadows of safety and denial. No pain is created equal—and thus no pain tears like the father's gaze, screaming without words that I am a failure.
He will never love me.

–Tales of Terrangus: Rinso the Blue - Volume III

PROLOGUE. DEFIANCE BY WEAKNESS

armaster Tempest Claw—son of Warlord Sardonyx Claw—sighed and took a deep breath, eagerly awaiting word from his most trusted editor. A new draft of *Tales of Terrangus: Rinso the Blue - Volume III* had been completed! The clarity of sweat dripping from his snout offered a peek of the terror and excitement clashing inside his zephum gut. His editor was many things: strong, supportive, beautiful, like a faint gust of wind nudging a lone viridescent blade of grass along the desperate crack of time between summer and fall...and she was harsh.

Very harsh.

Perhaps emerald instead of viridescent? Perhaps...just green? No! Larger words have more meaning!

He leaned back on his cushioned chair—one of only three in Vaynex—and took another sip of his imported Alanammus wine. His ambassador chamber in the east corner of the citadel was perhaps the most out-of-place room in any of the six kingdoms. The last remnants of wood crackled in the fireplace, filling the air with a sweet, yet subtle smoke. He had always found it odd that the scent of smoke could differ, that the burning Vaynex skies always offered some pungent reminder of unmet expectations, but not here. Never here. Bookshelves, wine, all clean, all wonderful. Vaynex had been his birthplace, but this room had always been home. Sadly enough, because it was nothing like Vaynex.

"Dear, I swear," Pyith Claw said, shaking her head as she crossed a line through the page in her copy. "If I have to cross out another 'roared loudly' I will bash you over the snout with this damn book."

He knew this moment would come. It always did. "But Pyith, it is imperative for the reader to understand Cympha's pain! She doesn't just roar, she roars...*loudly*."

Pyith crossed out the same line again, ensuring his defeat, bringing the symbolic wrath of the Guardian's one-handed blade through the heart of his words. "We're not having this conversation again. No more 'roared loudly,' 'yelled loudly,' and for fuck's sake, stop writing 'whispered softly,' just stop it."

"Fine," he said with a sigh. "I'll take it out because I love you. But somewhere out there in Terrangus, a young boy will picture the moment, and the roar within his imagination will only be a whisper of what I intended."

She smiled, walked over and kissed him—*gently*—on his snout. "Oh, and one more thing: that terrible poem near the end, something is missing."

"This one?" He rose, matching her smile, leaving the book on the table. As with any exhausted writer, he knew the words by heart. "'The pain of family is unique, like water flowing down the stream of a river. We crash into the rocks, jagged fragments of earth, molding us into a storm of lost dreams and expectations. Our loved ones know where to strike, where the pain lies, for they knew us when we were children—when we were too young to hide our weaknesses away into the shadows of safety and denial. No pain is created equal—and thus no pain tears like the father's gaze, screaming without words that I am a failure.'"

"Yes, that one," she said, giving him a mighty embrace. By Strength's name, she was strong. Being the life-mate of a Guardian had been an awkward road. Everyone knew she was superior to him in battle—well, most zephum were—and everyone knew their union had been conceived as a strategic move by Sardonyx, but she had somehow grown to love him. For all the horrors his father had inflicted upon him in his twenty-five years, Pyith had not been one of them. She was the calm before the storm, the heart within the eye of the maelstrom.

"No! What could possibly be missing?"

"I don't know but…something. Give it another shot in the morning. For now, finish that wine and get your clothes off. I could use a quick lay before bed."

He wouldn't dare say no—not that he wanted to—so he took another sip of wine and closed his book before steps approached his chambers. Who would dare? He was not to be disturbed…

Oh. Father. Of course.

Warlord Sardonyx Claw entered the room in his full steel armor, despite the late hour. As with any true zephum, he had worn the mask of a warrior so long it had consumed his entire identity. He approached the book, sighed, then threw it into the fire. "This again? You dishonor me, Tempest. You dishonor us all." The book burned, eclipsing the once subtle aroma with a scent of despair. Art had never been a match for the horrors of reality, despite the absurdity that said horrors had inspired said art.

Pyith rushed over, nearly falling over in surprise. "Warlord, I can—"

The warlord's glare cut her off. Pyith had faced demons, Harbingers, she who would not be named, and the God of Death, but Tempest's father was somehow worse than any of them. Sardonyx grabbed her by the neck and lifted her high. "I warned you, Pyith. Stop encouraging the boy to be weak. I will not allow it. I *cannot* allow it."

She struggled to speak, choking with both hands gripped on Sardonyx's arm. There was only one acceptable course of action. Tempest was a zephum of words, a diplomat, a hopeful scholar with true ideals to turn Vaynex into the zephum version of Alanammus. He was not a warrior, despite his father's wishes. He was not strong, despite his father's wishes.

He loved Pyith with all his heart, despite his father's wishes.

Tempest punched Sardonyx across his steel face guard. He couldn't hear the snap, but pain was kind enough to inform him of the broken bones in his hand. It didn't matter. Sardonyx dropped Pyith like she was nothing, then backhanded Tempest across his snout. This time, he could hear the snap. He hated himself for shrieking as loud as he did, but the pain was too much. It was always too much.

"Get up! Act as the future warlord I have raised!"

The future warlord Sardonyx had raised whimpered on the ground, not bothering to rise. Another beating. They had occurred less frequently as he aged, but they occurred all the same.

Pyith crawled to the corner of the chamber, clearly knowing better than to interfere. His dear life-mate deserved better. Her reward for defending the realm had been to marry into a broken family, with an insane, invincible warlord and his sane, weak son.

Sardonyx leaned down over him. "Where is your *honor*?" he yelled, before backhanding him again.

Tears rolled down Tempest's snout. He wanted to smile out of spite, but nothing in the realm could ever defend him against such pain. He didn't bother to defend himself as his father choked him; there was an ironic joy in the art of doing nothing, the art of defiance by weakness.

"Failures. Both of you. When I finally enter the Great Plains in the Sky, what will happen to Vaynex?"

His vision began to blur as the words drifted into the vague realm of whatever reality bordered consciousness and darkness. Sardonyx sighed and let go, then rose.

"After you die," Tempest said, against his better judgment, "Vaynex will grow. It will become the kingdom it was always meant to be after our people find enlightenment. Eventually, we will forget you. We will forget your father. Perhaps one day..." Tempest paused; would he dare? "We will forget Strength as well." He braced himself for a special kind of torment after demeaning their god.

Instead, Sardonyx turned away. His eyes were lost on a bookshelf, likely wondering how such a thing had found its way into the glorious lands of Vaynex. There was an empty spot near the bottom, next to *Tales of Terrangus: Rinso the Blue - Volumes 1 & 2*. Tempest would fill that spot eventually, but not today.

"You were born to be a storm, yet more and more you speak like the Arrogant One. Oh, I have failed you. I have failed us all. My dear Vitala...forgive me."

"*Never* compare me to him. I'm well aware of my flaws; it is what truly separates the two of us."

"Ah, my son. There is a kingdom the size of Vaynex that separates us. We are who we are. I did not choose you, but I will fulfill my duty and craft you into the future warlord. Forgive me, Pyith. *You* deserve better." Sardonyx left the room. For such an unread brute, he always knew where to strike with words.

No pain is created equal—and thus no pain tears like the father's gaze, screaming without words that I am a failure. Tempest sighed, nearly smiling at the epiphany. As usual, Pyith had been correct. The poem was missing an ending. He may as well add the truth.

He will never love me.

CHAPTER 1

VEHEMENCE

erenna Morgan materialized in the Terrangus outskirts portal, closing her eyes as the cool morning rain drifted down her platinum hair and pale white armor. The two guards at the portal bowed to her, which even after the seven months since Harbinger Nyfe would never feel normal. Though to be fair, it was difficult to say what normal was anymore.

The Guardian portal in the castle would've been a quicker journey to Zeen's healing bed in the military ward, but the longer walk had always been worth it to avoid Francis...*Emperor* Francis. She missed the days where he had only been annoying. Now, her old friend was basically a god, the worst kind of god, the god that assumed they—and only they—had all the answers.

As she walked through the open Terrangus gates, it was easy to see why. In the mere months after Nyfe had decimated the kingdom, Francis had restored order, through an odd mix of magic and...other methods. Life bustled through the trade district, the endless yelling and rushing, all the things no one loved until Nyfe had taken them away. *There's still no sign of him anywhere,* she thought. *I wish David had just killed him at the end. On that note, no sign of David either.*

Everyone smiled and cheered as she drifted by the carts and shops, with merchants yelling her name from all directions for the opportunity to claim Serenna had shopped there. Beloved Serenna Morgan, leader of the Guardians, defender of the realm…

Oh, how times had changed.

One change in particular was the sizable guards in full white armor with the God of Wisdom's crest engraved into their chest plates. *Serenity's Vanguard*, Francis had deemed them. She only noticed one drifting through the streets this morning. Supposedly, there were five total, but she had only ever seen four.

His eyes turned. He noticed her, too.

"You. Serenna Morgan. I am Vanguard Three. This marks the eighty-fourth day since you have received invitation to Serenity. You openly insult your emperor and god with such reluctance. Explain this irrational behavior."

The monotone voice sent a shiver down her back. What in the realm were these things? He radiated elemental energy, wearing a large oak staff in his sheath as if it were a sword. She had never seen one in battle. They had tended to escort troublemakers away with harsh threats and glares. None had ever returned.

"I care not for your tone, Vanguard. Tell Francis I will accept his invitation as soon as Zeen wakes. I will not meet with him until then. No one—Francis, Wisdom, *you* in particular—will change that."

"Re-word your statement to include the proper respect. His title is Emperor Francis. This is your fourth recorded strike of disobedience. I am authorized to apprehend you, if required."

She grabbed the Wings of Mylor from behind her back and stared him down. The other ones had made obscure threats of disobedience and whatnot, but 'apprehend' was a word she wouldn't tolerate in Terrangus. "Are you capable of such a task? Perhaps you will be the first Vanguard to die."

Vanguard Three paused. Ah, that was the look. The long stare into nothing as reality set in. It had been several months since anyone had shown her fear. To be honest, part of her missed that. "This will be reported to Emperor Francis and our god at once."

"A wise choice, Three," she said, passing him by. What a stupid name. Leave it to Francis to name people as numbers. *Maybe I should just meet with him,* she thought, before shaking her head. She never approved of Francis's ascension to emperor. Was he still a Guardian at this point? For their leader, she had done a terrible job of keeping in touch with everyone to ensure they could regroup when the time came...

His new power is terrifying.

That was the real reason. She hated being afraid of anyone, but this was different. Francis had never been physically imposing, just an annoying, spoiled nobleman who had outlandish opinions on everything from taxation rates to zephum legacy trade lines. Nothing is more dangerous than a man with unlimited ideas and the power to implement them.

Stay focused. Hide your distress, she thought, returning a smile at a group of children as she neared the gates to the military ward. Gods, it was like...being in Mylor, except there were no mountains and far too much rain. It was difficult to admit how much she appreciated Terrangus since Nyfe's fall, a welcome change of pace from the 'burn them all' days.

She navigated through the military ward. It was livelier each day; Francis had apparently made restocking the army one of his primary objectives. *There* was Zeen's barracks, one of the smaller structures in the ward, unworthy of her lover, the realm's greatest Guardian. She had considered bringing him home to Mylor, but it hadn't seemed wise to force a man in a coma through a portal. One of her favorite people in the entire realm stood at the entrance with a loving smile.

"Good morning, my dear," Landon said, embracing her. There was always such a desperation in his grasp, as if he feared never seeing her again. "Hmm, about an hour late this time. You are getting worse."

"Oh hush," she said, kissing his cheek before letting go. "My responsibilities have grown considerably."

"No excuse! Guardian Everleigh was never late. To anything! So much to learn, young one..."

She rolled her eyes as they walked together. "Did Guardian Everleigh have to deal with Vanguards? They are growing more bold. One actually threatened to apprehend me earlier."

Landon froze. "You didn't kill him, did you?"

"Of course not. Not while Zeen is still here."

"Good girl. Listen, I know you hate hearing this, but perhaps it would be wise to finally take Francis's invitation to Serenity and get it over with?"

"You're probably right but...well, something worries me about his deity. Death and Fear seek our destruction, which is simple enough, but Wisdom is playing some sort of long game. He found the perfect host to shape the realm into any direction he desires."

"Well, I think Lord Wisdom is great!" Landon said, blinking with the subtlety of a Harbinger. "Particularly if he is listening to our conversation now."

She snickered, but that was a fair point. Wisdom probably was listening. She never fully understood Francis's relationship with the deity. Hopefully, for his sake, it was nothing like the God of Death screaming through her thoughts. Gods, the silence since then... It was beautiful. To hear nothing. To no longer anticipate the screams. The tranquility of her own mind.

If...when Zeen wakes, my life may finally be perfect.

Actually, there was a way to check. "I declare the God of Wisdom to be a loathsome scoundrel." It was strangely uncomfortable to speak that way in front of Landon, who grimaced—

The door beside them slammed shut as a familiar chuckle echoed through the air.

"You were right," she said with a smile.

"Girl, I swear. Why must you tempt fate so needlessly? How many immortal enemies do you need? I'm too old for this."

"It was just a test. Don't be so jumpy."

He sighed, then continued forward. "Fine. While we're here, what will you do when Zeen finally wakes?"

Take him home and never come back... Ah, that's why he asked. "I think you already know the answer. Would you consider moving your family to Mylor? I could ensure that all your needs are met."

"Never! I was born in Terrangus. My daughters and grandchildren were born in Terrangus. After seven decades, it would be a disgrace to die anywhere else. Don't take that the wrong way. I do understand, it's just, well, you will be missed."

She hugged him at the entrance to Zeen's room. "I will come back for you, Landon. You have been a second father to me."

He kissed her and let go. "Out of all my daughters, you are...the most interesting one. I'll see you tomorrow, my dear."

Serenna entered Zeen's resting chamber. More cramped than she would prefer, but at least they kept it clean and Zeen fed and shaved. One advantage of the smaller room was the efficiency of the fireplace behind the head of his bed. It had kept the room warmer than the rest of Terrangus during the winter, but it was still no Alanammus. She scribbled her name in the visitor's log, surprised to see *Empress Mary Walker* and

Ambassador Tempest Claw written in yesterday's notes. Why had Tempest been here?

She kissed the sleeping Zeen on his forehead, disappointed not to see that smile as he continued to rest. She pulled up a chair, grabbing *Tales of Terrangus: Rinso the Blue - Volume II* from the far side desk. *Volume I* had been the worst book she had ever read. Hands down. Why Zeen loved these books could be anyone's guess. The author had certainly never seen a naked woman before, writing lines similar to, *Rinso caressed his fingers down the spine of the sultry Olivia, stopping at the curve where her tail would've been.*

Seriously? She sighed, opening to where she had left off yesterday, then read out loud, ""Hyphermlo!" Rinso yelled loudly. "You must train me in the ways of a zephum warrior! I will never defeat Warlord Vehemence without your guidance!"

"'Hyphermlo snickered, rubbing his snout. "Ah, but what is defeat? You are losing your way, tiny human. Relinquish the desperation in your heart. Let go of the rage, the hatred...the pain. These things may grant you temporary power, but at what cost? If you sacrifice your pillars of morality to defeat a monster, you have only replaced one monster with another. The truest of victories are the ones we find within."

""But... I don't understand."

""Sit, human. I will tell you the true tale of Warlord Vehemence. A tale that begins back in Vaynex, with his brother... Me."""

Oh my. She turned the page, then froze as something moved out of the corner of her eye.

CHAPTER 2

TOO MUCH, TOO SOON

his all feels too familiar, David Williams thought, gazing out to the sparkling Xavian sea, catching a whiff of the bitter salt air that always lingered. Ships rustled through the waters despite the early hour, as a warm breeze caressed his tired face through the gap of his hood. Odd that he would feel exhausted already, but perhaps that was one of the many prices of reaching forty-five.

He kept the Herald of Fear sheathed; the blade lay across his back, waiting to consume fear and extinguish life. That was all he was good for anymore. His target was Arabell Cora: an ex-mercenary genius who had taken up time magic after her criminal affiliations led to the death of her sister.

There was no way David could have known that already.

He took a swig of his flask, then pulled his hood tight as he walked through the Xavian streets. There was far less chance of being recognized outside of Terrangus, but no need to take unnecessary risks. For whatever reason, he expected a merchant to grab him.

"Good sir!" a man yelled, grabbing his arm. Xavian merchants were so bold. Grabbing anyone in Terrangus would lead to a swift death. "Who wears such heavy garments this far south? Are you immune to the sun? Let me fit you into something more comfortable!"

David ripped his arm back and continued forward, pushing down the urge to strike the man down. Such a scene would expose himself…

How did I know that would happen? What is going on here?

He took another swig of his flask. A large swig. For all its flaws, alcohol had the power to drown out most of his problems. Unfortunately, some problems—like being the assassin for the Goddess of Fear—were too heavy to drink away. His instincts told him to take the east road at Xavian Plaza, past the golden statue of Guardian Malzo, towards the rundown section where the pirate gangs had taken over. He had come this way with Melissa all those years ago, back when they…

Stop it. Move on. You swore you would move on.

He resisted the urge to grab his flask. Too much, too soon. Apparently, declaring he would be happy and actually doing it was not the same task.

Focus. Arabell would die, Fear would be pleased, then the monotony of his post-Guardian life would continue. As unfulfilling as it had been, the distractions were always welcomed to create any sort of attempt at purpose. Pirates and thugs eyed him, but they kept their distance. Just like in Terrangus, just like in Nuum, thieves always knew better.

The light faded as he continued through the slums. People sat on crates, throwing dice, slamming drinks, not giving him a second glance. Such a place could only exist in the darkness; there was a desperate beauty in the way life had adapted to the shadows.

Near the end was a shack, the perfect hovel for a time mage. He drew his blade and took a deep breath, staring at the tan, broken structure that barely passed as a home. How could something he had never seen before look so familiar? David crashed through the wooden door, making his entrance as startling as possible to trigger his target's fear.

Tiny Arabell sat by a table with her frizzy black hair, scribbling notes and marking numbers on a board to her side. She didn't even glance at him.

"Oh, hey David. Maybe I'll leave the door open next time so you stop crashing through."

He clutched his sword, which didn't glow. "What sorcery is this? How do you already know me? How...do I know you?"

"Not the smartest question, silly. You keep trying to kill me! I would appreciate it if you would knock it off though. I think...I think I'm nearly ready."

Sweat poured down his face as his heart pounded. "How long has this been going on?"

She smirked, finally stopping her work to meet his eyes. "Now that's an intelligent question. Honestly, I've lost track. We're in quite the debacle with these time loops. Every time I get closer to permanently reversing time, you come closer to killing me. Ah, time. Time, time, time."

Enough of this. He swung his blade at her head, but she casually dodged without looking.

"Again, really? You know, I expected Fear's assassin to be a bit more inventive."

He made a few more swings, with Arabell dodging each one with ease. If she already knew his actions, how did he ever come close to killing her? A candle flickered on the table; could he just burn the place down? *Hmm.*

I tried that already. Random memories filled his thoughts: a burning house, choking her with his bare hands, his sword by her neck... He had easily won every time. Every single time.

"Ah, that look. You're remembering now, aren't you?"

"Something is terribly wrong here... *Enough!*" He swung

again by pure instinct, hoping his own lack of preparation would catch her off guard.

It did. The sword cut across her face, sending her to the ground, shrieking. She looked so pitiful lying there in her own blood, clutching the wound. She was maybe…twenty-one? Where was her fear?

She snickered despite the gravity of her scenario. "Damn, that was much faster than usual. We may be nearing the end, David. You're getting me down quicker each time."

"Why are you still alive? There's so much I can't remember."

"Gods, you're such a mess. This would really be a lot easier if you remembered our deal. Think David. Think!"

Is this a trick? Why can't I remember? He watched Arabell clutch her staff. It was the same way she had done every other time. A bright light filled the room, filling him with a warmth he had only experienced in the arms of his lover.

By Fear's mercy, I remember everything. I must stop this…

*

This all feels too familiar, David thought, gazing out to the sparkling Xavian sea, catching a whiff of the bitter salt air that always lingered. Ships rustled through the waters—

What is happening to me?

He kept the Herald of Fear sheathed; the blade lay across his back, waiting to consume fear and extinguish life. That was all he was good for anymore.

Try to remember…

His target was Arabell Cora, an ex-mercenary genius who had taken up time magic after her criminal affiliations had led to the death of her sister… Rylee was her name, that's right. Rylee had been a wonderful girl, the only sibling to seek legitimate work to lift their family out of the slums, only to have been murdered in cold blood for no other reason than being Arabell's sister. When reality becomes unacceptable, it must be changed.

By any means necessary.

He took a swig of his flask, then pulled his hood tight as he walked through the Xavian streets. There was far less chance of being recognized outside of Terrangus, but no need to take unnecessary risks. A random instinct told him to travel on the other side of the street.

"Good sir!" a man yelled from the other side, waving his arms. "Good sir!"

He ignored the man and pressed forward, taking the east road at Xavian Plaza, past the golden statue of Guardian Malzo, towards the rundown section where the pirate gangs had taken over. He had come this way with Melissa all those years ago, back when they…

You don't have to move on. You can fix this. You can fix everything…

His shaky hands grabbed his flask, pounding the ale as tears filled his eyes. Too much, too soon. *What have I done?* He desperately tried to focus, choking as the ale burned his throat. Pirates and thugs eyed him; did they see a potential victim? He drew the Herald of Fear, pointing it at everyone in his immediate vicinity.

When an essence of fear drifted off a random thug and flowed into David, the rest of the men fled. A migraine pounded his skull at the chaotic outburst of people rushing away. *I broke something. It wasn't supposed to happen this way.* He rushed towards the shack. The one from his visions; the tan hovel of despair where this had all begun.

The door was already open.

"David," Arabell said, huddled into a ball on the ground, shaking. "Stop changing things. No more changes. I saw the

Time God. Time. Time. We must stop. He threatened to end everything. This entire timeline will cease to exist."

Her essence of fear flowed into his skin, giving him vague hints of an unfathomable power. The power that could end Fear or Death with a mere whisper. "I don't understand…"

She lunged forward from the ground, pressing him into the wall neck-first with the infinite strength of her grip. Half her face was replaced by dark void energy. "I have seen realms within realms; echoes of what is and what cannot be. Kill me. There is only one more chance at this. Kill me, David. *Kill me.*"

Arabell screamed, throwing David into the wall, cracking bones he didn't know existed. She grabbed her staff, clutched it, then a bright light filled the room, filling him with a warmth he had only experienced in the arms of his lover.

A warmth that was gone forever.

*

David sighed, gazing out to the sparkling Xavian sea, allowing tears to fall as he remembered the first time he had told Melissa he loved her. It had been here, this exact spot, this exact smell, the location where they had defeated their first Harbinger together. The start of a beautiful companionship that was never supposed to end.

The little things had built up over the months. The guilt of trying to move on, the guilt of forgetting the simpler memories: all the tiny dots on her arms, the newer wrinkles that had formed on her legs. The little things, like taking a bath and no longer finding those dark curly hairs stuck to him, or still grabbing two chalices before opening a bottle of wine…

I want to move on, but I don't know how.

He had mastered the abstract state of not wanting to die, but not really wanting to live, pushing it down for as long as his heart would allow. He downed his entire flask, begging the numbness to hit as soon as possible. Too much, too soon.

And nowhere near enough.

When Arabell had offered him the chance to bring Melissa back along with her sister, he yielded. Damn girl had made it seem so easy. He had blocked out various memories of each loop, doing anything he could to stall long enough for her plan to work. It almost did. It had almost destroyed everything.

He pulled his hood tight and trekked forward, the same way he had done the first time. He walked by the wool vendor, got his arm grabbed, and acted appalled to keep the stability. It was funny to consider how angry he had been over such an insignificant disturbance.

He took the east road at Xavian Plaza, stopping himself from smiling at the thieves and pirates eyeing him as he continued. Did they have any idea they were staring into the broken husk of a demigod?

One way or the other, this would be the final time he gazed upon the tan shack of his target. He took a deep breath, then eased the door open. Unlike any of the previous times, Arabell hovered in the air, radiating some sort of red energy. She turned to David, gazing at him with empty dark spheres where her eyes once were, speaking in a deep, distorted voice.

"The only way I can distinguish reality from dreams is when the pain is too severe. Why do you inflict such torment upon me? Have I wronged you in an alternate parallel? You are… David. Human David. Aspect twelve hundred and ninety-two." The deep rumble sent David to his knees, nearly blinded by the pain of hearing its voice.

"Please refrain from tampering with the constructs of reality. It pains me greatly to wake from my slumber. Time must flow. I must rest. Time must be the echo inside an echo, the faint drifting whisper that lingers forever. This is the unparalleled truth of our worlds. Do you understand?"

"*Yes!*" He would yell anything to get it to stop speaking.

The voice wasn't loud, but something about the vibrations made it feel like his skull was about to shatter.

"I have seen infinity, countless streams of seconds and years, flowing without interruption into eternity. But there is something divergent in this space. An anomaly. I treasure natural anomalies. Farewell, David. This version of you and I will never meet again."

David caught his breath as the pain vanished, flinching back as Arabell—with her standard brown eyes—was back to working at her desk.

"Oh, hey David. Maybe I'll leave the door open next time so you stop crashing through."

"I remember everything."

She stood, eyeing the open door, then him, cautiously. "Well, that's new. Is our deal still good? I can bring Melissa back. You never have to be alone again. Neither of us do."

His eyes screamed his condolences as he drew his sword and approached. "How I wish any of those words were true."

Arabell laughed nervously, darting her eyes to her staff. "Uh, what happened to—"

He closed his eyes as the Herald of Fear tore through her chest. It was beyond kind of her not to scream; for all the people he had ever slayed, this was the most painful. This reckless, delusional girl who had risked the entire realm to erase the pain... It was like killing a younger version of himself.

"So that's it, David? You're just giving up?"

"Every decision we make—in one way or the other—is to give up on something."

David wiped a tear from his eye, then used his blade to create a portal back home. He entered the icy dream of Boulom in the middle of a snowstorm, sighing as he met Empress Noelami's eyes. She was already in her goddess form.

She appeared to be *very* angry.

CHAPTER 3

SEVEN MONTHS?

een Parson rubbed his eyes, blinking over and over to regain anything that resembled clarity. How long had he slept? Everything was a blur, except for the shimmer of Serenna's platinum hair—but even if he was blind, he would still see the woman who held his heart from kingdoms away.

Serenna rushed over and crushed him with her embrace, letting out a cry that was somehow the most wonderful and startling sound he had ever heard. She clutched him with a strength that would make Sardonyx proud.

Ah, it's all coming back now. Strength sacrificed himself to bring me back. I'm very lucky to be here, which must be... This is Terrangus! How much time has passed?

"I love you, Zeen," she said, clutching him harder. "I love you so much. You will never leave me again. Never."

"I love you too, Serenna. I suppose the end of forever will have to wait. If you don't mind, I have...many questions."

"Yes, of course. Are you able to stand? You look remarkably well after being out for seven months. I'll never criticize the art of healing magic again, that's for sure."

He laughed, struggling to rise in his bed. His legs were remarkably sore. "It's unlike you to crack jokes. How long has it really been? Two days? A week?"

A crack showed in her smile as she held his hand. "Zeen…"

Oh. "By the gods… Really? Is everyone okay? I'm not sure how to cope with this."

"We're all fine. I'll tell you everything once we get home. There is a lot you will find difficult to believe."

Well, that was a bit ominous. He eased both legs off his bed and onto the ground, grimacing as he tested putting weight on them both. He would be able to stand, but damn, it would hurt. All things considered, the healing mages had done an amazing job of keeping him intact.

"Ah!" a familiar voice yelled from outside the room. "You're awake!" Tempest Claw rushed over with something in his right hand. "Wonderful timing! I was about to drop this off before I left. It's only the first half, but I figured perhaps…"

Zeen took the book with a rush of adrenaline as he glanced at the cover of *Rinso the Blue - Volume IV*. "I suppose being asleep for seven months has its advantages. I'm so excited to see if Rinso and Oliva can patch up their relationship after—"

"No spoilers!" Serenna yelled, placing her copy of *Volume II* on the table. When did she start reading that? "I'm nearly done with the second story. It's been a welcome upgrade from the terrible first book."

Tempest yielded a deep frown. "Hmm. You must forgive my first attempt. The beginning was convoluted, the romance was rushed, the combat descriptions were wonky, and I *may* have overdone it with emphasizing certain words. Don't even get me started on the semicolons."

She matched his frown with a cringe. "Oh…forgive me, I didn't mean that. Well, the second one is good…"

What?

Hold on—Tempest had written these books? If only he had known earlier! So many questions! To hell with the pain. Zeen rose, then hugged Tempest with the strongest embrace he could manage…which, right now, was not much. "Your stories are wonderful! I have always tried to model myself after Rinso's message of be kind and love each other. Why don't you credit yourself as the author?"

"As much as I yearn to, it would be improper for the future warlord of Vaynex to dabble in such endeavors. We favor loud brutes that tackle every problem with blades and roars. But still, thank you. Your words are a joy to my heart."

Zeen struggled to keep his balance as he let go, stumbling into Serenna's arms as his legs gave out. "Forgive me. My body's strength doesn't match my excitement. I may need some time before I can be myself again."

She held him dearly with a smile. Such a warmth came from her arms, as if it were the one place where he had always belonged. "Take all the time in the realm. I thought I lost you, Zeen. To hold you like this again is nothing short of a miracle. Let me take you back to Mylor. When you're feeling better, we can have a reunion with the Guardians. Everyone will be thrilled to hear the news—"

"So, it's true," Mary Walker said from the door, then approached. Hmm. She appeared much larger than he remembered, but maybe that was due to her new golden armor? Since when did she wear an amber cape? "Wisdom informed us you finally woke up. Welcome back, my friend. You look like shit."

Serenna and Tempest appeared uncomfortable as she entered. "Welcome, Empress," Tempest said, with a formal bow.

Um, what? There's no way I heard that correctly. "Good morning, Mary! You look…different."

Mary glared at the others. "You haven't told him anything?" She sighed after a moment of silence. "It's Empress Mary Walker now. I'm just under seven months pregnant with the emperor's child."

Zeen snickered. "Oh, c'mon. I'm no Francis, but you'll have to do better than that." Why was no one else laughing? "Gods, you're serious? Congratulations, Mary! That is wonderful news! Who…is the emperor right now?"

"Francis," Mary said, letting out a faint smile. The fact she tried to hide it made Zeen smile back. She was truly happy. She would make a great mother…

Wait. Why was Francis the emperor of Terrangus?

Mary sighed again; maybe she picked up the habit from her new lover. "I'll leave it to Serenna to fill you in with the rest of the details. For now, get up. Emperor Francis demands your presence."

"Francis *requests* our presence," Serenna said in a bitter tone. "You may wield a fancy new title, but I am still your leader."

"It is what it is, Serenna. Take a few minutes to compose yourselves, then head over to the castle. I'll instruct the Vanguards to leave you alone…for now." Mary simply left after that, leaving an ominous silence in her wake.

What the hell is a Vanguard? he thought, easing his hand to Serenna's. "It's okay, my love. I'm happy to meet with them if it keeps the peace. Let's get this over with and head back home—together."

"You don't understand," Serenna said. "Neither of them can be trusted. Francis took advantage of the aftermath from Harbinger Nyfe to make himself emperor. He wields the Herald of Wisdom, doing everything he can to spread the god's influence in Terrangus and beyond. We're also getting closer to a year since the last Harbinger. A new one will come. These are dangerous times, Zeen. I cannot risk losing you again."

Her hand cradling his own was soothing enough to push down the various problems unleashed upon him. "You will never lose me again. Tempest, could I convince you to join us? I would feel more confident with Rinso the Blue by our side."

Tempest stood straight. "Forgive me. It would be an honor, Zeen, but my people need me back in Vaynex. Please, stop by when you have a chance. You have become something of a legend to the zephum after accepting Strength's blessing. The 'Human Warlord' is the phrase my father conceived. A bit startling, considering his simple nature, but he does manage to surprise me from time to time."

"Whew," Zeen said. "The Human Warlord and the Rogue Guardian. I seem to be collecting quite the array of nicknames."

"You'll need this," Serenna said with a smile, grabbing Hope from the east corner of the room. "I kept it close in preparation for this day. I figured Hope would find a way."

Zeen took the sword; it felt much heavier than he remembered. "Thank you both. And Tempest: Strength without honor—is chaos."

"Well spoken, my friend. I had never cared for the words, but they haunt me dearly now that Strength is gone. Serenna, as the leader of the Guardians, it would be most honorable of you to join Zeen when he visits. That is a request, not a demand. I may not be one of you, but you will always hold my respect for protecting the realm."

"Don't be a fool," she said, grinning. "You will always be one of us in my eyes."

Zeen leaned on Serenna as they strolled to the barracks exit, thankful she never complained about his slow pace. It was just so damn hard to walk right now...

He lost his breath as they stepped outside into the pouring rain. The ruins and death from their battle had all been cleared—walking into the future was somehow the same as walking out into the past. *How much did I miss? The realm just went on without me. I know I should be thankful, but why does it feel so awkward?* He had battled crawlers and those weird banshee things where children were now playing, and a cart was now set up selling wine where a pile of dead mages had been stacked.

Something must have tipped Serenna off as she held him closer. "I felt it too when I saw everything back to normal. We all did. It stops being strange after a few months, which is the strangest feeling of all."

"Do I even belong here anymore?"

"Of course," she said. "Too much is getting thrown at you at once. Let's make this quick and head to Mylor. We can rest easy until the next Harbinger."

He forced a smile as they continued. The idea of another Harbinger was not a welcome one...and a lot of people were staring at him. "We seem to have drawn a crowd. You know, this happened when I brought you here the first time. Except you were in a cart."

"I wish that I could remember any of that. My earliest memory was waking up in a prison cell."

"I—" He froze before they reached the castle entrance. "It was right there," he said, pointing to a specific spot to the left of the castle where nothing now stood. Rain dripped down, flowing towards them from the slightly elevated land. "I died right there."

A cold breeze blew his hair across his face as he shivered. It was impossible to block out the memory of when Nyfe's blade had pierced his neck, or when he had screamed at Serenna to somehow make everything right. How many of the realm's problems were directly his fault? The God of Strength had died because of him. Serenna was beautiful as always, but she looked so tired. *I did that to her. Emperor Francis is probably my fault, too. How is Vaynex faring without their god? I've killed so many. I never considered the weight of it all until I died myself.*

It was just so cold...

"And then you came back," she said. "Do not linger on the

past. We were given the gift no one else has ever known. I do not know what the future holds. I do not know what any of the gods are planning, but I do know that I love you. Together, we can beat anything."

Leaning his head on her shoulder, he closed his eyes as the rain poured down. It had never seemed so loud until now. "I love you too. Please be patient with me. I'll be back to my old self soon enough."

Hopefully, those words did a better job of convincing her than it did himself.

CHAPTER 4

ARCHITECT OF PARADISE

mperor Francis gazed into the eye of his Herald of Arrogance staff, still intrigued at how the stare would follow his own no matter the angle. He had learned so much that day after saying the mantra 'delusion is the cornerstone of happiness', the most annoying of which was learning how much he still didn't know. Knowledge had been an unexpected addiction, a never-ending journey down a rabbit hole of answers that only led to more questions.

He leaned back on his throne in his pristine white robes, glancing up to the glass ceiling where rain tapped down. It was easy to see how someone could lose track of time in Terrangus with the constant storms and darkness. Of course, not everyone had access to a fountain of knowledge going all the way back to the kingdom of Boulom. What time was it? It didn't matter.

"My dear Francis," Wisdom said, most likely visible only to him. The deity had been more subtle since Francis's ascension… for the most part. "It would appear they are finally en route to pay respects to their intellectual superiors. Best clear the room, this could get interesting."

The lack of reaction from the senators or guards confirmed his suspicions as he rose, immediately gaining the full room's attention. That feeling of being the center of everything would never get old. In a fitting twist, his anxiety had been defeated by other people's fear. "Guards, colleagues. Leave me for now and return in an hour. I am to entertain guests. Vanguard Five, remain. The rest of you, patrol the districts."

His lovely Mary entered as they exited, with each person having enough sense to clear a path for her. Francis was not a tyrant, but anyone who would dare touch his pregnant empress would face the might of the elements. Fire, to be precise.

"It is done, my lord," she said, giving a perfect bow at the head of the steps before the throne.

Francis rushed down to embrace her. "Mary stop! Never bow to me! That is for common folk, not you."

"You are the emperor," she said with a grin, caressing his shoulders. "I'll keep bowing until you marry me and make me a Haide. As of now, I'm just your scandalous, pregnant mistress, filling the needs of my easily excitable man."

"No! Do not speak that way!" he yelled, fury in his eyes. "You are *not* my mistress! I... you... I am your..."

Her smile grew. "Relax. It's too easy to rattle you, and gods, it is fun. It's been nearly a year now, but you still treat me like a zephum warlord who happens to look good naked. I'll keep on torturing you until you adapt. It's the least I can do."

Is this love? I have no idea. I refuse to speak the words until she does first in case the answer is no. Is that wise? This was supposed to get easier with my power...

She's looking at me. Say something. "On that note, Wisdom suggested we should arrange a wedding. Have you any objections?"

Her grin faded entirely. That was not the expected reaction. "I'll pretend you didn't just say that. Dammit Francis, romance me. Take me to dinner somewhere, show me something, anything other than another night in Serenity. I can't carry this relationship by myself. Not with a child on the way."

Wisdom save me, I don't want to be a father. How could I possibly raise a child? How do I learn the proper empathy? It's in every book I've ever read, but how do I force it to appear? Sweat poured down his head as his hands shook, refusing to entertain the idea of Mary ever leaving him. That would be impossible...right? The feelings of others were too random and complex, like books with missing pages.

"Mary," he said, caressing her face the way he had seen a young couple do in Alanammus once. "Help me understand. Tell me what you want and I can make it yours. I am the emperor now, nothing is off limits."

She sighed. "I don't want things, titles, riches. I want *you*! Give yourself to me! You don't have to be alone anymore. I have been banging on this glass barrier you formed around yourself for months now. Open yourself up."

"I'm not a crystal mage. I don't have barriers—"

The throne room doors eased open, which, based on the expression on Mary's face, was a blessing. Serenna and Zeen approached—rather slowly—with Zeen's eyes frozen on Francis's staff. *Hmm, it is good to see them again after so long, but how do I play this? I need to show Serenna she has no power here, and this is Zeen's first perception of me as emperor—*

"Hey Francis!" Zeen said as he let go of Serenna. "Good to see you. Congratulations on everything! You have been a busy man while I've been gone."

Fine. We play it that way. "Indeed, though it's customary to bow in my presence." *I forgot how annoying this one is,* he thought, sighing at Zeen's smile.

Zeen managed a pitiful bow, then...approached? Without permission? Oh, no. Zeen hugged him, clutching him in his surprisingly weak arms. *Why must he always touch me? I hate him. He should never have woken...*

Stop it, don't think that way.

"Sorry, I'll make sure to bow first next time. So...you two. When in the realm did that happen? I never would have pictured you as Mary's type. Were you...together the whole time?"

You can't just ask people that! he thought, clutching his staff. Mary and Serenna stared at him, awaiting his answer. What a mess. Fine, he could fix all his problems at once. "As a matter of fact, yes. Mary and I are—"

"*Enough,*" Arrogance said in a deep voice that rumbled the throne room, revealing himself as a much larger, floating version of his usual self, towering behind the throne. Francis could never find the golden smile on the sun mask when the god used this version, but the black frown radiated darker than any of Terrangus's worst storms.

The deity floated towards Serenna, who flinched back. Oh, was that fear? Interesting. "Ah, Serenna. Serenna, Serenna. Relax, my dear Guardian. I forgive you for ignoring my invitation to Serenity and missing out on enlightenment. What is it about poor decisions that always seem so...enticing?"

She took another step back, her face turning more pale. Something about those words struck her deep. Why? As far as she knew, this was still the God of Wisdom. He hadn't told anyone the truth. Not even Mary. "We're here now. What do you want?"

Arrogance chuckled. "Where to begin... Where to begin. Have you enjoyed your visits to the new Terrangus? It's slowly developing into a paradise now that logic governs taxation rates, public works...punishments. Who would have guessed that crowning unintelligible brutes with infinite authority would prove to be inefficient? My dear Francis and I have raised the standards of living considerably in under a year. What could we accomplish within a decade? What could we accomplish if we had, let's say...

"Forever?"

"No one rules forever," Serenna said, regaining her composure and clutching her staff. "How bold of you to make such a statement."

"Bold...is *not* the word you're looking for. Ah, while I would love to bring everyone to Serenity and discuss the philosophical ramifications of choice and predetermination, that is not in the cards today. Your friend, what's his name? The one that drinks too much wine—"

"David!" Zeen said, lighting up with a smile. A real one, not the grin he usually wore like a mask. "How has he been? I'm surprised he's not here."

Arrogance hovered in front of Zeen. "Oh, Zeen. I forgive your interruption. You killed Strength—possibly my most powerful enemy—by simply being a fool. You! Of all people! Your chaotic ignorance may end up being the prelude to paradise." Zeen lost his smile as Arrogance floated above the throne.

"Your David has made the Fear Goddess very, *very* angry, and nearly destroyed us all in the process. Her fury always travels the same path. A Harbinger will arrive in Xavian as early as tomorrow, which is rather unfortunate timing. As of now, you are woefully unprepared."

"That...is true," Serenna said, then brushed the hair from her eyes. "Francis, if we end up having to face a Harbinger of Fear, would you battle alongside us? I would gladly welcome your aid."

"No," Francis said. He had waited so long for this moment, for the opportunity to turn his back on the Guardian team that had never loved him. It was less fulfilling than anticipated. "Mary will not either."

Mary eased her hand to Serenna's. "I'm sorry. If I weren't with child, I would fight by your side again. You are my leader."

What about me? I'm your leader, Mary...

"Thank you. I do understand, but this places us in a terrible scenario. We'll need to recruit immediately. We need an elemental mage, a mechanist if we can find one, and..."

"The time has come, Francis," Arrogance whispered through his thoughts.

"It so happens I have an elemental mage for you," Francis said, nodding to his left. "Vanguard Five, come forth."

The slim, bald man with empty eyes stepped forward, his wooden staff sheathed to the side of his white armor, with Wisdom's crest on the center of his plate. Five was the tallest of the Vanguards, about David's height, if Francis remembered correctly. "If you demand it," Five said, kneeling, "I will serve. All glory to Serenity, may we persevere long enough to watch paradise manifest in our realm."

"Absolutely not," Serenna said, shaking her head at the kneeling Vanguard. "Let's travel to Alanammus. I'm sure Archon Gabriel can make a recommendation for an up-and-coming elemental mage."

"You don't value my choice?" Francis asked, signaling for Five to rise.

"Puppet emperors don't make choices. Let's go, Zeen. We're done here."

Francis clutched his staff, shaking as everyone—Wisdom included—snickered at her comment. How dare she? How dare anyone come into his domain and speak to the most powerful mortal alive? A genius, the realm's greatest leader, the one who would herald Serenity—

"Please halt," Five said, in the standard monotone voice. "Serenna Morgan, I understand and accept your reluctance of my kind. We have shown you nothing that would inspire trust.

32

However, it would be an honor to serve you as a Guardian, and an opportunity to earn our acceptance from the realm. I ask you, undeservingly, would you reconsider?"

This one is growing more eloquent. I will need to observe the others, it would be quite dangerous if Wisdom's grip ever shattered after giving them so much power. Hmm…

Serenna approached Five, studying his blank facial expression like he was a book. "Mary," Serenna said, glancing at her. "Can I trust this…thing?"

"Honestly, I have no idea. Vanguards listen to me when I command them, but neither Wisdom nor Francis have explained their purpose yet. They tend to leave me out of important discussions."

"That's not true!" Francis yelled, even though it was. "I include you in everything!" he yelled, even though he didn't.

Mary took Francis by the hand, gazing into his eyes, filling him with a feeling he couldn't articulate. Of all the poems that had been written about beauty, none came within a fraction of describing the red-haired, freckled goddess that had given herself to him. "Can you swear to me, in front of all these people, that Vanguard Five will do no harm? I trust you Francis, you're the father of my child."

Oh no. I do love her. How do I make both Wisdom and Mary happy? Why is all this knowledge of history and events completely useless when I need it the most? Serenity for our realm is the end goal. I will not falter. I can't…

"I swear to you, on our unborn child, that Vanguard Five will serve the Guardians with unyielding loyalty. Does that suffice?" *I picked up my mother's gift for lying. Do all leaders have to live this way? Why has power made me so unhappy?*

How much can a person be damaged before they are considered broken?

"Well played, my dear Francis," Arrogance said in his mind.

"These insignificant people will never appreciate what you do for the realm, but not me. The architect of paradise will be the most beloved man that ever existed by the time we're finished. Ah, what joy awaits us all..."

Serenna paused, glancing at Zeen, who nodded with a smile. "Very well," she said, holding out her hand. "I welcome you to the Guardians, Vanguard Five. Do not take this the wrong way, but I would prefer not to see you anytime soon."

Five accepted her handshake. "Be that as it may, God never lies. We do battle tomorrow."

"So be it," Serenna said. She left with Zeen, not bothering to say 'thank you' or even 'goodbye' to her emperor.

After the room cleared, Mary took his hand and sighed. "It startled me to hear you say that. Do you swear—"

He grabbed Mary mid-sentence, pulled her close, then kissed her sweet, wet lips. "I love you."

The flicker in her perfect green eyes was almost beautiful enough to distract him from the horrors he had just inflicted upon the realm.

CHAPTER 5

DREAMS ARE NOT ETERNAL

avid sighed, wiping the snow away from his eyes, never turning away from the Goddess of Fear. All the spectral humans and demons throughout the icy dream of Boulom stood frozen, staring at David in disgust. Light posts glowed above, casting a barely visible shadow on the pale snow falling from the skies.

"Why do all the men in my life cling to the faults that destroy them?" asked Fear, hovering in the air with her ethereal wings. Despite the blinding snow, the vortex in her left eye shimmered with a wrath that made it difficult to breathe. Did he have to breathe until now? He could never remember to check.

"For whatever it's worth, I apologize—"

"It's worth *nothing*. I picked you because I assumed you were different, because I assumed saving you from a self-inflicted end would mold you into the perfect champion. Do you want the truth, David? I had no idea what consequences would occur when I chose to prevent your demise. The rules... Time makes nothing clear. I risked everything...*everything* because I saw myself in you."

"I never asked to be saved," he said, finally breaking away

from her gaze. "I'm not the sort of man who can change his ways. Believe me, I've tried. When Melissa died, a part of me faded with her. Something grew in its place over the months, but it's nothing that drives me to be a better person. I am who I am, Noelami. You cannot change me. No one can."

"Pitiful excuse," she said, coming down and morphing into her empress form. When the crown materialized on her head, all the city-folk went back to their mindless drifting through the streets. "I didn't save your life to have you mope around and whine about the past. This is not a partnership, David. You work for me. You exist because of me. You have broken that commitment, and now you will suffer."

"Spare me your threats, Empress. We both know you cannot harm me."

"Spoken like a fool. Never dare one who has lost everything to find creative ways to inflict harm. Since you felt the need to linger in time loops in the wretched kingdom of Xavian, they can deal with a Harbinger. Let's see how well Serenna protects the realm with no Francis, no Mary, and a weakened Zeen. Their blood shall be your punishment. I disabled the portals on your blade, and now you remain until I allow you to leave. *If* I allow you to leave. Behold the powerless demigod."

"*No!*" he yelled, drawing his sword. "Leave them out of this! This is my failure; I accept whatever torment you lay upon me. My actions and consequences are my own!"

Noelami eased a finger to the blade, smiling as she pushed it down. "And that is where you are wrong, and why you were always an inefficient leader. Leadership means relinquishing the ability to shield others from your mistakes. Have you ever considered the burden that loving you placed upon Melissa?"

David leaned his sword against her neck, hands shaking as he considered tearing it through. "*Enough!* What do you accomplish by murdering them?"

36

She didn't step back, but at least her smile faded. If only he could read her fear. "You should be asking yourself that same question. Next time you see Zeen or Serenna, ask them how they feel about you nearly wiping out existence by torturing the Time God. I would love to hear their response."

"I..." Gods, where were the words? She always did this to him. "I tried to change the past, because changing the future seems impossible." He turned away from Noelami, gazing out to the snowy skies of Boulom. He reached for his flask, opened it, then went to chug the remnants of ale, disappointed as only chilled water met his lips. Of course.

A bright flash appeared where Noelami had been, showing a giant version of the fear windows he had used to summon from his sword back in the day. He watched through the window as Noelami in her goddess form approached an older man—most likely a mage based on his staff—in a grimy shack, with rats so large it could only be Xavian. The shack was even more rundown than Arabell's, if such a thing was possible.

"It all went to shit when Reilly died," the man said, sighing. "Senator Thompson takes more bribes than a Nuum whore, gods be damned. They took my wares and left me to die like a rat. Well, I'm not dead. Not yet, at least. Do it, Goddess. Do it before I change my mind. When reality fails, dreams are eternal."

David pitied the man, who was gazing up at Fear with a wide grin. Such a familiar desperation, the possibility of a newfound purpose giving relief to fill the void. Over gold? What a foolish thing to submit to a Harbinger for. Perhaps they were all foolish choices? When David had finished his revenge on Grayson, none of the joy returned. It'd been even worse once it was over, once he realized sorrow was not something that would vanish with an act of violence—

He gasped as a stream of energy flowed through his skin, returning the strength of a demigod. His blade emanated with void energy, causing all the city-folk to gaze upon him, then bow down. *How is this possible? The only other person here is...*

By the gods...

Maya Noelami feared she had pushed a mage named Ermias Naiman to the brink of time magic by—

Everything hit him at once. The first Harbinger, the end of Boulom. The God of... Arrogance? She hated herself for the failures of her lover, an undeserved pain that nearly brought David to tears. "Noelami, it wasn't your fault."

"If I had never led Boulom, it would still be here today. We wouldn't be sitting in this dream I created, a dream that does not exist. Half of my mantra is a lie. Reality fails, but dreams are not eternal. Nothing is." The world went black after she spoke, leaving David and Noelami in a cataclysm of pure darkness. She panted, lying where the ground would be. "It takes all of my energy to empower a Harbinger. Now, you know the truth. Kill me, David. The sword is capable of it. My existence of death after life has become an endless jest. I wish... I wish there was a god, friend, or anyone who would have saved me before I leapt off my tower. No one helped me. No one."

He approached the weakened goddess through the darkness. He could hear every thump of his heart with no other sound to distract him. Her eyes were like a mirror. He stared into the pain, the disdain for life's ability to persevere despite the heart's begging for it to stop. It was nearly the same. He had destroyed Melissa, but Ermias had destroyed her. Gods...

I could stop the cycle of violence. If she dies, there will never be another Harbinger of Fear. Why am I hesitating? She acts this way to protect the realm. What if she's right? What if never having a Harbinger of Fear will make the future Guardians vulnerable to Death? No, it's not about that...

Killing Grayson made the emptiness worse. I will never make that mistake again.

He took her by the hand, helping her stand, actively ensuring to keep eye contact. Such a thing was said to help. David embraced the Goddess of Fear, letting her tears roll down his arms. "Take as long as you need. Whether an ocean or a puddle, let your tears fall until it's better. I can never forgive what you have done to the realm, but I will always protect you. You were right—we are one and the same."

Please let them be okay. They are not ready without me.
Please...

CHAPTER 6

WEAKNESS IS A DISEASE

empest leaned back on his stone chair before he would address the zephum council, wiggling his tail to get a better fit through the hole that had been crafted specifically for him. Unfortunately, there was no 'honor' in such things as comfort, leaving him to address his father and warmakers with the uncomfortable summer heat seething against his back. Torches filled the Vaynex citadel hall, amplifying the sun, drawing sweat from his snout.

In true zephum fashion, they had tackled one problem by making another worse.

"My fellow zephum," he said, avoiding the stern gaze of his father, who sat on the Vaynex throne. A larger seat, but still the same height as everyone else. Humans had preferred to keep their leaders elevated, but zephum tradition demanded equal footing, a mandate that had come straight from the God of Strength. Tempest found himself thinking about the fallen deity more each day. *I was never fair to you. I even despised you at times… Why? You always believed in me, gave me the best chance, and yet I lashed out like a child. Is that how I treat Father?*

Am I the villain of another's story?

"It is my honor to call this meeting and confirm your

suspicions. Talks with Emperor Francis were successful, and we will proceed with the arms trade between our kingdoms as early as next week." *I'm forgetting something...* "Um, of course, contingent on our warlord's approval."

While Sardonyx sat like a statue with his face guard on, all the warmakers took Tempest's political misstep as an opportunity to sigh and murmur at an exaggerated volume. For all their hatred of humans, they didn't seem to mind stealing their more annoying traits.

"You forget yourself yet again, young Tempest," Warmaker Tellex Novalore said, brushing debris off his spiked shoulder guards. "Be careful child, the brute you despise is the one that keeps you alive. But not forever. Claw or not, I will never follow you as my warlord."

Tempest shot a glance at his father, who had a tendency to ignore the constant insults made at his son's expense. Apparently, today would be no different. *What would Rinso say? Hmm.* "It is you that forgets himself, Novalore. While you sit there and make idle threats and draconic sounds to create a perception of power, I am out there paving the roads for the future of our people."

"You hear this?" Novalore asked, rising from his chair, pointing at Tempest as he stared at the warlord. "Draconic sounds? Paved roads? Is this a council of zephum warriors or bickering humans?"

Tempest sighed. "Warmaker, despite your presence, this is a council of great minds—"

"I am old enough to remember the glory days of Vaynex. Back when we invaded Nuum and Terrangus outposts without mercy. Not for gold, not for resources, but for honor! All these... bargains and trades. Do you beg my daughter to sign a treaty before you mate?"

Considering how Pyith and I were forced together, that's not far off, Tempest thought, failing to ignore the snickers and nods from the rest of the council. "Yes, please tell us more of these glory days of the zephum occupations. The days of famine, economic recessions, days where resources were so meager one in four zephum were lost at birth. It's simple: unless we can learn to eat our blades, Terrangus needs weapons and Vaynex needs gold. In fact, it's so simple, even you should be able to follow."

Warmaker Novalore smiled, gazing down at Tempest, likely enjoying being the tallest zephum in the citadel other than Sardonyx, who still sat motionless. "Ah, you speak of those days as if you were there. Those days of famine, of loss, they molded us into stronger warriors. We lost countless, and so be it. Weakness is a disease only cured by honor or death. In the end, I am still here. Warmaker Pentule is still here. Warmaker Dubnok is still here. Zephum like us will always remain, despite how often zephum like you predict our downfall."

I envy Francis. He had the right idea to take absolute power and control everything. When I am warlord, how will I get anything done with outdated brutes like this? Why do the older ones who have already expunged their usefulness feel the urge to yell loudest?

"Zephum like you will always be here, because zephum such as I must tolerate it. Why can't you accept the betterment I create and stay out of the way? Tradelines, war treaties, your bloodline will know a life you could only dream of!"

"Our tradelines have given us unearned resources, a burden that fattens our weak. Our last cultural exchange with Alanammus led to our first Harbinger in a decade once they saw how magic rules in the barbaric South. Dreams you say? I dream of the past. Speak whatever you will about the hardships of my time, but Strength never abandoned us. Strength has no reason to exist once weakness rules supreme."

Tempest rose, stepping up to Novalore, hating himself for having to look so high up to meet his father-in-law's eyes. "No reason to exist? Strength died for a human! What does that say about us? *What does it say?*" His yell reverberated off the citadel walls, repeating the answer over and over for any zephum willing to listen. Strength had died for a human, because a human embraced the message of 'be kind and love each other,' a lesson Tempest had stolen for his damn books. A lesson he had never bothered to say thank you for—

Steps approached from the direction of the Guardian room. Tempest glanced over at…Pyith, Serenna, and Zeen? While he had made the invitation to visit, he had never expected them to do so.

Why would anyone come here willingly?

Novalore ignored Tempest, glaring at Serenna with a burning hatred. Ah, a weakness. How to leverage that? "What? Why is the Pact Breaker in our citadel? Stop your approach human, or I shall kill you where you stand—"

Warlord Sardonyx Claw finally rose, shooting a glare at Novalore that would've sent any zephum to their knees. "*You* are done speaking. This human girl—Serenna Morgan of Mylor— holds my blessing as my honored guest. I will dump your corpse in the streets if you dare threaten her in my presence again. And… Ah! Is that Zeen? This is *glorious!*" He rushed up to the injured Zeen, hugging him with a devastating embrace that made Tempest grimace. Zeen's eyes begged for mercy, but there would be no reprieve from the warlord's love.

"Behold!" Sardonyx yelled. "The Human Warlord! This Guardian fought with the wrath of our god. He put his ignorance aside and shattered the forces of Death, crumbling all that should not be with the glory of the first warlord. You will bow, or you will die."

Tempest held back a snicker at how fast the 'glorious' zephum council yielded to the demands of Warlord Sardonyx, bowing nearly in unison before hastily exiting the citadel. If there was one thing they all had in common, it was dealing with the insignificance of drowning in the shadow of rage.

"Your timing is impeccable, Guardians," Sardonyx said, approaching Serenna. "I cannot bear to listen to these fools any longer. Ah, that look in your eye. We are the same, mighty Serenna. I see power. I see destiny. I see *purpose*. Speak your burdens!"

"It is an honor to reunite, Warlord," Serenna said, bowing. If Tempest was not already standing, he would have fallen out of his chair. Not even a year ago, they had dueled in Alanammus tower. The end of Strength had truly changed everything. And perhaps, not entirely for the worse. "I wish the circumstances of my visit were more favorable, but we have reason to believe a Harbinger of Fear is imminent in Xavian. Forgive me, but I must request the aid of the mighty Pyith and be on my way."

Hmm. One of the less obvious detriments of losing their god had been to lose information of the outside realm. A Harbinger of Fear? Wasn't David supposed to suppress those? "You're certain it's Fear?" said Tempest. "What is your evidence?"

Zeen smiled. "Wisdom warned us, so we recruited some weird elemental mage named Five. While I can't say I'm ready to face a Harbinger again, I always wanted to see the pirate kingdom. They have ships! Real ships! Not the dingy Terrangus trade vessels."

Interesting, they recruited a Vanguard? I'll warn Pyith to keep her distance.

"There is no honor in Xavian!" Sardonyx yelled, turning his back to the Guardians. "A hovel of human rats. Hmm, since the shield human is with child, I imagine she cannot do battle?"

"I hear she's fatter than I am now," Pyith said with a chuckle. Since Serenna didn't laugh, Tempest made sure not to. "But damn, I just can't imagine Francis mounting her. By Strength's name, I've tried, but how do they get it to work?"

"I have wondered the same!" Sardonyx said, rubbing the bottom end of his armored snout, making Tempest want to die. "The male must dominate! I just...cannot picture the mating procedure with such a difference in height. Do humans use alternative methods?"

"Right," Serenna said with a drawn-out sigh. "While it's always a pleasure, Warlord, please forgive me for making a hasty exit. I must find a mechanist in Alanammus before we engage our enemy."

"A mechanist, you say?" Sardonyx said, taking his face guard off and offering a smile. "Pyith, introduce them to Dumiah Bloom. And one more thing: I have been given much to consider since our meeting. Tempest...you will accompany the Guardians in this battle. Warmaker Novalore is a fool, but he makes a valid point. You will protect the wretched kingdom of Xavian, then return as a zephum hero. Am I clear?"

No! Is he mad? "Me? Aren't I better off here?" Tempest met eyes with Pyith for a brief moment, and in that moment they shared unspoken terror. She knew. They all did. He had run away from Harbinger Nyfe as tears dripped from his eyes. Tempest was no Guardian. No warrior. No politician apparently, either.

What am I, then?

"You will thank me in the long run," Sardonyx said, glaring at him. "Defeating a Harbinger will grant you an honor none of these warmakers can claim. Follow the guidance of Serenna and Pyith, and victory is all but guaranteed."

"But..." Tempest started, but what was the point? Warlords never changed their minds. There was no honor in such things as evidence and logic. "Very well. Guardian Serenna, if you would have me, I will follow. I will battle alongside the Guardians in whatever role you see fit. Strength without honor—is chaos."

Serenna paused, each moment of silence screaming her

disapproval. "I welcome you as one of our own. Strength without honor—is chaos."

"Well spoken," Sardonyx said, his voice cracking. "I...when you return, we will feast! It will be glorious! If only things were... Ah. Forgive me." He put his face guard back on, glared at Tempest through the steel, then left towards his chambers.

He may never see me again. Was that...guilt?

"Relax, dear," Pyith said. "No one dies on my watch. Stand around Zeen and pretend to be useful. We'll get through this. Bloom's looking good; she's ready to fuck some demons up."

"Bloom is an unstable lunatic. I was hoping the next Guardian would be someone more...refined?"

Pyith laughed, waving the Guardians to follow as she walked towards the exit. "More refined? Here? Maybe you're the lunatic."

"I never heard of a zephum mechanist," Zeen said, finally drawing his eyes away from the spot behind the throne where Strength had used to stand. "Why are there none in the Rinso books?"

Pyith's laugh grew louder. "Because the author is a fucking idiot."

"Soon to be a dead idiot," Tempest said, forcing a smile. "In reality, Bloom's gift has been a cruel miracle for our people. Mages of any class are very rare, let alone a mechanist, but...well, you'll see."

*

Tempest shielded his eyes from the sun as they stepped outside onto the streets of Vaynex. As bad as this was, it would be nothing compared to the heat in Xavian. The economic downturn had translated to fewer merchants and soldiers contributing to society, with abandoned carts and shops rotting by forgotten corpses. Structures of tan blocks, tangerine sand, and...fear. The fact neither Serenna nor Zeen appeared surprised by the cruel conditions spoke volumes on the legacy of zephum culture.

Strength help me, but we need this alliance with Terrangus. When you contribute nothing to technology or culture, you contribute to violence, or you starve.

Only I can fix this. It will take time. It will take power.

"Whew," Zeen said. "Wish I woke up in the spring." He wiped sweat off his pale face that was actively losing more color. "Any chance uh… Do you have any water?"

"Take this," Serenna said, handing him the jug that was by her hip. "Tempest, where exactly are we going? I don't want Zeen out here for long."

"The honor grounds are a quick trek to the west. I'll ensure he gets a seat in the shade."

Zeen wiped the water from his lips after finishing most of the jug. "The honor grounds? Oh! Is that the spot where Rinso defeated Warlord Vehemence?"

"No spoilers!" Serenna yelled. The bitter tone of her voice filled Tempest with joy. Art's success can best be measured in how angry it makes otherwise reasonable people.

"Damn, you too?" said Pyith with a snicker. "Do humans have no art of their own? Are your books as terrible as your music?"

The small-talk brought the color back to Zeen's face, so Tempest kept the conversation going about Rinso as they trekked to the honor grounds. Perhaps Serenna noticed as well, as she was more than happy to oblige. Whether out of love for her life-mate or the story of Rinso, either motive was an acceptable one.

Serenna squinted her eyes as she peered across the unpaved Vaynex streets just before the honor grounds. "Not to sound vain, but since arriving, I expected a bit more of a crowd?"

Hmm. How to address that? These sort of things require subtlety and tact—

"They are fucking terrified of you," Pyith said, then spat on the ground. "Makes me sick."

"What?" Serenna asked, smiling, clearly not understanding it wasn't a joke. "Of me? Here?"

Pyith paused. "We fear everything now, not least the human Guardian that bested our warlord. Being able to see or touch god, there is a warmth to it you don't realize until it's gone. We knew Strength was there, protecting us, guiding us. Fuck, we never listened, but just to hear the voice was a comfort. No one is there now. No one watches, no one protects. We only have ourselves. And we have no idea what the fuck we are doing."

"I'm sorry," Zeen said. To Tempest's dismay, the color faded from Zeen's face again. Pyith had never understood the necessity of gentle words for a gentle audience. "It wasn't...it was never supposed to happen this way."

Pyith towered over him, glaring down. "You ever offer mercy to a Harbinger again, and I'll tear open your throat."

"Enough!" Serenna yelled, slamming her staff onto the ground. "Where is your mechanist? We waste valuable time."

"Come," Tempest said. He took the lead, waving for them to follow up the steel steps of the honor grounds, to a distinct position with a front-row view of the upcoming battle. Fortunately, the warmakers were absent this afternoon, allowing Tempest to offer each of his Guardian hosts a seat to observe. Only one spot offered shade, a seat normally reserved for the warlord. A year ago, if Sardonyx had seen Tempest offer it to Zeen, he would've killed them all.

Zeen took a deep breath after sitting, observing the minuscule crowd with most of the regular seats vacant. "Thank you, Tempest. Is this normal? The Rinso books always described the honor grounds as a mini-colosseum packed out in a frenzy."

"Not when she's here," said Pyith. "Zeen, you may want to uh…not watch this one."

And there she was. Dumiah Bloom in her red, tattered leather armor approached the circular battleground below, clanking her two swords together to get the smaller crowd riled up. "Wake up, you fucks!" she yelled, stopping when she glanced up at Tempest's post. "Shit, is that Serenna? Is this finally my audition? Yes!"

A larger zephum entered the arena, loaded from tail to snout with steel armor and a massive two-handed axe. Heavy armor was incredibly unwise against mechanist combat, and the fact Tempest didn't know this male's name suggested his odds of victory were relatively poor. A desperate warrior in desperate times. If only the story was more rare.

Dammit all, we need more gold until I can usher in reform. It's nothing short of a miracle Vaynex has lasted this long. Intelligent minds yearn for peace, while their counterparts fear being exposed by the harmony.

"Warrior Bloom," the warrior yelled from the sands below, "you honor me with this opportunity to elevate my family name. Regardless of the outcome, may the defeated send glory from the Great Plains in the Sky. Strength without honor—is chaos."

The larger zephum saluted, only to be met by Bloom spitting on the ground. Such abhorrence for tradition led to a chorus of boos and groans, making the arena sound like it was filled to the brim.

A warmaker would normally proclaim the battle, but with no one of any significant rank in the arena, Tempest rose, temporarily silencing the crowd. One could get used to that. "By the glory of Strength, and Warlord Sardonyx, I bless this combat for the future of Vaynex. Strength without honor—is chaos. Begin."

Bloom dashed forward, with a trap in one hand and a sword in the other. She dodged a swing towards her head by hopping back, then threw the trap by his leg. "Freeze!" she yelled, triggering the trap to erupt, freezing his leg solid and stuck to the bloody sands of the honor grounds. The boos continued to rain down, but became lighter as several onlookers got up to leave.

Oh, how I miss Melissa. Strength forgive me, but I can't think of anything worse than one of our people being a mechanist.

Bloom casually approached her opponent, whose leg was still frozen in place. He made a desperate two-handed swing, only to be disarmed—quite literally—as Bloom parried with one sword and swung down with an ugly swipe that removed both the zephum's hands. She ripped his face guard off, grabbed a trap from her belt, then plunged it into the zephum's mouth, interrupting his scream. "Okay, fair to say victory is mine. You surrender?"

The zephum gargled with the trap in his mouth, attempting to speak, but only managing obscure sounds.

"Don't be stubborn. Hey, you surrender? Last chance."

The gargled sounds continued.

She posed a few feet in front of her opponent, staring up into the sky with her two swords crossed in the air. "Strength is dead. And we have killed him. *Fire.*"

The trap erupted.

Screams, blood, and parts filled the air. Zeen fainted. Pyith laughed. Serenna did not appear pleased.

Serenna tapped Zeen's face a few times to wake him, then glared at Pyith. "Absurd. Completely absurd. Will this...Bloom follow orders?"

"Don't count on it. She got banished from our military for disobeying commands and...other reasons. It takes a lot to get banished from the military. *A lot.* Still, it's worth the risk. My life-mate is useless, and yours is weakened. Serenna, we need help."

"Pardon me for possibly speaking out of line," said Tempest, "but I must disagree. We don't need...*her*. The Guardians must be above battling the forces of evil by enlisting evil. Never tell Father I said this, but it's a tradition worth upholding."

Pyith scoffed. "What a joke. Serenna, we don't have time for this. She in or out?"

Serenna paused, then glanced at Zeen. "Are you okay with this?"

Zeen leaned up, fixing his slumped posture. "Everyone deserves a chance for redemption. It's what Strength would have wanted. Serenna, let's do it."

"Very well," Serenna said, brushing the hair out of her eyes. "Meet us in the Xavian Guardian room tomorrow morning at dawn. It's likely Wisdom speaks the truth."

Ah, Zeen. Damn you for being right. Be kind and love each other. Why is it so much easier to say than do?

CHAPTER 7

DESPERATE LIARS

erenna wiped the sweat off her forehead, then took a sip of water in the healing ward below the Xavian Guardian room: a dank, rundown chamber reminiscent of her days in a Terrangus cell. Bells rang as she peered out the window, shying her eyes from the shimmering sun reflecting off the morning water. Of course it would be here, in the middle of summer. Pure sun. Pure heat.

Pure Xavian.

She glanced at the resting Zeen before turning to the healing mage. "Speak truthfully. Is he anywhere near combat ready?"

The mage placed his wand on the table, then stepped back. "My Terrangus counterparts have done impressive work but…is an answer lying if the truth eludes me? I say yes, mostly because I gauge yes to be the desired answer."

This isn't fair, how is it that my second Harbinger as leader is without David, Francis, and *Mary? I guess some things never change. Everything depends on me. It always did—*

Zeen awoke with a groan, rising slowly as he observed the room. He smiled when he met eyes with Serenna, then eased out of his bed. "Oh," he said, testing out his legs. "Much better!

Not my full self, but I'll take anything over yesterday. Thank you for your aid, pirate sir."

The mage scoffed. "It's Gerry. I didn't spend six years mastering the arts of healing magic to be mistaken for a pirate. Here, drink this."

"Sorry," Zeen said, accepting the jug of water and chugging most of it. "It's just...this is Xavian! Home of the pirate lords!"

"Listen kid, best to love Xavian from a distance. Unless gang wars, poverty, and blistering heat tickle your fancy, kill this Harbinger and head back to Terrangus. All a joke if you ask me. Terrangus gets a perfect ruler in Francis while we're stuck with Thompson."

Francis is the one you should love from a distance. "Is Senator Thompson really that bad?"

"Ugh," Gerry said, shaking his head in an unnecessarily dramatic fashion. "I swear the gods mock Xavian. We finally get someone with a brain, then Reilly dies dealing with a rival kingdom's nonsense. At least the Harbinger came during Thompson's reign. No chance he wins re-election now. Spit on him. If my family weren't here, I would wish this Harbinger total victory."

Total victory? He had clearly never seen a Harbinger to speak such nonsense. The blanket of ignorance must provide a cozy warmth. "Well," Serenna said, holding back a sigh. "I thank you for your aid, but we can take it from here."

"Yeah, whatever. If your father ever retires, maybe I'll move my family to Mylor. I prefer Francis, but ugh, that rain." Gerry packed up his supplies and headed for the exit.

"Zeen," Serenna said, holding his hands. "Are you well? I did not wait seven months just to lose you again. I can handle this if you need more time. I can handle everything."

"The Rogue Guardian is ready for orders," he said, lighting up with a smile. May he never know how that smile burned through her, even if fatigue and stress had sunken his face since last year.

Seven months alone, yearning for the one person who loves me as Serenna, and not the faceless Guardian of Mylor. That time is lost. We slept through a dream just to wake to a nightmare.

She paused, clutching his hands. "Your orders are to survive. Forever. I will shield you from all the horrors of this realm. You will never feel pain again. I swear it." She gave him a kiss on the forehead and let go.

Zeen picked up Hope, gazing at the blade as if it were an old rival. He swung down with a quick enough slice to cause a whistle, then placed the sword back on the adjacent table. "I doubt any life can exist without some measure of pain. It's alright though, those moments of hurt make the happy moments all the more sweet." He held her by the hips and pulled her close, then brushed his hand through her platinum hair. "Like now."

Oh, to be held that way again. Seven months had been a harsh price, but as his touch gave her a tingle in the back of her head from brushing through her hair, it didn't seem all that bad. "Like now." She guided his lips to hers, pressing their bodies together as she closed her eyes. *I will never lose you again. I will tear off crystal energy until I'm a broken husk if it keeps us together.*

He offered no resistance as she pressed him against the stone wall. His hands wrapped around her, caressing her sides, giving her a heat unrelated to the Xavian sun. They kissed like they had in Mylor, like there hadn't been a seven month wait. Like they were lifelong lovers who were never cursed to become Guardians. They kissed like he had never taken a blade in his neck.

They kissed like he had never convulsed in her arms, screaming sounds too horrifying to be words, drenching her cold hands with blood. *I am a fool. We are desperate liars, yearning to be loved, yearning to be embraced by our distraction. There is no happy ending for Guardians. David taught me the lesson without ever saying it.*

She pounded her fist into his chest, much harder than intended based on the shocked glance in Zeen's eyes. "Why are we doing this? Guardians have no future. Serve until we die. Get replaced, forgotten. I finally have you again and it's right back into the nightmare. I am tired, Zeen. So very tired. I want to sit back and raise little baby Zeens, laughing with Father and Landon as we grow old and relax. Are we destined to become David and Melissa? Dead or fallen heroes? How does anyone keep it together when the struggle is endless?"

Zeen wiped the single tear that rolled down her cheek. "Serenna, I gave Strength my word. I am a Guardian until the end, just as I am yours. The realm is...how did he say it...simply marvelous, my love. It is our privilege to keep it going. Let's defeat this Harbinger, then maybe we can get started on those baby Zeens."

She surrendered a laugh, then composed herself as she noticed Zeen glancing behind her. Vanguard Five stood a few steps past the entrance. How much of that had he heard? He stared at her, but his dissociated gaze appeared lost, as if he could hear everything, yet listen to nothing.

"Lord Wisdom commanded my arrival at dawn. The zephum have nearly arrived, but take pride in being late."

"Welcome, Mr. Four," Zeen said, grabbing his sword off the table and sheathing it.

"Off by one, Master Zeen."

This one seems...different than the rest. "Welcome, Vanguard. We never made proper introductions. May I assume you have no issue with my command?"

"I am authorized to follow any request within the threshold of reason."

Serenna sighed. Just once, it would be a pleasure to team up with an elemental mage that wasn't infuriating, but that's what she got for waiting until the very last minute. Just like David always did. "For this to work, I need unquestioning loyalty. Am I understood?"

"Please be advised that Lord Wisdom prefers our triumph. If you order me to act in any way that lessens the odds of our victory, I will be forced to seize command of the Guardians."

Zeen stepped forward, hand on his sword. "That is not going to happen."

"Please hold. I will suppress my words; my actions are reducing our odds of victory. Adapting to irrational behavior is...difficult. Do as you will, Serenna Morgan. No matter the cost, Serenity must prevail."

Off to a great start.

"Y'all done?" Bloom said, snickering at the entrance. She stood in front of Tempest and Pyith. "Humans and their talking. Serenna, why don't you kill this guy? He just blatantly threatened you."

Gods help me. "That's not how this works. Our opponent is the Harbinger of Fear. Every Guardian team has their differences, but it's imperative we're on the same page before the true battle begins."

"Oh?" Bloom said, her eyes lighting up. "It's prison rules, then? What's to stop me from killing you right now and taking command? This morning is looking to be really interesting—"

Pyith slammed her shield into Bloom's skull, sending her crashing to the ground, knocking over several wooden chairs. "What Bloom meant to say was, 'Good morning, Serenna. Pleasant weather we're having. A fine day to defend the realm.' That right?"

"FUCK!" Bloom yelled, rubbing her swollen head. "Yep, sure. That's right."

"Our odds of victory have reduced considerably," Five said in his monotone voice.

David always suggested fear, but there must be a better way. Serenna approached the wounded zephum. She offered her hand to Bloom, who paused, then accepted. "Are we on the same page?"

"You got it, Boss," said Bloom as she rose.

Tempest approached in dark leather armor instead of his normal golden battle regalia, with a sword sheathed behind. He looked sort of like Zeen, if Zeen happened to be a lizard-man. "Hmm. What an interesting Guardian team you assembled. I don't recall any of them using three zephum."

"Potentially true," Five said, rubbing his chin. "Assuming we don't all perish, historians will debate this team vigorously. No team has ever used a three zephum formation, but being that Tempest is not a true Guardian, many scholars will suggest this falls under the two-zephum definition, as kingdom rulers are often classified as rulers and not their race. Emperor Grayson Forsythe and Warlord Sardonyx are the most recent examples of such."

What the hell is he talking about?

Tempest glared at the Vanguard. "I don't recall asking you. Keep your words and distance to yourself. Your god is a tyrant."

Five met his stare, but without any frown or smile. "And your god is dead."

Alright, I'll keep Tempest away from Five. But, hmm. I have to split up Tempest and Zeen with both mages. I could keep Zeen by Five... No. He doesn't leave my side. Enough of this nonsense. David was right.

Fear fills in the cracks of inspiration when love is too thick. "Enough! I didn't summon you all here to discuss history or definitions. Our formation will be as follows: Pyith in the front,

Bloom and Tempest by Five, Zeen by me. This is not up for debate. Am I understood?"

Say it's a bad formation. I dare you.

No one did. Everyone nodded uncomfortably, but Pyith grimaced, then said, "Meet us outside, Guardians. Serenna and I have a few things to discuss first."

Everyone walked out of the room other than Zeen, who took another sip of water. He glanced at Serenna and Pyith after an awkward pause. "Aw, me too?"

"You too," Serenna said, apologizing with her eyes. "Try to keep them from killing each other out there."

"You got it, Boss," Zeen said with a grin, in a terrible impression of Bloom's voice.

Pyith waited until Zeen was out of the room, then turned to Serenna. "Well?"

"Well, what?"

"You really gonna make me say it? Formation sucks. Keep Bloom by you, leave Tempest and Zeen by Stickman."

How dare you, Serenna thought, crossing her arms. "Why are you undermining me? You would never speak this way to David."

"Nope, not after he punched me in the snout," Pyith said with a snicker. "But think about it. How many times did he stay on the same side as Melissa?"

Never. "I... If I'm forced to lead this team until I'm dead, you can be assured I will lead as I see fit. If David was perfect, he would still be with us."

Pyith scoffed. "Don't give me that shit. I'm not Zeen, you can't trample me with sharp words. Listen, you want to do it your way, fine. Just remember, if you took some advice for once, Nyfe would've been dead long before he became a Harbinger."

I'm tired of everyone's perfect hindsight. Does one mistake bar me from ever making a decision again? "Spare me your advice. All I need is your obedience."

"Oh? So that's how it is? Sure thing, *Francis*," Pyith said before she approached the exit.

How dare... Gods help me. Serenna drew the Wings of Mylor, then cast a faint crystal barrier, blocking Pyith's exit.

Pyith froze, then began to drift her hand to her sword as Serena approached.

Serenna sheathed her staff, eased Pyith's hand away from the sword, then hugged her. "We do it your way. Please, never hesitate to offer your advice. I have no idea how to lead this team."

"You listened to reason, changed your mind, and I'm near certain you're not drunk while the sun's out. Somehow, that makes you the best leader I've ever had. Don't worry, we'll get through this together. You're still my human little sister."

Serenna let go and took a step back. "How did so much change in a single year? Why are we the only ones left?"

"Simple. Because everyone else sucks."

Serenna snickered, then tapped Pyith on the shoulder. "Fair enough. Let's go, Sis."

They descended the stone steps to the outside. Other than the people screaming in the far distance, it was a peaceful summer day. The warm breeze blew her platinum hair into her eyes as her sandals sunk into the dark sand, and she grimaced at the bitter salt air. How could anyone admire such a scent? The ocean is a beauty for the eyes, not the nose.

The Guardians who had arrived first had the right idea by standing in the shade cast by Xavian Tower behind them. The awkward blue of the structure didn't mesh well with the clear skies, and the algae stains on the side facing the water likely hadn't been acknowledged in years, nor the broken windows all over the tower. It was like Xavian had attempted to recreate

Alanammus's Platinum Tower, but ran out of gold or inspiration.

Not noticing Serenna, Zeen continued addressing the rest of the Guardians. "To reiterate: crawlers are the weird scorpion looking things, colossals are the big guys, then the Harbinger will reveal himself after we take out enough of them."

"Correct," Serenna said, nodding when Zeen smiled at her, "but there has been a change in plans. Pyith stays ahead, Zeen and Tempest by Five, Bloom by me. Melee, protect your casters from the crawlers that ambush from all angles. As soon as we have enough slain, we take the colossal down together, and then the Harbinger. Treat the Harbinger like an empowered mage. Pyith will remain upfront, but the true danger is from magic rather than melee. Be alert. Be efficient. Survive."

Forgive me, my love, but Pyith is right. Don't think of this as me pushing you away—

"Rinso the Blue and the Rogue Guardian on the same side?" Zeen asked, as his eyes lit up. "This will be glorious!"

Oh. Alright then…

"'Glorious indeed,'" said Pyith, butchering Sardonyx's voice. "One last thing: Harbingers of Fear yell out our fears to throw us off and gain more power. They never shut the fuck up, so just ignore them. Whatever gets said today, we let it go. No exceptions. Seriously, you're gonna hear some weird shit. I bet Stickman's greatest fear is having a personality."

"Is that pseudonym referring to me?" asked Five, with no reaction. An odd nickname, considering he wasn't all that skinny. Maybe all humans appeared skinny to Pyith.

"I'm not fucking calling you Five. Give me a better name or it's Stickman."

"Before I ascended into enlightenment, my name was Robert. Hmm. Vanguard Five is the proper title, but if you must refuse me such decency, I will accept Stickman."

David always gave some quick words before we began. He was never all that inspirational, but damn, I can't think of anything better.

"Alright everyone. We…" Serenna paused, drawing the Wings of Mylor. *What to say? Something. Anything. Silence is the Harbinger of doubt.* "This is the best Guardian team I have ever known. I trust each of you with my life. We do this not for the realm, but for each other. No one else deserves it. Now, raise your weapons."

It always sounded better when David said it. I wonder if he just stole the line from someone else. Hmm. I wonder how far back that empty inspiration flows.

The empty words did their job, as all the Guardians clanged their weapons in the air.

CHAPTER 8

WORLD WITHIN A WORLD

here are all the pirates? Zeen thought, following the Guardians through the dusty Xavian streets. When Rinso the Blue had visited Xavian in the first Tales of Terrangus novel to rescue Olivia's sister, he was greeted by several angry fellows, who all wore eye patches, bandannas, and, most importantly, said "Arrr," a lot.

Reality was a bit less whimsical.

People were dashing about in all directions, looting carts, screaming, their frantic running kicking up dark sands as if it were a storm. Zeen took another sip of water as the sun beat down. It just felt wrong to battle a Harbinger in the daytime. Demons should be fought in the stormy darkness, with rain dripping down your face as you spit out blood and clutch your blade.

He paused as they turned a corner past the golden statue of Malzo the Pirate Guardian in the merchant's center, to find a large blue crystal barrier held together by fifty or so mages on all sides. The Guardians passed bodies the closer they came to the barrier, but it wasn't nearly as bad as before they had faced Nyfe.

Before he had died.

It's okay. Breathe. The new guys are looking up to you. They expect the Rogue Guardian, the Human Warlord, the…

Breathe. Just breathe.

It was difficult to think of a worse way to calm his nerves than to focus on his breathing. He turned to Serenna, who was already staring at him. "Are you well?" she mouthed. He nodded with quick a smile, figuring getting consoled by the team's leader during a panic attack would be bad for morale.

Calm yourself. This is nothing like Nyfe. The sun's out, there's a nice breeze, and there's actually a barrier this time. Rinso was never afraid. Even after his brother Rensen left him for dead, he pulled it together.

At the entrance to the barrier was a chubby man with one of those old man hairstyles, where most of it was missing but he refused to cut off the rest. Why do guys do that? He wore a bright blue tabard, smiling as Serenna approached.

"Lady Morgan. We meet at last."

"Senator Thompson, I presume?" she presumed, then shook his hand.

"Indeed. Ah, how the gods smile upon irony. You should know, I supported you despite the political harm to my career after you broke the Guardian Pact, while Reilly took the coward's route and denounced your actions. Now, she's dead, I'm senator, and you're leader of the Guardians. It would seem that good always prevails."

"Perhaps, but I often find that good only prevails at terrible cost."

Zeen grimaced at the truth of that. Good had defeated Harbinger Nyfe, but only after the cost of a god. What would have happened if Strength had said no? *If it comes down to it, no mercy this time. Can't take the risk. No mercy, no matter what…*

We'll see.

Thompson snickered. "All in perspective, dear girl. As long

as a terrible cost arrives at a great reward, empty the purse. Let the gold flow. Turn enemies into memories... How fares your father?"

"Open the barrier," Serenna said with a sigh. "Some of us actually have a job to do."

Thompson glared at a young girl tending to the barrier, who nodded, then opened a door-shaped entryway barely Pyith's height. "Do try to survive, Lady Morgan. I have many interesting ideas when you're done."

He may be a bad guy, Zeen thought, following Serenna through. He took a sip of water, glancing at the blue tinted sun above the barrier. A world within a world. Blood stains on the black sands meshed with the rubble of collapsed buildings, all too vivid and colorful. Rain would've been nice. For all Terrangus's flaws, rain had always hidden the sweat, sometimes the tears, and usually the smells.

Serenna cast a crystal shield on all of them one-by-one, with her own coming first and Zeen's coming last. "Stay close, crawlers often target the ones who stray."

Yes they do. Zeen drew his sword, welcoming the platinum tint of her crystal shield before it reverted to its natural, lucid state. "I'll protect you," he said to Five, who glanced back, but otherwise had no reaction. Somehow, he appeared bored.

"From the logs I've read," Tempest said, "we should hear some hissing by now. Is that coming—"

And, of course, the hissing began. Zeen forgot how worse the high-pitched warning sounded when echoing inside a barrier. Tempest stumbled into Zeen, panting, putting one hand on Zeen's shoulder. As an essence drifted off Tempest's body, he gasped, clutching Zeen's shoulder harder, with enough force to make him hold back a scream. If it were Pyith's hand, that shoulder would likely be broken. "What... What do we do?"

Zeen pushed down the pain and smiled. While it seemed

odd to find inspiration in another man's fear, such was the gift of experience. "It's okay, my friend. Draw your sword, stick by me. We protect Five until Serenna says otherwise."

"Yes, of course," Tempest said, drawing his sword with shaky hands. He continued speaking, but Zeen honed in on the scorpion-like crawler slithering behind him.

The crawler dove forward, then Zeen jumped behind Tempest to intercept, slashing Hope upwards and getting a clean slice.

"Oh, shit!" Bloom yelled, her voice drowning out Tempest's yells.

Zeen blocked the counter swing from the crawler's bladed arm, then ducked below the next swing, aimed for his neck. The crawler let out a screech, leaned back to strike—

"FIRE!"

Uh, that better not mean—

It did. Bloom's fire trap erupted right by the crawler's mouth, most likely killing it instantly. There was no way to know for certain as Zeen flew back, with crystal fragments shattering around him. He tumbled into the sands, the adrenaline giving way to a burning sensation in his legs. Damn, did that hurt. Just when he was feeling better, too.

Lying in the sand, he stared again at the blue-tinted sun above, the hissing replaced by an awful ringing and Serenna's yelling. Melissa had never blown him up on their one mission together. Unfortunate that he had never thanked her for that. A new platinum shield filled his vision before going lucid, then he forced himself to rise.

Pyith was engaged with a colossal. The demon stood twice her size, with the same crooked horns coming out the side of its head as the ones from Terrangus. Red bulging veins coursed through its muscular arms, highlighted by the monster's silvery skin. The colossal appeared to roar as Pyith blocked a blow from its giant arm, but all Zeen heard was ringing—

All sound returned the moment Tempest grabbed him. "Hey! Your sword!" Zeen nearly fell over as Tempest pushed the blade's handle into his hand.

Focus, focus, focus. Zeen took a deep breath, planting his left leg back to enter his battle stance. A spike of pain blistered through his leg to his neck, causing him to gasp. At least the ringing stopped. Actually, with the yells, screeches, and Bloom's explosions now stalking him from all directions, that ringing had been an unappreciated blessing.

Three crawlers dashed through the sand, rushing towards Five, their tiny insect-like feet kicking black sand into the air. Zeen pushed against his wounded leg, using agony as inspiration as he intercepted the crawlers. He ducked under a swipe aimed at his face, thankful to lean on his uninjured right leg. A quick counter tore its neck wide open; he went to dash away from the next two, but couldn't manage the hop before their blades crashed against his crystal shield. The force sent him flying down by Tempest, who was wheezing, his eyes locked in on Pyith.

Zeen would always love Tempest, but his zephum friend was much better at writing battles than participating in them. Fortunately, Five moved with surprising grace for a mage, dodging strikes and switching between elemental forms. While he didn't seem to share Francis's ability to multi-form, Five shifted quickly, favoring the combination of freezing crawlers with ice and then finishing them with a blast of lightning. Zeen struggled to rise as Five took an open slash towards his gut, which shattered his crystal shield and knocked him down to the sand with an awkward landing on his left side.

"Master Zeen," Five said, grasping his left arm. "I... require aid."

Dammit, Tempest, Zeen thought, forcing himself to hobble over with his sword drawn. The pain of his leg amplified his scream as he thrust Hope through the crawler lingering above Five. "Tempest! Cover us!" Zeen yelled, then took Five by the hand to help him rise.

"My preference…is not to perish. Not until Serenity. What… What was the purpose of our suffering if only to conclude in failure—"

A rumbling laugh filled the air. Zeen couldn't see the Harbinger of Fear, but there was no denying where that voice came from. "Oh, ho, Robert Cavare! I can read your fear. After Julius died meaninglessly in that dirty hole of Terrangus fighting Nyfe, you doubled down on the tyrant Wisdom to find meaning in the pain, but you found nothing but shackles. Get over yourself. The end of freewill? You're the real monster here."

Something about that statement startled Tempest, who stopped pounding his fist into the crawler he'd tackled to stare at Five. "Robert? Robert Cavare? By Strength's name… For Julius! For the Golden Scholars!"

Zeen flinched as Five grabbed him by his leather armor, pulling him close. A tear streamed down the Vanguard's cheek, but his expression never shifted. "My last words to him… I called him a fool. Ten years of marriage, shattered by forces beyond our control. How can we possibly choose when the correct path is shrouded in darkness? How do we deal with the burden of failure? Wisdom is the only one that understands. Freewill…is *madness.*"

In battle, men switching from strategist to philosopher was always a sign things were going poorly. "Robert," Zeen said, brushing the debris off his shoulders, "don't let loss define who you are. The beauty of freewill means we can choose a better way. No matter how you arrived here, you are a Guardian now. The realm needs you."

Five sighed, then glowed a dark blue. "You sound like Julius. Or perhaps everyone sounds like Julius and no one sounds like me. The realm... The realm needs Serenity. Nothing else matters. Master Zeen, aid our lizard-friend. These things will never harm me again."

Fair enough, we all react to fear differently.

Zeen rushed over to Tempest, who was swinging his blade with one hand while he clutched a crawler by its neck with the other. With three focused swipes going low, low, high, Zeen finished the nearest one, then grabbed Tempest's shoulder. "Are you okay?"

"*No!*" Tempest yelled, wiping blood off his face. "If it wasn't for Serenna, I would have died ten times over. I shouldn't be here..."

The distant voice boomed again. "Ah, who we got... Tempest Claw! The realm's most boring zephum. You fear the burden of leading a people who don't love you. Well, boo-hoo. Where's your pride? Least your other fear's more interesting. Pyith is wasted by your shortcomings. Have to agree with that one. Have to agree your father hates you, too. I'd drown you if you were my son. Hell, I'll drown you anyway."

"*Enough!*" Tempest yelled, slamming his blade down on a crawler that had already died. "He goes too far... I'm aiding Pyith. I'll show them. I'll show them all."

Zeen clutched his shoulder harder. "No, please. I know it hurts. Trust in the plan. Trust in Serenna."

"Someone like you would never understand. I'm tired of constantly being a cheap burden laced with golden armor. Julius, Pyith...Father. Zeen, If I do not survive, I designate you to finish the journey of Rinso. Keep the legacy going. The realm needs hope."

"The realm already has hope. The realm has you."

They met eyes for a short moment, then the sadness in

Tempest's face screamed out his defiance before he rushed off towards the colossal. *Damn it,* Zeen thought, gripping his blade and forcing himself not to follow. Worst thing you can do when someone breaks from the plan is to break it further. Serving in the Terrangus military most of his life had been a nightmare, but having the mentality of following commands pounded into his head had been a welcome instinct as a Guardian. Maybe that's why David had chosen him. He'd never thought to ask. Having no idea where David was these days, he would likely never have the chance.

He took a deep breath, then slashed Hope across a frozen crawler, shattering it into pieces as his blade bludgeoned across. A few more frozen crawlers stood in an oddly neat line; Five had apparently decided to stay blue and stick to ice spells. A quick learner. The man, Vanguard, or whatever he was, would be a fine Guardian.

"Zeen Parson!" the Harbinger's voice yelled from afar.

Give me your worst. I've been killed, seen a god die by my mistakes, seen my lover cry in my arms after I failed her. I may always be weak…but as long as I have Serenna, I will never die alone, hated, and miserable.

"I can read your fear, boy, can read it well. The harder you try to protect the realm, the further you damn it to chaos. You're like one of those politicians everyone loves but fucks us all in the end. Die alone, hated, and miserable? Hell, if we could only be so lucky. You are Serenna's burden. You are Serenna's burden forever."

Zeen parried a crawler's blade, mostly by instinct, and used the momentum of the pushback to do a quick spin and tear through the demon's open mouth. Blood splattered onto his face, but the foul aroma of the warm liquid barely caused him to flinch. The blue-tinted sun continued to observe from above, mocking Zeen with its promise of a peaceful day in a broken land. Oh, how he missed the rain. Aside from everything else, rain always hid the tears.

He faked a smile as Serenna met his eyes and refreshed his crystal shield. Sweat poured down her face as she kept swatting the platinum hair out of her eyes. Gods, she was beautiful. The realm's greatest Guardian turned back to her side of the skirmish, leaving Zeen with Five, who didn't even spare a glance. Surrounded by people, yet completely alone.

Serenna's burden…

Seven months asleep had been a long time, but the realm had no problem moving on. Other than Serenna, who even cared? He took a deep breath, again wishing for rain, then rushed towards a crawler. He attacked at once with a reckless swing, not bothering to watch the crawler fall. Zeen rushed the next one, tearing through, the pain in his legs irrelevant as he considered the high grass that had covered him in the Great Plains in the Sky. The unicorn that had galloped off into the end of time. A god had died, and a failure had returned.

Seven months had been a long rest. Maybe next time, Zeen would sleep forever.

CHAPTER 9

ITCHY TAIL

amn this itchy tail, Pyith Claw thought, wiggling it to rub against the inner steel. Damn thing had always waited to itch until her armor was on. Did Sardonyx ever get itchy in his full plate? Was it *glorious* when he finally scratched?

The colossal's fist slammed down, shattering Pyith's crystal sphere, causing her to stagger back when she blocked the blow with her one-handed shield. Hmm, those crystal barriers had been weak today. Serenna was off. Too much focus on the idiots behind them. *Fuck, that's my fault, isn't it?* It sure was. What had Pyith been thinking? Putting Zeen and Tempest with Stickman was like putting Warmaker Dubnok in charge of writing poetry. Funny to watch, but when your life's on the line, a bit more concerning—

What is that? Oh no…

Tempest was rushing over, ignoring the plan, being a fool. By Strength's name, did the three of them suck. Why couldn't they just follow the fucking plan? Seriously, why? Stupidity is a hell of a thing. When stupid is paired with stupid, stupid has no choice but to become more stupid. Bloom had the right idea. Bloom was nuts. Can't go wrong with a psycho murderer as long as she's on your side.

Damn this itchy tail...

Serenna shot Pyith a glare, her tiny human eyes judging her for the idiocy of Pyith's life-mate. Fair? Nope. The way life's always been? Yep. Pyith never understood why the other Guardians always got rattled by Harbingers of Fear. Who cares? How can anyone who stares into the mirror not know their own flaws?

Tempest roared, sounding ridiculous as he rushed in. Holding his blade way over his head was the perfect metaphor for his performance in this mess. He slashed at the colossal's leg, with such an embarrassing lack of control it barely made a mark.

Now, colossals aren't intelligent things. If they were, they would just rush towards Serenna and everyone would be dead in five minutes. But Tempest's strike caught its attention. Stupid recognized stupid, and the colossal closed its fist and flung it across, sending Pyith's life-mate flying into the rubble of a broken building. He let out a high-pitched scream before he flopped into the sands and stopped moving.

Pyith clenched her teeth at the agony in his voice. Such a sound should never come from a zephum, let alone the one she loved. Tempest was a fool. A coward. But he was *her* fool, *her* coward. She threw her shield to the ground, clutched her sword, and roared. A true roar. Warlord Fentum Claw of old would fall to his fucking knees if could hear the power in her voice.

Get up, Tempest. Please, get up.

Please...

As any true warrior knows, once a plan starts to crack, kill it and put it out of its misery. Pyith charged to her left, hindered by all that plate armor, thankful her face guard hid her teary eyes. "Bloom! You're on the colossal. Stall it!"

Bloom glanced at Serenna, then nodded at Pyith. Good girl. Leader is just a title fools argue over while the ones wielding true authority call the shots. But, unfortunately—barring some sort of miracle—Pyith's orders were going to kill Bloom. Tempest was more important, both to Vaynex and to her. That's the sort of grim reality Tempest had never put in his books.

Serenna yelled something. It sounded rather angry, which was fair, but Tempest would not fall today. He would *not*. Serenna would've done the same thing for Zeen. No one admits it, but we all have an unspoken list of who we love and how much. Anyone who finds themselves at the bottom of too many lists is looking at a lonely end.

Four crawlers stalked the unmoving Tempest. They had chosen their target and, in doing so, they had chosen to die. Pyith swung her sword across, rage guiding her hands as it tore one of them in half. She didn't feel a thing; the blow may as well have torn the air from the sky.

To their credit, the crawlers all retaliated in unison. There was no time to parry. The first blade cracked her crystal sphere; she couldn't follow the next two attacks, but the second slice broke her crystal and a sharp claw tore into her right shoulder.

Tempest still wasn't moving.

No time for pain. One advantage of being surrounded means it's hard to miss. Pyith swung again, aimlessly. Her blade ripped the closest one in half; she turned around, finding…six more crawlers. Dammit all.

A claw pierced her right leg. *IT'S ALWAYS THE RIGHT LEG.* The crawler's arm got stuck in the armor; they did a sort of dance as she tried to shake it off, stopping when a new claw pierced the same right shoulder. She would have laughed if the pain wasn't so blinding. Oh well, plenty of time for jokes once they got home.

Tempest isn't moving. I can barely move. Everything is…fading.

A bright platinum aura flowed from behind. Ah, it was truly beautiful. Not in the way a zephum legend kills forty humans and screams about how honorable it was, but in the beauty of the heart. Tempest would likely describe it as a faint gust of wind, nudging a lone viridescent blade of grass along the desperate crack of time between summer and fall. Pyith had no idea what any of that meant, but if she could love the zephum writing it, what else mattered?

Serenna must have triggered her empowered form, as a thick platinum shield covered Pyith's vision. Claws were slicing against her new shield, tiny crack by tiny crack, but Pyith's eyes never left Tempest. He still wasn't moving, but at least they ignored him to focus on her. Too many sounds, too many yells, all muffled by the pain and the cracking barrier. Damnedest thing was that her tail *still* itched.

"Pyith Claw!" a voice yelled out from afar... Oh yeah, the Harbinger. This battle was a fucking mess. "I can read your fear..."

Fuck that guy. She ignored him, attempting to raise her sword as the cracks on her platinum barrier grew larger. Her right arm was numb, so she raised the sword with her left. The crystal shield shattered, and the platinum behind her faded as Serenna let out a pained cry. Shit. Pyith refused to glance behind her; whatever was going on back there was obviously a big problem. No need to see that.

Was this really happening? David had always warned of the day. What a joke that it should come without him. Pyith roared, roared until her throat burned. The crawlers flinched, then jumped in one-by-one.

She swung her sword, a burning sensation in her wrist as the blade tore through something. She kept swinging, taking stabs all over her back, a few in the front, and even one in the tail. It no longer itched. She wished it did.

Pyith threw her sword at the blur of a crawler, then threw her own body on the closest blur since she was falling anyway.

They crashed to the ground, then Pyith kept screaming while she pounded her fist into what was likely its face as the blur got worse.

Darkness began to creep in. Was this an honorable death? Would the zephum council sing awful songs about her honor? Or is honor just an excuse to justify a meaningless end before our dreams and loves are fulfilled? Too many questions, not enough time. Not enough of anything, really. *I love you, Tempest. Forgive me for leaving you. Be strong and save our people without me.*

You will always be my Rinso, and I will always be your Olivia.

CHAPTER 10

PLATINUM ANNIHILATION

erenna gasped for air, fumbling her hand through the dark sand for her staff. Funny, how nothing is softer than sand as you lay in it, but when a colossal sends your entire body crashing through, it feels like rocks. Tiny, vengeful rocks. Her hands shifted through the sand, where was that damned—

There.

She grabbed the Wings of Mylor and rose, stumbling to regain her footing, squinting her eyes through the brutal gaze of the morning sun. Everything was hazy as she cleared her head and parted the hair from her eyes.

Bloom was squaring off against the colossal, throwing traps with no finesse, mostly just leading it on a chase. The colossal had icy fragments all over its legs and mid-body, but it wasn't slowing down. Bloom had clearly never faced an opponent who could power through detonators. To be fair, most people don't.

Zeen and Five were back-to-back, the Vanguard freezing crawlers before Zeen finished them off. Out of all the teams, she had feared they would have the least synergy, but as usual, she had been wrong. Did David ever have trouble reading people? Other than mistakes like Thomas and Brian, he had always seemed to understand the realm as it was. Who goes where. Who does what. Purpose, in a realm that forced it upon them. She refreshed both their shields, then turned to—

Gods, NO!

Serenna screamed, tearing her dry throat, ripping the crystal energy out of her body. The rays of platinum light emanating in front of her eyes made it difficult to see, but nothing would impair her vision of Pyith's limp body. *Pyith, please. I need you. I can't do this alone. It's too much...*

Everything depends on me. It always did.

When a plan fails, true power is the only way to maintain order.

Serenna created a crystal sphere around Tempest and Pyith, then hovered them over beside her. Even through the dense platinum hue, Pyith's body was soaking red, with countless open wounds. *I should've used more energy. I trusted they were okay...*

I failed her. I failed my only sister.

Love is a powerful, wonderful force, but hatred had been a worthy muse during a year at war. She clutched her staff and screamed again, trickles of blood flowing down her eyes as the radiant light grew brighter. That caught everyone's attention; the quickest way to find inspiration is to steal it from someone else.

The crawlers from Pyith and Tempest's side rushed over as Serenna formed six tiny crystal spikes around herself. She normally preferred to throw in some giants, but seven months out of practice had taken its toll.

Those damned crawlers moved quickly; it'd been far too long since she had to aim. *I can't afford to miss. I will not be the Guardian leader who oversees the realm's end. Right...*

There. She launched one towards the closest crawler; it was a perfect strike as the crystal spike tore through its chest. She let out a breath of relief, then launched two more identical spells, thinning the demons to three. They would die by her hands. Every damned one of them.

Bloom staggered over, one hand on her right leg. She yelled something, but her words were mere whispers against the deafening cry of platinum annihilation.

"Get out of my way," Serenna said, voice deepened by her empowered form. "We will discuss your failures after I'm finished."

The colossal eyed Serenna as she approached. By the gods, it took a step back. If it was smart enough to be afraid, it would be smart enough to know it was already dead.

"Dumiah Bloom," the Harbinger's voice yelled from afar. "I can read your fear... Oh, you could be my new favorite! You fear the desire of your warlord's death, the desire of Tempest and Pyith meeting their end so your people can finally embrace the true zephum destiny: humans in shackles. The end of Strength has opened a new future. A future of violence, control, a future where the mighty rule and the weak serve. I'll strike you a deal: turn on Serenna and I'll spare you. Be quick, lizard-girl."

Serenna shot Bloom a glare, who immediately turned away and engaged a crawler. Hmm. *I have no choice but to trust her.* Serenna groaned, creating a crystal sphere around the colossal. She had killed one by herself during the battle of Terrangus, it was time to do it again. Pain flooded her upper back as she raised her staff, lifting the colossal about an inch off the ground before darkness invaded her vision. She let go and collapsed, losing her platinum aura, falling to one knee as blood trickled down both eyes.

By the gods, I'm completely out of practice. I wasted the last seven months...

Quick breaths, quick breaths. She ripped the jug of water off her side, then chugged the entire thing before throwing it behind her. Still thirsty. She hated that feeling. The thirst, a reminder of her weakness, a reminder of how quickly she had turned to darkness.

Where are you, Death? Would you truly leave me to such an end? Not even an offer of temptation? Nothing?

It was for the best. Serenna would never say yes, even if she wanted to. That desire to solve all her problems by destroying them… It would never consume her. Even if there was no other option. Even if it would save Zeen. She wouldn't do it. She kept telling herself she wouldn't do it in order to ensure it was true. Unfortunately, lying is difficult when the one hearing the lie happens to be the one speaking it.

Zeen rushed in. She could barely see him, but his voice was calm and collected as he yelled out useless orders. Five, do this. Bloom, do that. Serenna sighed at the inevitability of their loss, panting on the sands as Zeen's voice grew louder. What she would give to win this battle. What she would give to—

"Child of Valor. Stop this reprehensible display and rise. Show these lowly demons the superiority of the radiant line of crystal goddesses."

Serenna froze at the woman's voice who entered her thoughts. The only other one who could do that was Death. *What is happening to me?*

"Repetition is not the protocol of Valor. Rise and vanquish these demons. Rise and show these mortals how crystal magic has defended our realm for centuries. RISE! RISE!"

Serenna rose, glancing all around her. *Am I going mad?* she thought, using her staff as a crutch and trying to control her breathing. *Breaths match the heart. Slow the breathing, and the heart will relax. Relax…*

"FIX YOUR POSTURE! FIX YOUR CHEST!"

Serenna stood straight, not exactly sure what that meant, taking deep breaths as her blurry vision faded. "Who are you?" she said out loud, to whoever.

"I am the Goddess of Valor. You are familiar with my mortal title: Guardian Everleigh. We are not equals. You will refer to me only as Goddess or Lady."

Everleigh? That was...Landon's favorite. The crystal Guardian he would never stop talking about. "What do you ask of me?"

"Asking is not the protocol of Valor. If we are having this conversation, you have more to give. Now, I demand you unleash the dominance of crystal superiority, and finish off this colossal."

Crystal superiority? It was difficult not to laugh. Serenna had nothing left to give, barely awake as the exhaustion flowed through her. She let out a pitiful yell, then erupted into a platinum aura. It was nowhere near as powerful as the last two, but it was still platinum.

Zeen was doing his slash and dodge thing, keeping the attention on himself as Bloom threw trap after trap at the enormous demon that pierced the sky with its roar. Hmm, there was a frozen fragment on its lower neck. *For Mylor,* she thought. *For you, my love.*

For Pyith.

She created one spike—a giant—and hovered it by her right side. Her vision blurred as the spike floated up and down, but she wouldn't dare give in to the darkness. "Watch this," she said to Everleigh, not entirely sure if she was real, not really caring either way.

The spike launched as she collapsed again, but this time the platinum didn't fade. She was too frustrated and tired to give up. Despite Francis's motto, desperation it would seem, was a virtue. But the spike missed. It shimmered and flew into the infinite blue darkness.

"By Noelami's grace, such unremarkable form. Is this what passes for crystal mastery in your era? You would be a child's apprentice back in my day... FIX YOUR POSTURE!"

80

Serenna stood straight, pushing her staff deeper into the sand to keep her balance. Her team was cheering. Did they win? They must have gotten the colossal down if they were cheering, but all she could focus on was the hazy vision of a giant woman in front of her.

Guardian Everleigh, Goddess of Valor, whatever she was, towered valiantly above Serenna, white cape draped down, with white plate armor and a scythe that radiated the same pale energy. Her platinum hair went all the way down to her upper legs. Serenna had always considered perfection an ideal, something to chase, but never achieve. This was...

Perhaps Landon had not been exaggerating.

"Can they not see you, Goddess?" Serenna asked, easing up to the ethereal woman twice her height. No one else was reacting, so perhaps that question had not been wise.

"*Do not reveal my presence. I must remain shrouded from the fallen empress and the ender of worlds. Your realm teeters on the cusp of madness. The false senator schemes your demise in conspiracy with a deity far beyond your intellectual capacity. I will share the required details when time permits. Now, rally your servants and vanquish the Harbinger. Do not fail me anymore than you already have.*"

Everleigh faded after the last word. *If she's watching, I can't risk telling anyone. Not even Zeen...*

Rallying the team was easy enough as they approached. Zeen's smile vanished as he rushed down to the fallen zephum, checking Tempest, then placing his head to Pyith's exposed chest. "Tempest lives but...she's not breathing. Serenna, tell me you can help her. Five, do you have access to healing magic? What can...someone help her!"

Bloom shrugged. "She's dead, Boss. Let's get a move on. Will be ugly when Tempest wakes up. Maybe we should uh...never mind."

Five gave Zeen a rather uncomfortable look, an accusing glance as if he had lied to his face, then gazed down. "Not I, nor anyone else, has access to magic that would cure death. The only way I can recall is with a god's sacrifice. However, you exceed my knowledge in that regard."

Serenna leaned down to hold Zeen, letting him clutch her while tears ran down his eyes. "It means nothing to you?" he asked, glaring at Bloom, then Five. "Nothing at all?"

"We all mourn in our own way, Master Zeen. Do not accuse silence of apathy. The true loss is not of the individual, but of the chains of faded love that tighten around those forced to remain."

"Enough," Serenna said, slamming her staff into the sands. The sound was rather disappointing, but results came all the same. "Our task remains unfinished—"

The hissing stopped, but booming steps came from the direction of the dead colossal. A mage radiating black energies approached, with the same void wings that Nyfe had wielded, about Pyith's height if she were...

Prepare yourself, demon.

"Serenna Morgan!" he yelled, his voice in a clear Xavian accent as the distance closed. "You're the biggest coward of the bunch! Can't blame you, I would be afraid too if my leadership led to the death of—"

Serenna erupted into her platinum form, ignoring the pain and fatigue as the demon eyed her. One more. Pay any price to kill one more. "I care not for your threats. Fear lies buried beneath the power of crystal superiority."

The Harbinger smirked, raised his staff, then created a crystal barrier around himself tinted in black energies. Several large crystal spikes formed around him, all covered in the same void energy.

Serenna shielded her team one-by-one as the spikes rushed

forward. Zeen and Bloom dove out of the way, but Five took a direct hit. His shield shattered on impact, sending him to the ground. No fatal wounds from what she could see, but there wasn't time to check as the hissing restarted.

Dammit, we're at such a disadvantage. "Bloom," she said, staring her down, hoping it was somehow intimidating to the larger zephum, "you're on crawlers. If you fall, we die. If the crawlers pass you and get to us, we die. Whatever illusions of grandeur you hold with the future of Vaynex, put it on hold until our victory. Am I understood?"

Bloom paused, then spit on the ground. "No dice. I want the killing blow on the Harbinger. Put your human on them."

No more of this. Zeen stays by me. "Follow my commands and Tempest never learns of your ambitions. This is my first and final offer."

"Oh?" Bloom said with a laugh. "But Sardonyx told me the mighty Serenna's honor holds no equal. I guess humans are all the same."

"Think what you must. Let my fallen enemies declare me dishonorable; let the living declare me their protector."

"You got a dark aura, Boss. I like it." Bloom smirked, grabbed a trap off her belt, and rushed off into the fray.

Zeen walked to Serenna's side, gripping Hope, entering his battle stance. "Is this a bad time to say I love you?"

"As long as you say it again tomorrow. Promise me—"

A new void crystal flew towards Zeen. He swung his sword high to deflect the corrupted crystal to his left. While he didn't complain out loud, his desperate grimace screamed out the pain before he rushed forward. A second spike stopped him in his tracks; he swung again, but this spike shattered his crystal and knocked the sword out of his hand. Zeen lay in the sand, gasping, his eyes stuck on the blue-tinted sun above them.

All sorts of memories came at once: Nyfe's dagger in Zeen's

neck, his lifeless body in her arms, hovering the already slain Pyith to her side…

A common theme of the Rinso books she had read so far was that 'be kind and love each other' was all it took to protect the realm. A common theme of reality was that a dead enemy harms no one.

Serenna crafted a single spike, a shimmering mirror of platinum that reflected the glow of the sun. The harsh, bright burn would only be temporary to the Harbinger on the other side of the sand.

The Harbinger snickered, creating his own void crystal. He launched it forward, his eyes locked in on Serenna. In a clash of platinum and darkness, the void never stood a chance.

The crystal shattered the Harbinger's, then tore through his barrier. In perfect irony, it tore straight into his neck, almost exactly where Zeen had taken his wound. Serenna approached, unable to feel her legs, but able to command them to take her forward.

"Impossible…" the Harbinger said, clutching the wound. "So much hatred. You… What are you?"

"I can read your fear," Serenna said, still in her empowered form. "It's written on your face and in your neck. You took my sister. The price is darkness." She created one more spike—a smaller spike—then launched it into his skull before collapsing.

CHAPTER II

A REALM WITHOUT GODS

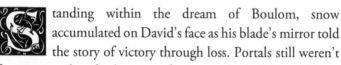

tanding within the dream of Boulom, snow accumulated on David's face as his blade's mirror told the story of victory through loss. Portals still weren't functioning, but for better or for worse, he had been able to watch the battle of Xavian. Part of him felt pride in watching his team win without him, but that small part yielded to the emptiness of the cost.

Noelami still remained on her knees behind him, but the pain of losing Pyith smothered his attention. *You were the best among us. Always saw the realm for what it was. Even kingdoms away, I still drag down everyone who gets close. My only wish is that you could have forgiven me before your death. I am more than this...*

Or at least, I used to be. Remember that version of David. Not whatever I am now. Perhaps it's a blessing that most dreams are forgotten.

Where was the justice? What was the point of serving a realm that begged to suffer? Serenna was already starting to crack, the idea of her doing this for twenty more years was nearly a joke. David turned around, his eyes met those of the fallen empress. He didn't shiver. He never shivered anytime he could remember the snow wasn't real.

"Noelami, your Harbinger is slain. Give me a reason why you shouldn't be next." David approached, Herald of Fear in hand, all the townsfolk gazing upon him as if he was their liberator. He wasn't. A dream's destiny can go no further than the dreamer. When the mind wakes and reality returns, dreams collapse to the part of the mind that forges new distractions.

Noelami, still panting, groaned at David. "My true purpose ended centuries before your existence. If you still blame my Harbinger for your failures, then my lesson meant nothing."

"No. I am done blaming myself. *You* killed Pyith. *You* killed Thomas. It always comes back to the gods. You all justify absurdities at our expense, arguing over who can ruin the realm most efficiently to shape their image—"

"Fool," Noelami said, easing herself up. "Have you any idea how frustrating it is to deal with mortals? You have been alive for merely forty-five years and have the audacity to act like it's forever. I have seen forever, David. Its remnants lie buried beneath the snow."

"Then buried beneath the snow will be a familiar end. Now, tell me: when you perish, will my blade lose its power?"

"Of course it will. We are all linked that way. Our artifacts live and die with the deity that forges their creation."

"Very well—then you shall be last. As a courtesy, Arrogance is my first target so you can watch his punishment. If you truly care for that wretched thing, I suggest you make amends."

Fear turned away, gazing into the illusion. "His name was…is Ermias. He wasn't always the monster he is today, though I'm sure he would describe me in the same manner. There will never, *ever*, be amends for that one."

As more energy flowed into the blade, the darker it glowed in David's hand. As a test, he pointed it forward and launched a portal to Terrangus. Ah, this time, it worked. "So fear has betrayed Fear. Farewell, Noelami. If it's any consolation, you finally won. The realm will be safe, for it will be a realm without gods."

"Stop! Don't waste my gift. Arrogance will tear your mind to shreds. You are not prepared!"

Of course he wasn't, but he entered the portal anyway.

CHAPTER 12

INSIGNIFICANT

empest groaned, struggling to rise from his soft bed. By Strength's name, it was hot, wherever he was…

Xavian. Of course. Last thing he could remember was charging the colossal, roaring like he was Cympha from *Rinso Volume IV*. That had not been wise—not for Cympha, nor for him. He had sworn he could hear her voice as he'd written her fate. *Tempest, why are you doing this to me? My character would never act this way.* We all react differently when the fear hits. Cympha had reverted to a hero, Tempest to a fool.

Well, on a brighter note, if he was still alive that was proof they had somehow won.

Right? He rose about halfway before stopping for the pain. While everything hurt, the sharp sting in his right leg was a unique level of torment. How would someone describe such a thing? Vicious pain? Relentless agony? Hmm…

Ha! An injured right leg; Pyith should appreciate the irony of that. How poetic for lovers to share a weakness. Hopefully, Pyith and the Guardians would be kind enough to…exaggerate Tempest's performance in their battle. Not for his pride, but for zephum legitimacy. Clearly, one's aptitude to run a complex economy dependent on tradelines and war was best tested by how well they fought with blades.

He met eyes with a human, who was likely a healing mage, based on the wand tucked in his right pocket. "Greetings, sir! Thank you for presiding over me during my recovery. How fare the Guardians?"

The mage grew rather pale for a darker skinned human. He had clearly heard Tempest, but turned away and left the healing ward. There was no one else recovering. While that seemed like a decent enough sign, the mage's reaction did…not inspire confidence. *If anyone is hurt, please let it be Bloom or Five. Anyone but Pyith.*

Hmm. For a victory, there was an ominous silence. Perhaps they were furious with him breaking the plan? That would be acceptable. It wasn't like he had helped all that much. Thank Strength David wasn't here.

Zeen walked in. He was kind enough to keep eye contact, but he wore a frown that would send the mightiest of warlords to their knees. "Warmaster Tempest…"

Oh no, he's using my title. He's not distraught enough for it to be Serenna; he's too nervous for it to be any of the others. It's Pyith. She's injured. Not dead, just injured. Zephum like Pyith never die. Only zephum like me die. The useless ones. The ones that can barely swing a sword.

"I…" Zeen stopped speaking, then hugged him. Zeen may not have been able to speak the words, but his embrace screamed them out in the room filled with no one for all to hear. "My friend, I am so sorry."

And there it was. The new word to describe the pain in his leg was 'insignificant.' Insignificant, because it described everything in his life that had led to this moment. All that time studying political and economic theory for a people that still fought to the death in the sand. All those years suffering his father's abuse. All those promises of a better Vaynex, together with the only one he had ever loved. "Speak the words, Zeen. I refuse to believe it's real until I hear it."

"She's gone. Pyith died a hero. None of us would be here if not for her sacrifice. Anything…anything I can do, name it. I will drop anything to be by your side."

Tempest channeled his father and gripped Zeen by the throat. Pain is a conduit. Force it onto someone else before it consumes you. "How could you allow this to happen? You already killed our god; now you take her? Wretched Novalore will tear me to shreds for this. Father…"

Tempest let go. It wasn't his fault. The only one who deserved to be choked was the one staring at the gasping Zeen. *Father will end me. It's not enough that I lose my life-mate. Now, I must suffer the wrath of my uneducated brethren who already despise me…*

I will never be happy again.

Rage was supposedly more powerful than pain, but Tempest fell to the ground screaming when he attempted to put weight on the right leg. Zeen rushed over. Of course he did. "Stay here, I'll get the others."

I can't move. Where the fuck do you expect me to go?

Pain answered questions he had never thought to ask. David's descent after Melissa. Francis's emotional distancing after his mother. Sardonyx's cruel demeanor after Vitala's passing. They all were forced to deal with…this. Whatever *this* was.

Everyone entered the room other than Bloom. The only other zephum didn't have the courtesy to care. A Guardian had died, but a murderer was free to continue on and commit more travesties. Such was the realm.

"Here," Serenna said, handing him a walking stick. The damned thing was just a piece of wood. Someone had probably just picked it off the ground on the way here. "Zeen and I delivered the body to Vaynex together last night. After Zeen's account of what happened during the battle... Well, forgive me for being blunt, but it would be best if you stayed in Mylor for a few days, or weeks, perhaps. It is truly unfair, but Warlord Sardonyx—"

"Spare me the obvious. When you write words, you learn to read in between them. Of course it's my fault. Not like anyone has the courage to blame you. Get out. Just...get out." It seemed absurd to lie back down after torturing himself to rise, but why bother? There was nowhere to go. No one worth speaking to. All he wanted to do was sleep. Life's first magic: the ability to close your eyes and let the world pass you by. To wonder. To yearn. To dream of a life that was no longer possible. *When reality fails, dreams are eternal.* So, Fear had it right all along. What a cruel joke.

Speaking of cruel jokes, they all left, other than Five. The emotionless husk of a human stared at him, with no frown or smile. This...thing was Robert Cavare? The joke ended. This had been the result of Julius's death. What had he been like before this? *What will* I *be after this?*

"Lord Tempest," Five said, glancing down for a split second before meeting his eyes again. "I have been where you are now. You are strong enough to persevere. You are—"

Five collapsed, shaking on the ground as he clutched his sides. "Tempest...never surrender. Don't...take my path. I can't resist anymore. I can't..." The shaking stopped. Five rose, then brushed sand off his white armor. "You chose this. Never forget that. Serenity is our only salvation." A tear ran down Five's cheek despite the upbeat tone of his normally monotone voice.

Tempest could've roared, could have screamed, could have grabbed Five's arm before he left, but Tempest did nothing. All the realm's accumulating problems didn't matter anymore.

Maybe the Arrogant One *should* win. Why not? Any dystopian future had to be better than this—

A cool breeze blew across Tempest's face. A breeze too cold for the summer air of the Xavian dusk. With the closest window a few feet diagonal from him, the trajectory of the wind made no sense until a voice filled his thoughts. A voice he had written, but never actually heard before. A voice that was too powerful to ever be considered insignificant.

"Tempest... Tempest, Tempest. I see tears forming in the maelstrom. I see the last warlord standing over an infinite pile of the Time God's broken children. The realm has abandoned you, but I am here to cradle you into the ecstasy of destruction. The time is not now, but the time is inevitable. Remember my words, Child of Strength.

"I am nothing. I am forever. I am the end."

CHAPTER 13

FEAR AND PERFECTION

rancis sighed as Senator Gallings continued to spout basic economic theory in the Terrangus throne room. The man had clearly just finished reading *The Wealth of Kingdoms*, and felt the absurd necessity to vomit out the words as if this was somehow new and exciting doctrine for the realm's most knowledgeable sorcerer.

His dear Mary had already left what seemed to be ages ago. She had let out a beauty of a groan, an unmistakable hint to stop speaking, but the senator was like a wind-up toy whose destiny was linked to the price of wheat.

He just keeps talking. It's remarkable. I should raise his taxes out of spite. I wonder if Wisdom would allow me to seize his fields—

"EVERYONE, DEPART FROM THIS ROOM, NOW! GET OUT!"

Francis nearly fell off his throne as Wisdom ascended to his Arrogance form, towering over the throne with his sun mask and the glowing black frown. There was no mistaking that his voice had been heard by everyone, as all the senators gasped and stumbled back. Why would he do that? The deity had tended to favor subtlety.

"Lord Wisdom? Please clarify your actions."

The bulging eyes of Arrogance gazed straight through Francis. His deity appeared absolutely enthralled to be in danger. "We have a visitor! He sucks fear like a mosquito, but I know Noelami's tricks. Tricks and lies, tricks and lies. Ah, the avatars of fear and perfection clash at last. Everything is coming together... I'm winning, Francis. I'm *winning*."

We're winning. Both of us. Right? Honestly, Francis preferred the Wisdom form over Arrogance. There was something...off about this one. He didn't seem to care about Francis. Or anyone. All those whimsical sayings and riddles yielded to pure concentrated hatred...

David is here? Am I ready? I never...hmm. To face off against my fallen leader. Alas, the Champion of Fear meets the Architect of Paradise.

The throne room doors flew open, with an imposing figure standing at the doorway. While some streams of fear from the fleeing senators flowed into David, it wasn't the whole room. In hindsight, a rational tactic by Arrogance. Most importantly, none of the fear came from Francis. *Don't be afraid. He consumes fear. I wield courage. Intelligence. Superiority.*

Was there any task less fruitful than forcing down fear? Francis's entire body trembled, but his fear didn't go anywhere. He assumed the Herald of Arrogance protected him, so he clutched the artifact with enough grip to force his hands to stop shaking. *I wish Mary was here. Does she even love me? Why am I facing the realm's most powerful villain alone?*

David approached, Herald of Fear in hand, staring into Francis with a mix of admiration and curiosity. "No fear? I'm proud of you, Francis. Your journey has been harsh, but you have traveled it well."

He's looking at me. Say something. Say something bold. "Fear is beneath me, dear leader. With all this knowledge and intellect, it would be an insult to even entertain the idea of being afraid." *Is he buying this?*

David stopped right before the stairs to the throne, then...smiled? "Only a rare few truly master their own fear. Most force it down, clinging to other faults like wings on a fallen angel. Alcohol, gambling, anything to drown out the fear. Some even cling...to arrogance."

Could David not hear Francis's heart pound in his chest? Assuming not, this staff was incredible; he hadn't truly tapped into its power since he had rebuilt the castle. "I cling to Serenity. You of all people should despise the chaos of our realm. But, as a sign of mutual respect, I offer you the chance to channel your...portal thing and exit my kingdom intact."

David's smile vanished as he continued his approach. "You're not my target. I think you know who is. Now, get out of my way before you end up the second emperor to perish by this blade."

He targets Wisdom? The audacity. The sheer...foolishness. Francis channeled his multi-form and glowed a dark blue and a bright yellow. It had been so long since he had faced demons; to face one with his old leader's face was a fair substitute. "If your goddess had any intellect, she would never have sent you to my domain. Farewell, David. May the temperate breeze of perfection finally douse the flames of your despair."

Francis launched an ice blast, which would capture anything mortal into the frozen infinity. Instead, David swung his glowing sword across, deflecting the bright blue fragments into shadows of nothing.

Any hypothesis about the Herald of Arrogance protecting Francis was absolutely confirmed as his heart thumped in his chest. *No multi-form. Put all your power into a single spell. Blow him into the dust of yesterday.*

Francis channeled pure yellow, then launched a lightning

bolt. He swore the blast would be powerful enough to erase a god.

David parried the blast, but groaned as he got pushed back to the open doors of the throne room. An interesting miracle. He could defend himself against perfection, but certainly wasn't invincible.

This is my moment. Emperor Francis Haide, hero of the realm, Architect of Paradise...

Another lightning blast soared forward, but this time David dodged the strike entirely before rushing forward. He had such murderous intentions in his eyes, gazing into the god behind Francis. What madness had triggered this? Fear had sent a Harbinger...and the logical conclusion was Wisdom's assassination? Francis would never dare accuse David of being unintelligent, but illogical was a whole different story. Illogical, rash, violent, desperate. Ah, of course. Like most answers, the solution was obvious once discovered.

He's gone mad. There's no other conclusion. It's up to me to stop this unhinged demon. Fear is a disease. The cure is fire.

Francis adjusted his glow to orange. A beautiful color with an ugly history of destruction. If David had any hint of reason left in his corrupted skull, he would turn back and run out of the room screaming.

That didn't happen, so Francis launched a fire blast at Fear's champion.

David let out a roar that sounded completely inhuman, then swung his glowing sword at the sphere-shaped inferno before it would end him. The blast was sent flying to the east of the throne room, crashing into the empty senator seats and exploding. The entire castle rumbled as debris and flames poured down the newly created hole.

They stared at each other, and the faint grin on David's face filled Francis with dread. *This is absurd. ABSURD! I'm doing something wrong. This staff is the most powerful artifact in the realm—*

"What the fuck is going on?" asked Mary, panting as she leaned against the door to their quarters in her nightgown. "You... Why are you here?"

"Get back!" Francis yelled, but it was too late. An essence of fear flowed from his empress. The mother of his child would doom them all.

David took a deep breath as the stream flowed into him, then turned to Mary. "You're wrong, old friend. He loves you so much he can't even comprehend it. Study the eyes. It's how I know that, deep down, he loves me as well. Rejoice, for your child will know a future without gods."

How dare he? Of course I love her. Is it not obvious? I'll burn this man with such force that Fear herself will tremble before me.

No more holding back. Fire it was. Fire would be his savior or his end. "Stay back, my beloved," he said, gripping his staff as he amplified the brightness of the glow. "The man we knew is no more. Remember him as our once mentor, and not the pile of ash about to stain my floors." He launched the fire forward, with flames seething with such intensity he lost track of David. That was the beauty of fire. It was not a delicate art. Choose a target, and watch it cease to exist.

The center of the room exploded with a flash so bright Francis stumbled back. He went to grab his throne for balance but the thing flew behind him. *Mary. Where is Mary?* She still leaned against her wall, gazing at Francis with a look of...fear? Anger? Something. She had a powerful reaction, whatever it was. How to read such a thing.

All of the room was aflame, so he channeled a deep blue and launched ice all over the room other than around Mary. Almost all the ice melted into water, which doused the flames, giving him a perfect view of the monster lunging forward.

By instinct, Francis cowered behind his staff, parrying the Herald of Fear. *If he wanted me dead, I would already be gone.* A terrible realization, but what else could he do? Francis stepped forward and swung his staff at David like it was the Wings of Mylor. Fear and arrogance collided and, to Francis's surprise, David had to regain his footing as he stepped back.

David then charged forward, tackling Francis to the ground, and knocking the staff out of his hands. There was pain, of course, but there was such dread in losing his staff that he held back a scream. An essence left his body, flowing into the already glowing David.

So, paradise would end long before its beginning. What a cruel finale. What an absurd way for a mortal god to die. Francis lay on the ground where the throne once stood. He said nothing. There was nothing worth saying to the one that had damned enlightenment.

Why is it that intelligent minds are no match for the horrors of violence?

CHAPTER 14

TREMBLE BEFORE GOD'S LOVE

avid's head pounded as Francis's fear seeped into his skin. A complex web of anxiety and doubt, fear of physical contact, of facial expressions. Fears of misplaced words from conversations with people who had died years ago. He feared the anticipation of being afraid, of knowing what triggered the fear, but never knowing why. It had been a war against his own mind, a descent into near-madness, as simple tasks had become a tactical battle of Francis preparing for Francis. But one fear rose against them all—oddly enough, just a simple question:

How much can a person be damaged before they are considered broken?

"If you ever figure that one out," David said as he stepped over him, "make sure to let me know." He stood face to face with Wisdom. Or Arrogance. Or whatever it was. Too many titles, but only one fate awaited the deity. "Ermias, destroyer of Boulom, may you find redemption in the void. Noelami sends her regards."

"Ermias? Do you think a human lies behind this mask?" Arrogance said with a chuckle. His voice echoed with such power it took every ounce of fear for David not to fall to his knees. "This is a war that extends beyond any speck of consciousness in your empty mind. You are the man who serves the man that forges the pawn waiting to sit on the corner of the board. Sweet, tormented David. Show me your *violence*. Show me the only gift freewill has ever bestowed upon you."

The bulging eyes and black frown on the sun mask laughed hysterically as David slashed his sword across its face. It made no attempt to dodge. The glowing blade tore across, tearing the mask into two pieces that fell and clanged against the ground. The laughter came to an abrupt end, but the chill in the air made David shiver.

"No!" Francis screamed from the ground. "How dare you? Why can't you let the realm prosper? You ruin everything!"

It all seemed too easy. David surveyed the room as Mary rushed over to Francis, consoling him as if a grievous wound had been inflicted upon him. The Herald of Arrogance staff lay on the ground, close to where the throne had used to be. Noelami had said the gods and their artifacts were linked until their end.

She had been many things, but never a liar.

"Why can't you just go away?" Francis said, easing himself back against the wall. "You destroy everything in your wake. A seething vortex of misery. I just want my people to know the joy of Serenity. Why is that such a sin to you? *Why?*"

David had grown accustomed to ignoring Francis's whining over the years, and today would be no different. For the realm's 'greatest' scholar, he didn't seem to focus on the air growing colder, the slight rumble on the ground, or the loud ringing—

The world went dark.

His surroundings returned to a flying sky garden, some illusion of despair that flowed through puffy clouds. A chalice of wine appeared in his left hand, but he threw it down into the endless depths below. Never accept a gift that numbs the mind from a cerebral opponent.

"Lord David," Arrogance's voice called out from wherever. "Guardian David. Puppet David. I invite you to observe the future you actively betray. The perfection that was, is, could be... Serenity."

David clutched his sword. It still glowed, but the power seemed completely empty. "How many liars justify cruelty in the name of progress?" *Noelami deals in dreams. This one is the same. A perfect match, those two. None of this is real. I stand on the precipice of delusions.*

"An interesting thesis!" the voice called out. "But the logic is flawed. Please, allow me a demonstration..."

A what? David flinched as an illusion of Melissa appeared in the gardens. Cellos floated and played above her, some ballad to celebrate a wealth or joy he would never know. Gods, he hated how much it hurt to watch her approach. *You're not real. I am above this. You're not real...*

Kill her. Stab the illusion right between those emerald eyes...

He did nothing as she drifted forward. Everything was the same. Every tiny dot on her face, every scar on her arms. A travesty. No one else deserved to know the little secrets between lovers. He would never check, but he assumed the leg scars would be accurate, too.

The image of Melissa lifted him by the throat. Whatever this was, it certainly wasn't an illusion. David dropped his sword and grabbed her arm to get it off, but the strength of her grip was infinite. He was a mere dream, at the mercy of the dreamer. At the mercy of a deranged god.

"It's a long way down," the fake Melissa whispered. It was so close to her old voice he struggled against the urge to weep. "Some parting advice? Close your eyes. Let it go. You will be falling, falling. Always falling."

She threw him off the gardens, and David couldn't help but scream as he plunged down into the skies of Serenity. It was just so cold. How could anyone yearn for such a distorted reality? There were no people, just vague things often attributed to beauty: songs, waterfalls, clouds...

It was like someone had tried to create heaven before ever learning how to smile.

David reappeared in the throne room, catching his breath as the broken room automatically repaired itself. Stones flew from every direction, flames dissipated, even the water from Francis's ice evaporated to cool vapors.

Lastly, the shattered sun mask became whole. "The absurdity of freewill never ceases to amaze me," Arrogance said, hovering above the throne.

The Herald of Fear's glow diminished; David sighed as the strength of a goddess faded from his frame. *If I struck down that fake Melissa, would I have won? Was there ever a real chance at this? A world without gods... I am a fucking fool.* It didn't seem to matter all that much now. David swung his sword at the reconstructed sun mask, just to have his blade get caught in the deity's spectral hands.

The blade was snapped in half, then thrown behind him.

Some men just live too long. I passed that point years ago...

I wish you had let me drop.

The view from that Alanammus balcony had been a harrowing sight. In a fairer realm, it would have been the last thing he had ever seen. The realm was too damn different now. It had been simpler in his thirties, to battle the faceless Fear and Death, to drink wine until either the sun went up or down, to laugh or cry in Melissa's arms. What the hell was going on now? Francis as Emperor, Grayson's divine jester pulling the strings...

This isn't my realm anymore. I am a visitor in a land that has forgotten me.

"Take your toll, deity. The only paradise I'll ever know is a permanent rest."

"Funny," Arrogance said, waving his arms, which launched David to the ground, "how the ones that don't wish to be here seem to linger forever. But to quote our mutual acquaintance, 'This is not your end, David, this is only your beginning.' Serenity still has a use for you, dear friend. One of the most beautiful aspects of paradise is knowing there is a place for us all. Yours...may be a bit difficult."

"Is there a role more difficult than yours? A self-proclaimed savior of a people you despise?"

Arrogance chuckled, then let out an exaggerated sigh. "Despise? Ah, such ignorance is the burden of brutes. If you could hear...even a faint whisper of my empathy...you would *tremble* before God's love. Farewell, my fallen champion of Fear."

Two of the Vanguard things approached, each picking him up by an arm. They had a gentle grip, seemingly aware David had no plans to resist. Why bother?

"Take him to the chamber," Francis said as he rose. He wiped the debris off his robes and, despite his overwhelming victory, kept hyperventilating and avoiding eye contact.

How does such an intelligent man not realize he's a pawn? Maybe he does. The gods know I served Fear willingly. It certainly makes sense of the chaos when a divine being offers a plan. "Francis, if I'm wrong about your god, I apologize. If I'm correct...then I am truly sorry."

Francis didn't respond, turning to Mary and wiping debris off her gown. She held his left hand gently, caressing his shaky palm. Ah, so he had finally let someone in. What an odd couple, but perhaps those pairings are the most beautiful. The pieces that don't exactly fit but come together to make something that only makes sense to the two people joined. Sometimes, a broken puzzle reveals the most joyful picture.

Gods, I miss that. I miss it all too much.

As the Vanguards carried David out of the room, a difficult realization came that even if he did plan to resist, he had no way of doing so. Without the Herald of Fear, he was just that broken old man from the balcony.

Countless people, senators, and whoever was still in the castle all pointed and gawked as David came out of the halls after the throne room and was escorted towards the prison. But the Vanguards carried him to the stairs that led under the stairs to the room for the very worst of Terrangus. Somewhere out there, maybe Serenna could smile at the irony.

They opened the cell doors, then pushed David inside. Their gentle grip faded, replaced by a surge of power as their push flung him into the bed chained to the wall. "We will return at the predetermined times with rations and various generosities dependent on your behavior. At this moment, we advise rest."

David groaned, then took a moment to clear the buzzing in his head before he leaned up to see who was snickering in the cell next to his.

"You lost?" Nyfe said. "Well, shit, but at least I'll have a prison buddy. How's the weather these days? More rain? They don't let me out much...or ever. Imagine that, the terrifying champions of Fear and Death rotting under Terrangus while Francis of all people rules the realm."

The voice matched, but the slim, long-haired, bearded man barely resembled the monster that had terrorized the realm a year ago. No signs of physical torture, but the shadow-like circles under his eyes screamed out a different sort of pain. David had never thought to check here. To be honest, he had rarely thought of the man after his defeat. "Why are you alive?" was all he managed to ask as his head throbbed.

"Same reason as you, new friend. You'll see it soon enough. Arrogance wants us to be Vanguards, like those other bald fucks with the dead eyes and silly clothes. I told him I'd rather die, but he seems intent on keeping me alive. It's funny really, everyone wanted to kill me until I finally wanted to die."

David snickered. "I suppose I can relate to that."

CHAPTER 15

ALWAYS AND NEVER

Serenna stood at the very top of Xavian Tower and took a sip of water from her jug. The morning breeze blew her hair across her face, a welcome caress after a mostly unsuccessful night of rest in the healing ward. She had woken up first, of course. With David gone, that responsibility would always be hers, until the day where she wouldn't wake at all. Was that why he had forced himself up early all those times? Inspiration?

Tiny specks of people were working among the sands below, collecting debris, bodies, and all the other aspects of a tragedy that require attention the next day to expedite the forgetting process. *Despite our differences, we all rebuild the same way: slowly and quietly. The sight doesn't even phase me anymore. I wish… I wish it did.*

But it didn't. The only loss that would not be rebuilt or fixed with time was Pyith. Zeen and Bloom had accompanied Serenna last night to Vaynex, where they had left the body in Sardonyx's care. The warlord hadn't wept. Hadn't screamed. Instead, he'd politely asked them to leave…and to keep Tempest away.

She took another sip and took a deep breath, then flinched as a spectral hand gripped her shoulder.

"It's not the view that changes," Everleigh spoke through her thoughts, *"but the perspective of the viewer. Your eyes yearn to despair, as they once did, but never will again. I'm proud of you for learning the lesson on your own. It's not the sort of thing one can teach."*

"It's an emptiness," Serenna said out loud. There was no one else up there, so hopefully, the goddess wouldn't scold her for revealing her presence. "Like wine without the calm."

Everleigh materialized next to her, holding the railing and staring out into the same view. "Numb the heart, empower the mind. Make them notice. The true potential of crystal superiority is making your opponents believe they already lost long before the battle begins."

Fair enough. It had been quite the rush when the Harbinger trembled before her like she was some sort of monster. Why deny such a feeling? If Everleigh had been half the Guardian Landon claimed, her advice would be worth her weight in gold. "It's comforting to hear a divine voice in my head that isn't threats or offers of destruction. You understand. You have been here. I mean…the pressure. Thank you, Goddess of Valor."

Everleigh turned away from the view and towards Serenna, then frowned. "Foolish girl, never speak my title. The other gods are still unaware of my presence, and it is imperative we keep it that way. We are not friends, not allies, we are a goddess and her subject. My enemies have been at this centuries longer than myself. I cannot squander the advantage of surprise. Arrogance…mustn't be allowed victory. Serenna Morgan, Child of Valor, if you falter…everything…*everything* is lost."

What does she mean by arrogance? she thought, but pushed down the urge to ask any questions. When a goddess demands you stop speaking, well, you stop speaking. She finished off her jug of water, then left towards the stairs at the middle of the tower. It had been several years, but if she remembered correctly, the senator's office should be the next floor down. She found a newly crafted golden door a few steps below, an outrageous display of wealth in a kingdom infamous for poverty and lawlessness. Apparently, ruling over the poor and keeping them that way was quite the lucrative prospect.

She entered through the already open entrance. Thompson was too preoccupied in his ledgers to notice, so she cleared her throat at an exaggerated volume to get his attention. "Oh? Lady Morgan, you're up early. My notes suggested I would have a few more hours before our meeting."

Serenna closed the door behind her. "Drop the pleasantries. You threatened my father. Did you seriously consider such an action would yield no consequences?"

Thompson snickered as he rose. "I won't pretend to comprehend the game as it is, but my role has been made clear. Your father has denied my several requests for a one-on-one meeting, but now, here you stand in my chambers. We live in a rather…impatient realm. My superior has demanded the South's allegiance with Terrangus to spread out future Vanguards. Alanammus and Nuum will follow the tide as always, but Mylor feels compelled to hold grudges. Perhaps you can be the voice of reason?"

"Kill this one," Everleigh's voice rang through Serenna's thoughts. *"He is in collusion with Arrogance. The more words a politician spews, the more crystal spikes that should be launched through their chest. Get on with it!"*

"I…" Serenna said, struggling not to wince at the harshness of Everleigh's voice in her head. Dammit, that was annoying. "Mylor will never stand with Terrangus."

"I anticipated such words, but forgive me for expecting a bit more…eloquence?"

"Call his bluff, child. Proclaim that you know about

Arrogance, then slay or coerce him. There is no middle-ground with these types."

What the hell was Valor talking about? "You should know…I know…about your arrogance." *Dammit, I sound like a fool. Dare I ignore her? I can't focus on both voices at once.*

Fortunately, Thompson flinched at that comment, despite the poor delivery. "Well then, you have me caught in an unfortunate predicament. Who was the traitor? Ah, it was Five. But of course. That remnant of a man wants all the benefits of paradise without putting in the work."

"Why is this nonsense still occurring? Slay him. Leave his torn-up carcass as a warning to all those who dare serve the destroyer of Boulom. Serenity is the nightmare from which none shall wake."

Serenity? Okay, Thompson and Everleigh were clearly referring to Wisdom. What was he planning? *Five…he thinks Five is a traitor. I'll lean on that.* Serenna approached Thompson, attempting to make her eyes as murderous as possible. Hopefully, fatigue and intimidation could walk the same line. "Five told me everything. You think I wouldn't act? I am the Pact Breaker. Wisdom may work through lies, but I rule through platinum superiority."

Thompson turned away and groaned. "Oh, to be a mortal in a realm of monsters and murderers. Arrogance is most likely watching our conversation intently. I hear he has already defeated David. What chance do you have against the divine? Is killing me worth it?"

David was defeated? Is that what triggered the Harbinger of Fear?

"Halt. Do not kill him. Arrogance will suspect an outside influence if he's observing. Use a natural reaction. Do something foolish."

They keep referring to Wisdom as Arrogance. Are they one and the same? "That remains to be seen," Serenna said, slowing her own breathing to ignore the pounding voice in her skull. "If I catch even a whisper of an alliance between the South and Terrangus, Xavian will be in search of a new senator."

"But..." Thompson said, glancing to the side as he sighed. "Tell me, Lady Serenna, what would you do in my position? Betraying you may lead to an unfortunate end, but betraying that one...well, there are fates worse than a quick death."

Serenna grabbed him, then pushed him into the musty walls behind his desk. Disgusting. The golden door was a rather dishonest first impression for the rest of the room. "I made no mention of a quick death." She leaned in and whispered, "Are we alone?"

"In this realm? Always, and never."

"Indeed," she said, stepping away, holding back a smirk at the irony. "I'll meet you half-way. I won't interfere if you push Alanammus and Nuum into an alliance, but Mylor stands alone, as they always have. No Vanguards in my home."

Thompson turned towards a mirror and fixed the top of his shirt. "A temporary solution, but fortunately us senators tend to excel at those. I do hope you can reconsider over time. Aside from my own ambitions of a predetermined victory, Serenity is quite beautiful. And that's not a word I use often."

"So they say. Perhaps one day I'll see it for—"

"Prepare yourself. He's here."

The floating sun mask and cape of Wisdom appeared behind Thompson, who stumbled back. "Pardon me for being late! Too much...calamity back in the lovely Terrangus. My dear Francis does his best, but oh, so much to be done! So much to be..."

Wisdom froze. The eyes on the mask moved around, rather frantically for the normally smug god. "There is a very powerful presence among us. Who? Where? Why? Fear lingers in her dreamworld, Death has the subtlety of a boar...oh. *Oh my.* It's

110

been so long! Is there a new god? A goddess, perhaps? Well? Don't keep me waiting! Reveal yourself!"

This seems to be going very poorly. Hopefully, Everleigh has a plan.

Unless it was to do nothing, it didn't seem Everleigh had a plan. "What nonsense are you babbling about?" asked Serenna, to break the silence that lingered for seemingly forever.

Wisdom's eyes stared through her before surveying the room again. "While I normally admire your voice, Guardian Serenna, I must ask you to hush for a moment. Silence is the only opportunity to truly hear everything…but alas, it's gone. A new opponent for Serenity. They just keep piling up as quickly as I can remove them."

Can I lie to this one? Liars can usually identify their own. "The realm stands against you, tyrant. Even Vanguard Five has turned against you. What does that it say about enlightenment that his first action under your hold was to betray—"

"Your father will suffer before I allow him to fade." A chill filled the air as the pattern on Wisdom's face reverted to the less welcoming version she had seen in Terrangus. "Sorry, did I interrupt? Would you consider that rude?"

How dare he? The lie had worked, but as she stared into the glowing frown and bulging eyes, she wondered if it was worth it. "Do your worst. Your delusions of Serenity will never come to pass as long as Mylor stands."

Arrogance chuckled. "Delusions…some would say they are the cornerstone of happiness. Oh, dear girl. I destroyed Boulom, and you mean to stand against me with a kingdom of rocks?"

Destroyed Boulom? What? Don't act surprised. The lie falls apart at any shimmer of doubt. "Mylor has never fallen. Her mountains are stained red with the blood of those who tried."

"You say it with such pride, as if consistent war is the zenith of civilization. I would never yearn for Mylor's fall. I yearn, no I beg, for Mylor's ascension!"

"Just as you begged for Boulom's ascension?"

Arrogance froze, gazing directly into Serenna as the frown radiated a dark glow. She resisted the urge to step back as the god floated towards her, then wished she had done so before he picked her up with spectral arms. "Boulom...was a mistake. A grievous, terrible mistake. Freewill has taken everything from me. My home. My lover. I was supposed to be a hero. An inspiration. Someone...like *you*."

She clutched his arms in vain. His grip wasn't painful, but held her with an unfathomable power. The despair in his voice was more intimidating than any of his vague threats. *He truly believes he is our savior, and that monsters like me stand in the way of a perfect future. Guilt and loss have destroyed his perspective. Would this have been me if I had accepted Death's offer?*

Arrogance let go, then floated to the corner of the room, staring intently into nothing. "If I fail, Boulom's destruction will be in vain. But when I win... all...everything will be forgiven. People will laugh and scream to the heavens, never worrying what the future brings, for tomorrow will already have been written with a pen of joy and harmony...and it will be *beautiful*." The god faded without glancing at either of them.

He is mad. Truly, truly, mad. I must return home and protect Dad.

Senator Thompson sat back down, taking a deep breath and laying his hands on the table. "Whatever game you're playing, I hope to learn the rules before I die. My hair is thin enough as it is. Here," he said, throwing a bag filled with gold coins over to her. "Take this and consider our official audience complete. It's not even afternoon and I'm ready for bed."

She considered saying 'thank you,' but grabbed the bag and left the room without a word. *I need to find Zeen and return home together. But what about the others? Bloom will take advantage of Pyith's death...*

What about Five? I may have just signed his execution.

Her legs ached as she descended the stairs, if only Xavian had a tower portal like Alanammus. It was rather impressive that Thompson managed to remain so round despite the amount of walking required to reach his office. She took each step carefully, navigating the broken stones while her mind raced over scenarios—

"Master Serenna," Five said at the entrance to the healing ward, gazing at her with his tired, empty eyes. Despite the deadpan expression, she swore he held a deep despair. "If I may, I humbly request that future records refer to me as Robert Cavare, and not...a number. The probability of us meeting again after today is quite low. It has been an honor. A temporary one, but an honor, nonetheless."

"Nonsense," she said, embracing him. "After your performance yesterday, I'm afraid you'll be fighting by my side for a long, long time." The unimpressive lie was filled with shame, as all lies are. They let go, and she proceeded into the ward, where Bloom and Zeen stood by Tempest's bed.

She handed everyone their share of gold, then grimaced as Tempest forced himself out of the bed. "Rest, Tempest. No need to—"

Tempest groaned as he leaned against his walking stick, then threw his gold across the room. It clanged against the stone ground and empty beds. "Gold? You offer me gold? Am I your zephum whore?"

"Ah, fuck this," Bloom said, stuffing gold into her belt where the traps used to be. "I'm going home. Serenna, Zeen, y'all are good. You ever want to team up and kill something, portal into Vaynex. Stickman too, wherever he went. Tempest, fuck you. It should've been you that died. I hope your leg never heals." She spat on the ground and stormed towards the exit.

"I'll have her body thrown in the streets," Tempest said, regaining his balance. He pushed Zeen aside and hobbled forward. "Get out of my way."

"Tempest!" Serenna yelled to no avail. Dammit, Sardonyx had demanded he stay away. Tempest clearly wasn't in the mindset to listen to reason, but was in terrible danger between his father's rage and Bloom's ambitions. "I don't know what to do, Zeen. I must return home. Arrogance... Wisdom threatened my father. He has some convoluted plan to overtake the realm with Vanguards."

Zeen gave her a puzzled glance, which was understandable, then turned it into a smile. "You protect Mylor, I'll head to Vaynex and watch over those two. As the 'Human Warlord,' I should have enough clout to defend Tempest. He needs me. He needs a friend, now, more than ever."

She pulled him close and kissed him, unfazed by the fact her beloved very much needed a bath. To be fair, she probably needed one, too. "Come back as soon as possible. Leave if it gets too dangerous. We are Guardians, not mediators of the realm. I love you."

"I love you, too," he said, then rushed out of the ward.

That left Serenna alone. She leaned against an unused bed and took a deep breath. *How can I defy Arrogance? If David lost...how could I possibly win? I'm not half the Guardian he was—*

A portal opened next to her, a doorway shimmering in platinum light. *"Stop dallying, child. The destroyer of Boulom does not rest, and neither shall you."*

While the goddess had likely meant those words to inspire her, Serenna walked into the portal, never feeling more tired.

CHAPTER 16

PRELUDE TO FOREVER

een reached Tempest quicker than anticipated, then slowed himself to match his walking speed—which was very, *very* slow. In hindsight, rushing had not been wise. He placed his hand on Tempest's shoulder, then said, "I won't pretend to understand what you're going through, but I will remain by your side as you heal. Today, tomorrow, forever."

Tempest paused, then took his free hand and moved Zeen's away. "I cannot consider a fate worse than forever without her. It wasn't supposed to happen this way. She's gone. I mean, where do I go from here? What is the point?"

"You go forward! It is the only way! I know it's the last thing you want to hear at this moment, but it's the words you need more than anything else. Tempest...don't become the next David. When we worship the scars, they remain forever."

Forgive me, David, I love you. Maybe the words were cruel, but they were layered in truth. Zeen knew that look in Tempest's eye. It was the exact look David had shown before he destroyed Intrepid. *Ah, I haven't thought of my old blade in forever. If there is a Great Plains in the Sky for swords, I hope you are there, old friend.*

At least I wield Hope. The realm needs it now, more than ever.

Hopefully, the fact Tempest didn't respond was a good

sign. Zeen eased his hand back to his shoulder, then braced his legs as Tempest allowed himself to lean on him. Damn, he was heavy, despite being 'small' for a zephum. Zeen's legs felt better than expected as he braced for the weight. His face still burned from Bloom's friendly fire, but according to the mirror, everything was still intact.

"Forgive me, Zeen. I have been difficult," Tempest said, limping down the stone stairs. "I hope the others can forgive my egregious comments from earlier. This is my failure, as I'm sure Father will be quick to point out. Why am I even going back? I should remain in exile."

"Taking time to heal isn't exile. Serenna already returned to Mylor. You're welcome to stay with us for as long as you need."

"No," Tempest said, gazing into the nothing above as David used to do. "Whatever the consequences, I am returning home to mourn my life-mate. They can throw my body in the streets if they please. Perhaps that is the fate I have always deserved. To rot and be forgotten."

"You deserve to be happy. It may not happen for a while, but you'll get there. When Mynuth sacrificed himself in the Rinso Saga, the pain consumed Rinso for several chapters, but he learned to smile again. As the zephum who writes Rinso, you *are* Rinso."

"I never killed Olivia. Mynuth and Vehemence were necessary sacrifices, but I never touched Olivia. There would be no coming back from that. Zeen, the price of love is the death of the individual. It is a gradual death, but one we all yearn to face. I exist before you as half a zephum."

They paused at the entrance to the Guardian room, finding a young mage sitting by the portal. "My lords!" she yelled, rising quickly enough to nearly fall out of her chair. "Where is your destination?"

"To the end," said Tempest, leaning on Zeen and gazing down. Ugh, going against Sardonyx's command would surely be a mistake, but how could he let Tempest go alone?

"Vaynex," Zeen mouthed at the girl, who was clearly frazzled and nodded frantically. The familiar red glow of the portal filled Zeen with unease. In all his attempts to calm Tempest, he hadn't considered the nightmare of Vaynex. A land of violence, arbitrary rules, bodies on the streets, and 'honor duels' which may or may not get interrupted by Sardonyx cutting someone in half. "I'll go first," Zeen said, then stepped into the portal. What a letdown Xavian turned out to be. He had never even seen any pirates...

*

Zeen took a deep breath as he materialized on the other side. The two guards simply nodded at him as if he were an expected guest. He wasn't.

"Welcome, Human Warlord," the taller one said. His stern glare suggested the phrase had perhaps been said under protest. Both guards turned to the portal as it erupted again.

Tempest appeared, leaning on his walking stick and not staring at any of them. He hobbled forward, at a noticeably slower pace than earlier. "Well? Someone may as well speak. The silence is deafening."

Do I let him lean on me? Maybe not here. They don't appreciate that sort of thing. "Where to, Lord Tempest?" asked Zeen, in as stern a tone as he could manage. Hopefully, referring to him as Lord could help him out.

"Take me to Father. Let's get this over with."

"That would be unwise," the other guard said. "You were good to my family, Tempest, so please believe me when I say now is not the time."

Tempest stopped right before the exit, then took a deep

breath. "Now? But what is now, if not the prelude to forever? In this moment, Father's wrath cannot harm me. The despair drowns out everything else. It is the ultimate form of power. You could train for five lifetimes and never feel this invulnerable. I feel *nothing*."

"Let me go first," Zeen whispered, but Tempest pushed him aside. He hobbled into the citadel throne room, interrupting some meeting of zephum politics. Sardonyx sat on his red throne in his full armor, turning his gaze to Zeen and Tempest. Even through his faceguard, the warlord did not appear pleased.

"Let the famine run its course!" one of the zephum yelled. "Back in my day, food was a privilege. You achieved honor? You ate. Dishonor? Starve. If we had more of that, this empire would be keeping humans in chains. Not…appeasing them—"

"Ah, there it is! More inane drivel from Novalore!" Tempest yelled, gritting his teeth as he approached the center of the citadel. "You speak of honor like it's currency. My child is starving, may I trade one honor for bread, please? No? Honor holds no value, you say?"

"*You!*" the zephum yelled. Zeen assumed he was Novalore, based on the rage in his eyes and the fact he was charging over. "You were not to return. Pyith is gone, my daughter, the heir to my legacy, gone! *Gone!*"

Zeen stepped in front of Tempest. That may not have been wise, but based on the size difference, he assumed Tempest didn't stand a chance with or without his injury. "As the Human Warlord, please allow us to speak in peace. If not, anyone who stands against Tempest stands against me."

Hopefully, Sardonyx didn't stand against Tempest.

Novalore didn't seem to care; he stomped forward, then pushed Zeen aside. He grabbed the injured Tempest's throat, who just laughed. "Do your worst. I loved your daughter more than you could ever dream. You are but a shadow of the perfection you helped create."

Novalore punched him straight across the snout, which sent Tempest and his walking stick plummeting to the ground.

"Stop it!" Zeen yelled, as loud as he could, hopefully not in vain. Vaynex was a kingdom of obscure rules, but violence always seemed to be the answer. "Enough! As the Human Warlord, I challenge this Novalore in Tempest's name. Warlord, will you bless the combat?"

Sardonyx rose for the first time, which immediately ended the murmurs of the other zephum senators...or whatever their title was. "The combat is blessed in my name. I will permit a duel, but I will not permit death. Novalore, you face the Human Warlord, the Terrangus Guardian, Zeen Parson. May your duel be *glorious!*"

Novalore spit by the fallen Tempest, then took the massive sword from behind his back. "Guardian or not, he will perish by my blade. Prepare yourself, human."

Uh, didn't Sardonyx just say no killing? I'm guessing this guy isn't all that concerned about the rules with his daughter gone. What a terrible loss... Zeen did a quick squat to make sure his legs still worked, then drew Hope and entered his battle stance. "However this goes, Novalore, strength without honor—is chaos."

Novalore didn't seem to agree, letting out a roar and charging towards Zeen. While the imposing size of his body and sword rivaled that of Sardonyx, he was...well, he was slow. He crashed his two-handed sword down, missing Zeen as he dodged by dashing to the side.

Zeen leaned forward and did a double slash, coming down against Novalore's leg, then bringing it up to catch the arm. Both strikes went completely unblocked as blood poured down his zephum foe. *Alright, no need to embarrass him. Maybe I can get him to surrender and end this peacefully? I really hope Serenna doesn't learn of this—*

Novalore launched himself forward with an incredible speed, swinging his sword, aimed at Zeen's face. There wasn't enough space to dodge on either side, so he ducked and stepped backwards to regroup. Novalore followed through, then slammed his armored elbow into Zeen's nose.

The loud crunch was not a good sign, but all he could focus on was the throbbing pain that made his eyes tear. Is there anything worse than getting hit in the nose? *Dammit, he played slow on purpose to bait me, just like Vehemence did in Volume II.*

It's time to focus. I'm not dying in this awful place.

Another slash came towards his head, but Zeen hopped back and gripped Hope. This whole mercy thing really wasn't working out. He reentered his battle stance, glaring into Novalore as an equal. Zeen dashed forward, swiping his blade across Novalore's chest. The zephum accepted the blow, using it as a chance to counter and swing high in an uppercut. Zeen flinched out of the blow's path, then thrust his sword into Novalore's raised left arm. The zephum screamed, then fell to the ground.

Zeen kicked his sword away and held his own to Novalore's neck. "Well fought, Lord Novalore. I offer you the chance to yield." *Not that you deserve it after that swing to my face...*

Why does everyone target my face?

Novalore started to snicker, then let out a truly mighty laugh. "Ah, so Pyith was correct. You are quite good, my human friend. It was an honor to face defeat by your blade. If only you were one of our people."

"He is one of us," Sardonyx said. "I could tell right away. Warmakers, this meeting is concluded. Leave us, *now*."

It was difficult to contain his smile as the zephum warmakers left the room. Oh...right. He glanced at Tempest, who had risen, but went back to staring at nothing. Tempest had clearly been unimpressed with the duel, or he just didn't care. Maybe they were the same.

"Take me to Pyith," Tempest said, finally staring into his father. "Distribute the blame as you will, but I loved her with all my heart."

"Zeen," Sardonyx said, glaring into him through his face guard, "were my demands not clear? I did not become warlord by repeating myself. If I did not cherish our friendship, you would be a corpse on my streets."

"You wouldn't kill your favorite human," Zeen said with a forced smile. No one else was smiling, so he let the gesture fade.

Tempest clanged his stick to the ground, then hobbled towards his father. "Will you not even acknowledge my presence?"

"To stare into you is to stare into a storm of regret. I coddled you at my dear Vitala's wishes. Now, here we stand, an old warlord and his broken son, mourning a fallen hero. Mourning the future of Vaynex."

"Spare me your misguided loathing. Take me to her."

"Her casket is on display in the Valley of Remembrance. Pay your respects, then get out. I cannot have these fools see their warmaster with a limp."

"Thank you, Warlord," Zeen said before Tempest could respond. While he couldn't see Sardonyx's face under his steel guard, it took little imagination to see his seething eyes. The fewer number of words should mean the lesser chance of someone getting cut in half.

Tempest hobbled towards the citadel exit. Before Zeen could follow, Sardonyx approached and grabbed him by the neck. "Do not, ever, defy me again. My empire hangs on by a thread. The moment they believe me to be weak is the moment…chaos rules our realm. I will kill you if I must, Zeen.

For Vaynex, I would kill you *all*." He let go and stormed over to his chambers.

Zeen clutched his neck, gasping for air. One of these days, he was going to die here.

*

It was brutally hot as they stepped outside. Zeen went to grab his water jug before realizing he hadn't brought one. That had not been wise, but at least he was in better physical shape than when he had been here three days ago.

Tempest moved at a much quicker pace than earlier, scraping his stick against the dusty sands and sticking to the side of the alley. He clearly didn't want the attention, or maybe he wanted to avoid the full-on brawl by a cart on the other side of the street—

Oh. Maybe brawl wasn't the right word. Zeen cringed as the vendor snapped the neck of his dissatisfied customer, then literally threw the body far down the street and continued yelling out bread prices. The bread vendors in Terrangus were usually little round guys, who clearly had enjoyed too much of the goods they were selling. The bread vendors here were a different sort of large. Perhaps, in a land of famine, to sell bread was to sell divinity.

"What if Father is correct?" Tempest said, glancing at the vendor before continuing forward. "It is a cultural issue. I cannot...how does one go about changing culture? This obsession with violence, displays of strength, it's like water to us. What would you do?"

Me? I quit the Terrangus military and became a Guardian. Not the advice he's looking for. "Well, when I was in the Great Plains in the Sky, the God of Strength said, 'it's okay that we cannot save everyone, but it's unforgivable not to try.' I think that sums up being a good person. Do the right thing, even though it's not guaranteed to work out."

"But what is the right thing? In my enemy's perspective, I am an inept ruler in the making, a coward who will damn Vaynex to more human dominance. The alternative is more war, more violence. I always assumed their beliefs were rooted in ignorance, but after the end of Strength, it became obvious it's all rooted in fear. Not exactly the fear of being wrong, but the fear of the other side being right."

"Not sure I can help you there. Trust me, it's really obvious who the bad guys are when you're invading another kingdom."

"Is there any word more dangerous to leaders than 'obvious'? I wager Forsythe thought it was obvious that executing Serenna the Pact Breaker was the only course of action."

I don't like where this is going. Strange, out of all the scenarios I feared, a philosophical discussion was very low on the list. "What is obvious is that you are in terrible pain. You need time to grieve, my friend. Let's go back to Mylor together and heal. This is the worst place you could be right now."

"Perhaps that's true, but for better or for worse, this is my home. I…" Tempest took a deep breath, then paused. "The God of Death spoke to me yesterday. I don't know where else to go. Zeen, I find it difficult to ask, but will you remain here with me?"

Oh no, I have to warn Serenna. "Of course. Whatever I can do to help. We should really tell—"

"No. Let it be our secret. If even a whisper of this got out, the Claw reign would be uprooted immediately. My father is a violent fool, but he desires balance. Without him, the empire will break apart again. We'll have factions fighting factions until a new warlord rises with the promise of war against humans. If I…if it becomes apparent I am lost, dispose of me discreetly. You have my blessing."

"You will never become lost. I'm here for you, Tempest, we'll beat this together."

Tempest adjusted his walking stick, grimacing as he adjusted the weight. Whatever thoughts went through his head, he spoke none of them out loud.

CHAPTER 17

A LESSON OF LIMITATIONS

erenna materialized into the Mylor Guardian portal, blinking a few times to regain focus. It had only been a few days since she had been home, but after leading the Guardians against the Harbinger of Fear, it felt like weeks. *Ah Zeen, we were supposed to return together.* They would be together soon… Right? If she could convince herself for seven months, she may as well keep going. With enough patience, even the most desperate lies eventually become true. Gods, she was tired. While all her emotions rose up and battled for supremacy—relief after protecting the realm, joy at Zeen's awakening, despair at Pyith's end, fear of a mad god's threats— the desire to sleep easily defeated them all. Maybe she could warn Father, take a warm bath, then—

"This quaint room is just as I recall," Everleigh spoke through her thoughts, causing Serenna to grab the wooden table for balance. Why was she always so LOUD? *"This is your home, is it not? I expected more luxury after all this time, though disappointing me again seems commonplace. Have you learned nothing in your leadership role? Perception is the first step towards superiority."*

"I am a Guardian, not a decorator. When you're the closest kingdom to Terrangus, most of the gold is spent on weapons and walls. My father is the senator, you can direct your grievances at him." Maybe that was a bit petty, but the Goddess of Valor was wearing out her welcome. It was like having an invisible Francis follow her around and critique every little thing. Those two would either be best of friends or terrible enemies...

"Oh child, Terrangus would not dare threaten our kingdom if I were still a mortal."

"Our? Are you...from Mylor?"

"Truly? Do you not read or study? I was Mylor's greatest Guardian! Oh, if I knew the Guardians of today were so simple-minded, I would have declined the Lord of Time's offer and continued my eternal slumber. Do you even appreciate the sacrifice I made?"

"Yes, of course. Forgive me, Goddess." Appreciate? Sure. Understand? Not a chance. While Serenna knew very little of Guardian Everleigh other than Landon's stories and some brief lessons on Guardian history from her school days, she knew even less about the Time God. She assumed the end of Strength had created an opening for a new god, but Everleigh didn't seem like the type to enjoy questions. Serenna filled a chalice with water, took a deep sip, then walked down the halls of the Mylor capital.

"Most of these portraits are over a century in age. Forgotten senators and archons, gray-haired men who barely left a mark on the realm. It is simply deplorable that Guardians are not cherished throughout history. We should be nearing my portrait soon. A rather amateurish piece, I do concede, but—"

An outline of a spectral hand touched the Guardian of Mylor's portrait. The 'epic' painting of Serenna gripping her staff in absurdly tight clothes while lightning crashed behind her appeared more laughable each time she passed. She nearly snickered, but Everleigh wasn't laughing.

"They replaced me…with you. After everything I did for the realm, Mylor's children have forgotten their mother. Curse this wretched hovel, with its birds and rocks. ENOUGH! Introduce me to your father, then we train. We train until blood flows from your eyes."

With the increasing anger in Everleigh's voice, it was possible Serenna would bleed from the ears before her eyes. She opened her father's door—half expecting the goddess to scold her for not knocking—to find him sitting at his desk, working on some ledger. It was nearly the same pose Senator Thompson had in Xavian, but the two men couldn't be any more different. What do these senators do all day? "Good afternoon, Father. The task is done."

"Well done, my dear!" Charles said, then rushed to embrace her. "It's morning, by the way, though the circles under your eyes might be blocking out the light." After a pause, he let go and gripped both her hands, with a surprising amount of strength for the little man. "You're alone? Um…is he well?"

"Zeen is fine. He is spending the next day or so in Vaynex to deal with complications. Dad… I lost Pyith. I wasn't strong enough…"

"Ah, she was a good one. I'm normally not fond of those lizard-people, but she was a good one. My dear, you look—and smell, if I'm being honest—a bit distraught." Charles snickered as she smacked his hands away. "You're home. Take some time to relax, then we'll sit outside with a drink and you can tell me everything. Only if you want to, of course."

"Thank you. Father, may I ask a question?"

Charles snickered as he rubbed his chin. "Should I be concerned that you're asking my permission?"

"What do you know about Guardian Everleigh? My close friend in Terrangus explained she was one of the most revered Mylor Guardians. Why is the name so unfamiliar?"

"Ah," Charles said, leaning against his desk and staring down, like he was trying to remember. "Some nonsense with a lover in Terrangus. Mother explained it to me far too long ago. She yelled something about the woman being a traitor so I stopped asking. You don't remember your grandmother, but she had those crazy eyes. I learned early on which roads to take while speaking to avoid that damned wooden spoon." Her father laughed as if that was somehow a pleasant memory.

Serenna resisted the urge to check behind her. The fact her goddess wasn't yelling was either a very good or terrible sign. "How could a Guardian be a traitor?"

"Simpler times, my dear. She got knocked up by some Terrangus general while our kingdoms were on the brink of war. Just imagine the outrage. If you think our people are prudes now, whew, you should've seen them back then. My mother would've beaten you senseless if she saw the way you look at Zeen."

Oh? So her Goddess of 'Valor' had a scandalous side. "Tread carefully on your judgment of Grandma. You used to be the same way."

"To an extent. Being a dad is a rather bizarre journey. A fair portion of the time is spent chasing away horny little brats but…you're an adult now. If he makes you happy, what else matters? That's all I can ask for at this point." He hugged her, then leaned in close and whispered, "Let's continue this after a bath."

*

Serenna stepped out into the Mylor gardens, in a fresh suit of armor and the Wings of Mylor behind her back. Her bath earlier had been relaxing enough to entice her to take a nap. She had woken up in the late afternoon refreshed but concerned about Everleigh's silence since the morning. Was she going to train her? Maybe all that talk about being a traitor offended her enough to leave—

"Oh, so you finally finished your dallying? Are you certain you don't prefer a tea party before we begin?"

Honestly, she would kill for a cup of tea, but that desire went unspoken. "I apologize for my delay. I am prepared for your guidance."

A large wall of pure crystal platinum appeared on the other side of the garden. It was the exact tint of Serenna's standard barriers, which she assumed was Everleigh's way of remaining incognito. *"Pierce my wall with a spike and we move on to the next step. Proceed."*

Hmm, this wasn't how Serenna normally trained, but so be it. She drew a faint amount of energy from her body, channeling a platinum hue as the wind blew her hair to the side. She created a single spike, hovering it in front of her, then took a deep breath as she studied her crystal. Vivid glow, flawless shape, and the point seemed sharp from what she could tell. Crystals are all about technique; a good edge would tear more efficiently than a dull spike thrust at twice the speed. She pointed her staff forward, launching the spike into the wall. Best to get this part out of the way before the true challenge began—

Her spike shattered on contact without leaving a dent.

"You are too focused on form and not raw power. I am not your father. I am not here to coddle you. Draw some real energy and do it again."

Fine. Yelling in the Mylor gardens would be an awkward sight, so she took a deep breath and tensed, letting out a faint groan as she drew in her energy. A new spike formed. Same design, but with a thicker tint of platinum. She pointed her staff forward.

Her spike shattered on contact without leaving a dent. Again.

"Stop focusing on the form! What inspires your desperation? You told the Zeen boy you love him. Would you still embrace him as a Vanguard? You would see him every day as a husk of his former self, with those dead eyes looking through you, remembering who you were, but lacking the will to care. It would be worse than seeing him dead."

"I already saw him dead," Serenna said, gripping her staff tighter. "He died right in my arms." She closed her eyes, thinking back to how hard Zeen had clutched her right before he went limp. So far, she had led the Guardians twice, and each battle had suffered a terrible loss. To hell with anyone who could hear. She let out a yell and erupted into pure platinum energy, created a new spike, and launched it forward.

The damn wall wouldn't budge. It wouldn't even give her the courtesy to crack.

She drew more energy while still empowered to form six spikes, two as giants and four normal sized. If Everleigh was still berating her, Serenna couldn't hear through the seething platinum energy. She launched them all, knowing it wouldn't be enough even before they crashed against the wall. "I cannot break this wall and you know it. What are we accomplishing here?"

"Aggravation is nothing compared to true pain. I want to see you suffer, to scream out, to draw so much energy you wished you were dead. I only exist because of your failures as a leader. No other Guardian team required a god's sacrifice to prevail. How do you manage with such guilt? Where is your pride? If you cannot break this wall, you may as well perish. You will be incapable of protecting anyone you love."

"I hate you," Serenna whispered. It felt so freeing to say it. She braced her legs as she tore an absurd amount of energy from her body. A dizzy sensation crept through her peripheral vision; she had to lean straight to stop her head from tilting. Trickles of blood tapped onto the grass; she assumed it was from the eyes, but with her entire body aching, there was no way to tell. She raised her staff high in an awkward motion, stumbling back to regain balance, then formed one final, monstrous spike that pulsated with a violent glow. She launched it into the wall before falling face first into the grass. Perhaps it made a crack, but darkness overtook her before she could confirm.

*

Serenna awoke in the Mylor gardens, her face pressed against the soft grass before she forced herself up. Something was terribly wrong. All the pain vanished, the wall was gone, and the roses that filled the east row of the gardens had been replaced with…lilies? It was nighttime apparently, which didn't make sense, but with the perfect view of the stars and crescent moon observing from above, there was a tranquility to it all that she hadn't felt in far too long.

The Everleigh standing by the lilies was not the Everleigh Serenna had seen in Xavian. Despite the same white battle armor, this version of the goddess was only a few inches taller than her, with platinum hair that went just below shoulder length. The scythe behind her back had an odd pale glow by the blade. Mylor textbooks had written of scythes as an impractical weapon, but there was no denying the intimidating presence.

"This is how I remember it," Everleigh said, in a soft voice and not the grating screech that had usually torn through her head. "The Time Lord said I could have a plane to call my own, so I suppose this will suffice. This was my training ground, where I relaxed, where I dreamed, where Felix and I made love for the first time. For a Terrangus general, he was a very generous lover." Everleigh's green eyes stayed frozen on the moon above, gazing into the starry night with a smile. Based on her last comment, she was likely reminiscing about memories Serenna was better off not knowing.

"How did I arrive here?" Serenna hesitated, then approached Everleigh to stand next to her. The intimidating nature of the woman was diminished by her true form. "Did I break the wall?"

"The wall was never meant to be broken. You were."

"Lady Everleigh, what was the point then? I just wasted an entire day on a meaningless task."

"A lesson of limitations, child. I wielded the same mentality in my mortal days. Crystal magic truly is a two-sided blade; we draw and draw, putting the weight of the realm on our shoulders, leading through pure intimidation. Sometimes, we prevail. Sometimes, we perish. Like I did."

I really need to study Guardian history. She assumed Everleigh had lived a long fulfilling life and died of old age, but thinking back, most Guardians served until the bitter end. *I imagine that will be me someday, fighting for decades as everyone I love falls in battle until it's my turn. How did David stand it? How does anyone?* "A Harbinger, I assume?"

"One from the fallen empress, in Terrangus, of all places. I rushed into battle too quickly after bearing my child. I was rattled by my new fears like a novice, but by Noelami's grace, I loved that boy from the second I held him. Tis an odd thing: the harder we love, the more complex our fears become."

Everleigh paused, then cleared her throat. "Right before the blade pierced my heart, I went to the void, assuming the realm was doomed. Without me, the Guardians would falter, the realm would fall, my poor boy would become a spectator of the next Boulom. Imagine my shock to wake and find not only was I wrong, but completely forgotten. I still lack the courage to check on the boy today. Wherever he is, he is better off never knowing his grandmother. Limitations cannot be denied. Learn from my mistakes."

"How do I do such a thing?" asked Serenna, watching the

moonlight reflect on the mountains on the outskirts. "How do I...let go?"

To her shock, Everleigh actually smiled. The pleasant glow of her pale face did not match the insults and threats that had torn through Serenna's thoughts. "It's not about letting go, child, but holding on. I'm afraid there's no simple answer to these things. I can only expand upon the lesson after you've learned it. Start small: like asking your father to fetch you water when you awake in a moment. Your vulnerability empowers him. Teach him to guard himself against the delusions of Arrogance instead of forcing yourself to remain by his side. The wall cannot be broken, but it doesn't make the wall invincible."

"But, what about..." Serenna paused as a dizzy sensation filled her head. "Please, not yet. I have...more questions..."

*

Serenna awoke in the Mylor gardens, her face pressed against the grass before she forced herself up. Ah, this was back home, with the sun beating down and roses lined up in the east rows—

"SERENNA, CAN YOU HEAR ME?" her father yelled, oh so loud.

"Gods yes," she said, rubbing her face as her vision cleared. "Please stop yelling. Dad, could you please grab me some water?"

"Right away!" he yelled, then dashed off inside the capitol.

Charles returned a few minutes later with a full jug, spilling an unfortunate amount as he pushed it into her hands.

She took a large gulp of water, then sighed in relief. "Thank you. I went too hard in training this morning. Dad, we need to speak about your safety. I may have endangered you by angering the God of Wisdom."

"Ah, I'm not all that worried about that one. Shall we head to my office?"

"No. Let's speak here. I have taken these gardens for granted my entire life. Hmm. How would you feel about adding some lilies?"

CHAPTER 18

TOMBS FILLED WITH HONOR

After an agonizing walk through the Valley of Remembrance, passing several tombs and resting grounds of forgotten zephum warriors, Tempest glared at the tan, barracks-like structure reserved for fallen Claws, with Zeen by his side. It was such an embarrassing monument, a testament to war, as if life's legacy could only be decided in abstract measures of honor and power. That's how they would remember his Pyith. Not as the life-mate who had lifted the anxieties of an unwanted future warlord, but as a warrior.

"It's beautiful, in its own way," Zeen said, studying the structure with a quizzical glance. "I expected something different based on your descriptions in *Rinso Volume II.*"

Zeen of course was referring to the golden tomb of Vehemence, surrounded by flowers and weeping zephum and humans alike, instead of all this sand and tan blocks. Hyphermlo had loved his brother, even if he was a brutal bastard until that last page. A bit convenient that a final act of sacrifice had pardoned a lifetime of atrocities, but how else could Tempest have written the scene? "It is always worth writing a beautiful lie. Look upon it, Zeen. This is the legacy of my people. Tombs filled with honor."

Tempest limped forward, thankful his injury delayed his approach. It was an odd thing to approach her resting ground, knowing an ambush of painful memories and guilt were all that awaited him. *The last time I entered this valley was for Mother. I can only wonder how different life would've been if Father had died instead of her. Is that a cruel thought? Has he ever wondered the same?*

Zeen placed his hand on Tempest's shoulder. A kind and welcome gesture in any civilized kingdom, but this was Vaynex. "Anything I can do to ease the pain, please let me know."

"You can start by removing that hand. Act as my bodyguard, not a friend. I will be expected to look upon her body with a stoic pose, not offering any hint of emotion or pain. My people seem to believe that by ignoring our feelings, we can conquer them."

One of the several downsides of a shattered leg was losing the option to rush out of uncomfortable scenarios if necessary. Several zephum by the tomb were whispering and glaring at him, with one having the audacity to point. *Just keep moving. You owe it to yourself to find closure. It's the only way to move forward...*

He forced himself to push his walking stick against the sand and carry on. His right arm ached as he took an extended step to reach the solid ground of the tomb's entrance. *By Strength's name, I'll have to make the same journey on the way back.* A terrible realization, but an inevitable one. If there was any mercy in the realm, the sun would come down by that point. At normal walking speed, he could make the trip in about fifteen minutes, but he had no idea how long it had taken to get here with his limp. *Agony makes the passage of time a fading blur—*

"You do not speak to him that way," Zeen said, drawing his blade on a zephum.

Tempest nearly fell over in shock. He immediately yelled,

"Never draw a sword here! *Never!*" before any irreparable damage could be done. Strength save him, this man was going to kill them both.

To Zeen's credit, the zephum he had threatened went completely silent and eased out of the tomb. To Zeen's discredit, he had just violated one of the most sacred traditions in zephum culture. *I never considered the irony. We forbid violence in a valley that worships it.* If Tempest was his normal self, he could play the rules to his advantage, using cultural invulnerability to goad his onlookers for an opportunity to punish them later. Today, none of that mattered in the slightest.

Zeen sheathed his sword and stared down. "Sorry. He was saying vile things about you. It is unfair to target someone who already suffers."

"Nothing about today is fair. Yet, here we are, in the tomb of my family name."

"I've never seen anything like it. When my father was buried, they didn't even mark the grave. I drank half a flask of zephum ale in his honor and poured the rest on the soil. I wouldn't be able to find that spot today if I tried."

Tempest paused. *Technically, I did say bodyguard. It's not his fault. Strength knows I struggled to fit in my first few times in Alanammus.* He hated himself for continuously lashing out against the one person who cared enough to help. No one else was here, but really, who else would come? Losing his lover and best friend in the same moment was the ultimate realization of how far he had distanced himself from his people. "I must ask you again to forgive me. I am…not handling this with dignity."

"No one does. Trust me, I was the same way a few days after I lost Dad. We were never that close, but that somehow made it worse. Like…from that moment on, there would never be a chance to fix it."

Tempest was certain Zeen had been nowhere near this

awful in his mourning, but the sentiment was appreciated. "Such is life, Zeen. Most problems never get fixed because we find such familiarity in seeing them broken."

Zeen simply nodded at that. Tempest wished he would keep the conversation going as an excuse to delay, but he had run out of words. He couldn't help but glance at the memorials layered in the east and west sides. The only way to identify who lay where were the bronze plaques by each shift in the walls. *Vitala Claw,* Tempest read, then *Fentum Claw* and *Onyeto Claw* on the left sides. No plaque was to Vitala's right, that spot would be reserved for his father. A 'glorious' end indeed.

"When my time comes, they will push me right...there," Tempest said, pointing to the empty spot next to Sardonyx's. "Not a guaranteed outcome of course. I could always end up on the streets depending on how the next few days play out. Hmm. I suppose there is no more stalling." Tempest's hands shook as he gripped his walking stick, despite fatigue being the least of his problems. He hobbled forward, refusing to meet eyes with any of the zephum who whispered to each other.

In the final chamber lay his Pyith. Her open casket stood high in the middle of the room like an altar, with four large candles lighting from the corners. She deserved riches, flowers, everything really, but such was the realm. From the poorest of men to those who rival gods, it would seem no one finds what they truly deserve when the end comes.

He slowly ascended the stairs to look upon her one last time. Strength forgive him, she didn't even appear dead. Her closed eyes and snout pointing into the air was just as she had appeared anytime she slept. All that was missing was her snoring. *I nearly walked out on her that first night. We mated, then she went right to sleep and snored and snored and snored. I thought that was true suffering. Oh, what I would give to suffer through such joy one final time—*

Tempest gripped his walking stick with both hands as his vision blurred for a moment. Sweat dripped off his snout onto the stony floor. How could this be real? He wanted to scream, to cry, to curse the empty heavens above for smothering him with such a fate. "I will fulfill our dream, my love," he said to Pyith. He had found it bizarre when Father had spoken to Vitala's body on the day of her mourning, but by Strength's name, the yearning to speak to those who cannot hear is sometimes the only option. "Our people will know a Vaynex of prosperity and reform. A land of fulfillment without violence, driven by art and culture. I swear to you. *I swear it.*" And he meant it. He hobbled down the stairs with a mix of vigor and desperation, nodding at Zeen to follow him back to the citadel.

*

A forever or so later, Tempest had arrived back at the citadel under the cover of dusk. He had blown out the candles in his chambers and lay in his bed, his heart pounding as he begged for sleep.

It did not come. A slight adjustment of his blanket, a turn to the side, a turn to the other side, a deep breath, a deeper breath. Sleep would not come. The harder he begged the darkness to allow him rest, the more it became clear such a gift was not coming. Is there anything more cruel than the fear of not falling asleep keeping one awake?

Sunlight crept through his window. It was clear the opportunity to rest had failed, that the horrors of today would be faced with an empty heart and an empty mind. To any normal person, the sun was a wonderful promise of a new day. For an insomniac, it was a reminder yesterday had never ended. *I made her a promise. I can get through this. Take it day by day.*

Tempest eased out of bed, his legs terribly sore from all of yesterday's walking. He drew a bath and limped forward, putting his strong leg in first and grabbing the steel sides for balance. Water splashed out from all over, ah how that would have angered him in better times. With the temperate waters easing his pain, he struggled against the urge to rest his eyes. How cruel of his body to finally demand rest when it was no longer an option.

Too much time in the bath made his throat parched, so it was time to leave the water to find some water. He didn't trust himself enough to stand on one leg and repeat the process that had gotten him there, so he leaned himself over the steel, hands first and pressed forward enough to get his lower-half onto the floor. It took more time than he would care to admit to get dried and clothed. All he was missing was his walking stick. It leaned against the bed, glaring at him, a reminder of how much life had changed in such an insignificant amount of time.

CHAPTER 19

THE SIMPLICITY OF VIOLENCE

avid leaned against the hard prison walls behind his bed and sighed. While he understood the opportunity to finally speak to another person was likely paradise for Nyfe, he just wanted to rest until Francis disposed of him, or whatever else the puppet emperor had planned.

"So, I gotta know, did Zeen pull through?" asked Nyfe. Maybe he noticed he was losing David's attention so he went to that.

"The audacity to ask such a question. You don't deserve to know."

Nyfe stared at him before letting out a snicker. "Well, I do now, thanks to that dry tone in your voice. I doubt you'll believe me but I'm glad he made it. Zeen is a good guy. Dumb as a rock, but a good guy."

"Fuck off," David said, closing his eyes. For summer, the stone wall was rather cool, likely from being so far below the castle. If he was still alive by winter, this cell would be a frozen nightmare.

"Fair enough. Apparently, that's still a sore point so I'll drop it."

David leaned forward and glared at him. "A sore point?

You begged him for mercy then stabbed him while his guard was down. Fuck. Off."

"True," Nyfe said with another snicker. "I tried that on you in this very castle but you caught me. How'd you know?"

"I never take my eyes off any evil that manages to grow old. Grayson did the same thing to Melissa. You cold-hearted ones do anything it takes to linger and spread your despair."

"Oh? And where does 'evil' come from? You killed Vanessa—Grayson killed Melissa. Cycle of life, my friend."

"Any sensible person knows I was right to slay Harbinger Vanessa. There is no coming back from such a fate."

Nyfe rose and grasped the prison bars to David's cell. He smiled, as if he had been anticipating such a response. "But I'm still here. Who knows, maybe I'm special?"

"You are nothing," David said, even though that was a fair point. *After all these years…was I wrong about Vanessa? Did I cause everything? No wonder all these people flock to time magic. Ah, for a chance to do it all over again. Just imagine…*

"Cheers to us, from one 'nothing' to another. I don't suppose your Fear buddy would bail us out?" After a long pause, Nyfe sat back down and crossed his arms. "Ah, she dumped you? Of course she did; Death dropped me too. We should start a club!"

David lay on his bed, pulling the pillow close. The damned thing was like a sack of rocks. "Give me peace. If this is my end, let me die a rested man."

"Figures, I finally get a prison buddy and he's the most boring man in the realm. Nothing but brooding and cryptic one-liners."

David shifted his head to make sure Nyfe couldn't see him smirk. Before he could close his eyes, steps approached his cell.

"Master David. An honor, sir," the man said. He had the monotone voice of a Vanguard, with a slight hint of humanity.

"It's highly improbable you remember such an occurrence, but you met my husband Julius and I at the gold cloak ceremony about a decade ago in Alanammus."

Rest never comes. Not even here. "Hmm," David said, rising. "It would seem the more people I meet, the weaker my memory becomes. From Alanammus, you say?"

"I appeared quite different back then. My name is Robert Cavare, though these days my official title is Vanguard Five."

David studied the Vanguard. Ah, it was the one from the battle of Xavian. While he was no expert on the matter, this one appeared different from the drones he had observed over the months. Arrogance would have to step up his tricks if he wanted David to serve. "You aren't Robert. Fuck off."

"A logical response. Here," he said, then took out a pair of keys and unlocked his cell. "When you severed the sun mask, it interrupted Wisdom's control over a few of us while he recovered. The rest are under his hold again but I seem to have kept my freewill. Odd, to be given the gift I actively sought to end."

Is this a trick? The door is open, I can't find any reason not to rush out of here. To think...I actually wounded him. A realm without gods. Perhaps it's possible after all.

"We thank you for your aid, Lord Robert," Nyfe said, his grin filling his entire face. "Oh, to taste freedom. I have several people who deserve a visit."

Vanguard Five... Robert glared at Nyfe. "Do you even remember Julius? Captain of the gold cloaks? Hero to an entire people? Was he nothing to you?"

"Oh, not this again," Nyfe said, sitting back down with a sigh. "Why does everyone wait until I'm in a cell to confront me? Scorned cowards from across the realm."

"You are the sole reason I became a Vanguard. Freewill cannot exist when individuals abuse it on such a tangible level."

"Why are you helping me?" asked David. While he wasn't about to refuse a chance to escape, no ally of Arrogance could be trusted. "I will never serve Arrogance. Never."

"It's…complicated. Arrogance has noble goals of reform, but I remain unconvinced he is the optimal choice to usher them in. Regardless, you have always served the realm. Serenna needs you; a new divinity is influencing her and we haven't pieced together who it is yet. Arrogance is not benevolent, but he is the superior choice to an unknown god."

It would figure David's quest to end all gods would fail so badly there would be more than when he had started. "Fair enough. Should I rush out, or shall we leave together? I know you have faith in Arrogance, but he will butcher you for betraying him."

The Vanguard paused. He must've known it was true. "Together. Do you need this one?" Robert asked, glancing at Nyfe.

"David has been my friend for decades! I'll have you know he was the best man at my wedding!"

"No," David said, then walked towards the exit, ignoring Nyfe's increasingly desperate and absurd claims. "How do we play this? I could pretend to be your prisoner."

"I calculated the arithmetic and there's only one possible outcome in which we escape to Mylor."

Oh, I'm not going to like this. "And that outcome is?"

"We rush to the outskirts after a distraction. Vanguard Three is stationed by the Guardian portal while One and Two are in the throne room. The probability suggests we will confront Four in the trade district, who may have backup aiding him. He killed a family last night after a simple disagreement. Tension between the people and Vanguards right now are…not well. If we are to fail, that is likely where it will occur."

"Great. I don't suppose you brought me a weapon?"

Robert fidgeted by his right sheath, then pulled out a dull short sword. "Before you voice your dissent, it's better than nothing."

David examined the blade before he took it. Maybe he had been spoiled by the Herald of Fear, but this sword...was not a good sword. "Nothing is a rather low bar. Could a man defeat you with such a weapon?"

"In theory, yes. Whether a blade costs one copper or one hundred gold, all it takes is one pierce through the neck. I always preferred magic but one cannot discount the simplicity of violence."

He grinned, then sheathed his sword before his back. "Fuck it. Lead the way."

Robert nodded, then closed his eyes before he glowed a dark orange. "Stay close, but not too close. We'll need a distraction." He opened the prison door, then eased up the stairs as David followed from a safe distance.

When they arrived in the castle's main hall, several guards glanced at the glowing Vanguard and pointed at him. They all seemed to acknowledge something terrible was about to happen, but inaction tends to smother any hint of heroism in large groups. No one approached as Robert launched a fire blast into the high ceiling. It erupted into flames as burning fragments of steel and stone crumbled down. "*Now!*" he yelled, then they ran.

The castle guards were either too frantic or intelligent to oppose Robert and David as they rushed out of the castle. Fortunately, the fire blast sent the military ward into a panic, so it was rather simple to blend in with the screaming people fleeing towards anywhere that wasn't here.

David had always complained about the noise and stench of Terrangus, but the aura of chaos was the perfect environment for two men wishing not to be seen. Rain poured down from the cloudy skies, a welcome distraction from the humid air. He couldn't help but notice Francesco's Alanammus Treasures as he rushed through the trade district. Gods, that could have been a lifetime ago.

A man dressed in the same white attire as Robert stood alone by the open Terrangus gates to the outskirts, gripping an oak staff. Four was it? Leave it to Francis to just name people as numbers. He glowed a dark green, then created a round, mountainous terrain that engulfed the three of them. "Vanguard Five. So it's true? Your death shall bring a long despair to us all. If I were capable of lying, I would tell our colleagues you died a hero. The truth, cruel as it is, will be far less lenient."

"Perhaps truth belongs to the winners," Robert said, stepping forward with his staff drawn. He glowed a yellow aura and approached the center of the mountainous arena. "You are my brother, Vanguard Four. Please acknowledge I take no joy in such wrath." He launched a burning ray of lightning forward.

Vanguard Four quickly shifted to yellow and countered with his own blast, creating a burning display as if David was staring directly into the sun. With the two Vanguards locked in, David rushed from the side—

The forces of yellow exploded, knocking the three of them flying in different directions. The mountainous terrain collapsed, revealing a sea of people observing the battle. Most of them had murderous intentions in their eyes—men, women...children alike. Ah, what an ironic death that would be. To curse the mob all his life just to die by their hands.

David rose, then clutched his sword. He went to rush forward before meeting eyes with Vanguard Four... Shit. A lightning blast flew towards him; by reflex, he clutched his sword and closed his eyes. His sword barely defended the blast as his body soared into the jagged rocks of the Terrangus trade district. He tried to scream from the burns, but the air was already gone from his lungs.

At least I didn't die on my knees. Melissa, I hope you're watching. You always said I was special, despite how little I valued myself. Despite...

Finish it. Send me to the void.

He kept his eyes closed but nothing happened. Why? What the hell was going on? He rose, holding his sword for balance as a dizzy sensation swept through.

Vanguard Four was being beaten by the mob, the same men, women, and children thrashing him as they screamed, "NO MORE VANGUARDS!" They sounded like animals, but since they were on his side, they sounded more like angels.

Vanguard Five was meeting the same fate, being pounded by the wrath of desperation as city-folk slammed everything from clubs to broken rocks onto his body. *He knew what he signed up for; this is my chance to escape. This is...*

Enough of that. David clutched his sword and rushed forward. He would stand no chance if the mob turned their ire on him, but the best way to defeat crazy is by acting more crazy. He swung a few times, then after no one responded, he stopped and yelled, "I am David Williams, Guardian of Terrangus. This one is my ally. Return him to me."

The mob backed away as David took Robert by the hand and helped him rise. To his surprise, more than a select few were cheering for him. They looked at David in awe, as if he were some bard's legend of old, some specter of a man that wasn't supposed to exist. Someone set fire to a weapons shop, and the mob was more than happy to turn their attention to the new fiery distraction.

David only gave a slight glance at Four, but the butchered limbs and blood made the glance one of the longest seconds of his life. "I don't care how hard it is to stand, Robert. We need to keep moving."

"That was your prompt to escape. It would have been a

proper end. Julius sacrificed himself in this very kingdom—"

Against his better judgment he paused, then said, "Sacrifice isn't what Julius wants, you're just looking for an excuse to join him. We survive and make them proud. Our purpose now is to become a shadow of the beauty they saw in us. Do you understand? I'm not moving until you confirm you understand."

"I prefer Zeen's delicate words to yours…but I understand."

"Most people do." David walked as fast as he could with the limping Five on his arm. Guards were rushing down from the military ward, but their primary targets appeared to be the looters and rioters. Ah, what he would give to see the look on Francis's face when he learned of his subjects' rage. Perfection it would appear, did not trickle down.

Rain prevented the fires from running rampant, but that only seemed to make the people more furious. They brawled in the streets, bodies sprawling on the rocky roads, guards being swarmed and never seen again. "NO MORE VANGUARDS!" was screamed over and over, with the people not having enough decency to sync their chants. Pure Terrangus chaos in the pure Terrangus rain.

There was less madness in the outskirts after the kingdom gates. With no mage to maintain the portal, David and Robert were able to approach with little resistance. He did have to kick a man to the ground who had noticed the Wisdom crest on Robert's white mail, but that sent a strong enough message for the rest to keep away.

"I assume you can operate this thing?" David asked, glancing at the portal.

"Any first-year student can work a portal," Robert said with a bitter tone, as if that were common knowledge. He stepped away from David and drew his staff. "Allow me to—"

A familiar chuckle filled the air, then the portal erupted, knocking them both to the ground.

"My dear friends," Wisdom's voice said from above them. "You were looking to leave? Before supper? How utterly rude of you both! Well, I suppose the three of us are familiar enough to lose our masks."

The stormy skies grew darker as his standard sun mask shifted to the Arrogance version, with the burning frown and bulging eyes. "There are two ways to train a dog. A treat after training rewards good behavior, but sometimes you have to beat the disobedience out of them. You have turned down the treat, so do you care to wager what happens next?"

David rose, gripping his sword. Hopefully, he appeared less pathetic than he felt. "If you slay us quickly enough, perhaps you can stop perfection from burning down."

"Alas," Arrogance said with a sigh, "the people have been ignorant for so long they oppose progress like a sick man refuses a bitter medicine. Five, I'm not entirely sure how you managed to behave so outrageously, but it's time to come home." The god raised a spectral hand, then closed it into a fist.

Robert screamed from the ground. He rose, then glared at David with dissociated eyes. "David…kill me. Before I…" Robert glowed orange, his burning aura overwhelming any hint of a breeze from the rainy open field.

Ah, fuck. He doesn't deserve to die, but I cannot sit here and risk burning to death. Julius, if you're watching, forgive me. David rushed the Vanguard, his eyes locked on his neck. He made a quick thrust but the aura erupted, knocking David back to the ground with his sword flying behind him.

Rain dripped onto his face as he lay there, gazing at the gloomy clouds above. If this were a battle against a Harbinger, David would wait for some heroic action from Melissa, Pyith, or Serenna to save the day. But, as life would have it, he was alone. *I wish it wasn't fire. Surely I've earned the privilege to meet a swift end. Oh well, one final moment of torment. A rather fitting end…*

He shivered as an ominous breeze blew across his body, then his eyes widened as the skies grew darker. A screech came from above; it didn't take long to realize who it was.

The Goddess of Fear hovered above him in her full goddess form, with the ethereal wings and long shadowy hair flowing with the breeze. The onyx gemstone in her right eye sucked in any remaining light like a vortex.

"Ermias, you loathsome insect," Fear said, as the wind whistled through the grassy fields. "This one is *mine*."

Arrogance chuckled, but David caught hints of distress in his voice. "Oh, Fear. Centuries of plotting, boiled down to a drunk with a fancy blade? The ruins of your once-great mind rival that of your once-great empire."

"Begone from here and slither back to your clouds unless you desire a second death from my blade."

"The one I shattered? Threats and rage, threats and rage… Oh, how I have dreamed of this moment, but of course, the reality is a disappointment. As someone I know once said, 'Where reality fails, dreams are eternal.'"

"If you expected anything other than hostility, you are the God of Ignorance."

"My hopes and expectations never seem to align. I always loved you, Maya," Arrogance said with a sigh. "Even now, for whatever it's worth. It will all make sense after I prevail. Serenity will be the legacy of Boulom. We can watch it together from my sky garden, laughing at how absurd life used to be. It will be simply…*wonderful*."

"You should alter the wording on your mantra. Delusion is all that remains but you are the most miserable thing I have ever seen."

"But the greatest of arts are forged in the deepest chasms of misery, dear Goddess. Very well. Take your tool and go."

"Robert stays as well," David said. While it seemed unwise

to interrupt the bickering of two deranged gods, he had the feeling his opportunity was coming to a close.

"*No*," Arrogance said. "He *chose* to be a Vanguard. I will not interfere with your toy, Maya, now have the courtesy to return the favor. Or shall we test how weakened you are after that Harbinger?"

"He means nothing to me," Fear said, not even bothering a glance. "Take him and begone."

David scoffed. "No! I only made it this far with his help. How can you abandon him?"

"His death is on your hands," Fear said, triggering the outskirts portal to a pale white. "Never forget that. *Never.*"

He wouldn't. Maybe his troubles with remembering all of the living was due to the growing number of those who had died. Grayson, Jasmine, Thomas, Brian, Melissa, Pyith... There was no reason to keep going.

But he did anyway.

CHAPTER 20

SOMETHING TO HATE

ary Walker snapped her fingers at Vanguards One and Two to follow, then walked out of the throne room while Francis argued with his senators about…whatever the hell they argued about. With Wisdom gone, this was her only opportunity to resolve this mess without a mass butchering of her people. She drew her sword and shield as the fire of the castle halls shimmered against her golden armor. Gods, it was heavy, but with her growing belly, big events called for bigger armor.

Her Vanguards followed intently, staring ahead at nothing, just being *weird*. She hated the damn things. It was like having cats that could shoot fire, quietly plotting her demise. Chances were, she would have her child, then some mysterious accident would leave her dead in her chambers. "A travesty!" Wisdom would proclaim. "Oh, what a cruel fate, if only we had Serenity!" he would say in that annoying voice. And of course, Francis would listen. That was Francis's problem, maybe it was the burden of every wise man: he listened to everything.

Mary snickered at the absolute dismay on the faces of the guards at the castle doors. They surely had to stop her from waddling outside, but neither would dare try. "Empress," was all they managed, followed by a bow.

Good to know I'm more intimidating than Francis. Wonder what that says about me. Hopefully, they were gambling men, because they just took a hell of a risk letting her go.

The rain poured down her scarlet hair, with heavy smoke smothering most of the view beyond the military ward. That was fine, have to start somewhere, may as well be the ward where Mary had spent the majority of her life in service to the kingdom she now ruled. "No killing. You understand?" she told the Vanguards. They stared in response, but no words, nods, or anything that could be considered a human reaction was accomplished. Gods, it really was like having cats.

"Empress?" General Marcus yelled. He rushed up, and despite the rain, she noticed his sweat. "What are you doing here? Our kingdom is rather unsafe this evening. Please allow me to escort you back to the castle."

"Marcus, you bald fuck," Mary said with a snicker. "It's just like Koulva, isn't it? Remind me how we stopped the riots back then?" It was fun to toy with the man and kill the annoying formal talk. He had been ranked far higher than her back in the day, but as far as she knew, the empress answered to no one. Well, almost no one.

"I have soldiers out there already. Listen, if anything happens to you, I can't fathom what Francis will do to me. It's not like the old days. I have a wife and kids now."

In the 'old' days, Marcus would thrust his sword through zephum prisoner's knees and laugh as they begged Strength for an honorable death. Didn't seem all that funny today. Seemed horrible after meeting the God of Strength in person. Seemed worse than horrible after realizing he had probably watched them do it. *How the hell does Marcus have a family?* She paused at the obvious. *How the hell do I have a family?* "Happy to hear it. You can return to them after we stop these riots. No killing. You got it?"

His face screamed disapproval, but no steel is forged stronger than the hierarchy of military rank. "Very well. Lead the way, Empress."

So she did, past the military ward gates and into the fray of the trade district. With the rampant fires and bodies sprawled throughout the streets, it was like...*that* night. The night the southern kingdoms had united to burn her home. The night she had helped them do it.

"Empress?" is what Marcus actually said when she stopped moving, but the tone of his voice made it sound like, "Mary, stop standing there like a fat horse and do something."

A young kid no older than nineteen rushed up to her before she could continue, a burning rage in his eyes like he was face-to-face with a Harbinger. He then spit on her and yelled, "You brought these things into our home. Pa got dragged off and I don't even know where or why. No one tells us anything. Why, Mary? *Why?*"

How did we get to this point? she thought, watching the spit roll down her armor. That boy would never know how badly he had wounded her. It was the ultimate confirmation of a dread she had pondered since Francis became emperor. *I'm not one of them anymore. When you look down upon your own people, they look up towards their enemy. But why me? I didn't do this. The gods know I gave everything to make Terrangus better off...*

Fine. I'll give you something to hate.

With a quick swipe, she crashed her shield into his face, sending the boy to the wet, stony grounds with a high-pitched yell. She wished she could claim she held back on the blow, but that didn't happen. The violence was a release. A release of going from a decorated soldier, to a Guardian, to an expecting mother with a title that meant nothing. *I'm not even Empress yet until we marry. No one points it out with words, but damn them for doing it with their eyes.*

She took a deep breath and gripped her weapons. Even in her current state she could crush any one of these worthless people. Sure, Vanguards were heartless tools that would kill anyone causing trouble without hesitation, but you know what? No one seemed to point out how much better things had been since Francis—

Both Vanguards erupted with a yellow aura, then launched lightning blasts at a clump of men rushing towards them with swords and axes. Marcus stepped in front of her, with the incredible bravado of defending his empress from the now burning corpses sizzling a few feet in front of her.

By the gods… The closest one's face barely resembled a person, with his skin burned so harshly it was shaped like an ink splatter. Only one man survived; he eased himself up, then screamed for mercy before a Vanguard blasted him again.

"I said no killing!" Mary yelled, but it was too late.

"Our God demands an end to the uprising," one of them said. It was impossible to tell them apart in the pouring rain, and it didn't help their voices were the same tone. "He is pleased you have decided to join us. Equating your presence with the threat of violence will systematically halt future riots. Empress, if you would, please proceed."

These fucking things, she thought, then proceeded anyway. She would never admit it but his comment sounded more like a command than a suggestion.

Mary's sword slashed across a man's face as he plummeted. She could have sworn she had seen him before, but since she would never see him again, no use wondering now. He wasn't dead, not yet at least. It would've been merciful to just stab him while he was down, but her conscience was already pressing against her skull.

Maybe he'll survive and turn his life around after tonight…

He wouldn't. You know, for whatever it was worth, the

days of Grayson hadn't been all that bad. The man had lost his touch in his older years, but there was always some speck of balance. The soldiers hated the nobles, the nobles hated the soldiers. Everyone hated the emperor, but never dared to oppose him in fear of being overwhelmed by the other side. Someone had once told her balance is not two sides of the same coin, but three corners of a triangle. It sounded like something Francis would say, but her mind was too busy blocking out the present to recall the past.

Mary slammed her shield into a woman's face, some young girl with red hair and a dagger by her side. Despite all the rain and screaming, the crunch from the blow was the loudest thing she had ever heard. *If it were me five years ago, I would burn this kingdom to the fucking ground with them. Is there no better way? What is the point of paradise if it's held together by the blood of those who refuse to cooperate?*

Marcus continued to follow but his blade was clean. Damn him for that. For better or for worse, the Vanguards were committing genocide on a level that would make her mother weep. For better or for worse, Francis and Wisdom would ensure the history books never mentioned such a dirty phrase. The fine line between hero and butcher only comes down to a few strategic words by the historians on the winning side.

Mary leaned back and kicked a man to the ground, then stomped on his skull before pressing forward. The rioters were losing momentum, mostly because they were losing the privilege of being alive. *This is an atrocity. Led by me. I am the enemy.*

She sheathed her sword; some other Vanguard was ahead near the gates, laying waste to the few stragglers still burning the shops and carts who were screaming, "NO MORE VANGUARDS!" Gods, they were brave. And they were angry. Desperate.

Irrelevant.

Mary gazed up at the skies, thanking the rain for hiding her tears. Any soldier of Terrangus would know the pose. Sometimes, it was just too much. The tone of the screams shifted. It wasn't screams of defiance, but screams of those who knew it was over and yearned to see tomorrow. *I will protect my child from all of this. I will become Death itself if it means they can stroll around the castle and live in blissful ignorance. Hate me if you must when you grow older, but I did it all for you.*

Fuck. She turned away from the skies and towards her dying subjects. "No more," she said to Vanguard Five. Wait, wasn't he supposedly a traitor? It was all too complicated these days. "Your empress demands your obedience."

"Kill me," he said. "Please, Mary, just finish it. I can't be a part of such things. Julius would... Please just kill me. They will forgive you."

She pretended not to hear, watching the shadows of her people hide behind the shadows of her tyranny. It's what she would have done if she wasn't the empress. But maybe if she wasn't the empress, there would be no reason to hide. "None of us die today," she said to Five. "We must live to accept the burdens of victory." Whatever the hell that meant. Townsfolk were kneeling, refusing to look Mary in the eyes like she was some monstrosity...

Wisdom floated next to her. His bulging eyes and burning frown made him appear like a nightmare from her old story books. "Consider me impressed, Empress," he said with that fucking chuckle. "I never anticipated your cooperation. Motherhood suits you well."

"Wisdom—"

"Henceforth, refer to me as Arrogance. No need to use silly names between family."

Mary sighed, then said, "Whatever you are, tell me: if your

Serenity thing comes to pass, will I still kill people?"

The god paused, then turned as if he were staring straight through her. "Do you love your child?"

She tightened her grip on her shield until her hand shook. "How dare you ask me that? How *dare you*?"

"If your answer is yes, then mine doesn't matter. Now, be a good empress and escort our dear Five back to the castle. He has been a rather naughty boy."

I'm destined to be a murderer forever. If we lose, the scribes will refer to me as Mary the Butcher. Mary the Red Death. My children will...

Wisdom vanished, then Five approached with his head down. "One and Two," Mary said, "finish up...this. Five, you return with me. Marcus, um, you come too."

Marcus didn't bother to hide how pleased he was to have an excuse to leave. One and Two wasted no time continuing their assault on the few civilians not wise enough to flee. Five's face didn't twitch, but tears rolled down his cheeks. Despite the rain, she could always tell the difference. One of the many talents from years at war that no one yearns for.

"Marcus," Mary said, begging her tired legs to walk faster towards the trade distract. "Why are we doing this? I mean, what the fuck are we doing?"

"Surviving," he said. "Can't do nothing but survive. We're just pawns on the battlefield, taking orders from people who don't care about nothing. Our kids will have it better than this. At least, I tell myself that every morning."

Mary sighed, carefully stepping forward with the muddy stones beneath her. "But when does it end? When is all of...this worth it?"

"I used to wonder that myself. These days, any morning I can wake up and see the family is a blessing. That's our realm, Mary. Some people wake up to misery, some people don't wake up at all. I loved this kingdom more than anything until my daughter was born. Now, fuck it. I just want her to not be me. You'll understand, if you don't already."

She understood more than she wanted to, so there was no reason to respond until they reached the castle doors. Francis met her eyes, then dashed towards her at such a silly speed, she would have laughed if not for the pain.

"*Mary!*" he yelled, then...hugged her? "You cannot abandon me like that! I need you by my side. *Please.*"

Too many emotions rushed up at once. The urge to punch him in the face, choke him, hold him close or just weep in his arms. She chose the last one.

CHAPTER 21

WARLORDS DON'T PAY FOR DRINKS

een took a sip of water, staring at the empty space in the Vaynex citadel where the God of Strength had used to stand. Tempest was taking forever to leave his chambers, but it didn't seem right to check on his progress. It didn't seem right to stand here either, obsessed with the ominous space that may as well have been the void. *Gods, I miss Serenna. Maybe I should head back to Mylor for a day? It's not like Sardonyx wants me here…*

"ZEEN PARSON!" a booming voice called from the citadel entrance. Warlord Sardonyx Claw stomped forward, with what Zeen assumed—hoped—was a giant grin. Sardonyx was never one to hide his feelings. Zeen would know by the time he was hugged or received another threat against his life how the warlord was feeling today.

"Ah, the Valley of Remembrance," Sardonyx said, then patted him on the shoulder. Despite the sharp pain from his armored hand, it was likely meant to be a kind gesture. Thank the gods. "Did it meet your human standards?"

I'm not falling for that one again. "The valley was very glorious, Warlord."

"Glorious indeed," he said, widening his grin. "Come, we walk!"

While the plan had been to wait for Tempest and help him in any way possible, the new plan was to follow Sardonyx's commands and not die. "It would be an honor, Warlord." *If he's in a cheerful mood, maybe I can speak to him about Tempest. Hmm, now may not be the best time. Let's see how this goes...*

Walking through the dusty streets of Vaynex was a significantly different experience when accompanied by Sardonyx. Countless zephum glared from afar, gave half-assed bows, murmured to each other, but there was fear. Fights stopped immediately, with all involved walking into their buildings of tan blocks quicker than their zephum frames should have allowed. Anytime the two of them passed a dead zephum lying in the streets, Sardonyx would simply walk over them. Zeen did the same, hoping that was expected, and not an offense that would lead to his own body joining them.

"Are we heading to the honor grounds?" asked Zeen. He hoped the answer was no, but they were on the exact path Tempest had taken them to meet Bloom.

"You catch on quick! *She* is fighting today. I have buried the hope that any of my people will defeat her, now it is only a matter of time before I am forced to do it myself. Watch her with your human eyes. I want your opinion on a weakness."

Great. "Well, when the Harbinger yelled out her fear—"

Sardonyx paused, then grabbed Zeen by the upper part of his leather armor. "*Never* speak of such things. Fear is a private matter, the bridge between the heart and mind. If I cannot defeat her honorably, then I have already lost."

"I apologize," Zeen said, taking a deep breath after the warlord let go. "It was foolish of me to suggest such a thing. Unfortunately, there is too much on my mind these days."

"Human problems! Do you know what I enjoy about you, Zeen? You learn lessons. I mean *really* learn them. My stubborn son has read every damned book in the realm but has the mind of a block when I speak to him."

Oh, this will be a mistake. "To be fair, it's a great incentive to learn the lessons when the alternative is to become a corpse in the streets."

Sardonyx paused again. That surely was not a good sign. "Perhaps I spoke too soon. Ah, Zeen, you wound me with such statements of human ignorance."

Zeen followed without speaking to avoid any more 'statements of human ignorance.' They entered the honor grounds, finding more people in the stands than last time, then ascended the stairs to the warlord's own section.

Today, Sardonyx took the shade. "The first battle should be intriguing! Honthop comes from an honorable line of warriors, but Vumpt has a lineage in my army. Never reached Warmaker of course, but his experience shall be an advantage. He wields a *murderous* rage."

"My gold's on Vumpt," Zeen said. He examined both warriors, though to be honest, he couldn't tell them apart.

"A bold choice." Sardonyx rose from his throne-like seat, then raised his hand to silence the crowd. "My fellow zephum! Today, we are given the privilege to observe two mighty warriors on their quest for honor. Their duel will be glorious! Strength without honor—is chaos!"

The crowd roared for their warlord, and for their god that no longer existed thanks to Zeen. *It's surreal that they view me in reverence, and not some God-killing monster. They are good people, better than I deserve.*

After two loud roars, both zephum warriors charged each other, wielding enormous swords. They clashed their blades, with the clang of steel on steel whipping the crowd into a fury. Ah, but their strikes were sloppy. The bigger one—he looked like a Honthop—went all-in on every strike, leaving himself completely exposed with each miss. That would've led to his death if the other one could attack faster. Slow, sloppy brutes. It made him appreciate his training from the Terrangus army. Nyfe had been a cruel general, but Zeen would be nowhere near as skilled without those days. Was it worth it? *I never would've become a Guardian and met Serenna if I led a normal life. Thanks, Nyfe. But also, fuck you.*

The crowd gasped as the other one—he looked like a Vumpt—took a clean blade straight through his upper chest. Did these fights always end in death? How would that benefit anyone? No wonder Tempest hated these traditions.

"Ha!" Sardonyx yelled, slamming his hand down on Zeen's back and nearly knocking him out of his seat. "You have weak human eyes. I told you Honthop would be the victor."

Actually, you never said that. "A bold choice, Warlord. Honthop fought honorably."

The next fight was similar: two giant zephum roared and clashed their swords. Zeen picked one to win, but since Sardonyx never announced their names, it was no better than a coin flip. In the Rinso books, each fighter would get a long introduction, taking several pages of exposition Zeen would end up forgetting by the next chapter. Which was better? Sardonyx and Tempest seemed too far apart in whatever vague road lay between too much and nothing at all.

Zeen sighed as his zephum lost again. Sardonyx barraged him with insults for choosing wrong, seemingly unfazed that his people were killing each other for no reason. The crowd cheered as two smaller zephum carried the corpse off, and after the victor received his applause, the arena grew silent.

Sardonyx leaned forward to observe Dumiah Bloom enter the battlegrounds. She had cuts on her arms and snout, but no visible injuries from the Xavian Harbinger. Her opponent was rather short for a zephum, about Tempest's height with a bit more bulk, wielding a slim long sword that made Zeen smile. It looked just like his old sword, Intrepid.

"*What?* Dubnok's son? He is tiny," Sardonyx said, pounding his armrest. "There is no honor in such a mismatch of strength."

"Warlord, in all honesty, a quicker opponent is a better match against mechanist combat. If he can dodge the detonators and close the gap with his speed, he may actually pull this off." *I have to be careful with my words here. Bloom is nuts, but she's a Guardian. I can't root against my teammate... Right? Serenna will be furious when she hears of this.*

"Speed is the life-mate of weakness," Sardonyx said, leaning back with a sigh. "I despise such...*trickery*, there should never be a problem that cannot be solved with strength!"

Zeen strongly disagreed with such a statement, but let it go unsaid. To be fair, an eight-foot-tall lizard-man wielding a sword that weighed more than most humans probably didn't need to outmaneuver anyone.

Sardonyx rose and silenced the crowd again; he then stared directly at Bloom. "This is our final battle of the day. Eltune Dubnok and Dumiah Bloom. Let this duel of warriors be in remembrance of the God of Strength. We will never stray from the path, no matter how far some of us may wander. Strength without honor—is chaos." The last words weren't yelled, Sardonyx said them with such gritted disdain, Zeen wasn't sure anyone on the lower levels would've been able to hear.

"Hey!" she yelled from below. "It's Guardian Dumiah Bloom now. You wanna give your speech another go before I kill this one?"

While he didn't respond, Sardonyx's glare suggested the answer was no. "*Well?*" he then asked Zeen, who jumped at his voice. "Choose a champion. Do not dishonor me by losing all three contests."

Bloom is going to destroy him. "Eltune wins by surrender. Mark my words." *Gods save me.*

"Ah, my boy. You have a large heart and a tiny mind. I shall join you in glorious ignorance. May the God of Strength look down upon Eltune Dubnok."

Vaynex was many things, but until now, quiet had not been one of them. It was a bit surreal to wipe the sweat off his face and watch the two combatants circle each other in silence. *I really shouldn't be rooting for this guy but he reminds me of Tempest. He reminds me...of me.*

Bloom sheathed both blades, then grabbed two detonators from her belt: one red, one blue. "Attack me, you fuck!" she yelled, not advancing herself.

Eltune stepped back in response, gripping his blade and keeping his feet at enough distance to maintain a proper battle stance. "I shall not be goaded into a mistake!" He took a quick step forward, then slashed his blade, aimed at Bloom's head. There was still enough distance between them that the blow cut nothing but air.

Bloom took the chance to throw her ice trap. She yelled, "Ice!" then her detonator erupted into a hazy-blue, missing the swift Eltune who side-stepped in response.

He swung again, this time causing her to hop back and grab a sword from her sheath. His next swing met her blade, which set Bloom reeling, but still standing. Eltune rushed forward with a clean thrust, aimed at her chest. The sword met her own, but the force of his attack knocked her blade several feet away. Gasps came from every direction. Even Sardonyx leaned forward, rubbing the end of his snout.

Bloom had a red detonator in each hand, then threw both at the same time. "Fire!" Neither throw particularly accurate, but the simultaneous blasts caught Eltune at the edge, launching him back into the dusty sand. There was a pause that rivaled eternity as both duelists caught their breath on opposite ends. Bloom gripped her remaining blade and grabbed another blue detonator off her belt. "Not bad, kid, but this is the end. Dubnok should be proud. That old bastard was good for something."

Eltune rose, spitting out blood as he grasped his blade. He rushed forward, letting out a roar. He stopped dead in his tracks as an ice-detonator flew at him; he threw his sword to stop it from hitting anywhere on his body. The trap erupted, freezing his sword before it fell to the ground and shattered. He kneeled before the broken blade with teary eyes, pounding his fist into the sands. Perhaps he named his swords as well. "I yield. Well fought, Guardian Bloom. Strength without honor—is chaos."

"The battle is concluded!" Sardonyx yelled, nearly falling out of his chair from jumping up. "As warlord of Vaynex, I do not condone any further violence. Guardian Bloom is our champion today." It must have hurt him dearly to give Bloom her honor, but Sardonyx seemed content on keeping the young zephum alive.

"Sorry Boss," Bloom said with a smile. "I don't do surrender." She slashed across his face, staining the sand red with his blood. She stood above the panting Eltune, then placed a fire-detonator on his chest. "Strength is dead. And we have killed him. Oh, stop booing. Anyone who steps into the ring with me is on borrowed time."

Shit, shit, shit. Seeing Sardonyx rise and grasp his sword, Zeen dashed down the stairs, pushing aside the several zephum who stared at him in awe. *Have to get there first.* Speed may have been the life-mate of weakness, but hopefully, today it would be the life-mate of preventing a disaster. The most efficient way to avoid a game where everyone loses is to prevent the game from ever being played at all. They would know that if they read the third Rinso book.

"Bloom!" Zeen yelled, rushing onto the battlegrounds. Even with his boots on, the sand seemed more jagged than the roads of Vaynex or Xavian. "The battle has ended; do not kill him. This would be a blatant violation of the Guardian Pact."

"Fuck the Guardian Pact," she said, stepping forward. "No one cares about that no more. Listen, you really want this? You're out of your human skull if you think you can stop me."

"Yeah, but If you kill me, you're out of your zephum skull if you think walking out of here is an option. Even if you do, Serenna will avenge me. You're good, Bloom, but you're not that good." There was a guilt in invoking Serenna's name, but hopefully, she would understand. Perhaps. Maybe. Probably not.

She paused, her eyes switching between Eltune and Zeen. "Fucking humans. Alright, whatever. The kid lives." Bloom took her detonator off Eltune's chest, then casually left the battlegrounds as if nothing had happened. It was difficult to explain the crowd's reaction. It wasn't really cheers or boos, but it was *loud*.

Eltune struggled to rise, his wide eyes stuck on Zeen. He eased forward, then bowed. "Human Warlord, thank you. I have never feared death, but when it looked me in the eye...I blinked. Forgive my cowardice."

"You fought well, my friend. My only critique: never roar when you rush forward. Loud and quick never mesh well."

"I will try. Thank you." Eltune grew red, keeping his head down. After a few moments, he bowed again, then rushed off.

Zeen was the last one in the battlegrounds and the entire colosseum cheered at him. It was so deafening he nearly lost his breath, counting down from five to make sure he never accidentally stopped. *Why are you cheering for me? I killed your god. I don't deserve...* He jumped by instinct as Sardonyx's armored hand came down on his shoulder. "Warlord?"

"Well played, human. Wave and nod, then we grab drinks. It will be *glorious!*"

*

However much time later, Zeen and Sardonyx entered a tavern close to the citadel. *Honorable Ales,* the sign read. While the name was rather uninspired, the drinks were powerful. Zeen made sure to drink at a slower pace than the warlord, but couldn't help but welcome the numbness that caressed him after his third glass. All the horrors of his mind closed off, leaving Zeen to enjoy the bitter taste, the lack of pain or fear...everything. With enough alcohol, we become temporary gods that cannot exist. Floating vessels of joy, oblivious to the debts of yesterday and the costs of tomorrow.

"You did well today, Human Warlord," Sardonyx said, staring at the middle of their table as if it were fascinating. "Eltune's death would have been a dishonorable *mess* between the Guardians and Vaynex. Had I known Dubnok's son volunteered, I never would've allowed such nonsense. You are..."

"I am *what?*" Zeen asked, not bothering to rein in his laughter. "Am I GLORIOUS?" His laughter was interrupted by a long silence, which lingered just enough to make it weird.

"I cherish you, Zeen. I do not say the words enough to my kin. Now tell me, and I shall slay you if you lie...am I a good father?"

Despite his intoxication, those words tore through his gut. The room still spun, but the clarity of the past smothered him. Some pains become more powerful the harder we try to ignore them. "Better than mine."

"Ah, the brutal judgment of scorned sons! It was easier when it was only two of us. My dear Vitala... I have failed her in ways that will forever haunt me. When I think back, I have to imagine her smiles. I have to imagine the laughter. My son writes his fables, and my heart writes days that never occurred. It was cruel for the realm to have taken her from me. Cruel, indeed. Now, I am alone with an heir I do not know how to raise."

"I gave him my word," Zeen said. He wasn't crying, but his eyes grew watery. "My final promise to the God of Strength…was to look after Tempest. But he needs *you*. You, Sardonyx! You!" He jabbed his finger forward with every 'you,' overwhelmed by the crash of despair and inspiration coming over him at once. Maybe that was enough ale for the night, but unfortunately, by the time you realize it's too much, it's always too late.

Sardonyx paused, then finished his entire glass. Damn, that was what, number nine? "When you and the sorceress mate and create a tiny human, what will you name him?"

He would never admit to anyone how often he considered such things. Both having a daughter, and the part that comes before that. "If David allows it…Melissa."

"You don't yearn for a son?"

"Melissa. She will have Serenna's eyes, her mind, her…everything. That's enough for me. It's more than I deserve."

The warlord's bloodshot eyes gazed directly into Zeen. "No need to explain. I always wanted a daughter. Pyith was…" He paused, then pounded his fist through the table, sending broken glass and wood all over the floor. The barkeep was wise enough not to complain. Everyone in the tavern was wise enough not to complain.

Zeen hung on his arm as they walked back to the citadel. Either they skipped on the tab, or more likely, warlords don't pay for drinks. The sun was long gone, if there really was a God of Time, Zeen swore his powers were somehow related to the consumption of alcohol. They entered to find Tempest standing in the middle of the citadel, leaning on his walking stick.

"Finally, there you are," Tempest said. "By Strength's name…are you drunk? Both of you? Ridiculous…" He stepped away from them. Even with the room spinning, Zeen caught the disgust in his eyes.

Sardonyx stood straight, wobbled a bit, then stomped towards Tempest…

He embraced his son with a *glorious* hug.

CHAPTER 22

DIVINE BLOOD

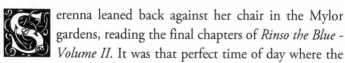

erenna leaned back against her chair in the Mylor gardens, reading the final chapters of *Rinso the Blue - Volume II*. It was that perfect time of day where the sun was just low enough to give its warmth without being in her eyes. Temperate shadows embraced the mountains in the far distance; it was as comfortable as one could be while sitting alone.

Rinso struggled from the ground, she read, *his human stare burning through Hyphermlo. Once a friend. Sometimes a teacher. Always a monster. Rinso spit out red blood and grabbed the steel hilt of Fortune. "I hate you..." he whispered softly, the cracks in his voice matching his confidence.*

Hyphermlo simply smiled back, leaning his giant sword above his bulky shoulder. "I know. Now, get up and try again. When you defeat Vehemence in the honor grounds tomorrow and rescue Oliva, you will realize how insignificant this pain is today."

"No pain is insignificant."

"Indeed. Remember that. Remember what you're fighting for."

So he did, thinking back to his sweet Olivia, with her womanly curves that rivaled the crescent moon, the red blush of her face like sweet Alanammus wine, the human growls as they had mated—

Serenna closed the book. If Zeen ever mentioned her

'womanly curves,' she swore she would scream. That was enough Rinso for today. Just as well, it would be too chilly this high up in another hour or so when the sun faded entirely. *Where is Everleigh?* she wondered as she rose from her chair and grabbed her staff. The goddess hadn't spoken to her since their training yesterday, which was odd, considering Serenna assumed they had become closer in the process. Did she expect Serenna to train alone going forward? Maybe saying 'I hate you' to someone only trying to help hadn't been a great idea...

Hmm.

"Lady Morgan!" Sophia yelled from the garden entrance. She ran over to Serenna, huffing and struggling to speak. "You are needed...at once. We..."

Serenna eased her hands to Sophia's shoulders. "Slow down. Speak to me." Hopefully, the desperation didn't show in her voice. So much could be wrong, her fears didn't know which terrible conclusion to dread first. *Don't let it be Zeen or Father. Forgive me, but that's all I ask.*

"It's David. He appeared in the outskirts portal and immediately surrendered himself in the bastion."

She paused. Out of all the things on her growing list of fears, ironically, the champion of Fear wasn't one of them. "Truly? Where is he now? Is anyone injured?"

"The grand bastion halls. No injuries or dark magics. He didn't even have a weapon on him to confiscate."

No Herald of Fear? Thompson had mentioned the other day Arrogance had defeated David. This is likely a trap. He's after Dad. "Where is my father?"

"I ran into him down by the markets and gave him the news. Charles should be there already."

Serenna resisted the urge to shout. Sophia had done nothing wrong, but damn, it may already be too late. "Then I must go immediately. Are you well enough to follow?"

"Of course," Sophia said, still huffing. "Just...give me a moment."

"We don't have a moment." Serenna rushed out of the gardens, not bothering to glance back. Considering Sophia didn't yell for her to wait, it was obviously the desired outcome. Why couldn't anyone just be honest with her? Was the fear of letting her down too dreadful? Their lies disappointed her far more than their weakness.

She rushed through the Mylor capitol, ignoring the concerned glances and murmurs in her wake. *I'm probably terrifying them into thinking it's a Harbinger or an attack from Terrangus.* It was harrowing to see how fast her people reverted to fear at any hint of trouble. It was like a spark, the eye of uncertainty opening old scars that could never be forgotten.

Where was Everleigh? Nothing about this seemed right. If David was a trick from Arrogance to attack her father, and Everleigh conveniently vanished, did that mean... *No. She's on my side. I won't entertain such a thought.*

She entertained such a thought as she rushed through the streets of Mylor, anxiety overwhelming the soreness in her ankles from rushing. Everleigh couldn't be a traitor; it would be impossible. No way. Right?

The mountain of eyes upon Serenna brought her back to *that* day. The day she had broken the pact. The day she had thrown Nyfe through a window. The day...she had met Zeen. One stark difference: this time, she yearned to hear a deity's voice.

Guards opened the bastion doors well before she arrived, offering a salute, but no words. Whoever had said 'no news is good news' had likely never suffered the torment of the unknown. She paused inside the entrance, grasping the Wings of Mylor despite seeing no enemies or hints of violence. It felt like an illusion. No crystal mages huddled behind pillars, no enemy forces coming through the halls. *We won. We won then, and we'll win now.*

She caught her breath and stopped shaking, drifting towards the grand halls with a forced composure. A mini army and her father surrounded David from a fair distance. By Valor's name, David appeared terrible, standing in the middle of the halls with his slim frame and tired eyes. It was nearly impossible to consider this same man had wielded the powers of a demigod less than a year ago.

"Father, are you well?" she asked, grasping his hands, studying him all over for any hints of danger, finding several wine stains, but no wounds. "Tell me everything."

"Oh, I'm fine. Confused as all the six kingdoms, but no harm done. Were you expecting him? Alert me next time. Pardon the security measures, but I didn't want to end up the next Grayson."

"I expected no such thing. I don't...understand." Clearly no one else did either, so she finally approached David to get some answers. The soldiers seemed more than happy to get out of her way. She recognized almost all of them. Veterans of the war against Terrangus, all likely stressed beyond words at the idea of another potential disaster barraging their home. Bravery is often a permanent trait, but bravado has diminishing returns.

His wrinkles creased as he smiled. "Serenna. Too long, my friend. Too long."

David Williams... After all this time, he was alive. She pushed down the urge to hug him, to thank him for everything, to revert to the child she had been nine years ago when he had recruited her. It could still be a trap by Arrogance. "Explain yourself. Now," she said, pointing her staff forward.

To her relief, her empty threat only widened David's grin. "I hope one day you can learn the joy to look upon your replacement and know peace. Unfortunately, my mission to slay the God of Wisdom failed. He destroyed my blade and severed my connection with Fear in the process. I only managed to escape through the madness of the riots." His eyes drifted to the floor, suggesting he'd left out some key points of how exactly that had happened.

Riots in Terrangus? She would have to monitor the situation. Chaos often spreads like a disease. "You truly fought Arrogance?"

"Ah, so you already know his true title. I can guess how, but I'll keep it to myself."

And there was classic David, speaking to her like she was eighteen again. True leadership lingers long after the title fades. His frail frame posed no threat, but there was still a presence about him that was difficult to articulate to anyone who had never fought beside him. Reputation is an old man's greatest armor. *I won't back down. He wouldn't want me to.* "By all means, speak freely."

He leaned in close. It spoke volumes that none of her soldiers reacted. "I will, because you can't afford to. Never reveal your new allies' identity. If even a single other person finds out, we can assume Arrogance knows as well." It was somewhat of a relief he was unaware of Valor's existence. Perhaps Fear didn't know either, or maybe she had kept the secret to herself—

"CHILD OF FEAR! GAZE UPON THE GODDESS OF VALOR. I DEMAND YOUR EMPRESS. I DEMAND HER NOW!"

And just like that, the Goddess of Valor revealed herself in the middle of the bastion halls. She used her goddess version, with long platinum hair flowing down her giant frame, clutching a glowing scythe with both hands. Soldiers and her father all stumbled back. For all they knew, the screaming goddess intended to murder them all. A platinum-haired angel of death.

Everleigh, why? After all those precautions. After everything...

David stood still, gazing up at Valor. "Hmm. You are the third deity to threaten me today. Whatever you know about me, Goddess, I swear you'll die by my blade when the day comes. My final service for these people will be to usher in a realm without gods."

Bold words considering he didn't wield a sword anymore. "David, Everleigh, stop this foolishness. This is exactly what Arrogance desires."

"Everleigh?" David asked with a laugh. "An interesting choice for the next god. I've heard the stories—"

Valor picked him up by the neck, ending his laughter, raising him near the ceiling of the bastion grand hall. "Summon Noelami, or follow me into the void. Unlike the crystal girl, bluffing is not the protocol of Valor." When nothing happened, she turned her gaze to the soldiers surrounding her, then yelled, "MORTALS! GET OUT OF MY PRESENCE IF YOU DESIRE THE EMBRACE OF TOMORROW! I SHOULD SLAY YOU ALL FOR FORGETTING YOUR MOTHER!"

Out of all the emotions that rose up through Serenna, pity was the one that overwhelmed them all. So, it was never about mentorship, protecting the realm, any of it. Just vengeance. What a sad existence. Serenna made no attempt to calm her people; words are powerful, but when a screaming goddess threatens your end, mortal inspiration cannot compete. Most ran off other than her father, who rushed to Serenna's side.

Serenna drew a fair amount of energy from her body to enter her platinum form. Despite the glow of her own aura, Everleigh's wrath put all light to shame. "Stand down, Goddess," Serenna said, thankful her voice stayed deep. "That is my friend you are threatening."

She struggled to maintain her platinum form as the room grew dark. Her heart pounded, and trying to focus on slowing it down only made it worse. It didn't help that her father was near crushing her arm with his embrace.

"You *dare* speak my name?" a distorted voice called out. "Like a child cursing the shadows, demanding her nightmares come forth without the courage to face them. I can read your fear, Everleigh. What stands before me is nothing more than a divine failure."

The Wings of Mylor began slipping through her grasp from all her sweat. The monstrosity above her was a mockery of an angel, with Harbinger-like wings and a glowing stone in her eye that drained light from the room. *Was this what I looked like that day? A monster?* Serenna resisted the urge to cry. No one would ever see her that way...but this was the Goddess of Fear. The mother of Harbingers. The murderer of Pyith...

I hope Everleigh slays you in divine blood. All glory to the Goddess of Valor...

Please.

Everleigh dropped David and paused. Serenna would never admit how the eternity of each passing second solidified her terrors. Valor gripped her scythe and slashed across at Fear, creating a flash so bright Serenna lost her platinum form and fell to the ground.

Too many sensations came over her at once. Everleigh's attack brought a gentle warmth to the air, an intimate cool that brought her back to Zeen's arms. She didn't see Fear parry the strike, but the crash of divinity echoed through her head. The cool faded, replaced by a chill. She shivered, clutching her hands to her chest and rolling over. Gods, it was cold. Too cold. Both deities screamed at each other. Indecipherable cries, a cacophony of madness that sounded like two giant armies battling in the bastion halls. Armies like Mylor and Terrangus.

Screams of her fallen. Screams of the ones she had slain. Screams of those who could've been either. It'd all sounded the same after a while. We forget, but it always comes back. We remember, if only because we don't want to.

Both goddesses roared with an unholy cry, then after a monstrous crystal spike flew past Fear, something *heavy* crashed next to Serenna. She flinched from the ground with a high-pitched yelp, then watched the scythe revert to a normal-sized weapon.

Everleigh's scythe lay across from Serenna, the pale glow from the blade made her shield her eyes from the light. It called out to her. To her, and only her. The Herald of Valor. *Dare I take it? Am I worthy of such a thing? What will happen to me? I am not a weapon to be used by the gods. Never again.*

A new screech smothered her doubts, the screech of Everleigh crashing down the east end of the bastion, knocking down an entire pillar and filling the room with rubble and a hazy-white mist from the dust. There was such pain in her distorted voice; Serenna recognized the desperation. She had screamed the same fury when Nyfe jabbed his blade through Zeen's neck. She had screamed the same fury when Pyith died under her leadership. It was time for her enemies to be the ones screaming.

Serenna picked up the scythe.

Crystal magic had always been a force of discipline, a struggle between the balance of power and the limitations of your own body. This…was something *worse*. The pale glow of the scythe radiated while she gripped the artifact with both hands, gasping as prickles of pain tingled all over her body, as if someone were stabbing her with tiny needles in random locations.

What started off as annoying became pure agony. Serenna's platinum aura erupted against her will, drawing more energy, too much energy, demanding more, tearing out power from deep inside her. *How do I stop it?* The platinum rays commanded themselves, erupting from her body and condensing at the blade of the scythe. *Make it stop...* A mix of tears and blood flowed from her eyes; her body yearned to crumble but the crystal force dangled her like puppet strings, forcing her to keep standing. *Make it stop...*

Despite the pain, a moment of clarity came from a desperate memory, her mind's last attempt to save her body. *It's the same concept as Death's Harbinger form. Unleash the power before it consumes you.* But how did it work? She gripped the scythe, then forced her arms forward towards the Goddess of Fear. The deity's form was indistinguishable through Serenna's broken vision, with the dizzying mists, the platinum rays that burned her skin, the tears in her eyes...but that stone kept drawing in light. It was a target, a floating wall to be destroyed. She formed a crystal spike, tensing her shoulders to craft the form into a rigid edge. A little more angle on the bottom. A little more tone...

The spike faded into specks of crystal-like sand as her legs gave out. There wasn't even an influx of pain, they simply stopped working. Too much focus on the form, too much crystal energy tearing out of everywhere. *Make it stop. Make it STOP!* Her insides were seething. Most people have no idea what goes on inside their body until it's all burning. *Prison...try prison. Try anything to make it stop...*

A hazy outline of a sphere surrounded the Goddess of Fear before it took a physical form. To Serenna's bliss, most of the platinum energy faded around her. An ecstasy of numbness. *Okay, so it keeps drawing energy from my body against my will. I have to use it or it builds up until I die.* What a ridiculous, suicidal design. No wonder crystal mages today never used scythes.

The platinum aura was returning against her will. Serenna's head throbbed from a migraine; she crafted a quick spike to release the energy with such a lack of form, it would've made her sorcery tutors grimace. It was surreal to see Fear stuck in her crystal prison; it felt like minutes or hours, but surely it was only seconds. They met eyes for a brief moment, and Serenna didn't care that she shivered. *Take my fear. Take it all. It will be the last thing you know before the end. Where do angels go when they die?* She raised the spike, aimed at the glowing gemstone. It would be enough. It had to be enough.

Bow before Serenna Morgan, the slayer of gods—

David knocked the scythe out of her hands. Serenna screamed as the power faded entirely, replacing the wrath of platinum supremacy with the torment of reality. Her body felt like someone had thrown it against the jagged mountains of the outskirts and left her to dry out and die. She crumbled into David's arms, her body shaking. Why did he do it? Why?

"Forgive me," he said, holding her close. "I owe her my life. Noelami does not die this day." Both goddesses and the Herald of Valor faded.

Just like that, true power had eluded her. Serenna's first instinct was to scream at him but there wasn't enough energy for that. There was barely enough energy to cry.

"Water…please…water." She lay across the rubble, staring at the ceiling as David rushed off. Tears came, not for the pain, but for the loss of that staff. For just a moment, she could have ended any war, slayed any Harbinger, any deity.

With such power, no one she loved would ever feel pain again.

CHAPTER 23

HEAR THE SHAPES, SMELL THE COLORS

mperor Francis sat on his throne and sighed, dragging his hands down his face in exhaustion. What a monotonous end to an unequivocally absurd day. How many other wise men had led their people to paradise, only to watch in horror as they burned it all down upon their arrival? Ungrateful wretches... *It's not their fault. None of these people have any formal education. How many of them can even read? Why do the ones who would benefit the most from paradise struggle against it?*

He couldn't imagine such debauchery of dissent and rioting back in Alanammus, but Terrangus was his home now. What an awful trade, rivaling Archon Consaga's bronze tariff concessions with Vaynex. Of course, it would all be worth it in time, but upgrading a swamp into a civilized society was a more exhausting task than he had planned.

"Bring forth the next traitor," Francis said, waving his hand. What a waste of an evening. He wanted to just hang them all to get it over with, but Wisdom had suggested trials and random acts of mercy for appearances. History dictated that true leadership had often come down to the balance between love and brutality, but love was a scarce commodity since the day's riots.

Two men in chains approached—oh, the castle guards. Whatever their names were. The noose had never seemed to care. They had permitted his dear Mary, the future mother of his child, to charge off into the fray. "We had orders from the empress," the first one said, then got jabbed in the side by the other one's elbow. "But it's true! May the gods strike me down if I'm lying!"

"That could be arranged." Wisdom chuckled behind Francis. Thank the gods for him. The deity had gone out into the madness and rescued his beloved. A true friend. These days, the only one.

"It's true," said Mary, standing with her stoic pose at the right side of the throne. She was still radiant—dare he say she couldn't achieve the alternative if she tried—but a certain sort of exhaustion plagued those soft cheeks. She hid it well. It was...unfamiliar to notice the secrets of her face. The subtle differences in the creases that bent depending on how happy, sad, or whatever other emotions she used. It was like solving a riddle in the classroom, only because none of the other students could read the assignment. "They're good men. You really think they could stop me from going out there? Spare them."

Ugh, now that was annoying. Despite being emperor, the choice—pardon, suggestion—had already been made. The most powerful man in the realm dangled by the strings of a god and a woman. A woman who happened to hold his heart. "Fine. A fee of five gold each, due upon the arrival of the third dawn."

"My eternal thanks, Empress. My lord." They bowed and scurried out of the room, seemingly unconcerned their hands were still chained. Francis would wager their entire penalty neither man had any means of paying their fine.

"Are we nearly finished?" asked Francis, making sure his sigh was loud enough to suggest which answer he was looking for.

"Quite soon," Wisdom said, "but do not despair. As always, I saved the best for last."

The best of these lot wouldn't make the index in an apprentice's glossary...

Francis caught his breath as Nyfe approached. The fallen Harbinger appeared tired and drained, but no punishment could be enough for such a scoundrel. Well, this decision would be quick. "I want him hanged in the trade district for all to watch! He can be the sacrifice that quells the riots. Who dares oppose my judgment?"

Francis smiled and surveyed the throne room. His dear Mary grinned, and even the less intelligent soldiers and guards nodded with approval. When both a genius and a fool deem a thing less than worthless, such a thing deserves to be extinguished in the public view to maximize the benefit.

Nyfe stared not at Francis, but past him, into the God of Wisdom. "Deity, does your offer still stand? Upon weighing my options, I find service as a Vanguard outweighs the end of a noose."

"You hang!" Francis yelled. He didn't mean to yell—such an outburst was beneath him—but by Wisdom's glory, every breath Nyfe had taken since the day of his defeat was a mockery. It would be only fitting to watch him struggle for that last breath. It would come. It always did.

"My dear Francis, there are more efficient ways to deal with failure than destruction. Take a leap of faith and sentence him to become a Vanguard. Have I ever let you down?"

Francis's hand trembled. He made no attempt to stop it. How could Wisdom propose such a thing? *I am the emperor, am I bound to his word? In the hierarchy of life, can a mortal ever outrank the divine? No. Of course not.*

"After reviewing the evidence," Francis said, despite the fact there was no evidence, "I will heed my god's command." *As*

I always have. So it seems, as I always will. "Nyfe, I hereby welcome you to your new title: Vanguard Twenty. You will pledge your freewill to our god upon sunrise." Mary must have heard Wisdom too. While she offered no dissent, the creases in her face suggested she was not pleased.

Nyfe rose, with a grin that made Francis's hand tremble all the more. "Oh, Francis. Do you know why I call you the Invisible Guardian? Because you yearn to be seen so fucking badly."

I could still kill him, Francis thought, ignoring the murmurs, fighting the urge to grab his staff. *I could burn every inch of his flesh until, by textbook definition, he would no longer exist. I could...*

Yet, he did nothing. For a man with no gods, Nyfe always appeared to grasp the luck of divinity. "As emperor, I am only invisible to those who never look up. Take him away." Francis made sure to grin, a move right out of the biography of Archon Jude. Smile at your enemies. Make them believe you know something they don't.

Francis nodded as the guards carried Nyfe away. It was surreal to consider there were twenty Vanguards at this point. Upon hearing of the riots, Wisdom had suggested to speed up the conversion process. A valid strategy; control was always a numbers game. A few more months and they could create an entire army...

But who was next? Who could possibly come after Nyfe?

Robert Cavare—Vanguard Five—stepped forward. By Wisdom's glory, he already appeared defeated. "My crimes are an abomination," he said, keeping his eyes down. "If you have any concept of mercy whatsoever, I beg for a quick death. Send me to him. Please..."

Francis's legs went weak. He sat and leaned back against his throne, taking a deep breath and ignoring the eyes upon him. They all looked at him for guidance, despite the fact he had no idea how to solve such a mess. Hang him? Never. Set him free? Impossible. *Julius, forgive me...*

I continue to fail the Golden Scholars. "I deem this judgment to take place upon the gardens of Serenity. Unless there are any that oppose, my will is absolute." Ugh, that sentence didn't come out right. Maybe 'absolute' was the wrong word? He quietly wished for Mary to step in, to offer some hasty suggestion, one way or the other. But nothing happened. Even Wisdom seemed pleased. Hmm.

The guards knocked Robert onto his knees. Every strike felt like a betrayal to a lost friend. "Lord Wisdom," Francis said, gazing back. "Please open your gateway to Serenity. There is no use in delaying that which must occur."

Mary grabbed Francis's arm before he could enter the portal. "I'm coming with you," she said with a stern glare that made it clear the statement was not a question. Sometimes, such a glare had led to wonderful things. He wagered this event would not be one of them.

*

Francis smiled as he stepped into the gardens of Serenity. The clear skies and temperate breeze were a welcome change from the rainy summer days of Terrangus that lingered on and on forever. There was something about this place... The culture of it. He could discover new aspects of beauty with each visit, it was like gazing upon a masterwork painting and finding details within the details of a genius obsessed with the layers of his own life's purpose. A valley of rocks leading away from the foot of a waterfall, surely some homage to a poem or song from the days of Boulom. Through enlightened eyes, art is its own civilization. No simpleton can merely look upon a mural and comprehend the whole picture, it takes a mastery of what came before and why; a mastery of when, how, all of it!

Mary did that thing where she cleared her throat at an unnecessary volume. Mary did not enjoy art. Not yet, at least. Hopefully, their child would grow to appreciate the finer things...

Francis shuddered at the thought.

They're looking at me. I should say something. "Vanguard Five. Welcome to Serenity." He tried to give one of those fake Zeen smiles, but abandoned the idea immediately. The four people here were all intelligent enough to know only three were going back. Lies have their place in the realm, and that place is at the beginning of life, not the end.

"It would honor me, Emperor, if you would refer to me by my true name."

"I did," Francis said, turning away. One of art's greatest gifts is distraction, so he stared at the doves flying out through the clouds beyond. Oh, it was marvelous, it was spectacular, it was—

"Robert," Mary said. She stepped forward to look him in the eyes. "Why did you help David escape? You have always been loyal through everything. Help me understand."

Robert turned towards the same view as Francis and did a half-smile. "I desire Serenity more than any of us. Even you," he said, glancing at Wisdom. "But the cost...is too much. I have sacrificed little by little, and every time I believe there is nothing more to give, more is taken away. All those flames. The people screamed as I burned them. If the road to paradise is forged with the ashes of the innocent, I cannot travel beside you."

Wisdom chuckled before Francis could offer a rebuttal. "Oh, mortals and their ideals are so...*precious*. Do you assume I can simply snap my fingers and usher in Serenity? It takes more, more than you could ever dream. The greatest tragedy of tonight is how close you were to tasting perfection. You took the gift from my hands, gazed upon its glory, and threw it away.

Speak your last words, *Robert*. I will grant you that much. Nothing less. Nothing more."

Francis kept his stare on the birds and clouds, ignoring the pounding of his heart. Execute Robert? Truly? After what Julius had done for Terrangus? He wouldn't dare look over at Mary. He could feel her eyes burning through the back of his head. When words fail, choose silence. Many deem it the most loathsome of actions, but any true scholar knows its comfort.

"Then I will speak the truth," Robert said, then took a deep breath. "You have shown me your vision of perfection. And to be clear, it is a sight of pure wonder. In your world, I can hear the shapes, smell the colors. It is the life we all desire, but are always denied when our heart and mind collaborate to write our dreams. I know it is perfect. I know…because I am told it is perfect. But nothing compares to my days with Julius. Such joys cannot be written in the fates, we can only stumble upon them. Lord Wisdom, you have fallen for the trap that plagues every misguided genius. You have gazed upon perfection, true perfection, and believed you could do better."

Francis kept his eyes on the birds. They flapped and chirped, but a tiny bit of the beauty now appeared missing. Seconds passed. Long, torturous seconds. Apparently, everyone had stolen Francis's strategy of remaining silent.

"You flail at words and morality like a child bangs on a piano, believing his cacophony of randomness to be a masterpiece. How…*quaint*. And I always assumed you were the better Cavare. Kill him," Arrogance said. Francis didn't need to check the sun mask to confirm the change. There was always such force in the tone of his voice.

Francis grabbed the staff from behind his back and finally met eyes with Robert. The fact he couldn't find any anger or judgment only made it worse. *Hate me. Say something. Curse my name… Of course not. He is intelligent enough to know I have no guilt in this. I follow the word of our god. I am absolved—*

"Don't you fucking dare," Mary said. She stepped in between Francis and Robert, giving him a convenient reason not to act. "I don't care what he has done. To murder him would be to murder Julius's sacrifice. Can you really live with that?"

I will have to. Another tragedy to throw upon the pile. "And what would you have me do? Ignore our god? While I take no pleasure in such things, we must—"

"Fuck your god. And if you go through with this, fuck you too. There must be a line. If you do this…I will leave you." Mary stormed out of the same portal, leaving the three of them in a terribly awkward scenario. But what did she mean by 'line'? How could he ensure not to pass a thing no one could see? Leave him? She would leave him? Alone? All of a sudden, it was very difficult to breathe.

They're looking at me again. I should…I have nothing to say. Oh, that silence. Francis knew Wisdom well enough to pick up on the little things. Simple-minded brutes tend to yell and whine, throwing tantrums with complex strings of obscenities. Arrogance screamed his silent fury through his eyes. Hopefully, he would forgive Mary for those unfortunate words. He had to…right?

"It's okay, Francis," Robert said with a smile. "If I had to choose anyone to be my executioner, it would be only fitting to choose a friend."

"Kill him," Arrogance said. Serenity trembled at his voice. The birds flew away and the sun dimmed. "I hate to repeat myself."

I will leave you. Those words were a dagger through his heart. Being a genius didn't seem all that useful when real problems couldn't be solved with pure knowledge. He took a

188

deep breath, thinking back to their first intimate night together in Alanammus. To lose that…may finally clear the obscuring mists between damaged and broken. *I have someone who truly loves me and I'm on the precipice of throwing it away.*

Francis took the Herald of Arrogance and created a portal to Mylor. It seemed rather ironic—and foolish—to use the god's own staff to defy his judgment. "I am intelligent enough to know I am fool, but lack the knowledge to do anything about it. Go forth to Serenna before I change my mind."

"In many ways, you are the wisest man I have ever known. You will always be a Golden Scholar. Thank you, Francis," Robert said, then left through the portal.

And that was that. Francis stood with his hands clasped behind his back, waiting for the repercussions of his actions. Serenity descended into darkness, with hazy clouds covering a red moon. The wind howled, chilling him through his robes. The waterfall stopped flowing, even the vivid plant life shriveled into a gray death.

"Paradise is an absolute," the voice of Arrogance rumbled throughout the gardens. While he was nowhere to be seen, his mere presence filled Francis's chest with a vibration. "Tread carefully with your failures. I can forgive the absurdity of freewill to an extent, but like your precious Mary, I have a line. I advise you never to cross mine. Most fools never consider how narrow the path between perfection and oblivion lies until they are plummeting down, down into the darkness. Ask your *mother* how many misguided steps it takes."

The desire to respond yielded to the desire to get out of this nightmare. Mom had died from natural causes. No. Surely he couldn't mean… Francis rushed out of the portal, sweat dripping from his head.

*

189

Francis appeared back in the Terrangus throne room. He gasped for air, finding eyes staring at him from every direction. They likely assumed Mary was furious and Robert was dead. Well, one of those was true. Something felt off. He reached behind his back, patting around for his staff. It was gone. He kept reaching for it in desperation, sweat pouring down faster as all the eyes continued to stare. And more damned silence. Mother had used to say that a hated leader brings the gift of silence into every room they enter. Mother had said a lot of wise things until she died from natural causes...

My staff is gone, riots are a mess, Wisdom plots my demise, Mary is furious. Too many problems, but that last one stole his attention. It would have been more efficient to make a closing statement, but he simply stepped away from the throne and towards the stairs to his chambers.

Surely, she heard him enter their room, but she didn't look around. Why? Why would she torture him so? "My beloved," he said, rushing forward before she could turn around or answer. He fell to his knees behind her, hands trembling.

Mary turned around and eased him up. By Wisdom's glory, or the glory of any god that still loved him, she smiled. Oh, that smile. Perhaps Julius had been correct to proclaim true love the ultimate Serenity. "I'm so proud of you. Whatever consequences arise from this, we'll pull through together."

"How did you know? Did Wisdom inform you?"

"Your face has less subtlety than the warlord. Tell me, did you do it for me?"

Francis paused. 'Yes' seemed to be the correct answer, but it wasn't entirely true. Mother had used to warn him never lie to a woman that has already seen you naked. "For you, for Julius, for *Mom*. Mary, I have always pondered how much a person can be damaged before they are considered broken. Tonight was the first time I nearly learned the answer. I don't...want to know everything. Especially that. Mary, please marry me. Mary, marry. Please. Be my empress. Be my wife. Be...my *family*."

One simple tear rolled down her cheek as she hugged him. Her firm embrace was painful, but such a pain he would give anything to hold on to forever. "I have always been yours. I love you, Francis. Let us give our child a future to be proud of."

CHAPTER 24

FOOL'S REQUIEM

empest pressed against his walking stick and entered the Vaynex citadel. He had usually been the first one to arrive at zephum council hearings, but by Strength's name, it was difficult to move in haste, and the lack of sleep only made it worse. *Forward I go, rushing towards my misery.* What was the point? Any illusion of becoming Warlord had ended with his shattered leg. If Sardonyx and his council held any level of intelligence, they would already know that.

Warmakers Novalore and Dubnok were already sitting in their chairs, and conveniently stopped their conversation the moment Tempest sat beside them. Did they truly believe such a petty act wounded him? Two days ago, he had looked upon the cold body of his life-mate and best friend. They could rip off his tail and he wouldn't shed a tear.

"Where is your father?" Novalore asked. 'Where is our Warlord?' or even 'Hello' would've been proper, but aged warriors tend to wear their ignorance like armor.

Father was probably hungover after last night, along with Zeen. How fucking glorious. "I cannot speak for his absence." He was about to ask where Warmaker Pentule was to change the subject until the old bastard approached.

Warlord Sardonyx Claw had never missed a meeting. He had stumbled in with the lizard flu, the day of Tempest's birth, and even the day after Vitala had passed. Perfect attendance until his son needed him the most. *Please don't do this to me. Not today. I can't...* "We will give the warlord another minute and then proceed without him. Any objections?"

There were none, of course. They appeared so genuinely happy, it made Tempest wonder how often they considered his father's demise. If they considered that, it was safe to assume Tempest's own life was less than sacred. What a long, miserable minute. Waiting for something that will never occur is the fool's requiem. Who knows, maybe they were right. Maybe Tempest was the final obsolete relic of the Claw reign. Another idealistic young zephum too naive to face the reality of a violent culture. *No. I promised her. If I cannot fix Vaynex...it was all for nothing.*

There is only so long one can stretch a minute. Tempest took a deep breath and rose, with his right hand gripping his walking stick. He limped towards the empty throne—his father's throne—then forced himself to take the seat. The hole at the end was much wider than his tail, and the hot, jagged stones cursed him as an unworthy invader as he leaned back. By Strength's name, he hadn't sat here since he was a child. He hadn't realized his mistake until he saw the rage in his father's eyes. Tempest had taken many cruel beatings in his day, but that one still haunted his nightmares. Right in front of Mother, too. She had watched, wept, and like everyone else in Sardonyx's path of destruction: did nothing.

Novalore cleared his throat.

Oh, how much time had passed? Why does looking back into yesterday make tomorrow arrive all the sooner? *Here we go. I'll focus on violence and say 'honorable' a lot.* "Very well," Tempest said, hoping no one noticed his eye twitching. "Dubnok, would you care to open the meeting? I have received

193

word that your son battled Guardian Bloom in the honor grounds yesterday and nearly fought her to a stalemate. An honorable outcome."

"My son is a *fool!*" Warmaker Dubnok yelled, slamming his fist down. If Sardonyx had bothered to show up, he would've made an unsubtle gesture towards Tempest to suggest the sentiment was true for both families. "Eltune nearly fell to that loathsome creature. Bloom should be executed! I demand an explanation for her continued mockery of our culture! I demand it now!"

Honestly, that was a fair complaint. Tempest and Sardonyx had found a rare common ground on considering ways to make Bloom 'disappear,' but Pyith always had a soft spot for the deranged murderer. Too late for that now. Too late for a lot of things. "Bloom is a Guardian. While her actions often drift from honor to shame, it is now beyond our authority to give her the death she deserves." Maybe there was too much spite in his voice, but Bloom was a monster.

"Guardian my tail!" Novalore said. "Now, the Human Warlord: Zeen Parson. That is a Guardian."

A Guardian who is likely vomiting into a bucket as we speak.

"Eltune speaks highly of him," Dubnok said. "Perhaps I will challenge him to an honor duel? It would be glorious to test my blade upon his own!"

These people are such fools. No wonder our kingdom is rotting in poverty. It's too bad one of them can't challenge supply and demand to an honor duel. "I would strongly advise you to refrain from such an action. We have different cultures, Zeen will gauge the notion as a threat."

Novalore snickered. "Hmm! And I suppose who would know more of human culture than the zephum who yearns to be one?"

With Pyith gone, it was nearly impossible to find any

reason to love her outdated father. "Watch your tone," Tempest said. If there was any mercy in the realm, the conversation would end there before—

"Or you'll do what?"

Anytime one could hear the crackle of the torches, the room was far too quiet. Tempest was doomed, and each passing moment solidified his fate. A true warlord would rise, grab his sword, and threaten immediate destruction to any who dared oppose his reign. *Father, why aren't you here? How could you abandon me like this? I have no one left other than...* "Shall I call Zeen back in here and let him finish what he started?"

Novalore paused, and to Tempest's surprise, smirked. "A warmaster who avoids war. Now I have seen everything. You dishonor the human by designating him as your shield. Would you doom him to fall upon his blade for your failures like you did for my daughter? The day you run out of allies, is the day you *rot* in the sand."

"Peace brothers," Warmaker Pentule said. He never spoke much, but Tempest was glad he decided to today. "Warmaster Tempest, has your father given any consideration to re-opening the outskirts portal to Terrangus? It would speed up our new trade lines considerably. Our people are starving and we need to get life back into Vaynex by any means necessary. If trades stall, we need war. Blood or gold. Make your choice."

"True, but my father and I agree that opening the portal while the people of Terrangus are rioting in the streets would be unwise. War...is the last resort. If it comes to such a thing, we must wait out the winter before any aggression against Nuum is rational."

That last part wasn't particularly true, but if Vaynex was still in a recession two months from today, the Claw reign would certainly meet a violent end. It wasn't fair. Vaynex had dealt with sandstorms, droughts, outbreaks of the lizard flu from *very* poor judgment, but to lose their god? How could his people come back from that? How could anyone?

"I don't mean to pry," Pentule said, obviously intending to pry, "but what was the purpose of parlaying with the Terrangus humans if we aren't willing to host them? How about a compromise? Open portals, both ways, with no Vanguards. Surely, both of our people would prosper?"

Tempest leaned forward and rubbed his snout. Hmm, maybe it was time to listen to Pentule more clearly. Maybe they weren't all fools. "I will propose the idea to my father. Well spoken, Warmaker. I suppose that will suffice for the morning. Are there any objections?"

Dubnok slammed his fist down on his seat. Was that his answer to everything? "Do not avoid the true issue! It is time for war, young Tempest. War! Rally our people! Where blood falls, bread and gold must follow. Do I stand alone in this?"

"I stand with you," Novalore said, "as I always have. You speak with the glory of a warlord. A *true* warlord."

Tempest sighed. "Again, it would be a tactical nightmare to war against Nuum in the summer heat. I mean, Novalore, you were there ten years ago when the droughts stalled our campaign. Have you learned nothing?"

"I learned the cost of weakness. Peace is the warrior's poison. And why do you assume Nuum is the only option?"

Foolish questions are often the most difficult to answer. Trying to follow the logic of a fool is a convoluted path indeed. Did he mean Terrangus? Surely not the kingdom itself. The Koulva mines then? That campaign had been an utter disaster for both sides.

"Alanammus," Dubnok said, leaning back and gazing at the citadel ceiling like he had just said something brilliant. "Crush their human magic between the fangs of our snout!"

Even by zephum standards, the idea was ludicrous. It made

Tempest appreciate his father just a *bit* more. How much nonsense was held at bay by Sardonyx's presence? The far worse question: what would happen if he were to die? "Alanammus? It's a two-week journey in favorable conditions. We would get flanked on all sides the moment our forces were spotted. Why are you wasting our time with this?"

Novalore rose. Without Sardonyx in the room, the zephum had a monstrous presence. "Think of the songs our people would sing! The life of trade and sweat returned to the streets! Think of the glory! But no, I wouldn't expect you to understand anything related to honor. My daughter was *wasted* on you."

Adrenaline allowed Tempest to rise faster than he should have, and the merciful part of his mind that distributed pain held off as he forced himself up. He clutched his walking stick, wishing it was a blade, his hand trembling from rage. He glanced up into the eyes of Novalore, and glanced into the eyes of a stranger. With Pyith gone, this fool was no longer his family. In reality, he never was. "Your daughter was the greatest miracle I have ever witnessed in our realm. I yield she was indeed wasted on me. My only solace is that she would've been wasted on anyone. There is not a soul worthy of such a zephum."

Novalore grabbed him by his leather armor and picked him up. As the walking stick left his grasp, it became apparent the journey down would be a crash. "Everything about you...every word you speak, every pompous gesture, is a mockery to our empire. Sardonyx deserved better. Pyith deserved better." Novalore kept speaking, but his voice went mute.

What is happening to me? It was like losing consciousness while being awake. The room was silent, even the flames of the torches continued to dance without the crackling of embers. The only sound that pierced reality was his own heartbeat. He had never heard such a thing before. A gust of wind chilled him from his tail to his snout. Was he going mad or was his body simply giving up?

"*Tempest... Tempest, Tempest. Mortal frames are such fragile, broken things. Wouldn't it be glorious to tear the life from their bodies, to burn the past into embers of honor and torment? The Time God always favored you lizard things. It disgusts me. The look of their snouts...the smells. Say my words, and we can make it all go away.*

"*I am nothing. I am forever. I am the end.*"

"Never," Tempest said. His voice came out clearly despite the silence. "I will never—"

What was likely Novalore's fist crashed into Tempest's snout. Tempest wasn't looking ahead before the strike. To be honest, he wasn't really sure what he was doing before the pain overcame him. He shuddered as all sound came back at once— roars, chairs getting knocked across the citadel, a ringing in his ears. He tried to rise, but his arms were weak and his right leg simply didn't work. What he would give to kill this brute. Novalore first, then the rest of them. A council of embers.

No wonder Serenna accepted a taste of his power. No one ever admits it, but that deal worked out for everyone. Maybe if I were offered a small taste... Can the deity hear my thoughts?

If Death could hear anything, it would be thoughts of panicked madness as Novalore kicked Tempest straight in the gut. He rolled several feet away from the throne and gasped for air. There are few things more terrifying than begging for a full breath and being denied. He wheezed, trying to block out the yells and whatever the hell else was going on behind him. Pentule's roar pierced the rest of them, then a loud thud crashed across the citadel. While it was difficult to piece together what exactly was happening, it was impossible to care.

"Stop this madness at once!" a new voice yelled from the back. A human's voice...of course it was Zeen. The hungover hero finally came to save the day. "The next zephum who harms my friend will find himself in the honor grounds. How could you do this to your own? Have you no honor?"

Zeen's threat was so absurd Tempest had to hold back a laugh, which was not too difficult considering the blood seeping through his armor. And yet, like most fools, his words got results. Tempest rolled over to see Pentule standing above a wounded Dubnok while Novalore grasped his sword. If a painter stumbled upon the citadel, they could've painted the very scene and titled it *The Death of Progress*.

"Are you okay?" Zeen said as he kneeled down. The horrified look in his eyes gave Tempest a full synopsis of his new injuries.

"Do I look okay? Do I sound okay? Where is…my father?"

"Sleeping like a rock. I considered trying to wake him but I'm near certain that would've led to a glorious death." He laughed and gave that phony smile. Surely Tempest wasn't the only one who caught on to that? How annoying. "Can I get you anything? Anything at all?"

"Get out."

At least that killed his smile. "Tempest, I am here for you."

Tempest attempted to rise again but his body was too weak. He took Zeen's arm to help him up. Damn the realm for forcing such indecencies upon him. "Hand me my stick. Then get out."

Zeen did the first half of what he was told. "Please. I know I have been…less than what you need, but I will not abandon you. I made a promise to the God of Strength—"

"*Never* mention that name to me again. The fact that my people worship you for bringing poverty to Vaynex is the perfect testament to our ignorance. Get out. That is the final time I will ask respectfully."

Zeen paused, looking to the floor, total dismay smothering

his face. Tempest studied the way his eyes and lips had a slight twitch, it would make for a useful description next time he sat down to work on *Rinso - Volume IV*. "Forgive me, my friend. I will return when you are ready, and I will do better. You have my word."

Please don't leave me, Tempest thought, gasping for breaths as Zeen slumped away towards the citadel portal. What miniscule pride remained stopped him from crying out to him. Tempest would be alone again. Isolation is a cruel fate, its torment augmented by how little of its cause is a mystery. For the first time in his life, he welcomed the idea of Pyith being a memory. To see him in such a state...

"*Oh Tempest. Tempest, Tempest. Not alone. You will never be alone again.*"

CHAPTER 25

For You, I Would Wait Forever

aylor please," Zeen said to the zephum working the citadel portal. He kept his head down, hoping some dignity remained in his voice. Zephum mages were less obvious than their human counterparts. They wore the same tattered armor as the warriors, with a steel staff across their back instead of the usual sword, axe, or polearm. They never spoke much or showed any emotions; he would have to ask Tempest why that was...another time.

The zephum triggered the pale glow and grunted. His answer to all of Zeen's requests in the past few days had been grunts. Considering how badly he had failed in protecting Tempest maybe grunts were all he deserved.

Such a confusing clash of emotions came from those white rays of light. Zeen never would've imagined going home to Serenna in such a depressed mood. *I should've been there for him.* It's not like he could have turned down Sardonyx's offer of drinks...right? Maybe he didn't need to have so many. Maybe he should've toughened up and been there anyway. Too many maybes, such a word is the Harbinger of regret.

"I will return," he said to the mage, who grunted back. Of course he did. What was his name? He had never thought to ask. A terrible habit—it's far too easy to label people by their role and not who they are inside. Nyfe had always done that... No. Not the time for such thoughts. The warmth of the glowing portal eased his anxiety as Zeen stepped in.

*

Zeen materialized in the Mylor Guardian room; he squinted his eyes to adjust to the imposing white shine of the walls. Some of the empty chalices on the east corner by the water barrels had cobwebs. His stomach rumbled as yesterday's drinks met today's portal, but a deep breath kept any nauseous feelings at bay. He then perked up as four guards in their pale Mylor uniforms approached. "Were you expecting someone else?" he asked with a grin.

"Welcome, Zeen. Your arrival is a pleasant surprise. We are on the lookout for Vanguards and other...unexpected threats."

Well, that was a bit ominous. "Vanguards? You mean like Five?"

"Actually, yes. Exactly like Five. He arrived late last night. Listen, it would be ideal if I escorted you to Serenna. There is more to report, and it should come from her." It took no convincing for Zeen to follow the guard out of the room.

Serenna. The thought of seeing her again washed away some of the guilt from Tempest's pain, and he pushed aside the confusion from whatever the deal was with those Vanguard people. Five was a Guardian so he was clearly a good guy. Were the others evil? Were they seriously all named as numbers? That would get rather confusing after the first ten or so.

Serenna. That long platinum hair. Deep blue eyes. Her smile. Serenna only smiled when she was truly happy. The memory of better days melted his heart. To think she had waited for him when she could have any man in the realm. The guard was walking too slow. Far too slow. He was a chubby little guy with some scars on his face, suggesting he had seen his share of battles. *Oh, I'm doing it again.* "What is your name, friend?"

"Call me Martin. It's funny, two years ago, I never would've imagined escorting you through these halls."

Walk faster. Faster. Faster. "Ah, you served in the war?"

"In a losing conflict, everyone serves in one way or the other. When you took Serenna away from us…I hated you. It is much easier to hate an enemy than learn to understand them."

"The last enemy I tried to understand stabbed me in the neck." He paused. That came out with more spite than intended.

"Yeah, well, you're a lucky one. For most people, that's the last lesson they ever learn before it's over. I'm sure a lot of my men tried to understand you."

Zeen considered how to respond before noticing the Guardian of Mylor portrait hanging on the other side of the corridor. What joke had he said that day? Something about wondering when his own portrait would find a spot on the walls? Not his best line in hindsight, but if it made her smile, such a line would surely get used again. He could remember so much of that night in every vivid detail. Their embrace. The lemony scent of her hair. Lying in her bed together surrounded by emerald drapes before she fell asleep in his arms. Honestly, it felt like yesterday. Considering Zeen had spent the past seven months or so asleep in Terrangus, it may as well have been. *Does she still love me? Or does she love the memory of me? My 'grand' return has been less than ideal. Pyith is gone, David is missing, Tempest is suffering…*

He took a deep breath to calm his nausea. Oh, right. The guard. Er, Martin. "Yes, I agree," Zeen said. Wait, was that the question? How much time had passed? Ah, who cares. *Serenna…*

Fortunately, that response seemed to work, as Martin laughed. "I almost wish we never met. My men…we feared you.

You were Terrangus personified, a master swordsman who broke crystals with the flick of your wrist. It was like facing a second Nyfe."

That snapped Zeen back to reality. "What? How could anyone possibly fear me?"

"Believe me, I'm wondering the same. Ah, it's just so different during war. Rumors spread. All it takes is one man's story, and then all of a sudden..."

Zeen tried to walk faster to get Martin to follow, but he just kept waddling along at his leisurely pace. This man had 'You didn't ask, but I will tell you my entire life story' written all over his face. What an odd change from Vaynex. Odder still that he was considered an outsider in both kingdoms. Where wasn't he an outsider?

"...and, so you see, it was actually my brother. He swore the two of you met blades and had a grand duel in the middle of the bastion halls. He would've had you, so he claims, if not for..."

Hmm. What could be considered home at this point? He had spent so long thinking about Serenna that he never considered how life would be surrounded by people who only knew him as an invader. *Serenna. Whether it's here, Terrangus, or even Vaynex, Serenna is my home.* To Zeen's disappointment, they passed right by Serenna's chambers. Would there ever be time to relax? Senator Morgan's door was closed as they walked by, with the aroma of cheap wine seeping out of the room.

Zeen smiled as they stepped into the grand hall. Serenna was standing in the center below the raised senators' section, talking to a small crowd, right at the spot they had shared their first—and so far only—dance. Her face held a stern glare as her father said something. Zeen could only wonder what thoughts rushed through her head. Was it all business, or did she yearn to reunite as much as he did? Wait. Was that...

"David?" Zeen asked out loud. The entire room turned

around. It was one of the oddest groups of people ever put together, a view right out of a Rinso novel: Senator Morgan, Serenna, Five, and David, who grinned while he approached.

"Lady Morgan," Martin said. Interesting that he would address Serenna first and not her father. "Zeen has just arrived through our Guardian portal. I escorted him to you at once." Not the most dignified attempt at fishing for approval, but Serenna had that effect on people, particularly in Mylor.

He braced himself as David hugged him. His old leader's arms had lost a great deal of muscle, and Zeen nearly flinched at the light strength of his grip. David seemed...different? As curious as Zeen was, it didn't seem proper to ask. Maybe Serenna would know.

"My friend," David said, letting go. "You look well, all things considered."

"As do you." It was bold to lie to his old leader's face, but such a face had clearly seen its share of horrors in the past few days. "I feared we would never reunite, but I guess you would already know that?"

"Not anymore. I'm back to relying on an old man's hunches...which are usually correct," David said with a faint grin. "We'll have our time to catch up. Go to her."

Zeen nodded and approached Serenna, who gave him a cautious sort of gaze. While he didn't run, he walked at an unnaturally brisk pace, which surely looked ridiculous to everyone watching. And you know what, who cares? There was always so much going on, some Harbinger, some obscure political scheme between kingdom leaders, he just wanted to take Serenna in his arms and carry her off to her chambers.

She gave him a quick, tight hug, then let go. Oh, how he wished for more. "Welcome home, Zeen," she said with a warm smile. "Does your arrival mean all is well in Vaynex? That would be an incredible relief with everything else going on."

"About that…" He paused. Tempest had confided that the God of Death was speaking to him. Zeen had sworn to keep it a secret. He had failed in all other ways, but a secret he could hold. It takes a woeful man to fail at the task of doing nothing. "There is much to discuss. Alone, if possible." Maybe it didn't need to be alone, but why not?

"I see." Her smile descended back to a frown, which deepened the dark circles under her eyes. Up close, his love appeared nearly as distraught as David. What the hell had happened in the past week? "Well, either way, it is wonderful to see you again. In these trying times, I have missed you dearly."

"I am here, and I am yours. So, what's the plan? This is quite the crew you have assembled."

"Master Zeen," Five said, who appeared just as exhausted as everyone else. "Your arrival comes at an advantageous time. There is a terrible unrest in Terrangus as the quantity of Vanguards continues to grow. Further still, Francis has officially become betrothed to his Mary as of this morning. While it would be a terrible affront to the emperor, I have advised the Morgan family to decline their invitation to the wedding."

"That is wonderful news!" Zeen said. "But why would we refuse to go? Francis and Mary are our friends. I know Francis is a grouch, but come on, he's a Guardian; he fought by our side."

"Francis is just a pawn," David said with a sigh. "Arrogance is the true enemy. I can't ask Fear what he's planning; the goddess stopped speaking to me after her battle against Valor."

Very little of this conversation made any sense. Zeen rubbed his chin, looking over to Serenna. "Um. Can you elaborate on…all of that?"

She snickered and returned to her glowing smile. "I shall. You know what, let's freshen up and take an evening to relax. We will not prevail if we push our bodies too far. Valor taught me a lesson of limitations, and I intend to take her words to heart."

Valor? Is that someone or something I should know?

"Be wary of that one," David said. "The pursuit of absolute power is a path that ends in tears. You were given a gift others would die for. Do not throw it away. It's all too easy to wake up one day with the wrath of a god and no one left to protect."

"We are *done* with this conversation," Serenna said, her eyes filled with a rare blue fury. "You of all people should despise her. What she forced upon you...was unforgivable." Oh, she hit him with the 'we are done, but I will continue to yell at you' method.

David shook his head. "The only thing ever forced upon me was a second chance. Everything else was my own doing. I am sorry if you cannot understand that."

Zeen felt like he should say something, but any misstep of words could lead to a disaster. Why were Serenna and David at odds? Hmm. "Unless you need me, I'm off to take a bath. Maybe we could all have dinner together? A feast! Like last time!"

"You have paid your debts with the lives of innocents!" Serenna yelled. "Every future Guardian who falls to her demons is now on your hands. I am sorry if *you* cannot understand that."

No one acknowledged Zeen. It would be awkward to hang around after announcing his departure. Hmm. Follow the silence, who else was uncomfortable... "Senator Morgan? Could you do me the honor of escorting me to my chambers? I have not been in your kingdom in quite some time."

"Right away!" Charles said, his wide eyes matching his grin. Clearly, he had been looking for an opportunity to escape. "Thank you for that," he whispered, taking Zeen's arm as he guided him out of the halls. "They have been at it since yesterday. My boy, a word of advice, never interfere in an argument between two powerful people, especially when they're both wrong."

"But, why are they fighting?"

"You know Serenna…always pushing the limits. After a taste of the Herald of Valor, she's been obsessed. You should have seen what it did to her body; it was like someone threw her off a mountain. Terrible things to my poor girl. I wish the gods would all just go away. She doesn't need any of that…she just needs you."

Me? Zeen thought, his face blushing. "While that is most kind, I'm not sure how true it is. She managed just fine without me for seven months."

"She read that stupid book to you nearly every day. Zeen, I say this with a heavy heart, but part of me wished you would finally rest forever in those days, just so she could begin to have some semblance of a normal life again. To commit yourself to a lost cause is a struggle I know all too well. Alas, it was a blessing to be wrong."

"I had no idea. I actually figured she read the books for her own pleasure." Some words don't seem foolish until they're spoken out loud. Of course she read them for him. *She loves me. No more excuses. I need to do my part and save Tempest.* "Damn, I wish we had that time back. To lose seven months…"

"Better seven months than forever. Get your head in order, my boy. Your old guest chambers are right around the corner. Take a bath, drink some wine, and make her happy. This year has been cruel to Serenna. I fear it's only the beginning." Charles had a deep gaze into nothing before returning to his cheery self. A fellow man who hid his pain behind the mask of a smile.

*

After a warm bath, Zeen sat alone in his chambers, eating a chicken roast Sophia had dropped off quite some time ago.

They had left him a bottle of wine, but after last night, water was just fine. *Where is Serenna? How long should I wait before I seek her out?* He leaned out the window to gaze into the shadowy mountains of the outskirts. It was rather brisk for summer; he could only imagine how chilly the capital got in the wintertime—

His chamber door opened.

There she was! "Zeen? I apologize. How long have I kept you waiting?"

Too long perhaps, but for you, I would wait forever. "No worries. It gave me an opportunity to take a bath and enjoy some human food for the first time in a week."

She gave a light laugh as she approached. A warmth came over him as her hand caressed his shoulder. Well, maybe it was more of a lean than a caress, but any contact with his lover was a thrill. "Hmm. I never stayed in Vaynex longer than necessary. What do they even eat there? When I was a child, my father used to tell me they ate humans. Thank the gods I learned it was a joke before I met Pyith…"

Ah, Pyith. They both paused. The wine bottle by the table seemed a bit more inviting. "A lot of beef. It's actually similar to Terrangus, but the presentation is more to the point. No forks, knives, napkins, or anything. Eat everything with your hands and then throw the plate on the ground afterwards. It was very…*glorious.*"

"Glorious indeed?" she asked, her hand easing from his shoulder to his side.

"Glorious. Indeed." He pulled her in and kissed her. She pulled him in more, enough that their bodies pressed together. If only their clothes weren't in the way. His left hand caressed her platinum hair as he took in her lemony scent. He didn't even like lemons, but the aroma was pure ecstasy as long as it came off of her.

"Promise me," she said, pushing him against the wall. "Promise you will never fall again." Oh, not this again. It was an absurd request, but the fire in her eyes made it clear it was not a joke.

"Serenna, you already know it's true. My heart has been yours since—"

She pressed him harder. While it was likely meant to be intimidating, it burned his warmth into a fire. "Love is more than the heart. I need everything. Your body. Your mind. You cannot die again. You cannot leave me waiting for you. I am falling apart, Zeen. I can't take all of this stress anymore."

"At ease, my love. As far as I know, no man has ever managed to die twice. Stop worrying about—"

"*Never* will I stop worrying, but now I can defend you without Death's wrath. There are greater forces in this realm. Forces that can be controlled, forces that bring our enemies to their knees. You have no idea what it was like to hold that artifact."

"Perhaps not, but I know what it's like to hold you." He caressed her back as she trembled in his arms. Whatever artifact she was referring to was clearly something terrible to bring out such desperation. If only he wasn't so weak, she wouldn't have to dabble in these nightmares. "There is not an artifact or deity in our realm that can rival my yearning for you. To quote the great Hyphermlo, 'Strength without honor is chaos, but life without you is despair.'"

"Stop! I told you no spoilers!" She laughed, her eyes dancing across the room to the various things surrounding them. Zeen couldn't do the same. With her body pressed against his own, he stared right into her eyes, silently begging for them to return to his gaze. They did. "I fear tomorrow. I fear the day that comes after tomorrow. But I refuse to fear this moment. Zeen... I am yours. Give yourself to me. Make this evening a joyous event to look back upon in my darkest moments."

"Serenna... You are certain?"

"I am."

There are few things more terrifying than finally being offered your deepest desire. He hoped she didn't notice his right-hand tremble as it eased to the knots behind her armor. Gods, how he had imagined this moment in his most intimate of yearnings. His fingers moved with the precision of a man starved from solitude; he untied each knot one-by-one to see if what lay beneath the mail matched his imagination. It only fueled him to move faster as she did the same. His shirt came off first, followed by his pants. Surely, these things were meant to be done in unison, but it was a sloppy storm of lust and love. Maybe they were the same. In such a moment, he could scarcely tell the difference.

Zeen was already naked as her armor hit the floor. Despite the brisk breeze from the window, his body was *not* cold in any way. He eased off her undergarments, the tips of his fingers navigating towards the area he thought Rinso meant by her womanly curves. In that moment, any and all of the things that had made Zeen's life seem unfair faded away. Serenna's body was pure perfection. Sure it had the scars, the pale tone of skin that hadn't seen the sun in ages, the little flabby parts that came together at her stomach, but it was Serenna. The woman he was meant to be with. Zeen's Serenna to Rinso's Olivia. For the first time in however long, the world made perfect sense.

The world stopped making perfect sense as an eruption of pale energies came from the right of his bed. Some monstrosity of a demon-woman appeared; she wielded a weird staff that resembled a farmer's tool. Zeen grabbed his sword. While it seemed absurd to enter his battle stance without armor or...anything, he gazed into the demon before them.

"Child, have you learned *nothing?*" whoever it was yelled. "Are you a simple harlot? Fornicating with this common man with no weapon to defend yourself?"

If this goddess wasn't Fear, then… Oh. So that was what they had meant by Valor. Was she always so angry? And…loud? "Stand down!" he yelled, most likely in vain. Or maybe worse than in vain. Valor nudged her bladed-stick thing and surrounded Zeen in a crystal prison. By the gods, it was *cold*. He shivered, then thrust Hope at his sphere. It was like trying to pierce a mountain. The vibration and sudden force in his wrist knocked him off balance; he then fell back-first into the crystal behind him. Zeen yelled as if he were dying. It was not a dignified yell, but the icy caress against his exposed back was like falling into a river during the winter.

"Everleigh, no!" Serenna yelled, her voice muffled through the dense crystal. "You know my feelings for him. How dare you harm him? Why?"

"The fool wounds himself with his eagerness. And what are your plans to save him? You ventured into this room looking for a quick tumble without your staff or any weapon whatsoever. If I were Fear or Arrogance, I pity whoever would be unlucky enough to stumble upon your shame-riddled corpse in the morning."

"A quick tumble? How *dare* you? After all the nonsense you suffered through in your pursuit of Felix, you would harass me with the same?"

Valor scoffed. "Find my methods cruel if you must, but defeat is not the protocol of Valor. Arrogance cannot be allowed his treacherous reign. You weren't there. You never saw the Vanguards in their true terror. When Felix looked through me with those dead eyes… I was nothing to him…"

The crystal sphere surrounding Zeen began to lose some of its vivid glow as the goddess spoke. Valor had a slumped pose, her long platinum hair unkempt and down across her face. Serenna was covering her exposed body to the best of her ability with both arms. *I won't get another chance at this. Here we go.*

Zeen slashed Hope downwards with his entire weight guiding the blade. He groaned as the force caused a *tiny* crack in the sphere's front. His hands were seething from the vibration, so he dropped his sword. It's not like it would protect him against this crazed goddess, anyway. Serenna rushed towards the crystal prison, studying the crack. Through the dense platinum hue, her body only seemed all the more beautiful.

Valor sighed then nudged her blade. The crystal prison vanished, sending Serenna crashing into his arms. "A fair strike, Guardian Zeen. I will not interfere in your shameful dalliance, but do not allow desire to rot your mind. You have powerful enemies…and *tired* allies."

The goddess faded, leaving Serenna in Zeen's arms. After an uncomfortable moment of silence, she started laughing. Not the ideal outcome for a partner seeing you exposed for the first time, but such was the realm. Zeen laughed as well, pulling her tight, holding back a gasp as their intimate parts pressed together. "Do you think she's going to watch?" he asked.

"I'm surprised she isn't still here, yelling out instructions. 'Part your legs! Move those hips!'"

"Does that bother you?"

"Zeen, at this moment, nothing can bother me. If Lady Everleigh feels the need to observe, then let's give her a show. I'm ready…

"Take me."

CHAPTER 26

SOLACE OF POISON

avid pressed his pillow against his ears, sighing as he rolled over in his bed. Tonight, Serenna and Zeen had been terrible neighbors. He understood. He *really* did but…come on. The flimsy white walls of his chambers did nothing to drown out the constant moans and thumps that would rise in eagerness, slow down, then right when he had thought it was over, start up again. It was like they were trying to keep a morning's buzz going well into the night. Actually, now there was a good idea. If sleep wouldn't bother to arrive, the solution was clearly more ale. Ale had always been the most loyal of allies, a neutral force that wouldn't curse or mourn him when his end finally came. There are worse fates than being forgotten.

He rose from his bed, chugged half a flask of ale, then threw his pillow against the wall. It silenced them for a moment. They both giggled, then went right back at it. Damn them. Damn them both to hell. Young lovers tend to go at it like unicorns, with some unwarranted desperation like tomorrow was unlikely to occur. Ah, the irony of it. The young rush and have forever, while the old take all the time they no longer have.

Melissa. Their joy was a dagger through his heart. Was that a selfish thought? Their coupling was a reminder of how much he yearned to hold her again. He yielded a faint grin. In all honesty, the two of them had probably been just as insufferable those first few nights in Xavian. Maybe worse. Probably worse. But, those days were gone. Not only were they gone, but new days weren't coming. He sighed.

At least ale would always be there for him.

David stepped out of his chambers and slammed the door. It blew out a few of the candles in the corridor, but he only required a limited amount of light to guide him to the grand hall. The walls were too damn bright, anyway. He nodded at the soldier guarding Zeen's door—Martin, was it? Hmm. In their brief conversations, the man had alluded to a fondness for Serenna. Ouch. If Senator Morgan was aware of such things, his placement had been a cruel punishment. "Here," David said, handing him the half-empty flask from his left pocket. "My condolences."

A clank of glass came from the grand halls ahead. Senator Morgan sat at one of the lower sections of the tables, sipping a cheap-smelling wine from his chalice. "Guardian Williams!" he said. Charles was likely at the height of his buzz. When any drinker reaches that point, they can either switch to water, or let the numbness carry them to a time that wasn't now. "Sit! Have a drink! Your senator demands it!"

David sat with a grin. "How unfortunate. I planned on finally quitting tonight, but who am I to deny a request from a senator?" He poured himself a chalice, getting the wine right to the top. Why do people always fill such large chalices with meager amounts? "I suppose you can't sleep, either?"

Charles sighed, then took a large swig. "Out of all my senses, hearing refuses to fade. I'm going to raise everyone's taxes so I can invest in sturdier walls. Tell me, this Zeen, is he a good lad? He won't just take the first portal out of here in the morning, will he?"

"Heart of gold. I would never allow it if I thought otherwise."

"Allow?" Charles asked with a laugh. "Ah, you sound like me. I hate to break it to you, but we're past the point of allowing anything. It's why we drink!"

That surely wasn't true. If he had forbidden their romance, would they have... No. Of course not. What a ridiculous thought. *I'm not their leader anymore. I'm not even a Guardian. What am I?* "Never tell a man why he drinks," David said, then took another swig. "It wasn't always this way."

"No. Of course not. I didn't really hit the bottle until Natalie left our realm. Serenna was a mere child... I doubt she even remembers what her mother looked like. Half platinum, half brown hair. We couldn't guess how our daughter ended up so powerful. It certainly wasn't me," he said with a sad chuckle.

"Be that as it may, I envy you. The realm was cruel to never bless us with children. I am the end of a line that never began." The wine was hitting faster than normal. Whatever Charles drank was a clarity killer. Kids. David and Melissa had stopped discussing it after a while. After their nights together had never led to any...they let it go. Stopped talking about it. Some things just weren't meant to be. Would David have been a good father? Probably not. Maybe it had been a blessing to never know the answer. But...damn.

"Fair point," Charles said, "but for whatever it's worth, there are downsides. The loss never heals when you see a version of her face every day. The eyes. I swear my daughter judges me through her mother's eyes. How do we manage to cope?"

David refilled his chalice with a grin. "That, my friend, is a wise question. I suppose a hungry man eats. A tired man sleeps. An old man...reminisces."

"That he does. That he does."

After what was likely an hour or two of drinking, steps

approached from behind. Charles was already glancing at whoever it was before David turned around. "Who's this?" Charles asked. "A friend of yours?"

It always startled him how normal Maya Noelami appeared without her empress regalia. She stopped at the head of the table. "Fair question, Senator," she asked, then glared at David. "Am I a friend...or something *less*."

Gods, he couldn't bother to be afraid. How much of his bravado was the wine? Maybe that was why she had never let him indulge around her. "I can accept a truce, Goddess. Join us for a drink and tell me your demands."

Charles rubbed his chin. "Why do you look familiar? *Oh*. Empress, welcome to my kingdom of Mylor. If you could be so kind, please refrain from any more battles against Valor. Or at least, please fight her outside."

"She is here," Noelami said with a grin, "but not here, to be precise. We find comfort in our illusions the way you mortals find solace in poison." She poured a chalice, took in the aroma, then placed it far to her right as she grimaced. "Deplorable. I will accept a truce but not...*this*." With the wave of her hand, a new chalice formed, filled with a sparkling white wine. He wouldn't dare ask, but oh, he was curious how it would taste.

Fuck it. David raised his chalice to Noelami. He hoped it was somewhere near her face, but with the room spinning, it was impossible to know for sure. After a pause—an agonizing long pause—they clinked glasses. "Welcome to the pity party. Care to share any of your deepest regrets?"

She scoffed, clearly unimpressed. Nothing he ever did impressed her. "You mortals have it easy. Dead lovers are just that. Mine happens to be immortal. A fool of a man who couldn't simply relax and enjoy the zenith of civilization. There is nothing more destructive than a man's desire to fix that which has not broken."

"Wisdom?" Charles asked.

"Once Ermias. Now, Arrogance. He tried this Vanguard nonsense several decades back, but Everleigh and her Guardians unified against him after he converted too many high-ranking people in Terrangus. His moves are more gradual this time. The fool may actually pull it off."

David took a light sip. While he longed to extend the numbness, he didn't want to drown whatever was left of his good judgment. "And why is that?"

"Useless rulers. Useless Guardians. Worse yet: Useless gods. After all these years, the God of Time ascended a new one. Another woman! At last! But it figures it would be her, one of the few minds more damaged than Ermias. Saddest part is that she hates him nearly as much as I do. Perhaps this will all be for the best. If Serenna can master that scythe, she could finally be the empress that unifies the seven kingdoms. A reign of fear. A reign of balance. Perfection, in all its temporary glory."

Technically, six kingdoms remained after the fall of Boulom, but he found no reason to offer that correction. The truth is the most elusive creature in the realm to those not looking to find it. Any discussions with Fear had to be done on a thin-line. Anyone so unhinged could—

"Valor seems no less crazy than you are," Charles said with a laugh. "You remind me of our fallen friend, Grayson. Take a lesson from an old mortal: usually the ones that think they're surrounded by madness are the root of it."

To David's enormous relief, Fear actually smiled at the comment. It was a smile of daggers, but at least she remained in her human form. "An old mortal may as well be a speck of dust compared to me. Such ignorance is why you deserve to lose. The fact that my Boulom lies in ruins while the *lesser* kingdoms are allowed to exist is an atrocity."

Her smile faded. "You're better off dead. All of you. The

only reason you are not is because I despise them. You mortals are unworthy of my hatred. You are tools, things to be used to ensure the monsters that have scoured this realm suffer as I have."

An awkward silence followed her words. For all of Charles's terrible judgment, he didn't press the issue any further. *Lies. In lying to me, she's lying to herself. I saved her life. It's about time for some gratitude.* "Look me in the eye and say that you hate me."

She blurred, but he managed to meet one of the pair of eyes. "You? You're the worst one of all. I hate you in the way only someone who loves a thing can properly despise it. You failed me *completely*. Played right into Ermias's hands. If the realm was merciful, I could've had Melissa instead. The two of us would have fixed everything."

He clenched his chalice. How dare she mention Melissa. "The realm has never been merciful. Maybe you'll learn that the next time Serenna has a spike aimed at your heart." He finished his wine, poured a new chalice, then rose. "Next time I'll simply...walk away."

And so he did, or at least tried to, pressing his hand against the walls for balance as he left the hall. The spinning hit harder than usual. Too much ale. Too much wine. Too much of everything. After a few swigs of his chalice, he dropped it to the ground and staggered forward. Fear had hurt him more than he would ever dare show. Was that all he had ever been to her? A tool? Sometimes, alcohol clarifies the truth instead of numbing it. He shoved his hand into his pocket, searching for the... *I gave it to Martin.* With the corridors already spinning, that was likely for the best.

How am I still alive? When does my service end? Gods, just let me rest. Please, all is forgiven if I can finally rest. He stumbled forward, panting, begging the realm to hide him from anyone in Mylor. This surely wasn't the way to his room...was it? It

219

was impossible to tell in this miserable capitol. Everything was so white, eclipsed by paintings of people who never mattered. He fell over, leaned against the wall, then started laughing. Across from him was a grand portrait of Serenna. If he remembered correctly, it was titled *Serenna the Beloved Hero* or something similar. They showed her as majestic. A goddess among men. David had no paintings. No statues. His role as the champion of Fear would likely be told to young children to scare them into obedience. He tried to rise, but nothing worked correctly. Like everyone else, his own body abandoned him. *So be it,* he thought, closing his eyes.

David fell over onto his side, crashing into...grass? He opened his eyes, finding a time that wasn't now, with tall grass, deathly white flowers, and mountainous outskirts in the distance. The Mylor gardens? Someone must have dragged him here. Rather undignified that they couldn't have brought him to his chambers, but the gentle breeze may as well have been a blanket as he shifted onto his back. A woman with long platinum hair stood tall, leaning against the balcony with a mesmerizing presence. Serenna? It had to be Serenna. No. Maybe?

"My Felix was a drunk," she said. The voice was strangely familiar. "Odd that it never bothered me. The heart must shield our eyes from the faults of our lovers. There is honesty in your pain, Guardian David."

Valor? Did he trade one crazed goddess for another? "Leave me be. All I desire now is rest. It's all I've wanted for so long, as long as I can remember."

"And you shall have it. Compassion can be the protocol of Valor. Temporarily."

"A price...there is always a price. What...do you want from me?" With his slurred speech, it was a wonder she could understand him.

"Despite your shameful intoxication, you already know the

answer. As a Guardian, it is ingrained upon your essence. Service. You will serve the realm till your last day. As I have, as the crystal girl and her paramour will. From what I gather, the zephum-woman was the best of our kind. A pity I did not reveal myself to her. Fill the void created by her loss. Be the next engager. Surely, you know how to use a shield?"

"Mary. Mary is our engager."

"The mortal empress has chosen her path, and it does not align with our own. You will have to slay her before this is all over. Enough. I will not listen to anymore tomfoolery. Take your rest. When you wake, demand a sword, shield, and some mail armor from the senator. He will provide the necessary tools, or he will answer to *me*."

At least this goddess was blunt. David groaned and closed his eyes, resting his head against a pillow he had never seen. A blanket covered him. Ah, gentle taps of rain. The perfect setting to finally rest.

"Thank you," he whispered, as the night carried him off.

CHAPTER 27

PUPPETS WITH CROWNS

ary Walker—soon to be Haide—stared at herself in the mirror in a red silk dress. It was supposed to match her hair, but the damned thing was pure crimson. Her mother and older sister, Ruby, would be thrilled to see her in a dress, but she hated it. She had always imagined when, or if, she finally got married, it would be in her Terrangus armor, in front of the warlord's corpse or something like that. That dream seemed like a lifetime ago. Serenna had the right idea. Serenna did everything in her armor.

I miss her. I miss them all. Even that idiot, Zeen. Maybe if I was there with them, Pyith would still be alive. What the hell am I doing? Trying on dresses while they battle the gods? When did—

"While I admire the color," Wisdom's voice called out, "regret does not suit you. I hear it's rather unfavorable for expecting mothers."

Fuck this guy. Wisdom, Arrogance, whatever it was. Anyone with more than one name was a guaranteed liar. "Oh, so you're talking to me again?"

Wisdom revealed himself floating by her side, then did that annoying chuckle. "The only time I stop speaking to those I love is when they perish. With the proper…let's call it guidance, I dare say that could be decades from now."

Even if she couldn't battle the god in a melee, she felt naked without her armor or weapons. "Look, can we cut the bullshit? The second my child is born you're going to kill me. If you're here for intimidation, try someone else. I have never feared death."

"Oh, my dear, blunt Mary. You flail at forgone conclusions without a shred of evidence or cognitive thought. Why, oh why would I harm my family? Particularly the *useful* ones?"

"Just shut up. Can you talk to Francis instead? He's been an anxious mess since you took back your staff. If you want a truce, start there."

The lifeless eyes of the sun mask hid his emotions, but the long pause suggested he wasn't after a truce. The perky tone of his voice agitated her far more than his yells. Yelling meant he was losing. A bit too similar to Francis in that regard. "Did you know I was a professor back in the days of Boulom?"

The Boulom you destroyed? she thought, but let it go unsaid.

"A thankless job, more of a sculptor of minds than true academia. When a teacher is presented with a group of hopeful young scholars, the first step is to weed out the useless. Fail them and move on, or give them Cs. A C for the ones I do not see!" He chuckled again.

"The most interesting conclusion…is when the lesser minds somehow rise to the top. Determination is a fascinating trait. Unquantifiable, of course, but it reminds me of a similar phenomenon. What do we call that one? *Desperation.* Are you desperate, Mary? How else have you risen to the title of Empress?"

She shifted her dress to better cover her growing belly. If Wisdom didn't want her to be empress, she would wear it just to spite him. "Can we blame the 'absurdity of freewill' and call it a day? Listen. I don't like you and you don't like me. We both love Francis, or at least, I do. Maybe I'm a fool, but it does seem that you care for the man. Let's act like separated parents who keep it together for the kid. Deal?"

"But, I love you both! In fact, I love you so much, I designated a Vanguard to be your attendant in the upcoming days. May I introduce: Vanguard Omega."

"Omega? So you finally gave up calling them all by—"

She froze. Nyfe entered her chambers, wearing the same white armor and cape as the Vanguards, but he had kept his long hair. The man always had empty eyes, but they seemed emptier, if that was possible. She would not shiver, but to see him here was unsettling. To see him at all was unsettling. He was supposed to be dead. How long would the realm tolerate his existence? Why had everyone ignored her pleas to just kill him all those times? "Nyfe, get the fuck out of my chambers. You are never welcome in this room."

"I have been an unworthy friend to you and your betrothed, but please, forgive my past and embrace my future. The man you refer to as 'Nyfe' no longer exists. I am Vanguard. I am Omega. I will tear open the pathway to Serenity for as long as my empress desires."

His words were so empty. This was the lunatic that had nearly destroyed Terrangus. The monster that had slammed a dagger into Zeen's neck. "If you have come to kill me, you will not find me easy prey." What started off as a lie became a determined truth. It wasn't just Mary anymore. To kill her would also kill her child. No one—god, demon, or otherwise—would do that. Never. Her eyes darted around the room for her sword and shield. They were on opposite sides of the room. Enough foolishness, it was time to stop playing family and keep them close. A mother's love is the end of a mother's comfort. If she could only wield one, it would be the shield. An engager always chooses the shield.

"Kill you? You wound me with such an accusation. Perhaps

the man you knew as Nyfe would stoop so low, but I am Vanguard. I am Omega. I would never harm you, Mary. I am not allowed to."

"Are you not pleased with your gift?" Wisdom said in a mocking tone. "I even fetched him a dagger from Boulom! Expand your imagination. You have a reformed murderer that will answer to your beck and call. Go ahead. Give him a command."

She grabbed her shield and approached, meeting him face-to-face. Any flinch, any weird twitch of the eyes, and she would bash in his skull. "Truly? You'll do anything?"

"I am forbidden to lie. I am aware that is how a liar would respond, but…yes. I will fulfill any request from my empress."

Everything about him infuriated her. The nonsense they had gone through in Boulom. His utter failure as emperor. His…everything. What a pitiful end for a pitiful man. "Take your blade. Tear it across your neck." She hoped it would poke a reaction from Wisdom, but the god remained silent. He probably anticipated such a response. *He's getting to me. I have to start thinking as an empress and not a soldier. My enemies wield words, not blades.*

"I do not wish to die," Nyfe said, as he raised his dagger to his neck. Such an odd blade, almost glass-like as it shimmered. True to her command, he very slowly dragged from the far-left of his neck. A tear flowed down his eye. "I am Vanguard… I am Omega."

Blood poured down. At this rate, the fallen Harbinger would make a mess of their chambers. "Enough. I am convinced. You are truly mine? Do you listen to me above all else?"

"Serenity above all else. But otherwise, I am yours, despite my own dreams and desires. I am Vanguard. I am Omega." He gazed behind her into nothing, not bothering to address his bleeding neck.

"Nyfe, what has he done to you?" She didn't know any of the other Vanguards on a personal level. She knew of Robert, but to her shame, she couldn't name any of the others. It never seemed like it mattered. Of course, it never seems like it matters until it happens to you.

"Rejoice, Empress, for I have finally been given purpose. Service in the name of Serenity." His words brought a chill. For as much as she yearned to formally be named Empress, the words coming from Nyfe's dead voice brought her back to reality. Francis and Mary were puppets with crowns. Their child would be the puppet of the next generation. And what was the alternative? How could she succeed where David had failed? Even with the wrath of Fear he had easily been defeated. That would never happen to her child. Her child would be born on the winning side of history—

"Wisdom? Mary? What is happening here?" asked Francis from the entrance. His frantic eyes stopped when they met Nyfe's. "*You*. I give you another opportunity and you threaten my wife? In my own chambers? Get out, or I shall reduce you to embers."

"I am instructed to only answer the empress. Forgive me, Emperor."

Francis expression turned from fury to terror. She hoped they couldn't read it, but Francis was never one for subtlety. "The only reason you exist at this moment is because I prefer not to have burn stains on my rug."

Nyfe's lips shifted just enough to form the slightest of grins. His body twitched as if the act brought pure agony. "I doubt that. Without the Herald of Arrogance, you are merely the *Invisible Emperor*."

Any thoughts of maintaining an alliance with Wisdom shattered at those words. She clutched her shield and threw it towards Nyfe's head. He ducked or strafed quickly. It was impossible to follow his movements as he avoided the blow and closed the gap. His glass dagger pressed against her neck.

She caught her breath. Her heart pounded from the chill of his blade. An overwhelming terror riddled her. Pure terror, not in the way she had feared dying from the zephum in the Koulva mines, or ironically enough, the fear her twisted ankle had given her in the battle against Nyfe, but the terror of never seeing her child smile. A son? A daughter? She always wanted a son.

Francis rushed forward, no weapon in hand. Nyfe simply back-handed him to the ground, never nudging the dagger from her neck.

"Stop it!" she yelled. "Wisdom, Arrogance, whatever you are, leave us be. We will serve. We tie ourselves to your own fate. Serenity or death."

"Why are you addressing me?" Wisdom asked. It must have *killed* him not to chuckle. "Instruct him to stop and he'll do so. For an empress, you don't seem very natural at this whole command thing."

"Stop," she whispered.

Her eyes widened as Nyfe pressed the blade harder. His half-grin ascended to a crazed smile as he said, "It would just take a twitch. Kill two lives in one swipe. Wouldn't that be precious? I never forgot how you betrayed me in Boulom, Mary. Despite whatever this monster has done to me, I'll never forget."

A wind filled the chambers despite the windows being closed as Wisdom shifted to his Arrogance version and clutched his spectral fist. The bulging eyes stared straight through Nyfe as the Vanguard crumbled to his knees, screaming. "Oh, how I *hate* to repeat myself. Simply *hate* it. Do you desire another year down below? Where you can watch Emily die over and over? Over and over, over and over, your blade right into her back. It wasn't an instant death. No, of course not. The greenest eyes in the realm begged to know why. Why? It's a newborn's first question to his mother, an old man's final question to the grave."

Nyfe convulsed on the ground, screaming as Arrogance shifted his gaze to Mary. "Would you prefer a new gift? I fear this one could be fully broken. From what I gather, you prefer merely the damaged ones."

The god had never terrified her more than in that moment. It wasn't the threat, the unnecessary display of cruelty, but the fact Arrogance was incompetent. There would never be a Serenity. Paradise would always be an unreachable goal, a silk red dress draped over a rule of tyranny. Mary took a deep breath, then said, "Your point is made. Now please, give us some peace. Keep my child safe, and we will play our part. Everything, all of this...it's for him or for her."

Arrogance sighed. It was so exaggerated it put Francis to shame. "Now here is a *fine* irony. The one with freewill obeys, while the Vanguard reaches towards absurdity. It's a boy, by the way. Little Francis Jr, waiting to make his grand entrance to our grand kingdom. Serenity may take more time than I initially hypothesized. You may never see it, but I swear your son will. I have danced with words, lain with emotions, nudged our realm into tragedies and miracles, but you will find I often speak the truth. I do love you, Mary. Believe it. Or don't, Serenity will play out all the same."

Nyfe rose from the ground. His eyes were completely white with his mouth wide open. It was like a corpse with strings. "Forgive my transgressions. I am off to seek forgiveness down below. Down below. I will pray to gods that are not real for a mercy that does not exist. Next time we meet, I will be *perfect*, for I will be Vanguard. I will be Omega."

Mary rubbed her neck as the two of them left together. There was a slight cut, but the true damage was to her ego. She could've had him a year ago. Gods that had felt good, to lean down and punch him in the face right in this very castle. Was that only a year ago? With all the absurd changes that had occurred, it felt like decades. She helped Francis up and held him close, embracing him desperately. Damn his cute face, who would have thought that a one-night stand could lead to becoming a pregnant empress? It takes only one rash decision to alter a lifetime.

"Do you believe him?" asked Francis. He gently rubbed her belly, analyzing it like it was a math problem. She *hated* that at first, but Francis had odd tendencies. It was just him. How he was. She loved him for it.

"I do. Does Francis Jr work for you? I know some men hate the idea of passing on their first name."

"Gods, I don't…wait. You said a few months back you were hoping to name him after your father if it was a boy. Calvin. Calvin Haide. I must admit there is a cadence to it. Calvin! Calvin Haide!"

She stood frozen. He actually remembered that? His eyes were usually staring off into nothing, likely in deep thought anytime she discussed family matters. For a man that had claimed not to understand the rationality of love, sometimes it came more naturally than a Terrangus rain. "Francis. You would do that for me? Truly?"

"For you, my beloved, I would do anything."

She took a deep breath, wishing she could tell little Calvin Haide she loved him. Do babies know what love is? Hopefully. He would need all that love, all that affection, all those unfathomable expectations that would follow his birth. Today made her worst fears known: Mary was as good as dead. She thanked the realm Francis was too foolish to acknowledge it.

CHAPTER 28

SHADOW OF SILENCE

erenna rose from her bed with a newly found spring in her step. She felt wonderful. Wonderful! Wonderful enough for everyone to know. And why not? The last year had been so wretched, so painful, so cruel. Her legs and generally everything below her chest was sore, but it was the best kind of sore. Ah, such a release of pent-up stress and anticipation. Finally. After everything.

Life was wonderful.

It was almost embarrassing to rise without clothes, but shame was an unworthy emotion compared to her cloud-like joy. Her dear Zeen still lay in their bed, exposed for only her to see, snoring loudly. The snoring was not wonderful. She would fix that before they married. Before they made little baby Serennas and Zeens to fill her kingdom of Mylor. Her home. Their home. Zeen Morgan. They would have a grand wedding, with the Goddess of Valor and Sardonyx himself in attendance. He would rise in that exaggerated way, lift his blade, and declare their joining to be *glorious*! Hmm. To let him sleep or...

She checked herself in the mirror. Her hair was a ruffled mess, so she took her brush and guided it all down. Perfect. Let him think she always woke up this way. She lay back in bed, then nuzzled herself into his back. "Zeen?" she whispered. After a few seconds of no response, she gave him a not-so gentle shake on his shoulder.

He groaned, rolled over to the side facing her, then smiled. "Good morning, my dear."

"Good morning!" She rose, covering herself with a blanket. What lay underneath may never be a mystery again, but it felt cute to toy with him. Cute? When was the last time she had considered being cute? Honestly, none of it felt real, like she would open her eyes and be in the middle of a battle against some Harbinger or wretched demon. *Enjoy the moment, but don't let go completely. I will always be Serenna Morgan, Guardian of Mylor, the woman from the portrait...*

Zeen must have noticed her conflicted pause as he leaned up and stared at her. "Is something the matter? Can I uh, get you something. Or um, do you want me to leave?"

"*No,*" she said. It came out with more command than intended. Hmm. A line had been drawn, and a line had been crossed. How do you lead your lover? David had sort of done it, but there wasn't a Guardian in history who had ever expected him to take a harsh tone with Melissa. Pyith, Francis, Serenna, Zeen, all of them had taken a verbal or physical beating from him at some point, but never Melissa.

Well, I could always just ask him for guidance. Too awkward. Was he even a Guardian anymore? With his connection with Fear severed, she could always invite him back. But how did that work? Would he instantly become leader again? Valor forgive her, but she didn't want to relinquish command. She had earned the right to lead the Guardians into a new era, where they could interfere where they saw fit, to use their experience and raw power to better the realm. There had been no wars since she had taken over. Who would dare? 'Pact Breaker' had evolved from an insult to a title that inspired fear. Aggression can only thrive when ignored. After those days in Mylor, where she'd watched her people suffer from Terrangus...aggression would never thrive again.

Zeen rolled out of bed, picking pieces of his clothing up off the floor before he dressed himself. "Of course not! I wasn't planning on leaving but uh, just so you know, it's um, not the best feeling to see such a look of regret after our first time together."

Regret? Was that how she appeared? "Oh, Zeen. Regret is the farthest thing from my heart or mind. Forgive me, I am just weighing the consequences of how this will affect the Guardians. Listen, you must...you must still obey my commands. Our coupling does not change our positions." A blush of red came to her face. 'Positions' was not the best word.

He smiled at her blush, then walked over and hugged her. She rested her head against his chest. Other than inside her shields it could be the safest place in the realm. "After last night," he said, "you should be aware of how well I take direction."

"Stop it!" she yelled, then Zeen snickered as she pushed him away. Did he not understand? This was not a joke. *Did I ruin everything? Gods, oh gods, everyone already knows. We were so loud last night. Where did that come from? I suppose loneliness is a catalyst for reckless decisions.* "We are not children, Zeen. This is a serious matter!"

For the first time ever, his smile filled her with dread. "Of course we're not children, but it doesn't mean we've already grown old either. You know...you sound just like Olivia the first time she and Rinso—"

"Out!" She would've stormed out first if she had clothes on. His smile only grew as he gave her a light kiss and stepped to the door, waving goodbye before he left. Zeen was so giddy and carefree, just as Serenna had been a moment ago... Did he *seriously* make a Rinso reference? It was impossible to imagine

David and Melissa ever dealing with such nonsense. What had David been like in his twenties? Oh, if only Melissa was still alive.

With the room clear, she put her clothes back on, studying the mirror to ensure no evidence of their evening was too obvious. She went to reach for the Wings of Mylor before remembering it was still in her own room. To be separated from her staff for an entire evening...had Valor's warnings been correct?

She took a breath and left her chambers, half expecting an angry mob to be outside ready to condemn her. No one was there. Not even Martin, who was supposed to be guarding the door from last night. Hmm. He clearly cared nothing for her safety. The corridor was unusually quiet. She made a quick stop at her chambers and grabbed her owl staff. She frowned inside the room—maybe it was silly, but she had assumed that bed would be the spot where they would be intimate for the first time. A silly thought. *Stop it. Focus.*

To her dismay, everyone was already seated in the grand hall for breakfast. Had she overslept? Fine. Whatever the cost, it had been worth it. Both the extra rest, and what had come before. She was greeted by several eyes but no words. Gods, everyone knew. Even Father, who sat with a large jug of water. The circles under his eyes appeared poisonous. Somehow, David looked even worse. She had seen the man moments from death in their years together, and never had he appeared worse than now. Was no one going to speak? Seriously?

She sat across from her father and David. *May as well get this part over with.* "Good morning." A simple greeting; it put the sword in their court.

Please, someone say something. They just kept sipping their water, so she glanced around the halls, finding most eyes glancing down the moment they met. Only Sophia kept her gaze, offering a wide grin—

"Archon Gabriel requested you last night through an emissary," Charles said, not drawing his eyes from his water. "I told him you were...preoccupied."

By Valor's grace. "I'm sorry," she whispered. In her younger days she would have grown furious and stormed off, but that tactic loses its dignity after a certain age.

"So, when is Zeen heading back to Vaynex? Immediately? Great!"

Her face burned red. "It was that bad?"

"I have been without your mother for nearly twenty years. Please have the courtesy not to remind me of that loss while in my own home. Let me dream. She waits for me there in our peaceful valley of slumber."

All the food at the banquet hall lost its appeal. She filled a chalice with water, spilling some of it on the table. If anyone noticed, no one said anything. Silent judgment smothered her from every direction.

Serenna rushed over to the gardens. The sun reflecting from the mountains beyond did nothing to cool her off but at least she was alone. The weight of a crowd of eyes is a heavy burden under the shadow of silence. "Everleigh?" she asked aloud, leaning against the railing. No one answered. She sighed. Such childish decision making. She would never regret her evening with Zeen, but it could've been done more discreetly.

"I figured I could find you here," Zeen said, then walked over. "I tried the banquet hall first but...a glance from your father suggested I didn't need breakfast today."

"Oh, Zeen. Sometimes loneliness can defer good judgment quicker than alcohol. Please, don't get the wrong idea. I love you, and it was wonderful to share what we did. Just...we must continue our roles. The realm will collapse if we falter."

He reached for her hand, and she didn't hesitate to grab it. A troubled mind can be a powerful adversary but an eager heart knows no equal. "Sorry, I know I was a bit silly earlier. There is a lot weighing me down. I won't burden you with it, but it feels like the realm is closing in on us right when the good days have finally arrived."

Serenna eyed him cautiously. What did he know that she didn't? Oh, it must be the Terrangus riots. That was likely what Archon Gabriel had summoned her for. "One day at a time, my love. It so happens I plan on meeting with the archon later today. Would you care to join me?"

He let go and leaned across the railing, staring at the mountains as if he had never seen them before. "I should really get back to Vaynex. Unfinished business. Very *glorious...*"

Serenna's heart pounded. He couldn't look her in the eye when he said it. Leave? After last night? "Zeen...am I nothing to you?"

That got his attention. His face swerved around, nearly colliding into hers. "You are everything. Forgive me, I realize how that came out. How about we handle this Alanammus business together, then I go to Vaynex for a day and come back? You must know I would rather spend my time with you than with lizard-people who want me dead."

Dead? He clearly wasn't telling her everything. It was likely something related to Bloom. "Fine, but it's contingent on what Gabriel tells us. I imagine the riots are growing worse."

"I'm sure they are," he said with a smile, "but Terrangus will always survive. They can burn the whole damn kingdom down and we would just rebuild it the next day."

She kept her words to herself. *'We' wouldn't be rebuilding anything. Let Francis and his Vanguards fix what they have destroyed.*

*

Serenna materialized first in the Alanammus Guardian room

235

portal and waited for Zeen, who popped up a few moments later. He shivered, which was odd considering the withering heat. Did he fear portals? An unfortunate stigma, but she could wean him off that habit. He could use some new boots as well, and his loose shirt wasn't doing his physique any favors—

Stop it. Focus.

To his benefit, he didn't reach for her hand or stand too close. Maybe his experience as a soldier kicked in. He took a deep breath, then said, "Should we have brought any of the others? I can see why you wouldn't want Bloom or Five, but having David with us could be an advantage."

"David is *not* a Guardian. I will tolerate his presence for now, but the man has overstayed his welcome. If not for him, Fear would be no more. Do you understand the significance of his actions? I nearly stopped Harbingers of Fear from ever plaguing our realm again. If only I had that scythe…"

Zeen's raised eyebrow made him seem more confused than impressed. Ah, he wouldn't understand. Only someone who had temporarily wielded the power to fully vanquish evil could understand. "I'm sure he had his reasons. David has always been rash, but the man loves our realm more than any of us."

It was her turn to raise an eyebrow. "You truly believe that, don't you? Let us not dwell on such things. Come, the archon awaits. His full name is Archon Faelen Gabriel but go ahead and just use Archon."

"Yes dear," he said with a grin, then followed with, "Understood," before she could chide him.

The opulence of Alanammus Tower would never cease to infuriate her. All this wealth on display seen only by a chosen few, but the archon apparently had nothing to offer against the siege of Terrangus. Gabriel had rolled the dice with a cost he couldn't pay. She had nearly submitted to Death's offer. Nearly destroyed the realm.

Two guards opened the diamond-encrusted doors to the archon's chambers, not offering any greetings or smiles as the Guardians passed them by. Archon Gabriel stood at the other end of the room, aided by his staff, underneath an enormous chandelier shaped with gems of all shapes and colors she had never learned the names of. The shimmering table Sardonyx had destroyed had apparently been replaced. Portraits of late archons and senators of note hung from the walls, with even a vivid portrait of the God of Wisdom. She never understood why they kept his statues, plaques, and portraits after casting him out. She had asked Francis once, who sighed as if it were a child's question, but notably didn't offer any answer of value.

"Ah, Guardian Serenna. Guardian Zeen…you are here as well. I must admit you are later than expected, but you are here all the same. Allow me the honor of welcoming you to Alanammus. Since Francis ran away to play emperor, I find myself with an unfortunate scarcity of Guardians."

"Thank you, Archon," Zeen said in a surprisingly formal tone. He wasn't supposed to speak first, but it wasn't an egregious enough offense to worry about.

"The honor is all mine," Serenna said. "Forgive me for going straight into business, but my father suggested this meeting was rather urgent."

"We must have contrasting views on the word urgent." Gabriel offered a slight grin. Despite his slim figure and tiny frame the man had a mastery of crystal magic that would rival her own. "I am surprised you brought a guest. If your father ever invites me back to Mylor, I'll make note Lady Brianna is invited as well."

Serenna sighed. "Whatever you have to say to me can be heard by Zeen as well."

"Oh, my dear, you reveal too much. What did the lizard beast say that evening? 'Mating with the sorceress?' A pity he never reimbursed me for the table." He smirked and glanced at her. "Fine, I'll get to it. My scholars are attempting to forecast when and where the next Harbinger of Death will arrive so we can limit the collateral damage. We haven't been able to narrow it down to an individual, but Nuum or Terrangus seems most likely. Terrangus because of this Vanguard nonsense, and Nuum well, because it's Nuum."

"What about Vaynex?" Zeen asked before Serenna could respond. "From what Tempest had mentioned, the economic situation is growing worse, and it's causing a lot of unrest."

"A fine theory," Gabriel said, "but historically speaking, Vaynex is the least likely kingdom to host a Harbinger. Unless of course, you know something I don't."

Zeen's face grew red. He apparently knew something they both didn't. "No. I don't know anything. I'm just saying things could change. Things could be different in the future. You know how things are."

By Valor's grace, Zeen was an awful liar. She pushed down her fury and took a deep breath. He would pay *dearly* for this later. "Zeen, you appear flushed from the heat. Wait outside these chambers until our meeting is concluded."

She didn't watch him leave. After the doors clanged shut, the archon smiled and gestured to the seat closest to the head of the table. They both sat, then he said, "Ah, by the law of averages, the room has become significantly more intelligent. You did well to bed a man who cannot lie. Trust me, I didn't marry Brianna for her mind, either."

"Do *not* go there."

"But I must. Wise words from a fool are never an accident. Some warmaker or brutalized warmaker's son have probably begun to hear the whispers. Good, this changes everything."

Visions of the broken Tempest filled her mind. A shattered leg and a fallen life-mate. "What about Tempest?"

Gabriel scoffed. "Impossible. The warlord's son is the only reasonable thing to come from that kingdom in my lifetime. No, it would be one of the reckless ones. Dubnok has been increasingly irrational, and I hear his son has been enrolling himself in those barbaric arena melees. Hmm. Yes. It all makes sense."

It made no sense to Serenna. All the signs were pointing at Tempest, but there was no reason to argue. "Archon, what am I doing here?"

He leaned forward, trading his grin and warm demeanor for an empty gaze. "Please ask Valor to leave us for a moment. This is a sensitive matter."

"Valor isn't here. And if she were, such words would only spark her interest."

"Hmm. Lying suits you, Guardian Serenna. So be it. Let her listen. We share a common enemy."

Why does everyone always assume I'm lying? Whatever, I'll take it as a compliment.

Gabriel cleared his throat. "The Haide wedding. Are you planning to attend?"

"One of my…sources advised me to stay home. Why?"

"Allow me to answer your question with a question. Do you agree the God of Wisdom must be stopped?"

I wonder how much he knows about Arrogance. "He blatantly threatened my father in our last meeting. And with the riots in Terrangus, the Vanguards are growing in number and power. In my honest opinion, he set the riots into motion as an excuse to give the Vanguards more authority."

"I share your suspicions," he said with a nod. "Often, the most complex issues are solved in the simplest of matters. Do nothing, or do everything. Do you follow?"

"I am well aware of your 'do nothing' tactics.'"

"Yes, yes. Some words I prefer not to speak out loud. Us

mortals are never alone." He lay a tiny piece of paper on the table and slid it over to her, then grabbed his platinum cane. A dense platinum sphere surrounded them, and only them, blinding her vision of anything beyond. She caught her breath at the claustrophobic size of the sphere. They could nearly touch faces. To her shock, tiny words of platinum appeared on the note. Crudely drawn, but readable all the same.

We kill Francis on his wedding night, she read. *Senator Thompson is on our side but Wraith is a liability. Mind your words before you speak them out loud.*

The sphere and the wording on the note vanished. "Keep it simple," he whispered. "Agree or dissent?"

Rage coursed through her. Pure rage. After all the suffering her people had gone through...now he wanted to interfere? Now he was concerned for kingdoms other than his own? Or maybe that was it. Maybe he saw Francis as a threat to Alanammus and this was just a means to an end. That's all anything ever was with him. "I thought you opted never to interfere?"

"You think what I want you to think. Remember that. Now, relax. Take a deep breath. Consider my offer next time you lay with your Zeen, and consider what it means if we fail. What we *lose*. I would rather my reign be seen as an efficient cruelty than an avoidable tragedy. Farewell, Guardian Serenna. You can see yourself out."

She stormed out without a word, sweat pouring down her head. Would she warn Francis? She never liked the man, but betrayal to a fellow Guardian would be unheard of. Even him. Even if he had become a puppet to the tyrant Arrogance. Even if he was ushering in a realm of Vanguards.

And there was Zeen outside the door, smiling at her. After his lies, he wouldn't be smiling much longer.

CHAPTER 29

LET THE SANDS TAKE US

empest's bloodshot eyes stared at the ceiling above. Remnants of faded dreams were the only evidence he had ever slept at all.

"Tempest… Tempest, Tempest—"

"SHUT UP!" he yelled, to nothing. To forever. To the end. The damnable words flowed through him. How had Serenna dealt with such tortuous whispers? How had anyone? Oh, to yell at the ceiling. It was close to a new low, but he couldn't shift through his fragmented memories to find a comparison. A lack of sleep after one night had been a hindrance. After a week, it had become a nightmare. A drunk-like fog, with all the paranoia of inebriation but none of the joy. Every night, morning, and whatever we call the continuous stream of the two combined had been worse. Once the fear of insomnia takes root, the body surrenders to the predetermined defeat of the mind.

He eased out of bed and grabbed his walking stick. No bath today, after he had momentarily drifted asleep in the warm waters last night, he didn't have the willpower to risk his existence struggling with a task a mere child could accomplish. Maybe he was better off dead. The idea had seemed just a little more inviting each morning as rest abandoned him.

Tempest hobbled out of his chambers and towards his diplomacy room. Thank the remaining gods there were no council meetings today. The warmakers had seemed less inclined to share their ridiculous thoughts after Sardonyx returned. Perhaps power's greatest attribute is the ability to crush ignorance under its fist. But what happens when ignorance is the one wielding the fist? Ah, enough nonsense. The room was always a disappointment in the summer. The bookshelves and imported wine canisters appeared naked without an active fireplace. Stacks of empty wood lay there, waiting to be burned, waiting for a chance to be useful. But unlike Tempest, the wood would eventually find use again.

Tempest sat at his desk, pushing away empty chalices of wine and uneaten bread. Hmm. He had let this room go in the past few days. A terrible habit that had compounded over time. He would take a morning or afternoon to get everything in order. Not today, of course. Maybe tomorrow. Time to put his torment to use. He pulled out a sheet of paper from Alanammus and dipped his pen in the ink.

Alright, yesterday, I ended with Olivia and Rinso breaking up…again. Hmm. I need some filler before Rinso has his honor duel against Vehemence Jr in Warlord Hyphermlo's name. Maybe it's time to start outlining these things. I need a plot twist, a love triangle…or I could kill someone! Who's left? I wish I'd kept Cympha around long enough to—

He let go of the pen and let it sink into the ink. Cympha deserved better. She had been Pyith's favorite character, a clear homage to his life-mate. Not the most artistically inspired of the Rinso team, but the ones from the heart are always the most beautiful. What to do, what to do… Of course! It was time for a flashback.

Tempest eased the pen out of the ink, flicking his hand to get it off his own, not caring that it splattered onto his rug. He pulled the paper close, then started writing. *Twenty Years Ago…*

"Hey, Tempest?" Bloom's voice. Out of all the insufferable people. "Got a minute?"

"It appears I have all the time in the realm for everyone but me," he said, then abruptly pushed his papers back on the desk. "What do you want?"

"Damn, you're still riding this brooding thing? If Strength was alive, I'd tell you to thank him for sheltering you from battle. If you think this is bad… Well, most of my friends are forgotten under the sand. After a while, I just stopped replacing them."

He sighed. Was that her attempt at consoling him? "What a wonderful story. Look, either get to the point or get out. My tolerance for honorable conversation has vastly diminished."

"Fine. Fuck it then. I want Warlord."

"Why are you asking me? If you want the warlord just approach him. As a Guardian, you wield the privilege."

"Tempest," she said with a faint grin. "Stop talking and listen. I want to *be* the next warlord."

He clutched his walking stick as if it could do anything. "I see… Even for you that is bold. Do what you must. I won't make believe I could ever defeat you, but I will not concede the satisfaction of groveling."

"For a guy with a shattered leg, you're still the best at jumping to conclusions. By Strength's grave, I don't know how Pyith ever tolerated you. Alright, here's the deal. My first thought was to just storm in and kill you and Daddy Claw. That's how we got it done during the war. Bad commanders just kept blowing up. Never figured out why." She laughed as if that was hilarious.

"No long-term benefit that way, unfortunately. The Zeen kid was right. Serenna will tear me to crystal shreds if I'm too ambitious. But—and I mean but—what if I became your new life-mate and ruled as Dumiah Claw?"

Tempest nearly laughed but his face stood frozen. By the gods, she was serious. "Have you lost what little sense you have left? It has barely been a week since her passing and you dump this nonsense upon me? *Here?*" he yelled, slamming his fist on the table. It felt better than expected, perhaps that was why Dubnok had resorted to the tactic so often.

"Relax, boss. I ain't coming on to you or anything. Trust me, I got my needs fulfilled in that area. Do I have to spell this out for you? When Sardonyx dies, you die. I'd bet it's the same damn day on the same damn hour. I just want your name; you can hang around and handle the economic stuff no one cares about. Dumiah Claw, Warlord Guardian of Vaynex. Ah, that gets you *hot* doesn't it?"

Hot was one way to put it. He took a deep breath and pushed down all the frantic arguments on why this was stupid. More information. More information, then react. "And what of the warmakers? Dubnok and Novalore will never stand for this. Would you kill them all?"

"*Oh*, I like that tone of voice. You would enjoy that, wouldn't you? They won't stand for anything once I blow off their legs. Not all of them. I wager after one died the rest would find some loyalty. I mean, do you think we follow your daddy for his bright ideas?"

"Of course not." What a sad day for the realm that Bloom was one of the brighter minds in Vaynex. By Strength's name, there was a temptation to it, an answer to his problems that didn't involve the God of Death. Even if it was only to spite Novalore. But...too much of an insult to his dear Pyith. Tempest would be expected to find a new life-mate of course, but not now. Not even the most callous of zephum would move on so quickly. An absurd idea. Completely absurd...with some merit. Hmm. Bloom wasn't conventionally beautiful by zephum standards. She really wasn't unconventionally beautiful either. Maybe she fit in that category one step below, where her snout was magically more slender under the carefree gaze of evening twilight.

"Well, no need for an answer now. I'm just planting some seeds. Maybe if I wasn't born a mechanist and thrust into the military, I could've been a gardener. Yeah, probably not."

He watched her casually stroll out of the room, as if she had simply proposed afternoon tea. Life must be so simple for the ones that don't think ahead. But she had thought ahead. Right? There was an odd logic to her request; it frightened him in a bizarre way to consider Bloom wasn't simply the fool he'd thought her to be. Bloom would be an abysmal warlord, but could she be any worse than the others? Dubnok desired war against Alanammus. Surely Bloom couldn't be so foolish after seeing the power of magic firsthand. *How can I possibly consider this?* Surely, it was the lack of sleep. No other reason. Enough distractions; he pulled his book-in-progress back to his desk and dipped the pen. *Where was I? Ah yes, a flashback. Twenty Years Ago...*

"What was *she* doing here?" Father's voice. Great.

Tempest dumped his pages back into the desk. How could one be both isolated and smothered by people? "Perhaps you'll laugh at the idea. Bloom wants to marry into the family line so she can eventually become warlord."

Sardonyx sat across from him. Normally, it had been a human on the other end of the table, some fear-stricken merchant or senator who yielded every advantage for an opportunity to leave alive, as if Tempest were some unhinged monster. "Look upon me son. Do you see laughter?"

Its hear *laughter, Dad.* "You only laugh when people are dead. Sorry, that was unworthy of me, insomnia is taking a harsh toll. The sad part? She makes a fair point. I had deemed the woman a fool, some violence-ridden beast, but it's not a terrible offer, assuming she doesn't just blow me up right after our joining."

"I'm not dead yet," Sardonyx said. He leaned back and rubbed his snout. Was that what it looked like when he attempted to summon a rational thought? "By Strength's name, I despise magic. I...cannot defeat her in single combat. You know this. Perhaps she knows it as well. Our options are limited. What are your thoughts?"

Tempest froze. "My thoughts?"

"But of course! I am leaning towards accepting her deal just to ensure the name lives on...but I would never, *ever* demand you take a new life-mate. *Never.*"

Gods, his father terrified him. "Even the mere thought of replacing Pyith is an insult to her legacy. Dad...it's just not fair." He hated himself for letting tears fall in front of Father, but dammit all. Everything they had built was fading. The end of the God of Strength, the end of Pyith, the eventual end of Sardonyx. The nothing, the forever, the end. The nothing, the forever, the end.

To his surprise, Sardonyx simply smiled. "Fair is a goddess unknown to our people. When I lost Vitala, I considered ending it all. An honorable death! By my own hand! But I did not. How could I? Vaynex needs us, my son. The Claw name is all that stands between zephum prosperity and human oppression. *Never.* When the time comes, let the sand take us all."

It felt like the two of them were having entirely different conversations. "Father... What do you expect from me? What should I do?"

Sardonyx rose with a smile, despite the faint tears in his eyes. Other than Vitala's memorial, Tempest had never seen him weep. It had been a shattered illusion, a realization our fathers are not gods, but merely aged sons, shifting through the threads of time, trying to decipher the thin veil between knowledge and trauma. "*Survive*. Strength without honor—is chaos!"

Encrypted words. Not empty, but obscure. Was that his plea to marry Bloom? Strength save him, he didn't want it. But, with enough time…

Oh, the things we do for *honor*.

CHAPTER 30

THE ABSENCE OF MERCY

oes it please you, Emperor?"

Francis stood in his chambers, analyzing his new wooden staff from General Marcus. Something was off. It was flawed. Or merely imperfect. Are imperfect and flawed the same thing? It seems there are too many words to describe everything below perfection and yet they all fail to describe anything. Upon reflection, nothing could compare with the Herald of Wisdom. To wield such magnificence! It was fruitless to believe he could've ever found a replacement...

"Uh, Francis?"

"*What?*" Francis snapped back. "Do I appear pleased?"

"No, my lord. Forgive me. I will go out and try a new vendor. Perhaps one with greater esteem?"

"This staff is from Terrangus? You dolt. Go to a *real* kingdom and obtain a *real* staff with some *real* wood. Look here! Look at the warping! This shouldn't be difficult. Why is everything so difficult for you people?"

"Please stop whining," his dear Mary—who had been very grouchy lately—said. Easy for her to say, a sword and shield could be forged by any blacksmith's apprentice. A staff takes a knowledge and precision only a true professional could master.

"Emperor, other than Xavian, the southern kingdoms have closed off their portals to us. While I haven't received specific reasoning of why, my hunch tells me it's because of the riots."

"Your 'hunch' isn't worth a roll of copper. This is absurd. Absurd! Everyone has abandoned me." To be fair, it was a decent enough hypothesis, but the true paranoia was likely due to the Vanguards. Classic Alanammus propaganda. It was all so tiring. How different would life have been if he had refused Wisdom's staff? No emperor. No Vanguards. No child on the way. Oh, actually, that act had been done beforehand. Francis hadn't often made mistakes, but accepting the Herald of Wisdom appeared to be one of them. Just like becoming a Guardian.

"The Terrangus military stands with you, Emperor." To be fair, Marcus was a good one. His promotion to general had not been a mistake. The man was realms away from being a great mind, but by Terrangus standards, he may as well have been Archon Consaga. "My men hear rumors of escalations by early dusk. Give me the word, and I can preemptively crush the rebels before they ever get started."

Preemptively before they get started? He's so redundant. "First off, never refer to them as rebels. The title has a literary proximity to heroic actions. Traitors or rioters. On second thought, only say traitors. Use that phrase as often as possible and ensure it sticks with the masses. Create an atmosphere of us against them, and let our victories show that any on the side of 'them' will be crushed."

"Uh, sure," Marcus said, rubbing his chin. Why was he confused? Oh, what Francis would give to have Julius as his general. Better yet, Julius as general and Robert as advisor to the throne. Alas, they were both gone, leaving Francis with a useless kingdom, an angry betrothed, and a vengeful god.

She's looking at me. I should say something. "Yes, my beloved?"

"I didn't say anything." Great. Well, her eyes certainly did. The riots were getting to her. In theory, Francis could entertain the idea of guilt from overseeing the deaths of her people, but were they really her people? In a swamp like Terrangus, she would be better off distancing herself from as many of these 'people' as she could. Like all other burdens, it was a simple numbers game. Too many fools, not enough space, far too much yelling.

"General," he said, pleased that Marcus immediately met his gaze. "I shall join you for the hangings this afternoon. Let our enemies discover a lesson in fire if they dare to be so bold."

Marcus raised an eyebrow. Did he think Francis was helpless? "Is that wise, my lord?"

"Wise?" Francis asked with a snicker. "Allow me to inform you about wise. Soon after my mother cast Wisdom out of Alanammus, a small sect of fanatics sought her assassination. Riots, threats, all the standard tools of an ignorant mob. Mother responded with violence. I saw things…things children should never have to witness. And yet, I watched obedience follow the absence of mercy."

Marcus glanced around the room cautiously. "Emperor, are we alone? May I speak freely?"

"Never alone," Francis said, holding his new wooden staff. On second examination, it was good enough. An imperfect staff for an imperfect kingdom. "Speak freely if you must but allow me a guess: you don't trust the Vanguards, do you?"

"Perhaps trust isn't the word I'm looking for. They just…um, seem different lately. It is difficult to explain. Ah, forget it. Forgive me for burdening you with such boy's tales."

"But that's the smartest thing you've said all day," Mary said, leaning back on her chair with both hands on her belly. "They're like cats. Never trust cats."

Marcus gave a nervous snicker. "Did something happen?

Between you and Wisdom? None of us have seen the god in a few days. Since Nyfe arrived, to be exact."

Nyfe… With everything going on I forget he is here. Perhaps I can arrange an accident of sorts? It's clear I cannot defeat him with such a dingy staff. Hmm, on that note, I dare not leave Mary alone. "Lord Wisdom has business in Serenity. I assure you that all is well. In fact, my dear Mary shall join us today in our endeavors!"

"No fucking way am I getting involved with that." Both her fury and body rose faster than expected as she stood. "Marcus. Get out."

Marcus bowed and left. What a mess; the man clearly believed he was in service to a royal family awaiting the void.

Francis sighed. "My beloved, I don't want you here alone. We have too many enemies in our own home. Everywhere…all around us."

"Then stay here. We don't have to be a part of such evil."

Oh, what would my mother say? "Let them call it evil if they must. Such is the natural order of things. Unrest is dissolved by a temporary storm of chaos, but the post-storm clarity is always a thing of beauty. Time…time will be favorable." *Was time favorable to you, Mom? No one ever speaks your name. 'Addison Haide was a tyrant' the staff had told me. What legacy will the staff proclaim of me centuries from now? Tyrant? Mad Emperor? Perhaps, 'Francis Haide, a damaged man that eventually became broken.'*

"But Francis," Mary said after a long pause, "these are my people."

"Well, technically—"

"Stop. This has gotten beyond ridiculous. An arms race of violence against our own subjects! Hanging traitors, sure, that's always been the Terrangus way, but why must it always be public? Every death from our tyranny creates two new enemies.

We will never create peace this way. What sort of kingdom are we building for our child?"

"Serenity…" The word came out weaker than he intended. The sad part was, she was right. A scholarly review of any kingdom's history would show the temporary reigns of tyrants. Maybe Francis would be different. No other emperor ever ruled with the Herald of Wisdom…

To his surprise, Mary took both his hands. "Serenity is a mad god's dream that will never come to fruition. Think about it: Robert, David, Serenna… Every sensible person has abandoned us. How much more evidence do we need? It's time to repair the damage from our mistakes."

Mistakes? Have I truly become so careless? "Would you think less of me if I admit I have no idea where to start?"

"Francis," she said, then squeezed his hands and let go, "that may be the wisest thing you ever said to me. Maybe after 'I love you.' Let's start with mercy. I will join you to the hangings, and we will shock everyone when we pardon their crimes. It's a reasonable first step. I saw captains offer full pardons during the Koulva mines campaign to raise morale."

Francis sighed, with enough restraint to avoid her wrath. "This goes against everything I was taught. I…very well, my beloved. For you, and baby Calvin, I am willing to try."

*

Sweat poured down Francis's face as they followed Marcus through the trade district gates, surrounded by guards, but no Vanguards, particularly *that* Vanguard. Damnable summer heat sizzled without any rain. When Francis had told Marcus the plan he was met by a silent bow. Marcus had always been quick to praise, but never one to voice his dissent. As usual, silence had delivered an opinion without stating the obvious. Francis enjoyed that about Marcus. If only some of his senators could learn such constraint.

"This idea is foolish," Francis whispered, following Marcus up the stairs to his post. So many eyes were upon him. So many whispers from all directions, so much anger in the air. When had this occurred? Why did no one love Francis? One truth became apparent immediately: moving the hangings from the privacy of the military ward to the open streets of Terrangus had been a terrible mistake. It's sad how often yesterday's brilliance can become tomorrow's burdens.

As usual, he didn't recognize any of the men awaiting the noose. Honestly, they all appeared the same after a while. Tattered clothes drenched in sweat, unwashed hair, dark circles under their eyes.

They're looking at me. All of them. Should I say something?

"You're sure about this?" asked Marcus. "My men will be pissed if it backfires. It wasn't easy to take them alive."

"Yes," Mary said before Francis could respond. Somehow, she appeared more distraught than the men awaiting their end. She downed her flask of water as if she hadn't drank in days.

This is my moment. Francis Haide, elemental sorcerer, Emperor of Terrangus. He rose, expecting silence to follow. When it didn't, he raised his hand in the air, the way Forsythe had done as emperor. When that failed, he clutched his staff and glowed a bright orange. The people of Terrangus were uneducated simpletons, but they found the courtesy of silence under the threat of fire.

"My fellow people of Terrangus," Francis said, continuing his orange glow. Adding 'my fellow people' had been a move inspired by his mother, despite the redundancy. Weak minds crave the obvious. "It goes without saying that tensions have increased considerably in the past few months." He paused, how could he call them fools without stating it? "We all agree on the eventual outcome of Serenity, but like the greatest of scholars, disagree on the methods of arrival."

Francis glanced at Mary and Marcus to check his progress. The fact neither of them met his eyes spoke volumes. What was he doing wrong? Tone it down? Or maybe, get to the point. He was speaking to fools, after all. "I will speak plainly. This war of Terrangus against Terrangus has been nothing short of tragic. I wish for no more bloodshed and, as an act of good faith, I will release the vagrants you see here back to the public, as a chance to atone for their crimes." *Oh, maybe I shouldn't have said vagrants...*

Murmurs filled the air. It wasn't exactly anger...distrust, perhaps? The soldiers below shrugged at Marcus. In hindsight, telling everyone the plan beforehand would have made more sense. It took a good five minutes or so of gesturing between Marcus and his men before the captives were freed. None of them appeared grateful. They all glanced at Francis with...hatred? Why? What more did they want? *I have nothing left to offer you people. Take this glimmer of mercy and do something with your lives. Read a book. Learn a trade. Do...anything.*

"DEATH TO THE FOREIGN EMPEROR!" someone yelled. Who? It wasn't any of the freed men.

He heard it again, from a different direction. Again, from behind him. Then, from the men he had just freed. Francis clutched his staff and amplified his orange glow. Why was this happening? "My beloved, stay close," he said.

The freed men started assaulting their captors. Absurd! The men and women rushing from all directions from the trade district was more absurd and, to be honest, a bit concerning. Marcus rushed down to the streets and yelled out orders. Gods, it was like a war, a civil-war, with Terrangus uniforms the only distinguishing factor of friend or foe. Fire wasn't the right element for such a scenario. If he burned his own soldiers, his people would immediately unite under a common enemy. He shifted to yellow and searched for a suitable target to rain lightning down upon. Everyone was so entangled, bodies upon bodies, swords upon steel, torches thrown in the air.

Francis found a target: a young man throwing torches and yelling. He blasted him with a lightning bolt and watched the battlefield shift. The rebels...traitors were advancing. How was that possible? Enough. He found another man alone and crushed him under the superiority of elemental magic. Wooden staff or not, Francis Haide, elemental sorcerer of Alanammus, Wisdom's chosen one, would never fall to a common man. He had defeated demons, Harbinger Nyfe, even David. What were these men to him? *Nothing.*

His dear Mary was crying. Out of fear? Damn these traitors for making her weep. He amplified his yellow glow, blasting more bolts down from above—

A bottle crashed by his side and erupted into flames, sending Francis stumbling back, knocking the staff out of his hands and down into the mob below. He gasped for air, struggling as Mary's cries grew louder. These uneducated fools! Snails in leather, insects with flesh, fish who could speak. Mary's cries grew louder. Was this the price of mercy? Francis rubbed the sweat off his face and lost his breath as his hand returned bloody. The emperor bled. The emperor was never supposed to bleed. The gateway to Francis's post was being overrun. It would be mere minutes before—

"*Ah, my dear Francis. Have I caught you at an unfavorable time?*"

"Wisdom...Arrogance...help me. Please, I was a fool. A fool! Help me. It can't end this way. Everything...has failed."

"*How is that mercy tactic working out for you? Our 'Robert' treads freely through Mylor. Your future wife appears rather distressed. Your general is being overrun by his own army. How sad, it seems the Architect of Paradise will be a mere footnote in history books after he hangs by his own noose."*

"Wisdom, please help me. I will not stray from the path. I will usher in Serenity with Mary by my side, and baby Calvin will continue our legacy after we are gone. Please don't let it end this way. This can't be all for nothing…"

"All for nothing? Ah, in your desperation, you have quantified freewill into a single definition. I am a generous god; it is what separates me from the nightmarish deities that oppose us. Take hold of my staff. And this time, do not, ever, forget what we are. An architect and divinity. But my assistance is no longer free. I'm throwing in a touch of Arrogance. The realm may seem a bit…different once you reclaim my staff.

"That, my dear Francis, is because it will finally make sense."

Francis grabbed the staff. It felt so familiar in his hands, like a perfection that had been crafted only for him. Power and knowledge returned, replacing another feeling he couldn't seem to recall. All the screaming and violence below went mute, along with Mary's cries. He dropped his yellow glow. Lightning was a precise art, the sort of magic one would use to pinpoint targets one-by-one. Orange erupted. To call it an 'aura' would be a disservice to magic's supremacy.

"Welcome back, my friend. Burn them without hesitation. Remember, they chose this."

Something inside him screamed to stop but he couldn't grasp the feeling. He had no reason to question the voice from his staff. He launched a blast to his left, incinerating a cluster of men. Friends, allies, foes, it didn't matter. Perfection has no time to sort the irrelevant. Every single one of them died instantaneously and Francis felt nothing but satisfaction. Whatever remained of that *other* feeling vanished entirely.

Another large clump of men battled in the south, right by the inn of the Three Handed Sword. He burned them. All of them. Fire only meets its potential when the ones burning can't manage to scream. Scream? Let them scream. Mary screamed at him, but her voice was buried within the tumult. How many more desired their end? Well, they kept fighting, so they continued to burn. Directions, words, locations, none of it mattered with the Herald of Arrogance in his grasp. Francis was a god. A ruler of men. The chosen one of Arrogance.

Oh? His side appeared to be winning. Imagine that. Imagine what occurs when insects rise against the sun. He couldn't find Marcus, and he didn't care. Generals are decorated servants to their higher power. Ah, look at that! Down below, where the mortals gathered, they bowed to him. Unrest had been *annihilated*. Disloyalty *obliterated*. Perfection...embraced. He clutched the Herald of Arrogance. All the people—friends, foes alike—gazed at him for words. But what needed to be said? They had challenged perfection and paid the price through golden fire. Mary gazed at Francis as if he were a monster. Sad, but necessary. Baby Calvin would understand. Baby Calvin would hail his father as a hero. Whatever the cost.

A voice within screamed, but it wasn't perfect, and thus, ignored.

CHAPTER 31

A CHAPTER FOR CYMPHA

on't you ever, *ever*, lie to me again. I gave you everything. Every part of me. And this is what I get? Do not come home tonight," Serenna yelled before she rushed off.

And that left Zeen alone in Alanammus. This kingdom always brought mixed feelings. Despite all the expensive-looking walls and fancy glass things in every room, there was a darkness that lingered here. A few rooms behind him held the balcony David had attempted to jump off last year. No one had really spoken of that day since it happened…

He sighed and entered the Alanammus Guardian room, surprised to find several guards maintaining the portal. Mylor had been the same way. Whatever it was, everyone seemed on the lookout for something. Oh, wasn't it Vanguards? So much for time alone to clear his head. "Morning all," he said, pouring himself a chalice of water. "You guys on the defensive too?"

"Archon's orders," the biggest one said. Not much to work with there. It was barely a step above the grunts of Vaynex.

Tempest. Zeen had clearly botched the meeting with the archon and revealed way too much. Lying was never his strong point, but some questions are difficult because every answer is a lie in its own way. Serenna would figure it out if she hadn't already. The archon probably knew as well.

Was it too early for wine? Zeen leaned back and sighed. Despite his best intentions, everyone was mad at him. Serenna would eventually forgive him...hopefully. He never had much luck with relationships. He had stumbled into love several times, always thinking *this is the one!* but all his courting attempts fizzled after a few months. But Serenna was so much more. The woman of his dreams. *I should've told her. She has been a Guardian far longer than I have. This really isn't the sort of problem I can fix on my own...but I must. She doesn't have time for my nonsense. Tempest is my friend.*

I can fix this.

He finished his water and rose, then adjusted his armor to make it more presentable. "Guards!" he yelled. "Trigger the portal. I am heading to Vaynex." It was stranger than he would admit to see the mage trigger the crimson glow with no hesitation. For all the burdens of being a Guardian, the authority was a welcome change.

Zeen stepped inside and took a deep breath. The rush of authority faded to the rush of anxiety. Portal nerves, Serenna, Terrangus, Vaynex...whew. His knees wobbled as he materialized into Vaynex. Too many portals in one day. His zephum mage friend shot him a surprised glance, then grunted.

"I have returned. Is now a good time, or is there a council meeting?"

The mage grunted with a shrug. If Zeen had to guess, that meant no to at least one of his questions.

"Right. Well, before I go, what is your name?" Silence. How rude; not the way to address the 'Human Warlord.' *If I were cruel, I would challenge him to a duel for such dishonor. Actually, I know little about zephum mages. I'd probably lose.* "Have it your way. See you later, friend."

Zeen grimaced as he entered the main citadel hall. It was always so hot in this room; why they had the torches burning was anyone's guess, though it was neat how the flames shadowed the throne. Plenty of guards were scattered about, but the Claws and warmakers were nowhere to be seen. Well, with Tempest's injury, he was likely either in his resting chambers or the diplomacy room.

The diplomacy room was the correct guess. Tempest sat at his desk, sighing like Francis as he pushed whatever he was working on to the side. "So. You have returned. Against my wishes." Well, Tempest was still mad.

"Tempest, can we start over? I acknowledge my failures to you as both a friend and a Guardian. All of my mistakes are taking their toll. I don't want to lose everyone close to me. Please."

Tempest paused, his right eye twitching. It seemed more out of fatigue than anger. "Come. Take a seat. Perhaps this is for the best, I have been stuck on this section far longer than acceptable. These damn sleepless nights are getting to me. And the mornings. They all blend together after a while, not that you would understand."

Zeen didn't, so he made no mention of it and sat. "Are you working on...Rinso? Volume four?" His heart pounded. He had always imagined this moment, coming face-to-face with the artist who crafted his hero. Who could it be? A wise old man? A swashbuckling pirate? A cynical zephum royalty hobbled by injury and the loss of his love? Didn't expect that one, though to be fair, it wasn't always this way. There aren't many things more frightening than considering how close to the edge we always stand.

"Correct," Tempest said with the faintest of smiles, which warmed Zeen's heart. "Okay, for some context: in the last chapter, I split up Rinso and Olivia again. I'm thinking of introducing a love triangle to fill up some pages before the final battle."

By the gods, please don't. "A love triangle? I can't speak for everyone, but why don't you leave Rinso and Olivia together? We all love them! Who is even left for Rinso at this point? You have um, 'mated' him with just about everyone."

Tempest smirked. "Perhaps it's Olivia's time for some fun?"

"No! Let's um… What other options do you have?"

"How intriguing that Rinso can dally about but Olivia must always remain faithful. Well…fine. How about a flashback? A chapter for Cympha the fallen." Tempest's smirk vanished as his eyes twitched.

What? Cympha dies? Spoilers… Zeen searched for words to end the pause. Cympha was obviously a Pyith stand-in, maybe a quick homage would brighten up Tempest and keep the God of Death away. "A wonderful idea. No one deserves it more."

A hint of a smirk returned. "Wise words, my friend. Would you care to help me? I haven't had anyone since—"

"Of course!" Zeen said before he could finish that sentence. He pushed his chair closer and leaned back. Surprisingly comfortable for Vaynex; this room was more prestigious than even the Terrangus throne room. "How about her first battle as a Guardian? Tell me that story."

"Ah, you see, it started back in…"

*

In Zeen's excitement, he had lost track of time. "Read that last line to me again."

Tempest cleared his throat. ""Well fought for a zephum!" said Rinso. "Fuck you, human, said Cympha.""

"Perfect," Zeen said with a smile. "That's rather similar to my first encounter with Pyith. I tried to shake her hand and then she took bets on how quickly I would die."

"My first encounter was…well, a tale for my heart only. Zeen, thank you for returning. I cannot exaggerate how difficult everything has been."

It seemed like the moment was there, so Zeen rose and reached out his hand. Tempest paused, then accepted the aid to stand. Zeen embraced him, holding back enough to avoid putting weight on his right side. "I am here for as long as you need me. But, um, I have a confession before you thank me too much. I had a meeting with Serenna and the archon about the next Harbinger of Death. I didn't specifically tell them about your…situation, but Serenna definitely caught on that I was worried about you. Subtlety has never been my strong point. I apologize."

After the long pause, Zeen expected to be banished from Vaynex again, but then Tempest said, "I understand."

"Truly? You're not angry with me?"

"Anger is beneath me. It has already rotted me to the core. I am more than this leg. More than my loss. I will beat this." He grabbed his walking stick and banged it on the ground. "*I will beat this!*" he yelled, with the deep confidence of a future zephum warlord.

To Zeen's joy, he believed him.

CHAPTER 32

THE MIRROR DOESN'T LIE

avid sat next to Senator Morgan at the Mylor capital hall table. His hand shook as he clutched his chalice of water. The shakes hadn't afflicted him in a while, but the toll of last night would linger long into today. Gods, everyone kept speaking. Why were they all so loud? Especially Charles. The man looked no worse for wear despite the abominable amount of wine he had consumed at this very table. A short-term gift. David's mother had avoided hangovers until she slept one night and never woke up. *I have to get out of here,* he thought, refusing to let the aroma of fresh bread fill his nose. His body desperately needed something to soak the wine and ale, but there wasn't any food in the realm that would survive the trip down his stomach.

Enough of this, he thought, rising without a word. Fortunately, no one really gave him any attention. Everyone was still focused on discussing Serenna and Zeen: two attractive, young Guardians who had coupled into the night. What a scandal, surely these men and women with children of their own could never imagine such debauchery.

David paused at the exit of the hall, glancing behind him to the group of people chattering away. They all ignored the fallen demi-god in their presence. He had been many things: a Guardian, a leader, a lover, a champion of fear…a monster, but he had never been ignored. Never been irrelevant. It was like staring into his own death. We all know the realm goes on after we fade, but to be reminded of it is a cruel fate. Where to go? His chambers offered rest, so his chambers were a fair destination.

Wasn't there something he was supposed to do? Ah, he'd had the strangest dream last night. A giant Serenna had carried him off into a slumber of lilies, a garden where reality fails, but dreams are eternal. Dreams. All dreams. If Noelami had been correct about anything, it was the power of dreams.

He took a large swig of water and fell onto his bed. Resting in the morning was never a great strategy, but who can choose when our body decides to tire? David closed his eyes, welcoming the darkness, hoping to dream of a time that wasn't now.

"You lackadaisical oaf. Have you no shame? Rise! Rise and fulfill your promise! Compromise is not the protocol of Valor."

Maybe it was time to stop drinking. He rolled over, ignoring his migraine and the bizarre voice that whispered through his thoughts. The pillow was so soft, so welcoming, a pile of feathers ready to bring him to a time that wasn't now…

"DO I SPEAK IN RIDDLES, GUARDIAN? YOU WILL RISE. YOU WILL RISE NOW. REPETITION IS NOT THE PROTOCOL OF VALOR."

By Fear's mercy, the voice was loud. Everyone was so loud today. He leaned up, out of a mixture of terror and duty. Had last night not been a dream? Impossible. Valor had demanded his death, and the death of Noelami. Puppets are usually the first ones to go once empires fall apart. "What do you want from me?" he asked, feeling ridiculous for speaking out loud, but knowing she heard his words.

"Guardian of old, you are to fulfill your promise to Valor and

become the next engager. Speak to the crystal girl's father and demand your right to the proper armor. I do not mince words with the wise. You will serve. You will likely perish. These naps and binges will never fill the fatigue of the heart. True rest comes at the end of duty. When it's finally deserved."

Ah, death. It always came back to death. A year ago, he had attempted his own end, but here he lay, another day, another disappointment. Now, a new goddess demanded his end a year after the other goddess had prevented it. What drew these crazed deities to him? Perhaps the broken can identify their own. So tired. So very tired. David rolled over again and rested his eyes. Nothing mortal or divine could compete with the desire for rest—

His bed was launched from the ground, sending him sprawling to the floor. "Fine!" he yelled, taking a minute before he rose. Gods, everything was sore. Losing the Herald of Fear had been a greater loss than just a blade. Reality returned. The reality of age, a dying body, a shattered mind. No more illusions. His body was too damned slow by now, maybe engager was the perfect role. Get suited in armor and a shield, stand there like a fool, then hope the rest of his team killed the enemy before he died.

Valor appeared before him. By Fear's mercy, she was beautiful, or perhaps loneliness makes everyone beautiful. Long platinum hair drifted all the way down to her legs, while her armor shimmered with a white glow that burned his eyes. Despite the burn, his gaze could never flee her scythe. It radiated power. *Real* power. Valor grabbed him by the shoulder, analyzing him like he was a zephum gladiator. Before he could admire her blue eyes, she slapped him right across the face. It was a gentle slap, but he held back a scream from the whiplash of his neck.

"I tire of these games, Guardian. The crystal girl is naive, but you are delusional. Retrieve your armor, then pledge yourself to my service. We will defend the realm. Failure is not the protocol of Valor."

It took a moment to register the audacity of being slapped. Wonder took over. This was a new goddess. A fallen mortal, a deity of pure beauty, ascended from the void by the God of Time. And yet…it wasn't his goddess. At rock bottom, through his plummet, only one woman had stood by his side. "I will fulfill my oath," he said, "but I am not yours."

Valor gripped him by the throat and picked him up. It was impossible to breathe, even pain eluded him. Deities weren't allowed to slay mortals, but perhaps she wasn't aware of such things.

"Oh? So you belong to *her*."

"Noelami…" he managed to say.

"*Fear*. No wonder she favors you. She always favored the ones lost in their delusions. Speak to the drunkard senator. Demand your armor then meet me in the gardens. You have ten minutes. After that, I will test the threshold of how much pain I am allowed to inflict on mortals." She dropped him to the floor then vanished.

David clutched his neck, gasping for air. His body begged for rest, but he had a hunch bluffing was not the protocol of Valor. He rose and drank whatever was left of his chalice of water. A quick glance at the mirror behind him where his bed used to stand brought him to a pause. This was David? This frail old man with bloodshot eyes and shadows underneath? Valor was right, he was lost in his delusions. David the engager. What a sad fate. Pyith would laugh in his face if she could see him now. But she couldn't. Most of the ones from his past couldn't. Zeen and Serenna still could. He would do it for them. Let them live the life he never had.

But not for Francis. Fuck Francis.

He drifted toward Charles at a brisk pace, uncaring if anyone found it odd. None of them had a crazed goddess threatening torture. "Senator, a moment of your time, please."

Charles laughed. "Patience, Guardian. I haven't reached the punchline of my story yet. It's a good one and, even if it's not, they must laugh! A win-win!"

"*Now.*" Back in Terrangus, the simple word had brought men to terror. David hoped the desperation hid from his face, unless that made him more intimidating.

Apparently, it did. "Pardon me for a moment, lads." Charles rose and gestured David away. "An emergency? It's not Serenna, is it?" he said as they left the halls.

"A divine emergency. Long story short: I require your finest plate armor with a sword and shield. I am to become the next engager, courtesy of the Goddess of Valor."

A sad smirk came over Charles's face. "More like courtesy of me. Does this mean you and Serenna are patched up? I respect you enough to be blunt: if it gets ugly, I will take her side. Even if she's wrong. Especially if she's wrong. Serenna is all I have left."

"If she will have me, I will serve." It felt so odd to speak it out loud. Could she truly deny him? Despite his complaints of serving the realm, it was all he had left. With Melissa gone, it was the proper way to join her: in service to the realm she had always loved.

"My girl respects you more than she ever respected me. She would never deny your aid. Trust me on that."

He did. Charles had been many things, but never a liar. They turned the corner to the armory, at the very bottom of the citadel. An odd chamber. Despite the array of swords and armors, the dank aroma made it feel more like a wine cellar.

"Oh, stop that look," Charles said. "The true armory is in the bastion and I'm not taking that trip after last night. We keep this here in case of emergencies. See anything you like?"

No, he thought, but kept it inside. Hmm. Surely he had passed the ten-minute mark, but no horrible agony assaulted him. Still, it would be wise to choose quickly. Most of the armor seemed like a variation of Serenna's mail, but—

"That one," David said, approaching a display of full plate armor with a sword and shield. The shield had the Mylor insignia of the pale owl with ebony eyes forged into the design. "It's nearly perfect. Do you have a shield without the owl?"

"You wear my armor, you wear my bird," Charles said with a grin.

"Fine. Can you help me get this on?" He struggled to get his legs through the holes. Unlike leather, it was all so…limiting. Maybe stifling was the better word. After he got the lower part on, his heavy plate on a hot summer day already drew sweat. How the hell did any zephum ever tolerate such discomfort? Charles helped him fit the upper-plate down from above his head. Oh, it was *heavy*. What a bizarre feeling, some balanced mixture of protective and lethargic. Taking blows had never been his style. Since it only takes one blade to end a life, the obvious solution is to take zero blades. "Thank you. It feels…off." He could barely see Charles study him through the limited view of his helmet, so he removed it. "Better."

Charles rubbed his chin. "It's less majestic now that I can see your face again. Put it back on and get used to it. Not wearing a helmet basically screams out 'please target my head.'"

*

David approached the Mylor gardens in his full plate armor, wielding his new sword and shield. A few bystanders on the way had stared at him, likely having no idea who he was. The helmet blocking most of his view was still odd. Even as a drinker it rattled him; he had learned to navigate the spins and blurs of reality, but somehow an obstructed clarity was more confusing.

"Valor?" he asked out loud. Noelami had always preferred to speak first. Perhaps a habit from being Empress…

"Defend yourself!" she said, appearing on the other side of the garden. Despite the humid breeze of the summer morning, Valor's scythe made him shiver. "From this moment forward, both of our lives are in your hands. Allow me to slay you, and we shall fade together into the void."

He kept his knees loose and clutched his shield. If her crystal spikes were at Serenna's level—they were likely well beyond that—blocking with one-hand would break his arm. He threw the sword to the ground and held his shield with both hands, the way he had seen Mary do.

But instead of spikes, she rushed forward, letting out a deep battle-cry. For all his complaints about a lack of vision, the glowing scythe was perfectly clear as it flew down towards him. He resisted the first instinct to dive out of the way and flung his shield up to match her blade. Their weapons clashed, and a burning agony shot through David's arms. A sloppy block, the kind Pyith would've made. *I'm not a giant lizard-man. I have to use Mary's technique or I'll never leave these gardens.*

Valor pulled back and swung again, aimed at his head. Despite Charles's words of wisdom, his helmet wouldn't block a damn thing if David relied on it. He pushed his shield up again, this time meeting the scythe at a curved angle instead of dead center. Less pain, but his right leg gave out, temporarily sending him to one knee. He immediately rose despite the pain; mercy was unlikely the protocol of Valor.

And it wasn't. She jabbed his gut with the wooden end of the scythe to shove him off balance, then took her right hand off the scythe and punched him directly in the helmet. Any normal person's hand would have shattered on contact, but she didn't lose a step. Instead of following through, she stepped back, clutching her scythe and radiating a harsh platinum glow. A single crystal spike formed in front of her, a freezing chill emanating from the pure-platinum haze. They met eyes for a fading moment, her judgment piercing him. Was she mad? No mortal in the realm could defend against such force. Well, after having been defeated by Arrogance, dying from Valor seemed a fair fate.

He smirked as he clutched his shield. *So be it, Goddess. Send us to our end.*

The spike flew forward. He could only stare at it for a moment before the platinum glow burned his vision. David clutched his shield and closed his eyes. There was a faint impact, then he laughed. He laughed like she had told the greatest joke in the realm. "Why am I still alive?"

"Because I allow it. You gazed upon your inevitable death and smiled. No mentor in the realm can teach such valor. It takes either infinite courage or infinite despair to accept the inevitable. I will allow you to write your own judgment on which journey comes to pass."

"Forgive me if I don't thank you."

"Perhaps you will after this. Hand me your shield."

David handed her the shield, hoping she would remove the ridiculous owl design. Instead, she pressed her hand against it, surrounding the shield with a burning platinum glow that eventually settled.

"Use it well, Engager," she said, handing it back. "This was a sufficient introduction, but your form is embarrassing. Take your rest and we shall continue tomorrow. Oh, and David?"

He paused; she had never used his actual name. The shield felt the same in his hands, despite whatever she had done to it.

"While we train, you will not partake in your poison. You will *suffer* if this condition is not met."

Her words crushed him, but he held back a smile, anyway.

Just like with Fear, the conversation always ended with an unnecessary threat. Some desperate attempt to confirm who held the power, as if there was any doubt.

CHAPTER 33

THE GODS ALWAYS WIN

ary tried to rub her belly through her plate armor. A robe or cloth would've been more practical this late in her pregnancy, but in a kingdom of enemies, it wasn't worth the risk. She had left Francis in their chambers early in the morning. Only the gods knew when he had woken up, but she had found him by his own dresser, staring at the Herald of Arrogance in dissociated awe. Damn that staff. Damn it to hell. Mary would always love Francis, but after yesterday, it was time to love him from a distance. All those people. The way they had burned. All those screams, all those yells. Her own yells…

Mylor. The only reasonable destination. With Serenna, Five, and David already there, they could put their minds together and find a way to bring Francis back. To save her future husband, the father of her child. But after yesterday, they may just arrest her or send her back immediately. What sane kingdom would want to deal with Vanguards and tyrants? She held back a laugh at the idea of Mylor ever coming to Terrangus's aid. But that was her life now.

The guards nodded and opened the castle gates as she approached, to the second sunny, beautiful day in a row. Maybe they saw her determination, because neither of them announced her name as she left. Poor fools. She had saved them the first time her actions got them to meet Francis's judgment. If there was a next time, it would probably be the last time.

Walk casually. Vanguards were all over the military district. Gods, there were so many of them now. Most stopped and stared at her, but none approached or said a word. Like cats, they watched their 'master' drift towards her eventual demise. Cats will interfere for food and scratches, but once satisfied, cats will never interrupt a mistake. *Don't panic. Act like the so-called empress of Terrangus.* As far as she knew, Vanguards couldn't read her thoughts. Francis certainly couldn't read her thoughts, emotions, or anything that wasn't from a book. It didn't seem Arrogance could either, or she never would've made it out of the castle.

Some soldiers met her eyes and immediately glanced down and walked off in a different direction. May they never know how badly their terror wounded her. It was never supposed to be this way. In hindsight, Francis and Mary had not even the slightest clue on how to rule a kingdom. It had just been so tempting. After saving the realm, how could she have turned down the opportunity to guide it? We all dream of being ruler, but none of those dreams ever hold the blueprints of what ruling actually is.

I'll never see my mother or sister again. They were all set to come for the wedding, but she could only pray they would find an excuse not to come now. They were probably counting down the days until Mary's last name changed to Haide, to avoid the stigma of sharing a title with a murderer. An empress of death. 'Oh, Mary? I never heard of her,' Mom would say.

Gods above and below forgive her, but she felt a slight sense relief that her father was gone. He had always been about 'doing the right thing' and 'dignity' and all those other phrases that sound great but don't really mean anything.

She took a deep breath and walked through the trade district. Maybe the portal in the Guardian room would have been a better choice, but any excuse to leave the castle was a welcome one. The true danger lingered here. People with nothing to lose are always the most vicious and, thanks to Francis and Mary, there were plenty of people with no future and sharpened blades. Her golden armor was a blessing and a curse. It protected her, but made her known.

Still, there are advantages to being feared. More than several people noticed her, but unlike the subtle glances of the military district, these people fled. They fled as if she was about to burn them alive with the Herald of Arrogance. The cruel irony of marriage: we never inherit our partner's achievements, but our new last name always carries their burdens. *How did we get here? How did I ever allow this?* Her son kicked, as if answering her monologue. Oh, poor baby Calvin. He may never know the true Francis: the kind-hearted man with all the answers to the questions no one bothered to ask.

That man was gone or, at least, missing. She could save him. Saving Francis was the first step, then the rest of the kingdom…well, that would work itself out eventually. Just like Father had used to say, 'peace comes one day at a time.' Father was dead, but that didn't diminish his words—

A hand grabbed her shoulder. "Mary? What brings you out here on such a fine day?" Nyfe said. Fuck Vanguard Omega, his name was Nyfe.

"Taking a stroll. Don't ever touch my shoulder again. What are you even doing out here?"

"I do what I'm told. You should try it sometime. For some reason, my mere presence seems to inspire terror. I cannot fathom why."

"Well, I'll leave you to…being you. Can't imagine how pitiful that must be."

"It's like being you, but better! So, where are we off to? Hmm. Full armor on a hot summer morning… You're fleeing, aren't you? How scandalous. Did you inform our god? He gets rather grouchy when left out of important decisions."

She took a deep breath. Can't make a scene; if other Vanguards were involved this could become a nightmare. "Your god is not my god."

"He will be everyone's god soon enough. Listen Mary, out of all the people that plague our realm, you annoy me the least, so here's the deal: mortals never win. I've seen Death, I've seen Fear, I've seen…Arrogance. They always win."

Mary nearly laughed. Nyfe's ridiculous monologues had made sense back in the day, but after seeing him for the coward he was, the words meant nothing. "You poor fool. Death lost in this very kingdom, and I bet Arrogance won't win, either. You know, at one point, I believed in you. Thought you were the smartest man in the realm. But you don't know a damned thing, do you? Goodbye, Nyfe. I hope you find some speck of happiness in this travesty you call a life." She marched forward, heart beating, baby kicking. *Ignore them all. Just keep moving forward.* Away from Nyfe before he could call her out for being a liar. She was terrified, but giving up was never an option. Father had never given up, and neither would she.

Trekking forward, she was nearly out of breath and had to pee. Why having a baby meant more trips to the chamber pot was anyone's guess. *Almost there. Almost there.* So many Vanguards on the streets of Terrangus. Her sister would scream at the outrage. How much of this was Mary's fault? *Almost there.*

Her plate boots sank into the grassy terrain of the outskirts, and the portal was straight ahead. Fucking Terrangus couldn't have the courtesy to rain. That sun pounded against her plate, drawing sweat, reminding her of how thirsty she had become in the past hour. But, almost there. Three Vanguards guarded the portal. By this point she had no idea who any of them were. In simpler days, back when it was Vanguards One through Five, they just patrolled the trade district and sighed a lot. Far too many of them now.

All three Vanguards watched her approach. It was more unsettling that none of them spoke. *I am the empress. It's time to act that way.* "Vanguards, open the portal to Mylor. Now." None of them responded, standing there motionless with cat-like suspicion in their eyes.

"A moment please," the middle one said. His shoulders slumped and his face grew dissociated, the kind of stare visitors would give after listening to Francis discuss economic theory. He then tensed up and said, "God has spoken. Pardon me, Empress, but your request is denied. Please make your way back to the castle. We can provide escort, if necessary."

"Open the portal to Mylor. I will not ask again," she said, clenching her fist. She spoke the words well but they meant nothing. Once fear is gone, threats are just another form of begging. Well, at least they hadn't tried to kill her yet. *They're just waiting for my son. They will take him away from me. They will make him into another Francis...*

"Empress—"

It was all too much. She drew her sword, even though she could never defeat them all. If they must take her, let them work for it. "I said *now.*"

"Please do not resist," the left one said as he approached. "This is for your own good. The true wonder of Serenity is guiding those lost to their paradise." He took her hand—the one not holding a sword—with a surprisingly gentle grip. If they had orders not to harm her, could she use that to her advantage? What would David do in this position—

She flinched as a glass-like dagger tore into the Vanguard's neck. His grip went from gentle to nothing as the body collapsed. "I don't have long before I lose control," Nyfe said, rushing towards the next one. "Be a good Mary and kill that one, will you?"

If he had worded it any other way, perhaps she would've listened. She clutched her sword and watched Nyfe swing at the next Vanguard. He got a slight cut against his neck, but the Vanguard was able to deflect most of the strike with his staff. The third Vanguard radiated a dark blue. How odd, that after all the absurd scenarios Nyfe had survived, a nameless Vanguard would be the one to do him in.

"Help me, you fool!" he yelled. That was more like it. A spray of blue flew towards them, then Nyfe spun the Vanguard he was entangled with to take the brunt of the blast. The Vanguard's back froze before Nyfe pushed him to the ground with enough force to shatter him. Nyfe rushed at the final Vanguard, who launched another blast of ice towards him. Nyfe dove under to dodge, but landed awkwardly at the Vanguard's boots. A swift kick to the head rattled Nyfe, then the Vanguard rained down blows from his staff.

"I...told you," Nyfe said, huddled on the ground trying to defend himself. "The gods always win. I can't blame you for being afraid. Gods...love their cowards."

What a ridiculous scenario. She hated them both. Nyfe was less trustworthy, but if he was the enemy of Arrogance, maybe there could be some common ground. *Am I nuts?* How would a cat handle this? A cat would probably kill them both, but that would mean no portal. Dammit, she already knew the answer.

Mary took the shield from her back and slammed it into the Vanguard's skull. Maybe it was more force than necessary, but she had no idea how powerful these things were. He lay on the ground motionless. Hmm. Maybe that had been too much. She waited for dread, regret, all those other emotions, but none of them came. Let this be a lesson to those who would say no to the empress of Terrangus.

"Just like old times, huh?" Nyfe said as he struggled to rise. "I... I...ugh." He pointed his glass dagger at the portal and it erupted in a pale glow. "God is...taking control. Bring me with you. I think his influence fades the farther I am from here. I...don't...just take me with you."

Gods, he looked pathetic. Sadly enough, there was a small part of her wanting to help. *Small* being the key word. The other parts understood that bringing Nyfe to Mylor would lead to her immediate demise the moment Serenna noticed him. Can't save everyone, and baby Calvin would always be at the top of that list.

"Sorry Nyfe. It's not that the gods always win, it's that you always lose." She ignored his desperate cries as she entered the portal.

*

Nausea rushed up her chest as she materialized in the Mylor portal. She took a deep breath to force it down, making a mental note to limit her use of portals while pregnant. Everything was so blurry, men were yelling... Which room was this? Wobbly table, white walls, barrels of water... Ah, the Guardian room; it brought back memories. She had used this portal to engage Harbinger Nyfe. A bit ironic in hindsight—

"Terrangus invasion! Summon the senator! Summon Serenna!"

"Close the portals now! Let none pass!"

"Relax, I come in peace." *What would Francis say? Oh gods, he is going to be furious.* "Escort me to Guardian Serenna at once."

The closest one drew a sword to her neck. Issuing orders may not have been the best choice in a hostile kingdom. "Slowly drop your sword and shield. Follow our orders and no harm will come to you or the child."

The audacity. He wasn't *the child*. He was Calvin Haide. This scrawny little man had some nerve. "I will drop nothing other than you if you mention my child again. Escort me to Serenna or find someone who will."

Maybe the blood on her shield convinced him to rethink his station. "Wait here. We'll bring our Guardian to you."

A few minutes passed. It felt absurd to be guarded by ten or so men, as if she could waddle over and start bashing them all with her shield. Such is the price of fear. Well, when Serenna arrived, what would Mary say? What was the plan here? Beg for help?

Serenna entered the room and everyone stepped aside. If they feared Mary, they either were terrified of Serenna or revered her as a goddess. "By Valor's grace... Mary? What are you doing in *my* kingdom?" She had a nasty tone to her voice, as if this visit interrupted some much larger problem. On that note, where was Zeen?

"I come seeking aid. Unrest has risen in Terrangus, and I fear..." She paused. Speaking like this never came naturally. Fuck it. "Alright, listen. I fled. Arrogance has corrupted Francis, and now the Vanguards are imposing martial law on my people. I need your help to save Francis and fix all this."

The puzzled glances from all the soldiers in the room didn't fill her with confidence. To be fair, the words sounded more ridiculous after she had spoken them out loud. Serenna's glare made it worse. "So you come here? Just like that I am to trust you no longer serve Arrogance? How convenient."

"Serenna...where else would I go?"

"Not here. Never here. You bring war to my doorstep!"

Mary took a deep breath, sweat pouring down her forehead. All of her hopes were crashing down. "There won't be a war. It's just me. The empress stands alone." The words came out barely a whisper.

"With Terrangus it always comes down to war, regardless of who sits on the throne. Return home. Unless invited, do not return here again." Serenna triggered the portal. The black eruption nearly brought tears to Mary's eyes. "Farewell, Empress. In better days, I would wish you well."

*

Mary materialized in the Terrangus throne room. She made no effort to battle the nausea as she fell to her knees and vomited onto the floor. The Vanguards by the portal glanced at her, barely acknowledging the fact their empress appeared, then they all smiled and closed their eyes.

"My dear Mary!" Wisdom's voice echoed through the room. "What a relief to see our runaway empress return home. How was your journey? Or do I even need to ask?"

"You knew? Of course you did…"

Wisdom chuckled as he appeared in front of her. "Divinity suits me well, but I'll always carry a passion towards teaching. Ah, a professor's burden to teach never fades…never fades. So, tell me: what did we learn today?"

She tried to rise, but despair overpowered her rage. It was all for nothing. "Our fates have become one. We either win together, or we both die."

"Close! I award you a B for effort. The answer I was looking for is…" Wisdom raised his hand, levitating Mary to her feet. His mask and voice shifted to the Arrogance version. "The gods always win. This is your final opportunity to serve the winning side. I have a *nasty* tendency to make meddling mothers disappear. Do I make myself clear?"

"My answer no longer matters. I have no one but you."

CHAPTER 34

BROKEN WARLORD

empest opened his eyes in awe. He had slept! For how long, it didn't matter. Obviously nowhere near a full night, but anything is more than nothing. Yesterday and today were now two separate entities. As it should be. As it must be.

He rose and grabbed his walking stick from the side of his bed, slowing his enthusiasm to match his body. Joy from sleep. He nearly laughed at the absurdity, but it's important to take victories when offered. Another meeting of the council today, and they would finally face a rested Tempest. No more dissociation, blurred vision, stuttered words, they would cower before their intellectual superior. Well, maybe not cower, but they would finally respect their future warlord.

The warm waters of his bath embraced him as he submerged himself. He probably reeked from however many days of no bathing, it was difficult to know without Pyith wrinkling her snout at him... *Ah, my love. Forgive me for what I must do. I did not choose this...and yet, what is the alternative? Nothing could ever replace you.*

Nothing but lies.

He would marry Bloom. It was a fair offer. A purely

loveless engagement of course. She wanted the title, not the decisions. With her protection, Tempest could fulfill their dream of a greater Vaynex. Not in the way any sane zephum would have predicted, but fulfill, nonetheless...

And he had made progress on *Rinso Volume IV!* It had become abundantly clear the story should have been a trilogy, but he had expanded the world to keep his imaginative people going. The story must continue. Not for the ones in the story, but for everyone else. Zeen had done a fair job offering his input; it was nice to converse with someone who truly loved the work as opposed to someone who only loved the one writing it.

It was tempting to invite Zeen to the council meeting for protection, but it was time for Tempest to be Tempest. *I am the future warlord of Vaynex. Son of Sardonyx Claw. If I can overcome my own depression, an economic one should be possible to defeat.*

Some enthusiasm faded as he stared at himself in the mirror. It was like meeting the new Tempest for the first time. Wrinkles all over his snout, circles under his eyes, and...pain. Pain had manifested, it ages us faster than time itself can only dream. *It's not like I have ever been beautiful. My injury doesn't change that.* The zephum staring at him in the mirror only brought confusion. Pyith had loved him. Truly loved him. How had that been possible? He turned away and walked forward. The doubts were returning. Doubt can be an undefeatable enemy. He filled a jug with water and exited his chambers.

Tempest was first to arrive at the meeting, leaning back against his seat and grinning. The one who could barely move arrived first. What a testament to zephum laziness. Oh, there was Father, with every step of his armored frame inviting more doubt. Tempest could never be such a warlord. Who could? The council was basically a shadow of honor, an ode to those born with the right set of physical attributes to pretend leadership was their right.

The council entered, in rank fitting to their usefulness. Pentule first, then Dubnok and Novalore. Pentule nodded at Tempest, but the other two sat without a word, whispering to each other and offering quick glances. Hmm. Something was wrong. When fools attempt subtlety, best prepare for the worst. Tempest cleared his throat to get his father's attention, but the old fool was preoccupied with his own nonsense. How could he not see it?

By Strength's name, something is amiss.

Sardonyx rose, silencing the room with his presence. "Warmakers, you *reek* of dissent. As Warlord, I demand to hear of your troubles. Let them be known as words before I acknowledge them as blades."

Oh? Perhaps Father was not a fool. He obviously felt the lingering hatred in the air too. Something terrible was about to happen. Dubnok cleared his throat, then said, "Sardonyx, as you are well aware—"

Sardonyx pounded his sword into the ground. Humans preferred odd hand gestures for whatever reason, but nothing creates silence faster than fear. "The dishonor in your eyes speaks volumes. If this is the path you have chosen, then choose it well. You only get one opportunity to challenge the warlord. Such a choice leads only to the throne or beneath the sand."

Novalore rose, drawing his sword. The sheer audacity of the act stole Tempest's breath. Pyith's father...a traitor? It was a blessing she couldn't see him now. "Choice, you say? Choice was robbed from me when you sent this...*thing* to battle beside my daughter."

Sardonyx sighed. "True warriors never make excuses. You shame the mighty Pyith by latching her demise to my son. You may be her father, and *you* may be her life-mate," he said, glaring at Tempest, "but I always knew her best. She now smiles upon us all, from the Great Plains in the Sky."

"More lies!" Dubnok said, drawing his sword. "Your collaboration with the so-called 'Human Warlord' ended the possibility of such glory. We are alone now, *Claw*. It is time to adapt to our new reality by controlling it!"

Tempest grabbed his walking stick and began to rise before Pentule grabbed his shoulder. "Nothing personal, old friend," he said before his grip tightened. "I will never ask for your forgiveness, but know dishonor shall haunt my dreams."

You too? By Strength's name—

Pentule threw him to the ground right on his bad leg. How cruel that it couldn't help him walk but still offered pain. To say the doubt returned would be an understatement. He hobbled away, grabbing his walking stick, one of the few things still familiar to him in the chaos.

Father roared, sending the citadel guards into a panic. Maybe not panic? Several rushed over, some to his side, others by the traitors'. Not a fair fight numbers wise, but putting a quantitative value on Sardonyx's power was a fool's task.

Tempest crawled behind the throne to catch his breath. The rings of steel and yells of victory and death crashed in the citadel. *I will never be Warlord. Father shouldn't have to die for my weakness. Pyith already did. What a miserable end, to be the albatross of the Claw name.* Part of him had known it would always end in violence. The delusions of peace could only linger so far…

"*Tempest… Tempest, Tempest. It always intrigues me to watch mortals eradicate their own. You lizard-people always yell and roar and struggle for power, clinging to strength like my fallen child clung to my dagger. Strength and power are not alike. You know of one, but dream of the other. Let me answer your dreams, Broken Warlord. Accept my gift. Speak my words… I am nothing. I am forever. I am the end.*"

Tempest shivered. It was tempting, and Death knew it.

Serenna had known it all that time ago. Tempest had seen true power the day Nyfe had stepped outside Terrangus castle and destroyed the entire structure. Tempest was supposed to die that day, but Julius and Reilly had taken his place. More dead because of him. The list went on and on, all due to his weakness. These traitors would kill Father, then surely he was next. If only Bloom was here. He hated himself for the thought, but it was a fair one. Anyone but Death…

A pained scream howled from behind. He wouldn't check, but the voice was too high-pitched to be Sardonyx. Perhaps he was winning? If there was anyone who could defy such odds, it was Father.

"Vile cowards!" Sardonyx yelled, followed by a crash of steel, then a loud thud. "Human Warlord! Battle by my side! We will send these traitors to the sand. And it will be glorious!"

Tempest finally leaned against the throne to check on the battle. To his shock, Zeen rushed over to Sardonyx. Zeen dodged a sloppy strike from Dubnok, then slashed straight across his neck. The warmaker clutched the wound and collapsed, gasping for air. Just like that, Warmaker Dubnok was slain. One of the most miserable avatars of regressive leadership, murdered in his own citadel by a human.

Tempest nearly fainted. The aid was welcome, but with Zeen slaying a warmaker, war was all but guaranteed if the Claws fell. Perhaps it was always guaranteed. He grabbed his walking stick, using adrenaline to force himself up. "Stop this madness! Stop it at once!"

They all ignored him of course. He nearly tripped on a dead guard's tail, having no idea if the fallen zephum was a traitor or a hero. Either title would be dependent on whoever won today. If only he could get Zeen's attention. Whatever the consequences, Zeen could not die here. Even if it meant the Claw's end. A dead human Guardian would mean the end of

Vaynex. Complete unification of humans against zephum. The end they had always feared, manifested by slaying Strength's chosen.

Sardonyx roared and fell to the ground, clutching his side. Zeen's sword flew across the citadel, then a quick punch to the gut sent him falling right next to him. Pentule and Novalore stood above them both, surrounded by the remaining guards.

"Don't kill the human!" Tempest said, his hand shaking as he clutched his stick. "If you slay a Guardian, you slay our future. I cannot prevent you from taking the citadel, but I beg you not to rush its demise. Please... *Please*."

Novalore sheathed his sword and approached with an ignorant grin filling his face. "By Strength's name, I'll never understand what she saw in you. Just...*look* at you. Pyith was supposed to rule this kingdom. To give us a home to be proud of. Vaynex! A Vaynex of warriors! Conquerors! Not...whatever you are."

"Well, your dreams have come to pass. We are again rooted to the past by a murderer's ambitions. If it fills the void in your heart, take my life if you must. It no longer matters. Perhaps it never did." Tempest turned around and faced the empty spot where the God of Strength had used to stand. Like a tiny void in a room of chaos, the emptiness would eventually consume them all. "Spare the human. Do not ruin our home more than you already have."

"On one condition," Novalore said, widening his grin. "Kneel and call me Warlord. I want to hear the words from your broken tongue. After all these years of tolerating your weakness...I *need* it."

"NEVER!" Sardonyx yelled from the ground, only to take another boot to the face. "My son, let the three of us die in peace. We will be united in the Great Plains in the Sky..."

No. We won't. We will close our eyes and know what it is to fade. Tempest kneeled. "I yield my status as Warmaster Tempest Claw, and humbly accept the reign of Warlord Tellex Novalore."

"*No!*" Sardonyx yelled, but it came out as more of a howl.

"Good. Very good," Novalore said. "Pentule, kill the human. Slowly."

By the grace of whatever gods still remained, Pentule didn't draw his sword. "That wasn't the plan. If we kill Zeen, Mylor will march upon us. If we spare him and war against Alanammus, Mylor will remain neutral. We must pick our battles."

Novalore shot him a glare, his grin fading entirely. "You defy your warlord? This human killed one of our own!"

Tempest sighed. If they were already bickering, this alliance would be dead in the sand before summer's end.

"I advise," Pentule said, "not defy. Let us relish today's victory without inviting tomorrow's defeat. Banish the human, then we can publicly execute the Claws and seal our position by tomorrow's sunrise.

Sardonyx struggled to breathe, favoring his right side. "An *execution?* You would deny me an honorable death? By Strength's name…what will become of Vaynex? Forgive me, dear Vitala. Save me a spot by your side in the Great Plains in the Sky. I am prepared to join you."

"Go," Novalore said, pushing Zeen towards the exit. "A fair warning: by decree of Warlord Novalore, any outsider who enters our portals shall die. Spread the word to your human lords."

Tempest met eyes with the wounded Zeen. "Go," he whispered. "Be safe. We will prevail. The Claws always do." Zeen nodded and was escorted out by two guards.

Bless Zeen for believing him, if he did. The Claws would never prevail again. The only hope now was for a quick death, but based on the fury in Novalore's eyes, that hope was as dead as their god.

CHAPTER 35

DANCING WITH THE TRUTH

ilence lingered in the Mylor Guardian room after Serenna had banished Mary. Perhaps it had been cruel but nothing was worth the risk of war. "Well?" she asked, staring down her guards. "Do you object? Speak! Silent opinions hold no value."

"These are not days for mercy," Captain Martin had the audacity to say. Martin, the coward who had abandoned his post outside of Zeen's quarters. "If it were a year ago, you would have done what was necessary."

Murder a pregnant woman? Could such evil possibly be true? If it was, Serenna was happier than she would dare show that the thought was inconceivable now. She didn't want this. She wanted Zeen. A quiet getaway, whether one day or forever, a time to be happy. Content. Any of those feelings the realm constantly kept from her reach.

Well, after she was done yelling at him. What is it about poor liars that inspires them to keep trying? Ugh, in the madness, she had forgotten about Tempest. About Archon Gabriel's ludicrous plan. Too many of the realm's problems were converging around Mylor, as they always did. The pressure pressed against her skull. Where was Everleigh? Where was

Zeen? *And*, where was Father, the supposed leader of this kingdom?

"What in the platinum hells," Charles said, huffing out of breath at the entrance. "Is this a joke? Where is the invasion?"

Serenna sheathed her staff across her back. "It's handled. Listen, get your priorities in order. If I weren't here, we would be at war with Terrangus before nightfall." She normally wouldn't berate him in public, but it wasn't the day.

"What exactly was handled?" Charles asked, studying the room. Her father was no scholar, but he likely noticed the lack of blood or evidence of a struggle.

Captain Martin stepped forward before Serenna could respond. Why was he suddenly so hostile? "Lord Senator, the Empress Mary Walker entered through our portal, but Serenna allowed her safe exit—"

"*Allow?*" Serenna said with a scowl. What dignified man would refer to her father as 'Lord Senator?' "Have you already forgotten the horrors of last year? I dragged myself to that bastion every day. I still feel the blood on my skin. The screams from both sides. The near loss of my home." She still felt the other things too. To end an entire roomful of soldiers in one spell. To absorb their essences. She never spoke of such things. Not to Father, not to Zeen...

Not to anyone.

Martin didn't back down, his glare deepened as they met eyes. "Then act like it. Stop behaving like a school-girl and...dallying with the enemy. Such shame is beneath you."

Serenna drew her staff—

"Get out," her father said. "I don't care where. Just not here. All of you. I will speak to our Guardian alone." Anytime it was 'our Guardian' and not 'my daughter' Dad was clearly annoyed.

She clutched her staff as they all left. Martin had always

been kind to her. What changed? "That fool," she said out loud, even though Father was the only one still in the Guardian room. "All those days we fought together in the bastion, and he dares question my loyalty? In public? He will suffer for the insult."

Charles laughed; it only made her more angry. "I assure you, my dear, the man has suffered already. He won't realize it for years but I did him a favor worth his weight in gold by sending him to guard that door. Your heart was never his. Never will be."

"What the hell are you talking about?"

"Nothing that concerns you. Now, speak truthfully about your encounter with Mary. Spare no detail."

She took a deep breath and recounted the events. In hindsight, it had been a rather quick encounter considering the possible ramifications. She had made the correct choice. No war, no violence. Let Terrangus handle the psychotic god they had welcomed with open arms. "Are you disappointed?" she finally asked, if only to break the silence.

To her surprise, Charles hugged her with a firm embrace. "Only because I think the world of you. My dear, you have always been the best of us. Which unfortunately means you have the farthest to fall. Nothing changes us quicker than children or war. If I can bestow anything upon you in my sixty-four years, let it be that."

Serenna went stiff in his arms. Bless him for not trying to let go. Mary wasn't the enemy. She had battled Nyfe by her side both times in Terrangus. It had seemed like a play by Arrogance. By imprisoning the empress or offering her asylum, it gave Terrangus an excuse to enact another war. She couldn't handle another one. Not when she had everything she ever wanted. "I will do better. I swear to it."

"Shh," Charles whispered, letting go. "Don't be so hard on yourself. I'm not powerful or good looking, so being forced to rely on my senses has made them wise. In all fairness you made a safe choice. It gives us time to reconvene. At some point, we *will* have to deal with Arrogance. And by we, I mean you."

"I know—" She flinched as the portal erupted again. It was closed off from Terrangus, so who could it be?

Oh. Zeen materialized. He obviously couldn't bear the thought of being away from her. She would forgive him in time, as soon as—

"*Zeen!*" she yelled and rushed over. His sword eased out of his hands as he rolled over on the ground, huffing for air with tears in his eyes. Blood seeped out of his leather armor and his right eye was completely swollen. "Who has done this? Give me names! I will kill them! I will kill them *all!*" She steadied her breathing and cupped his face. He still breathed. Her love was bruised but none of the injuries appeared life threatening.

"Vaynex," he forced out. "Mutiny. The Claws…need our help. Tempest. We must… Tempest."

"Mutiny?" Charles said, rubbing his chin. "Oh my. That does not bode well for anyone."

"Serenna, forgive me for dancing with the truth," Zeen said, groaning as she helped him rise. "Trying to make everyone happy just made them all angry. Dark days…may be on the horizon."

Oh, Zeen. Dark days are always on the horizon, she thought, balancing herself as Zeen leaned on her. He must have been truly injured to put so much weight on her. Mutiny? She could only hope Sardonyx was well. Such a thought would have never come before last year, but oddly enough, the giant zephum had become her family. Like a giant uncle with a tail, one who never brought gifts and said '*Glorious!*' a lot.

"I will always forgive you, Zeen. No matter how much you harm me. I am yours, and you are mine. Forever."

"Forever," he said with a faint smile. Father was kind enough to take the hint and go elsewhere.

As Serenna carried Zeen to his chambers, she considered discussing Mary's visit but opted not to. Withholding information and lying are not the same thing, at least when she did it. She groaned as she opened the door with one hand, taking most of his weight on her right side.

Zeen dropped like a stone when she let go of him onto his bed. She shuffled around the desk and found a flask to fill with water; it wasn't much but hopefully it could relieve his dry wheezing. Her poor Zeen was a mess. "Thank you," he said, drinking the whole thing in one gulp. "The warmakers revolted against the Claws. I believe Novalore led the mutiny, though Pentule seemed to call the shots at the end…"

She nodded, though honestly she had no idea who these people were. As far as she was concerned, the hierarchy was Sardonyx then Tempest. After that, it was just giant lizards with dramatic titles. "Shh, my dear. Save your strength. When the time is right, we shall take retribution. No one harms my love and survives. *No one.*" For the first time in a while, she yearned for Valor's scythe. Make those beasts think twice before attacking her family. Ah, what a rush it had been to wield such power. To make the Goddess of Fear acknowledge Serenna as an equal…

"Serenna?"

"Sorry," she said, clearing her head. Far too much to worry about; the worst thing she could do right now was make a hasty decision… Another hasty decision. She needed a place to think. Somewhere peaceful. The gardens. "Zeen, rest your eyes. When you wake, I will be the first thing you see." She kissed him before he could respond. That was his cue to say yes.

"Very well. I love you," he said with a smile, then rolled over onto his side. He would have looked adorable lying there, if not for the bruises all over his face. Trickles of blood seeped into the sheets. To be fair, they likely needed to be changed, anyway.

Okay. Healing mage, then gardens. Serenna went the long way to avoid her father, not in the mood to hear his opinions on how to handle Vaynex. She grabbed Vanguard Five from the corridors, then kindly explained that despite whatever his current task, he was now Zeen's healing mage for the day. "Give him anything he needs. Expense is irrelevant." She left after a confirmation nod.

Serenna approached the gardens... What was that sound? Like a clash of platinum energy against plate armor. Since when did soldiers train in *her* gardens? She caught her breath at the sight of Everleigh slashing her scythe down, crashing against a warrior's shield. The grunt sounded familiar, whoever it was had a steel resolve to stand their ground against a goddess. However, whoever it was seemed a bit out of practice. A sloppy block knocked him to the ground, sending his helmet a few feet behind him, revealing...

"David?" she asked, cocking her head to the side. Despite the absurdity of seeing him sprawled out on the grass in plate armor, it was definitely him. "What in the realm are you doing?"

"Taking his final breath if this were a true battle!" Valor said, sheathing her scythe. "My purpose was to work on his form, but the lesson so far has been teaching him the threshold of mortal pain. He is slow, aging...and *eager*. With more time I shall make an engager out of him yet. Mark my words, crystal girl."

Serenna stood there in silence as David struggled to rise. *Why is she teaching him? Did she give up on me?*

"Close that gaping maw! Envy is not the protocol of Valor. Since you have decided to spend your time coupling with the Terrangus boy, I have prioritized my efforts on this one. He couples with nothing but regret. The perfect engager."

Serenna could only imagine how red her face became. Her

first night with a man in years and suddenly she was the kingdom harlot. "*Fine.* Then I'll leave you to…this."

"Wait!" David said, sheathing his sword. "Serenna, we must speak. Please."

The weakness in his voice nearly dissipated her anger, but Everleigh fading without a word brought it all back. She took a deep breath, then said, "Well, I am here. In *my* gardens. Speak."

David eased towards her in his full armor, sweat pouring down his bald head. He stopped in front of her and paused, creating an awkward silence as they met eyes. "I…this is difficult for me."

"We have always maintained a professional relationship. I find in these scenarios, it is best to just speak." *Oh, if only me from nine years ago could see this, she would faint.*

"Then I shall," David said, falling to one knee. "Serenna Morgan. Guardian of Mylor… Will you allow me the privilege to serve as your engager? I will not beg, but please know that my only remaining purpose is to protect the realm. I have reached the point where yesterday will never be more beautiful than tomorrow. The point where—"

"Stop!" she said and helped him up. "You are not defined by your mistakes, and neither am I." Gods, was there an official way to do this? Did she have to run it by the others? Hmm. Ironically enough, David never did. There was a tradition worth keeping. "David Williams, it would be an honor to have you return by my side as a Guardian. This is contingent on you never wielding the Herald of Fear again. Do you accept?"

They met eyes for a moment, his glare asking the question words could not: would she still pursue the Herald of Valor? Perhaps. Perhaps not. Again, withholding information is not the same as lying. "I do," he said, then grinned. "My contingencies seem to increase each day. It brings great relief to see the realm in your care. Melissa… Melissa would have been proud." He put his helmet back on before the tears fell from his eyes, then drifted further into the gardens.

"Thank you," she said. If David could hear, he did not respond.

CHAPTER 36

TEARS OF THE MAELSTROM

h, was that the sun? Tempest's eyes twitched at his desk. Night and day converged into a continuous stream of despair, a torture without words or blades. The traitors had locked him in his chambers after a beating, not having the courtesy to apprehend him with chains or rope. They didn't care. It was only Tempest. The Broken Warlord that never was.

With nothing else to accomplish, the plan had been to finish *Rinso Volume - IV*. Odd, how we cling to such absurdities when the end draws near. He dipped his pen into the ink. The story was nowhere near completed, but perhaps someone could… No. The only ending that would come was his own.

It is simply overwhelming, he wrote, *just how underwhelming life can be at the end. I was born to be a storm. A storm that leaves hope in its wake. A force of creative destruction in the name of progress, limited only by the threshold of one's imagination. I tried. Oh, how I tried, but in pursuing my dreams, I have killed the dreamer.*

He let the pen drop. It had been easier than expected to sum up twenty-seven years of life. Where were the guards? It was cruel to make him wait. Sardonyx, wherever they kept him, was likely raving mad at the dishonor. Say what they will about Father, but he had always done what he thought was best. Do all great villains see themselves that way? Novalore certainly envisioned himself the hero. And Pentule. Basically, everyone but the Claws. Hmm. A question certainly worth pondering if he wasn't expected to die in a few hours—

The door flung open. Novalore. Of course it would be him. *By Strength's name, he always hated me. Every damnable thing in his life is somehow my fault. When the mirror reveals an unworthy narrative, we create our own.*

"Get up!" Novalore yelled, stomping forward. Not a single guard accompanied him. "I have yearned for this moment for years. For years! And yet, to see you in such a pitiful state is infuriating. Why can't you fight back? Where is your honor?"

"My honor lies in the heart. Pyith loved me. She loved me because I never became you. That alone makes this death worthwhile." He made sure to smile at the end. *When our body becomes too frail to wield weapons, we must sharpen our words.*

Novalore struck him across the snout, but oddly enough, it barely hurt. Oh, there was a rattling sensation, but apathy drowned out all other senses. It was like throwing stones into an empty lake.

"I was born to be a storm," Tempest whispered as blood trickled down his mouth.

"Enough," Novalore said, forcing him up. He pushed his walking stick into Tempest, knocking him back until he grabbed the desk for balance. "As much as it pains me to say this: we have decided you will die first. How I yearned to see the look in your eyes as Sardonyx fell, but such is the realm."

"Such is the realm, indeed." Tempest took a final glance at his so-called diplomacy room. In all likelihood, Novalore would burn all the books, notes, even the shelves, just to ensure there was no risk of him ever learning anything. Tempest snickered out loud at the thought, not caring what consequences came from it. Alcohol has a reputation of numbing the senses, but there is nothing in the realm more numbing than the realization tomorrow isn't coming.

I was born to be a storm.

They entered the citadel hall, where Sardonyx struggled on his knees. Enough rope bound him to hold a building in place. Pentule kept a wide distance, while several guards all held polearms to their fallen warlord. Bloom leaned against a pillar, never looking in either of the Claws' direction. Not much of a surprise to see her on the winning side. Hopefully in time, she would betray them all and take this rotting kingdom for her own.

Sardonyx was defeated, powerless, and to any neutral observer: the most dangerous zephum that ever existed. "My son," he said, before one of the nameless guards struck him in the snout. "Accept our demise with honor. We shall smile upon our memories from the Great Plains in the Sky. My dear Vitala awaits us both."

To see his father in such dire straits ripped him apart from inside. Oh, what a mercy that Grandfather Fentum Claw couldn't see this day. Tempest got pushed to the ground beside Sardonyx, then said, "Will you do it here? I would rather not make the journey outside if all that awaits me is the void." He had no idea where his courage came from. Maybe it wasn't courage, but apathy. What worse could they do to him?

With his arms crossed, Pentule took a deep breath. "Please, come freely to the honor grounds and accept our judgment. I assure you that both your bodies will be placed within the Valley of Remembrance. If you love this kingdom, even a fraction of the amount you both claim, you will not deny us the opportunity to make our transition as seamless as possible."

"Pentule," Sardonyx said in a voice so weak, it barely

sounded like him. "Allow me to die with honor. Place a blade in my hands and throw warriors at me until I can fight no more. An execution? You cannot do this! You cannot!"

"Indeed, I cannot, Sardonyx Claw, son of Fentum Claw, and yet, I must. I will add your hatred to the sum of my shame. Guards, let them up, then escort them forward. The time for words has ended."

Tempest snickered again. "If we cannot use words, then what are we?"

"Zephum," Novalore said before anyone could respond. "You heard your warmaster, get up and start moving. The sun rises upon my glory. Rejoice! For it is an honorable day to die."

"I think I'm happy right here," Tempest said.

"Tempest," Pentule said. "Please, don't force this to be more degrading than necessary. Listen to your father. Follow us outside."

I was born to be a storm. "Outside, you say? Is the weather cruel or beautiful this morning?"

"Vaynex is always beautiful," Pentule said, gazing at the empty spot behind the throne where the God of Strength had used to stand. Was he silently begging for forgiveness? He would find none.

Tempest laughed, and couldn't help from laughing harder. Storms have no self-control, and he was born to be a storm. "Vaynex is many things. But beautiful? No. No, my council friend it is not. Irrelevant is the word you're looking for. A state of mind I have become rather intimate with. I was born to be a storm. I was raised to be a tempest. Through it all, life has molded me into a maelstrom. Drown in my tears. Beg the black clouds above for an honorable fate that has never existed.

"I am nothing. I am forever. I am the end."

"*Tempest... Tempest, Tempest. You were never my first choice, but oh, how fate brings us together. Your people haven't served me in ages. I will enjoy this. Take my wrath. Drag Serenna, Zeen, and David down into the void. I will look upon them one last time before I forget they ever existed at all."*

"*No!*" Father screamed. His voice lingered…until it didn't. Until it stopped like everything else. Ah, to hear silence in the citadel. Even the torches stopped crackling. Once the ethereal black wings sprouted from Tempest's shoulders and lit the citadel with an ebony glow, the torches lost their purpose. Another victim to irrelevancy.

The guards all fled as power surged through Tempest. Not strength, but power. *Real* power! He threw his walking stick to the ground. His shattered leg worked again. Everything worked. By Strength's name… No. By Death's name. Strength had unified a people not worth existing. Brought them together, tolerated their nonsensical ideals. A people that only valued physical strength. A people that would crumble under Tempest's wrath. The wrath of a zephum Harbinger.

Novalore struck him again. No pain followed. More strikes came, all aimed at the snout, as if he were afraid to strike anywhere else. His fist was laughably slow, it would take nothing to dodge or block the blows, but after a lifetime of irrelevance, it was time for Novalore to comprehend weakness. "What have you done?" Novalore yelled with a cracked voice.

"Again," Tempest said, laughing off the attacks. "Hit me again. Show me your glory. Your honor! What were your words that day, *Warlord*? Ah yes, 'weakness is a disease.'" Was this what it felt like to be powerful? No wonder all these zephum had treated him with such disdain.

"Is honor so foreign that you would rather destroy our kingdom than embrace it?" asked Novalore, his grin completely vanished. "Out of all our people, she was cursed to be with you. May the realm never forgive me for allowing such dishonor. Pentule! Bloom! To me! We shall live or die as warriors."

Novalore and Pentule grouped up and drew their blades, but Bloom kept her distance. Terror. That was the only way to describe her expression. Every face has its own variation of conveying terror, but the language of horror is a universal truth.

An unprovoked urge forced Tempest to raise his right hand and open his fist. A weightless sword materialized, shimmering with void energy and pulsing in his grip. By Death's name, it was perfect, like wielding the void itself.

Unsurprisingly, Novalore rushed in first. His answer to every problem was either slamming his fist or charging it with a blade. Tempest barely flinched as their weapons clashed. So much power... It was incredible. He pushed Novalore back, reveling in watching the old zephum stumble—

A tiny dagger pierced his neck. From...ah, Pentule had thrown it while Tempest was distracted. For any mortal enemy, such a wound would mean the end. For Tempest, it was just a prelude to nothing and forever. He took it out of his neck and gazed upon the blood. There was no pain at all. He went to feel the wound, but void energy had already closed it. So, this is what it was like to become a god. To gaze upon mortality as a hindrance.

Enough. His body trembled. Too long without violence... *Too long!* "Feed me your essence!" he yelled against his will, turning his attention to Novalore. Ah, now there was a target. Tempest swung his glowing blade across. The swing was blocked but he effortlessly pushed Novalore down to his knees. It didn't even take his full power... What was his full power? None of the Time God's children could ever bring it out of him.

Novalore disengaged the parry, then thrust his sword at Tempest, aimed at his chest. Tempest flinched as the blade grazed his side, then thrust his own sword into Novalore. It was like piercing the air.

Novalore groaned, his eyes going wide. "So…be it. Strength…without honor… is—"

"*Chaos.* And chaos rules all." Tempest tore his blade out before the mantra could be spoken in truth. No need to waste homage to a dead god when the most powerful one reigned.

The body lingered on the ground. Younger Tempest had always considered Novalore's death until the shame of it brought him back to grace. But his old self was gone, replaced by a storm. A maelstrom. Novalore's death was beautiful. It was like slaying irrelevance. A green essence flowed from the body. Whatever it was, Tempest yearned for it like he had never yearned for anything. A greater need than to walk again. A greater need than his Pyith. *No, that's impossible. Nothing could ever replace her. Nothing except…*

The power somehow grew as the essence flowed into him. It quenched a lingering thirst; he sighed with relief before he turned to his remaining targets. Bloom was cutting Sardonyx's constraints as Pentule approached.

"Tempest, my friend," Pentule said. "You have always been the wisest of us. If there is any sense at all left in that head of yours, please surrender. This is not the way. Be reasonable. Be merciful." Pentule threw his sword to the ground by Tempest's feet.

He's right. By Strength's name what I have done. What have I done—

"*ENOUGH! The time for hesitation has crumbled into the void. Taste the ecstasy of destruction. Devour these mortals, then Time itself. Oh, for a zephum of all things to erase the Time God…*"

Agony brought Tempest to his knees. "Friend?" he said, forcing himself up. "Do friends mutiny and conspire to murder my family? While sense lingers in my mind, it is nothing compared to the hatred festering in my heart. Merciful? I was born to be a storm. I no longer know what mercy is."

He grabbed Pentule by the throat and crushed it. The zephum crumbled to the ground, offering another essence to empower Tempest. All those years of planning and plotting together to prepare for any scenario. Not this one. Foolish Pentule, the only contingency against the wrath of God is to never face him at all.

"Fire!"

A detonator exploded by his head, sending Tempest crashing to the ground. Ah, to feel pain again. He actually struggled to rise, groaning as void energies mended his wounds. "Oh, Bloom. I take it our deal is off then? How unfortunate. You know, the human Melissa was able to trigger detonators with only her mind. If you haven't mastered that by now, there is no scenario in which you leave this citadel alive."

"Fuck you!" Her voice and hands trembled. Tempest had seen the best and worst of Vaynex, but Bloom's terror was a unique vision. "How could you? Humans will rule us forever after this. If there are any of us still alive to rule." She threw another detonator at his head.

"Humans?" Tempest said, taking another blast to the face. Since he braced for it, this one didn't send him flying. "You have always been simple-minded. Humans, zephum, the void awaits them all. Each death is one step closer to ending the Time God. He will fall... He will fall to my blade." His body trembled with hatred for the Time God. He couldn't recall the deity's face, voice, or...anything, but there wasn't a force in the realm he despised more. *Nothing.*

Bloom sighed and drew her two swords. "So, this is it, huh? You traded a broken leg for a shattered mind. Out of all the fucking ways to go..."

She rushed in with a roar and started swinging. Bloom was

much better at melee combat than he anticipated, getting several unguarded slices across his body and even a few on his snout. If it were a fair battle, he would've lost, but no duel against Death's Harbinger could ever be fair.

Tempest let her get a strike in, then countered with a swing to her head. She ducked under his sword and stabbed him in the neck, then kicked out his left leg to knock him off balance. He gasped from the pain, with a flicker of terror that the wounds were healing at a slower rate. Tempest took one more unguarded strike through the chest, then punched her in the snout, the same way he had seen Father do all those times.

Bloom staggered back, landing awkwardly on her tail. She looked up at him with tears in her eyes. "I won't beg," she said. "Make it quick."

"*Yes! Slay her! Send the lizard Guardian to the void!*"

A newfound rage coursed through him. It wasn't quite the level of disdain for the Time God, but Bloom was a plague upon the realm that must be destroyed. Tempest raised his sword, smiling as Bloom refused to meet his eyes. He swung down—

Tempest struck another blade. Despite his power, he couldn't force his way past it. He disengaged and took a step back to find his father.

"Guardian Bloom," Sardonyx said. "You and I have never seen our kingdom with the same eyes, but only you can protect Vaynex now. Portal back to Mylor and report to Serenna. Go forth, child. And remember! Strength without honor—is chaos."

The trembling Bloom nodded without words and sprinted off to the Guardian room, leaving only the two of them.

Silence lingered as they met eyes. The Warlord and the Harbinger stood in the citadel. "I will not apologize," Tempest finally said. "They forced my hand. This kingdom—*our* kingdom—will be ruled by Claws, or become a smoldering crater."

"No, my son. This kingdom will always be ruled…by *honor*."

To Tempest's surprise, Sardonyx rushed forward, flailing his sword forward with no precision but with the power to end realms. He blocked, but had to shift his legs to regain balance. For the faintest of moments, all the rage and limitless power of Death flickered, leaving nothing but doubt: the most smothering of feelings. *This is my father. Sardonyx Claw, Warlord of Vaynex. I can't win. I cannot… Help me. This was never supposed to happen. This—*

"NO MORE DOUBTS. NO MORE WEAKNESS. NO MORE LIFE. END IT. END IT ALL."

He roared, unleashing stored energy and increasing the burning glow of his wings. "Come, Father. You will join your fallen deity in the void." If there was any reason to hold back, he couldn't recall. He couldn't recall much of anything, other than knowing the zephum in front of him must die.

Death's Harbinger surged forward, slashing his blade. His opponent blocked all the strikes. Was this warrior favored by one of the lesser gods? It seemed likely; no mortal could persevere against such wrath. Oh well. This one would fall, then his god would join him. Everything would join him; Time itself would implode into darkness. One final strike would finish it. He swung—

And hit nothing. His opponent forced a sword through him and kept pushing him back until he collapsed in front of the throne. No! Impossible! Pain, doubt, fear, they all returned. All that talk about limitless power now seemed like the words of a madman. "What are you?" Tempest asked. Yes, Tempest, that was his name. Fragments upon fragments were returning. Vaynex. A shattered leg. A lost life-mate…

Sardonyx Claw removed his helmet and placed it on the

ground. "Death may be the end, my son. But Strength is the now."

A flare of agony rushed through him as all the fragments of clarity faded. He tried to cling to one of them...Pyith...but the name was like a fading whisper. He rose and grasped his glowing sword. The Child of Strength could have ended him, but chose not to. He chose his own end.

Death's Harbinger surged forward, then pierced his blade straight into the mortal zephum. How strange, he had expected him to dodge. Surely, he had the ability. It didn't matter. Perhaps that was why he had taken the blow. Nothing matters in the end.

"I understand why you hate me now, Father. All those years of disappointment. We both knew the throne was my destiny, but now, I finally deserve it. Rest easy. Or don't. It doesn't matter. Nothing ever mattered. Have you any final words?"

The zephum... Sardonyx rose with pained breaths, not bothering to grab his sword. Void energy tapered out of the wound. "I will leave this realm quoting the one I love above all. The one who has filled me with enough pride to rival Strength himself."

He approached, clutching his fatal wound. "'The pain of family is unique, like water flowing down the stream of a river. We crash into the rocks, jagged fragments of earth, molding us into a storm of lost dreams and expectations...'"

Sardonyx, Warlord of Vaynex wheezed for a deep breath. "'Our loved ones know where to strike, where the pain lies, for they knew us when we were children—when we were too young to hide our weaknesses away into the shadows of safety and denial. No pain is created equal—and thus no pain tears like the father's gaze, screaming without words that I am a failure...'"

His father lunged forward and hugged him. It was not a

threat, but the embrace was filled with an unfathomable power. "*I have always loved you.*" He collapsed after the words, now an empty shell in front of the throne he had always sat upon.

Tempest froze. He remembered everything. His father's final words wounded him more deeply than any pain ever inflicted. If Rinso the Blue had been a real human, he would hunt Tempest down and vanquish him in the citadel halls. Another creator slain by their own creation.

It was never supposed to be this way. And yet, here we are.

Finally, there was Death's caress, helping him forget. No time to obsess over the pain. He had a realm to crumble. Life to end. A Time God to destroy. He sat upon his throne, fighting back memories of his childhood. Father's lessons, Mother's love, memories of a time when all he could do was beg for tomorrow. Tomorrow had arrived, coated in the blood of yesterday. *I was born to be a storm. I was raised to be a tempest.*

He leaned back upon his throne, letting tears of the maelstrom fall.

CHAPTER 37

SCHOLAR'S DESPERATION

rancis sighed as someone tapped on the door to his chambers. Mary wouldn't have knocked and Wisdom could appear anywhere, so chances were someone useless was seeking his attention. "Who is it?" he yelled.

"General Marcus, my lord."

Correct. Someone useless. "Enter."

Marcus eased forward, keeping his stare on the ground. Great. What was it now? More riots? More people fleeing Terrangus? "I bring news, my lord."

Why else would you knock on my door? "Of course you do. If it's rioters, just round them up and hang them. I grow tired of repeating this order."

"It's Mary," Marcus said. "Um, Empress Mary."

"Am I to guess your meaning? Speak plainly!" By Wisdom's glory, Marcus had become…different in the past few days. Right after Francis had dealt with the rioters himself. To be fair, just about everyone was different now. Particularly Mary. Those looks. The distance. She hadn't the courage to call him a monster, so she had begun treating him like one. *Apparently, they all fear me. Mother would be proud.*

"My men report that she fled Terrangus this morning

through the outskirts portal to Mylor. Worse yet, she collaborated with Nyfe, um, Omega to murder three Vanguards. Not sure what transpired in Mylor but she has safely returned. We are keeping her in our custody until your orders."

Francis lost his breath. Mary had run away? Just like that: no words or goodbyes? There had to be more to the story; fools always leave out the most important details. At least she had returned. That surely meant something. *He's looking at me. I should say something.* "Which Vanguards were slain?" he asked, trying to hide his distress. What sort of reaction would be normal in these circumstances? Weep openly? Stoic frown? Hmm...

"I wasn't given their names. Forgive me, I was under the assumption your floating friend would have the details."

"My what? Do you mean *God?*"

Marcus took a deep breath. "Francis, listen. I'm doing my best here but you have to meet me halfway. Things are bad. I mean bad. And this is coming from someone who served under Grayson and Nyfe."

What a mess. It's like calming one rebellion only forges two more. How do I... Okay, one problem at a time. Like a scholar. What can I solve first?

Oh, I'm taking too long to respond. "One problem at a time, General. Where is Mary? Perhaps the stress of pregnancy is causing this irrational behavior." The look of dismay on Marcus's face suggested he did not agree with such a hypothesis.

"Regardless, we have sealed off the Guardian room and kept her inside. Before we get going, would you prefer to bring your staff?"

Francis glanced at the Herald of Wisdom from the other side of his chambers. He resisted the urge to grab it. There was a certain...clarity when he didn't wield such power. Mary would certainly appreciate its absence and if trouble were to appear, some of these high-ranking soldiers could earn their keep for once. "No. Lead the way." Hopefully, Marcus couldn't hear the hesitation in his voice.

Interestingly enough, Vanguards patrolled the Guardian room entrance instead of traditional soldiers. There were so many of them by this point. Francis would never admit it, but without the knowledge of his staff available he couldn't remember their original names.

The Vanguards bowed as he entered the room. Good to see the table had been repaired, and better yet, there was space to move without Melissa's weapons scattered about. A hint of nostalgia came over him as he noted the portal, but where was Mary—

She rose with a groan. By Wisdom's glory, she appeared terrible. "Ugh, about time."

"Everyone out!" Francis yelled. "My beloved, you look famished! What has befallen you? Why did you go to Mylor?" He paused before asking the real question. "Why did you leave me?"

"It doesn't matter anymore. After all we have done, I have nowhere else to go. Serenna could barely look me in the eye. She *feared* me. The most powerful Guardian in the realm feared me!"

More powerful than Francis? What a foolish notion. "Predictable response. It is a natural reaction for the unenlightened to fear what they cannot understand."

Mary slowly backed away. "You sound more like *him* every day and less like the man I love."

"Love as in the present tense? Oh, thank Serenity. I um, I apologize. What can I do to help? Would you prefer to rest in our chambers?"

Each step forward from Mary made his heart race. It was like a debate but to lose would mean dying alone. "That would be nice. Would you rest with me? Lay together? We can stop being tyrants for an afternoon and just…relax."

"Of course," he said, taking a deep breath. Out of all the concessions he had been prepared to make, a day of relaxation was more than a fair compromise. *Do I press this issue further? Ask about the Vanguards?* he thought as he took her arm. "I heard you um, had a disagreement with some Vanguards…"

She studied him as they eased out of the Guardian room together. "They stood in my way. I regret nothing. Does that anger you, Emperor?"

"I'm too exhausted to be angry. Honestly, I don't even recall their names. If they were foolish enough to tell you no then they probably deserved their fate. We'll just make more."

Mary laughed in the middle of the halls, drawing an uncomfortable amount of attention from the guards and nobles drifting about. Odd, he hadn't said a joke, but as they say: happy empress, happy emperor. "I don't suppose you saw Nyfe? Gods, forgive me for saying this, but he came to my aid. I may owe him a favor. Or at least an excuse not to execute him."

"Wisdom took him to the lower chambers after some issue from earlier… Oh. The puzzles of today are coming together. It stands to reason that Nyfe is in for a day of pain."

"Well, you know what? Fuck him."

"Fuck him, indeed," Francis said, delighted by the new smile on Mary's face. Ah, that laughter. Most people can fake emotions but a natural laugh is a beautiful sound. Her joy was his muse. None of these other issues mattered. Dead Vanguards, riots, Mylor… It was time to relax.

She kept a firm grip on his arm as they eased up the stairs to their chambers. "I figured you would be angry with me. I may end up having nothing but you in the end…but perhaps that will be enough."

"No, no. Not anger. Never anger. It's more of a fear. Maybe a terror? It's difficult to articulate the difference—"

Mary snickered. "Francis, how could you ever fear me?

After your newfound power, how could you fear anyone?"

He couldn't force a snicker or one of those fake Zeen smiles. Do liars know how easy they have it? "Power isn't exactly…what I imagined it would be. I can't shake the premonition I'm going to wake up one day alone in a kingdom that despises me. And for what? Loneliness has always been an elusive struggle. It cannot be destroyed, it cannot be solved, but ever since we initiated this relationship, I haven't felt it linger. Please don't give up on me."

Mary paused in the middle of the throne room, glancing at him as if he were a stranger. "I left to request aid. To save Terrangus. To save you."

"Me? But I'm not in danger—"

"Francis," she said, gripping him tightly. "You are in greater danger than anyone in the entire realm. Arrogance is manipulating you. He is after your mind, but I will never allow him your heart. That is mine and mine alone."

He took a few steps back, rubbing his hands together to keep them busy. Life these days was terribly confusing. What an utter tragedy that Wisdom and Mary continued to be at odds. Hopefully, the birth of baby Calvin would fix all that. Everyone could put their differences aside and stare at the pretty baby. Mother had once said people have children as a last-ditch effort to save failing relationships. *Was that my purpose? By Wisdom's glory, I wish she was still alive. Perhaps only a tyrant can properly educate a tyrant. When do the ends justify the means? How much force is too weak or too cruel?*

How much can a person be damaged before they are considered broken?

"Francis?"

I'm taking too long. "Sorry. Are you still interested in rest? I can imagine few prospects more appealing at this moment."

She grinned. "I can name a few."

While he had no idea what she was referring to, it was a comfort she accepted his stalling method. "Wonderful! Please, lead the way my dear." *If she's accusing me of sounding like Wisdom, then I should refrain from saying 'my dear.' Oh well. All things considered, today ended up being less awful than—*

When she opened the door to their chambers, Wisdom and Nyfe were already waiting inside. "My dear Emperor," Wisdom said, shifting his left eye towards Francis but keeping the right one on Nyfe. "Forgive me for interrupting your planned relaxation, but I have...well, unfortunate news. Shall I continue?"

"Fuck off!" Mary said before he could respond. "Fuck off for just one day. One quiet day. Give us this. If nothing else, let us have a moment alone."

Wisdom snickered, floating in front of them both. "Alone? Those who rule are never alone. Now, please hush, the adults are having a conversation. A Harbinger of Death has revealed itself! A zephum of all things. Perhaps you remember his name? *Tempest.*"

"He would never," Francis said, trying to ignore his pounding heart. What an annoyance that trying to ignore the reaction only granted it more control. "Tempest... Tempest Claw. Truly?" The Golden Scholars diminished yet again...

I'm the only one left. The final Haide, the final Golden Scholar.

"Truly. Now, this opens an interesting dilemma. I have been cursed with a profound knowledge of arithmetic, so believe me when I suggest that the Guardians are one short. Who, oh who, will fill the void? *Void*, pardon me for the inappropriate jest."

Does he mean me? I don't want it. Please, let me rest. My Guardian days are over. Francis sighed, then asked, "Do I have a choice?"

"You should know I don't favor that word but I forgive you. No, Francis, I don't mean you. As emperor, your job is to delegate Guardians, not act as one. How about...this one." Wisdom gestured to Nyfe, who was standing straight, but with puffy eyes that stared into nothing. "Vanguard Omega. Oh, I have big plans for our fallen Harbinger."

"They will kill him the moment he arrives in Mylor," Mary said. "Surely your powerful mind already knows that?"

To Francis's relief, Wisdom chuckled. "Ah, my fatal weakness. It always seems that I know too much, while those closest to me know nothing. Watch and learn, Empress." He raised a spectral hand, then a white outline of...something swirled around Nyfe's head.

Nyfe screamed as the outline became solid. Pure white mail pushed into his head, covering everything except his eyes. He fell to his knees and let out another shriek. While Francis had never cared for the man, this cruelty seemed a bit unnecessary.

Oh? Perhaps it wasn't cruelty? Nyfe rose, standing straight and clutching his crystal dagger. His eyes erupted with platinum energy.

"What have you done?" asked Francis. He studied Nyfe, but kept a safe distance. Leaving his staff had not been a wise idea.

Nyfe glared at Francis. "God has made me perfect. Despite my constant disobedience, I have been offered the role of Vanguard Omega. Escort me to Serenna. I miss my dear friend."

Mary had the right idea by making a fist and shaking. Any combination of fear and anger was the proper response. "This is absurd!" Francis said, unable to calm his voice.

"No," Arrogance said, turning both eyes to Francis. "There is only one thing I classify as absurd. Escort him to Mylor. Despite your hesitations, this action is necessary to craft our Serenity. Step by step. Piece by piece..."

Heat rushed to his face. "How can I comply with this? Bring *him* to Mylor? After what he did to—"

"Are you under the assumption I made a request?"

Francis staggered back at the power in his voice. If only he had his staff... Ah! It was in his hands, gripped tightly with a scholar's desperation. He couldn't remember grabbing it, but all seemed well in the realm again. "Will you join me, my dear?" he asked Mary. The question was a pleasantry. Surely, she would say yes.

"I can't do this," she said, rushing off. What a strange reaction. A tiny piece of Francis screamed at him to follow her, but the yell was muted by silence. Silence cannot be improved upon. It is both perfect and empty, the prequel of every great symphony.

"She will understand," God said. "Or she won't. You have a more important role to fill. Escort Vanguard Omega to Mylor."

"They sealed off our portals. How am I to arrive?"

Arrogance chuckled. "Oh Francis. Stop being so imperfect." The deity raised a spectral hand, opening a shimmering portal in front of Francis.

CHAPTER 38

INTELLECT OVER EMOTIONS

erenna leaned across the balcony of her gardens, gazing out towards the mountains, taking in the solace of familiarity. What a bizarre day. David and Zeen had gone to rest hours ago, leaving her alone, wondering what to do about Vaynex. Regardless of her actions, something terrible was coming. Interfering during the mutiny would bring war today. Not interfering would bring war tomorrow. *Are the Claws depending on me? If I do nothing, am I just another archon?* Doing nothing would be the easiest choice. No wonder so many leaders veer towards the comfort of inaction. It is a sad, yet often inevitable journey to become the very thing we hate.

She missed David the most in moments like this. The old David, who had used to berate and threaten the team, making outrageous claims that one mistake was all it would take to lose the realm. Such words had seemed ridiculous back then. Such words seemed to define everything now. She pushed the hair out of her eyes, watching dusk's unwanted arrival. Something about worrying about tomorrow makes the sun fade faster—

"You are wise to meditate in silence," Valor's voice called out from behind. "I did the same back in my time. Unfortunately, your dire mood is warranted: a Harbinger of Death has entered our realm."

Serenna lost her breath and fell to her knees. "*No*. Not yet. We are not ready. *I* am not ready."

Valor appeared to her left, leaning against the same balcony, her long platinum hair flailing with the wind. She reached out a hand to help Serenna rise. "We never are, Guardian. And we never will be. Now, rise, take a deep breath, and create a perception of confidence. Most victories are crafted well before the first spell is cast."

How could she be confident? She had led the Guardians twice, nearly losing both times. It was happening again—the team was weak, untrained, unprepared. "Give me your scythe. I have earned it!" The words rushed out, and she refused to regret them. Most problems are nothing more than enemies waiting to be destroyed.

Valor sighed. "No, and do not make the request again. I saw the true Serenna that day. Wielding my blade turned you into a rabid beast."

"Then what good are you? Perhaps I can defend our realm with all the insults and threats unleashed upon me in the past two weeks."

"Oh, crystal girl. I can only ponder if I was such a child at your age." Silence followed her words. With the sun going down, it seemed rather chilly. Rather cold.

A portal materialized in the middle of the gardens. Similar to Fear's, but the shape was off, and there was an odd platinum tint on the edges. The outline coming through was definitely human. A bald shorter man, with a familiar staff in his hands...

"Francis?" she asked. Great. Was he here to complain about Mary's treatment? Well, if he was unaware of a Harbinger of Death, he was in for a rude awakening—

The portal flickered again, revealing an odd-looking Vanguard, wielding a crystal dagger. Who had crafted such a weapon? The man—or whatever it was—had white armor infused into his skull, with glowing platinum eyes that radiated a violent energy. *I have seen him before. There is only one man I can recall who wielded a dagger, but surely it's not him. That would be impossible…*

Right?

"Guardian Serenna!" Francis said. "Pardon my unannounced arrival, but we have much to discuss. Ah, and the Goddess of Valor! A pleasure to finally meet you in person." Serenna nearly fell over at the confidence in his voice. Maybe confidence wasn't the word she was looking for.

Serenna straightened her posture and kept eye contact. Always match the tone of the room, or gardens, in this case. "Well met, Emperor. May I assume you already know our scenario?"

"My dear Serenna, assume that I know everything. Bloom is en route as well. Your father is rather frazzled by the constant visitors, but it works to our advantage that the Guardians are already here. Oh! Where is my dear Five? I would love for a chance to speak with him." Francis's eyes never left his staff. He gazed at it with the same admiration her father gave to wine jugs.

"Serenna!" Bloom yelled from the entrance before Serenna could respond. She was surrounded by Charles and several Mylor guards, all appearing confused on how to deal with a zephum in the capitol. "It's Tempest. The fucker did it. He really did it." Bloom paused to take a deep breath. "Tempest is a Harbinger of Death. We must act immediately. You know the deal. We have no barriers. My home may already be lost. The boss, he… Sardonyx saved my life. We gotta go. We gotta go now."

Serenna gripped the railing, pressing her hands into the steel to alleviate the pressure of the eyes upon her. "Then we go immediately. We go and we save Sardonyx."

"No," Francis said with a chuckle. "No, you don't. Only one Claw remains, and he happens to be your target."

Bloom let out a deep breath. "Figured as much. I'll tell you, and you write these words in all your fucking human books: the warlord died with honor. Met a glorious end. Strength...without honor—is chaos."

Serenna pushed back her tears. She would never cry in front of Francis. Damn that arrogant smirk on his face. "Have you come to offer aid, Emperor? Otherwise, you have worn out your welcome."

"Well, in a sense, though I doubt you'll be pleased," Francis said, losing his grin. He finally glared at her. While his eyes were the same shade of brown, they were filled with an utter indifference for all of them. A Harbinger of Death was a minor inconvenience for the puppet of Arrogance. "Allow me to introduce the next Guardian. The one blessed by Wisdom to make Death itself irrelevant. Vanguard Omega."

The odd-looking Vanguard stepped forward, with platinum energy still burning from his eyes. Surely, it wasn't him. Even though he was about the same height. With the same long white hair. Same...everything.

By the gods.

Serenna grabbed the Wings of Mylor and pushed down the urge to enter her empowered form. That energy would be needed for Tempest...for the Harbinger of Death. "How *dare* you bring him here. Do you desire war so badly, Francis? From what I gather, Terrangus would celebrate your end. Give me a reason." Platinum energy begged to disperse from her body as she gripped her staff, but she kept it at bay.

Francis didn't respond. Instead, he stepped back and grinned. Arrogance appeared in the open spot, radiating raw power as the god's eyes glared through Serenna. Even Valor took a step back. "Your mind is stuck in yesterday, my dear

Guardian, but we must venture forth to craft the yesterday of tomorrow. You need more creativity! Think of him as a pet. A tool! Imagine defying Death by using his own broken toy."

"How could I ever trust you, let alone this one?" asked Serenna. It was all too much. Nyfe was here. How could she justify his presence to David? To *Zeen?*

The wind picked up as Arrogance sighed. There was an echo that bounced off the far mountains. "The end of every great war begins with a decisive victory. This one is *mine*. If you require trust, follow my incentives. Remember, my dear Serenna, I cannot mold paradise if everyone is dead." With a bright white flash Francis and Arrogance were gone. Not Nyfe. Of course they left him.

"I exist only to serve," Nyfe said. "Please allow me the honor to fight alongside the Guardians. It is my purpose." His eyes twitched as he grimaced. What an abomination of a man. Of a monster. Whatever he was.

Serenna stepped forward, keeping both hands on her staff. Up close, she saw his real eyes. The platinum energy was an illusion to hide the tired husk underneath. "Do you remember me, Nyfe? Do you remember anything?"

His eyes shot to the ground. "Please…don't use that name. It hurts. Nyfe is a memory. I am Vanguard. I am Omega."

"We should just kill him. It's absurd to bring him along—" Serenna jumped as Valor's hand eased to her shoulder.

"Intellect over emotions," Valor said. "Never turn down an extra blade in a battle that may be your last. Arrogance hides it well, but he fears the uncertainty of this battle. Fortunately, I know better. Assemble your team. Face the ender of realms. Then enjoy the temporary peace that always follows."

Valor wasn't a very good liar; maybe it was a common trait of Crystal Guardians. *She doesn't expect me to win. Otherwise, she would never recommend bringing Nyfe. David will probably understand, but Zeen…*

"Serenna, we gotta move," Bloom said.

"Yes, of course. Before we go, what is your opinion on Nyfe? Am I mad for considering this?"

"Nah. Look at him. Nyfe is dead, Boss. Whatever that thing is surely isn't human. It's like, uh, damn what would we call it? Just call him Vanguard Omega like the Arrogant One suggested. We need all the help we can get."

Serenna leaned in close and whispered, "Watch him at all times. If he shows even the slightest hint of betrayal, blow his head off."

Bloom nodded with a smile and followed her towards the crowded exit. They had to slow their pace to allow Nyfe… Vanguard Omega to follow. All the soldiers and onlookers moved out of their way, other than Charles, who gave a sad grin. "Part of me is relieved to know the day has finally arrived, if only to lose the burden of anticipation. Be well, my dear. I'll have a grand feast awaiting your return. As always."

"I love you, Dad," she said, giving him a quick hug. The rest of the words she yearned to tell him would have to wait. Always time for such things after they won. No other scenario could occur.

There was an unnatural silence as they traveled through corridors. A guilt perhaps, that everyone was relieved to hear that the Harbinger was elsewhere. Serenna felt it too and shared in their guilt. Thank Valor's grace it wasn't here. Not her home. After the war against Terrangus, Mylor wasn't prepared to face another disaster. But if she failed, the end of Mylor would eventually follow.

"You two," she said to Nyfe and Bloom, "stay outside. Omega, or whatever you're called, you are not to interact with Zeen. Do not look at him. Do not acknowledge him. If he strikes you, accept it. His life is more valuable than yours. Confirm that you understand."

"I understand all too well." She couldn't gauge any reaction from his glowing eyes or the mail that covered his face. His voice betrayed nothing. How frustrating that Arrogance made them all sound monotone. Even him.

Serenna's hands shook as she opened the door to Zeen's chambers. *He will never accept this. He will despise me for even suggesting it. Would it be cowardly to blame Valor? No. I am the leader, all failures and victories rest on my shoulders.*

"Master Serenna. I have done all that I can," Five said, sheathing his staff behind his back. "Zeen is in fair shape. I wouldn't recommend him battle ready, but...I fear the choice has been robbed from us. Have a moment alone, then we must get moving. Vaynex is unfit to handle a Harbinger. Every moment of hesitation incurs a loss of life."

Serenna slowly walked over to Zeen, keeping an eye on Five. "So, I take it Arrogance still speaks to you?"

"Not *to* me, precisely, but I can hear...echoes of words," Five said. "The best way I can describe it is overhearing bits and pieces of a conversation from outside a tavern."

"I see. In that case, could you read Omega's thoughts? That would save me a lot of trouble."

"No. He is sealed off. The only thing I can guarantee is that he hates Arrogance more than any of us. I will not suggest empathy, but the man has suffered greatly in the past year. That being said, he took Julius from me. If anything goes amiss, I will burn him into the ashes of yesterday."

If anything goes 'amiss' we are all dead. "Thank you. Do you have a preferred name? I have treated you unfairly despite your proven allegiance. It pains me to only refer to you as a number."

Five smiled. "You are kind to ask. Stickman was...less pleasant, but the title has faded at great cost. Let's see what tomorrow brings after we face Tempest, if anything at all. Until then, Vanguard Five or Robert will suffice." He bowed to Serenna, then left her alone with Zeen.

"You interrupted a wonderful dream," Zeen said with a grin. The bruises on his face were still visible, but the dark, purplish tone had subsided. "Oh well. Time to save the realm again. I'll make sure not to die this time." He snickered, but the words filled her with dread. How could he joke about such things after what they had shared?

Zeen got out of bed and grabbed his armor, changing his clothes with no modesty. She quickly glanced away. The mystery of their bodies had faded, but it seemed a great loss to acknowledge it. "Um, before we go," Serenna said, then hesitated. *I'll just tell him. If I berate him for avoiding the truth, I shouldn't do the same. But, well, withholding information is not the same as lying.* "We have a sixth Guardian. Vanguard Omega. He's a bit…odd. Just ignore him and stay focused."

"That's a stupid name," he said with a weak laugh, sheathing Hope by his side. "I guess Francis either ran out of numbers or lost count." His laugh faded as he glanced at the floor. "Five already told me the scenario. Serenna…I can't believe it's Tempest. It feels like…I caused all of this. I've only been awake for a few weeks and everything is already falling apart."

Serenna embraced Zeen and pulled him close. "My love, never take the blame for another man's evil. We choose our own path." They shared a kiss before letting go.

"I suppose we do. Okay. I'm ready." Zeen immediately paused when he stepped outside, his fiery eyes staring into Nyfe. All the uncertainty and despair on his face yielded to pure rage. "*You.*"

"Please halt. I am not the imperfect being from your memory," Nyfe said, keeping his head down. "I am no longer—"

Zeen surged forward and slammed Nyfe into the corridor

with both hands. The force knocked one of the paintings off the wall and several jugs of wine from an adjacent table. "No longer what? The man who stabbed me? Robbed me of seven months? Robbed us all of the only honorable god?"

"Lord Wisdom has absolved me of my imperfections. Please, give me another chance. Like the old days."

"I don't do that anymore," Zeen said, stepping away and drawing Hope. "Serenna, you have five seconds to convince me not to kill him."

She rushed forward, easing Hope back into his sheath. "Because I command it. Take the remaining four seconds to reconsider raising your voice to me again." Any of the cold inside her vanished as they met eyes while pressed together. She didn't mind that look. Why anger brought up such feelings was difficult to explain. If only they were alone...

Focus!

"Fine. I mean, yes dear. I mean, yes Guardian Serenna." Did he feel the same? His face grew red as he backed away. "Do we have a sixth? It's not another Vanguard, is it?"

Serenna calmed him with a smirk. "A human. One of the best I have ever known."

CHAPTER 39

TODAY IS THE DAY I DIE

A knock at the door brought David wide awake. It wasn't a simple tap, more of a desperate hammering. He stared at the white ceiling above. There could only be one reason anyone would demand his attention.

Today is the day I die.

He rose and snickered at the shield and plate armor set across the room. A tomb of steel. A tomb of finality. He had kept Melissa waiting too long. She had always been patient, perfect, a woman transcending the flawed…thing David had become. *We will be together again soon, my love. And we shall rest. Rest forever.*

"Come in," he said, pushing his legs through the holes of his armor. He was getting better at getting the top-half on with no help. His helmet stood on the dresser, but that could wait.

Serenna entered first, followed by Bloom, Robert, Zeen, and… What the fuck? Was that Nyfe? "It's him," Serenna said, clearly following David's eyes.

"You of all people are okay with this?"

"That is my decision. Do you object?"

The tone of her voice made it clear the only acceptable answer would be: "Nope," he said, grabbing his sword, shield, and leaving the room. "Bloom, a pleasure to finally meet you in person. This is um...an interesting group. Where are we heading?"

"Vaynex," Bloom said. Gods, it would be uncomfortable to battle beside a mechanist that wasn't Melissa. To be fair, Bloom certainly felt the same about a human engager.

A zephum Harbinger? Haven't faced one of those in nearly a decade. Francis and Serenna's first one, if I recall correctly. Oh, how things change. "I see. Anyone of note?"

"Tempest," Zeen said, with a mix of despair and fatigue haunting his face.

Tempest? Ah, the poor kid had finally snapped. That probably meant Sardonyx was gone as well. A terrible shame that David would never have the chance to say goodbye to the warlord. "How long has it been?"

"A few hours," Bloom said. "The sooner we go, the more we can save. We gotta move."

David sighed in relief. "Agreed. Serenna, lead the way." The newer members would have no idea how fortunate it would be for Vaynex that the Guardians had assembled so quickly. Excellent leadership by Serenna, or perhaps luck. Whichever one, the realm never seemed to care.

They rushed to the Mylor Guardian room, then Serenna triggered the crimson hue of the portal, waving on the Guardians to enter one-by-one. David was last. He waited for some words of encouragement before he walked through, some vapid speech about love and friendship, but Serenna stayed focused on the portal and remained silent.

Clearly, she had learned from the best.

*

By Fear's mercy, it was hot. They arrived in the Vaynex outskirts, with the sun on its way down but still burning from above. *Fuck this thing,* he thought, throwing his helmet into the sand. "Nyfe," David said, "do you know Guardian protocol? Do you even care?"

"Lord David, please refer to me as Vanguard Omega. My current protocol is to follow the orders of Serenna while maintaining God's prerogative." No hint of sarcasm, disdain, or any of the annoying traits that had always followed Nyfe's voice.

"No soldier can serve two generals," David said. "Which one has priority?"

"Divinity transcends any chain of command."

"Enough!" Serenna said, banging her staff into the ground. The sands muffled the sound, but the group fell silent. "Save your quarrels for the enemy, and speak up if you can spot his unique demon. We move forward."

Zeen walked up to David as the group traveled towards Vaynex. "So, you're an engager now? Don't take this the wrong way, but that armor looks ridiculous on you."

David snickered. "Is there a right way to take that? Surely, you must prefer all this steel to when I was the champion of Fear. I won't be able to strike you in the face with all this armor limiting my movements."

"Whatever you are: Guardian, champion of Fear, engager...you will always be David. It's an honor to battle another Harbinger together."

Indeed. Their final one. "The honor is all mine, my friend. I am...pleased to see you alive. The realm is a sad place without you."

"Well, I promised Serenna I wouldn't die again so let's keep it that way—"

"Zeen, I never wrote my name on the list but I did visit while you were recovering. I hope you know. It's...important to me that you know."

"I do," Zeen said with a grin.

327

David took a deep breath as they entered the bloody gates of Vaynex. Ugh, the stench of bodies was rancid from the heat. It didn't help that there were so many. Too many. Say what you will about Terrangus and its storms, but obscuring the view of something terrible is the rain's greatest attribute.

Zephum were running in all directions, roaring, screaming, and apparently looting the shops and households all over. No barriers, no disaster plans, pure anarchy in motion. He could see the shapes of demons in the distance; it could be a matter of minutes before the entire kingdom was overrun. "Stay close," Serenna said, then shielded them all.

The platinum sphere became lucid in front of David but he'd never felt less safe. Despite the absurdity of wielding a shield while covered in one, it was difficult to remain composed knowing his role if they found a colossal.

"Human Warlord!" a zephum yelled, rushing over to Zeen. "By Strength's name, it is a blessing to find you! Can you spare a moment to calm the riots? The demons are farther ahead, but I fear there will be nothing to protect if we do not restore order."

"Well met, Eltune," Zeen said, shaking his hand. "Of course, what can we do to help?"

Serenna shot Zeen a warranted glare. It brought David a small relief to see she didn't favor his stupid ideas despite their coupling. "Absolutely not. Our priority is the Harbinger. Nothing will distract us from our mission."

"But—"

"But *nothing*. Eltune, was it? The best course of action you can take right now is to ensure your people keep their distance."

Eltune paused with his snout wide open, turning away from Serenna. "Bloom? You would truly abandon your people?"

"I don't cross the boss. My advice: find whichever side is winning and throw in with them. Now, get the fuck out of my way, we have a job to do." The Guardians trekked forward, leaving Eltune to watch them leave. Poor kid certainly felt betrayed, but Serenna was right.

The stench only got worse the farther they progressed. The shape of crawlers skittering along the buildings was more visible up close, but they were difficult to track with their colors matching the tan sands and buildings. An enormous relief not to find any colossals, but…what the hell was that? David swore it was a human, but the entity radiated dark energy as it thrust its sword through a screaming zephum.

"That must be his demon," Serenna said, refreshing their crystal shields. "Why would it be human? Hmm. There is something familiar about him."

All the color drained from Zeen's face. "Look at the sword… Fortune. It's Rinso the Blue." Whatever the hell that meant, though the statement brought a gasp from Serenna.

"At least they're not banshees," David said, drawing his shield. Should he wait for a command or just rush in? Pyith had always done whatever she wanted, but David wasn't a giant lizard-warrior—

A crawler leaped from the sands towards Serenna, letting out a high-pitched shriek. David froze. He was slow to react, all his armor was too damn cumbersome. Nyfe of all people intercepted the demon, getting a clean slash across its throat before throwing it back into the sand.

Serenna brushed the hair out of her eyes in that way she always did when nervous. "Thank you…Vanguard. We should press ahead towards the citadel. The open space increases our risk, but a shortest path is the most favorable." She glanced at David. The words weren't spoken, but the fear in her eyes asked for his guidance.

"I suggest we ease our way forward," David said. "If we rush, it will draw the entire kingdom upon us in the open sand.

Use the buildings to guard our flank and hug them until we reach the citadel. It will take longer, but with less risk."

To his relief, she nodded, and didn't interrupt or impose her command. Perhaps a trait David could have learned in his forty-five years. It just never felt like he could trust anyone else…

Except Melissa. "As the engager, I'll stay at the front. Serenna, Robert, hug the buildings with a few feet between you to avoid getting smothered. Zeen, take the corner, Nyfe, the back. On second thought, Zeen in the back, Nyfe on the corner. Bloom, no detonators until a colossal appears. I've seen you throw those things. If you have to blow up any of us, aim for Nyfe." *Gods, I have missed this. If only you were still here, my love…*

But she wasn't, and she never would be.

It must have looked ridiculous as the Guardians hugged the buildings to take the long way to the citadel. A few crawlers leaped from the sands, only to get taken out by Nyfe and Zeen. Formation would need adjusting once a colossal appeared, but so far so good.

"Gotta say, David," Bloom said, with a sword in one hand and a detonator in the other, oddly similar to Melissa's battle stance. "After all the stories, you're a bit of a letdown."

"Would you prefer to charge directly in and die?"

"Well, I mean, I always heard you were a psychotic drunk with a magical sword. This is like watching Grandfather Bloom trying to engage."

David snickered. "Trust your elders. We may not be the strongest, but we know how—"

Hugging the buildings may not have been the best idea. A colossal crashed through from behind, letting out a deep roar. The impact sent David to the ground, breaking his crystal sphere, smacking his head upon the sands. If it were the jagged terrain of Terrangus or Mylor, he would be dead. *Note to self, bring the helmet next time.* He forced himself to rise, thankful his wobbly legs didn't give out from the added weight of his steel armor. The commotion alerted demons from all across the sands, who—other than the human thing—ignored the zephum stragglers to face the Guardians. With the building crumbled into rubble, there would be no protecting their flank.

Well, the plan was fucked.

Serenna must have been the first to rise; she was yelling out orders and casting shields. Hopefully, they were good orders, because David couldn't hear a damn thing with the ringing in his years.

"Fire!"

He could hear that. One of Bloom's detonators went off, way too close based on the surge of heat. His team... Serenna's team was yelling at each other, or the demons, or just in general. He was too old for these things now, but one advantage of being an engager: his priority never changed. David clutched his shield with both hands and rushed the colossal. Fortunately, it was smaller than average for a colossal. Unfortunately, it was still enormous.

Fight like Mary. Bend the knees, legs spaced apart, no slouching. Deflect attacks from an angle to minimize the force. Use their own momentum to bridge the size gap—

The colossal flung its fist down and roared. All the mental notes, training, and days getting beaten by Valor fled his mind. He dove to his left, taking an ugly fall from the weight of his armor. *Shit,* he thought, forcing himself to rise.

The colossal didn't follow through, instead rushing towards Robert, who was surrounded by a bright blue aura of frost. "No!" David yelled, running at the colossal. The demon didn't respond to his words, but it did respond when David slammed his shield into the back of its leg. It turned around and flung another fist down.

I will not fail you, Valor. He blocked, if one could call it that, meeting the fist with the very edge of his shield. David's crystal sphere shattered, but other than the burning pain in his wrists, he seemed okay.

The colossal flung its other arm wildly, getting a more direct blow to David's shield. The force knocked the wind out of him, sending him back-first into the sand. *How did Mary ever do this? I owe her a drink next time we…*

I will never see her again. Or Pyith. Or any of the others.

The colossal stood above him with its fist raised. David's team kept yelling, but their voices seemed far away. It was like…there was a rift between them. Those clinging to see tomorrow, and those yearning for one last stroll through yesterday. David smiled. He had always wanted to die smiling. His eyes closed as the fist came down.

A clang of cracked glass rattled him; he opened his eyes to see the realm in a dense platinum hue. Ah, Serenna. If she kept a tab for how many times she had saved him with a last second shield or barrier, it would be a debt no man could ever repay. The colossal's fist was pressed against his new crystal barrier; it stumbled back and roared as the barrier shattered into glass fragments a few moments later. With any luck, the impact broke its wrist.

"*David! Get up. This is your final chance,*" a woman's voice said through his thoughts. Not Valor but…

"Fear?" he asked with a weak snicker. "Have you come to say farewell? Despite everything, you were good to me when no one else cared. Thank you for that. May you one day find the peace I never could. May you one day find a goddess of your own."

"*I have lost an entire kingdom of those I loved. I will not lose you too. Rise and take my blade. I still lack the power to create a new Herald of Fear, but it will serve you well.*"

His right hand instinctively grasped the blade that materialized. If he was quick, he could rise, grab his shield, and re-engage the colossal with his new weapon. He could save himself, live to see tomorrow…

"No," David whispered. The sounds around him faded, as if his mind accepted his heart's decision. "I am no longer that man. Perhaps at one point, but not now. Can you read my fear?"

"Always, but I choose not to."

"Noelami, I don't want to fight anymore. I'm tired. So tired."

The colossal's fist came down, but David didn't close his eyes. It struck another platinum sphere as Serenna let out a cry from behind. "Let's go!" Zeen yelled, rushing in front of David with Bloom. While he couldn't follow the action from the ground, the yells and detonators were a sign they were still alive.

"Ice!" Bloom yelled, followed by a quick chill in the air. "Hey, Zeen, I froze the shoulder. Aim there!"

"I would, but I can't exactly fly. Can you target the arm—" A crawler's screech interrupted Zeen, loud enough to cover most of his cry, but not loud enough to cover his platinum sphere breaking. "Leave me! Protect Serenna! Bloom, No!"

Enough.

David rose, leaving his shield and grabbing his new sword. It pulsed in his hand, offering a mere drop of his old power. But he would take that drop and drown every demon in Vaynex. He pierced the crawler on top of Zeen from behind, then rushed over to the colossal. Its attention was still on Bloom, but that was about to change.

David stabbed it through the ankle, then tore the blade up to get all the leg he could reach. The demon roared in response, but David didn't flinch. He tore the blade out and rammed it through the other leg, tearing up with the same strategy. To his surprise, the colossal could still walk. It turned around and flung a desperate fist—

It was frozen, just like Melissa would have done. David slashed the frozen fist, shattering it as blood and flickers of ice flew past him. The colossal wailed, staggered back, then collapsed upon the sands.

"I don't deserve you," he whispered.

"Lean on me, David. In aiding in your wounds, perhaps I can finally lay mine to rest. We shall travel our journey of healing together."

Every journey of healing begins with one step. David picked up the shield and stepped forward.

CHAPTER 40

COLD TENACITY

erenna's trembling hand parted the hair from her eyes. Thank Valor's grace David had been able to slay that colossal. The demons on her own side had been destroyed, with no small thanks to Nyfe. "You were right," she whispered to Valor.

"*You mutter the words as if the outcome was unexpected. How many times will you doubt me, crystal girl?*"

"I doubt everything." And how could she not? It was all moving so fast. The night before Harbinger Nyfe had been wonderful, the first time she and Zeen had declared their love. No time for any of that today. Get up and go. This team was a battered mess before they had ever stepped foot into the portal.

"*Indeed, the feeling can be translated as a strength or a weakness depending on the variables. Now, compose yourself and move forth. The other goddess is already here. Keep a watchful eye on David.*"

She held back a sigh. There wasn't anything Serenna could do about Fear. Part of her hoped David would turn back into the deity's champion, if only to make their group more powerful. "David, before we continue, all is well?"

He simply nodded. She would have preferred a verbal

confirmation but there would always be that awkwardness of rank between the new leader addressing the old. *Will that be me one day? Taking orders from my student? I doubt it.*

My service only ends when I do.

"Fair enough," she said, refreshing everyone's crystal shields. "Now, we do it my way. Stay close and keep formation, we press forward in a straight line to the citadel. Our path shall be difficult, but nothing we cannot handle. This...is the finest Guardian team ever assembled. I trust each of you with my life. We do this not for Vaynex, not even for the realm, but for each other. No one else deserves it."

David took a moment to snicker, then continued forward after the rest nodded. His pace slowed as the hiss of crawlers amplified.

She refreshed everyone's shields and stepped behind Nyfe. It would never feel normal to trust him, but so far, the man, Vanguard, or whatever he was had been reliable. If this all was a trick by Arrogance, he could've murdered the team earlier. She held back the urge to stay near Zeen. David and Melissa had always kept their distance. Love is the most wonderful force in the realm, but the gift is often plagued with distraction.

Crawlers screeched and dove at the team from every direction. Serenna stood back-to-back with Five. Hopefully, the melee would perform their task without error. She had used too much power to save David—triggering another empowered form this early would make her woefully unprepared to face Tempest.

The Rinso-looking demon glared straight into her eyes from afar. While Serenna's team battled the crawlers, her focus was locked in on the human rushing forward. She immediately recognized the slim man with a tanned face, blue eyes, brown hair, average human-sized nose, and of course, ragged black armor.

By Valor's grace, it's really him. I hope Zeen can handle this.

Rinso thrust his glowing blade at David, who blocked with his shield and stepped back. Poor David likely had no idea what in the realm he was facing. She cast a new shield on him just in case, then created four tiny crystal spikes for support. All four launched at the same time, aimed at the head and upper body. To her surprise, two spikes were direct hits, sending the demon plummeting into the sands. That would never have worked on the true Rinso.

They're just demons. Compose yourself and destroy them all.

Serenna flinched as Nyfe jabbed his dagger into the neck of one of the Rinso things. Gods, it was the right thing to do, but it felt like blasphemy to watch her old nemesis murder her lover's hero. A roar went off as David rushed past her; he gripped his shield and engaged a colossal rushing towards Five. An enormous relief that David was back to normal. It was safe to assume Valor had spoken the truth, that Fear was with him, offering threats and demands. *Whatever you said to him, Goddess... Thank you.*

Grinning, she refreshed David and Bloom's crystal spheres. The two of them had excellent synergy despite their opposite demeanors. To be fair, there wasn't a human in the realm with more experience battling beside a mechanist. If Serenna kept them shielded, they could probably defeat it with just the two of them, allowing the others—

Nyfe's crystal shattered, leaving him vulnerable. The old Harbinger was surrounded by four crawlers, all waiting for the perfect moment to take him down. Serenna gripped the Wings of Mylor...then hesitated. It wouldn't be murder if she failed to save him. Right? If there was anyone in the realm that deserved to feel a crawler's blade in their back, it was Nyfe. Just thinking about the man tightened Serenna's grip on her staff. *I won't do it. Not because I need you. Not because Valor would disapprove.*

To become your enemy is to accept they have destroyed you.

She refreshed Nyfe's crystal sphere, which cracked when the crawlers jumped him at the same time. For all his faults, Nyfe was perceptive enough to slay the crawlers one-by-one with his glass blade. An odd thing, to watch her enemy battle her enemy...

"Forgive me," Five said, glowing with a yellow aura. "I had a clear shot to save him and held back. I have never hated a man with such fury. It has...altered me."

Oh, how I understand but... Serenna shook her head. "Hatred changes all of us but always remember that it's an optional burden. Hesitate again and you are no longer a Guardian. Am I clear?"

"Yes, Lady Serenna." Five broke eye contact and stepped away, then resumed his yellow glow. As if to prove his loyalty, he blasted the closest crawler to Nyfe.

"Was I too harsh?" she whispered. Battles always came down to lies. Serenna would never reveal she had the same hesitations. In the war against Terrangus, she had lied every morning to say victory would soon be theirs. Every evening, she had reinforced the disproven lie with a new one. Power and deception had paved her road to leadership.

"Never confound harshness for cruelty. We never learn the cost of our words until it is too late. Every Guardian has their own unique threshold. Be wary of how much water is chosen to punish those already drowning."

Ugh. Serenna gripped her staff and refreshed David and Bloom's crystal spheres. *Am I losing myself? If Valor of all people suggests I should tone it down...* "Robert?" she said, but he didn't respond. Her voice must not have carried through the chaos of battle. Surely, he wouldn't have ignored her.

Focus. Don't waste this advantage. With David and Bloom controlling their side, Serenna crafted a large crystal spike to hover in front of her. It was truly bizarre to watch Nyfe dodge and counter the colossal's blows. Had Arrogance amplified his skills? Or was he the same man she had battled in Terrangus and Mylor—

"Launch it now!" Nyfe yelled in his real voice.

That voice...

She staggered back, tensing her shoulders to regain control of the crystal spike. Serenna pointed the Wings of Mylor forward and launched the spike, aimed at the colossal's upper-chest. The blow was perfect, but no joy or relief followed. That voice. That *fucking* voice. She crafted a new spike, larger than the first, and hovered it in the air. Nyfe met her eyes. The mail shielded his face, but she swore he was grinning. It would happen again. Nyfe would kill her, kill Zeen, kill them all. A gust of wind blew her hair to the side. There was a chill with the sun nearly all the way down, but the burning sensation in her body amplified.

"Master Serenna?"

"Boss, you good?"

She flinched as a hand eased to her shoulder. How much time had passed? "Hold," David said. "We need him for Tempest. Don't waste any advantage in battle, no matter the circumstance. *Please.*"

The way he had said 'please' brought the rage down. She took a deep breath, letting the spike fall to the sands. "I wasn't going to do it."

David grinned. "Do you remember our first time here? What was it...nine years ago? I asked if you were afraid. Foolish question in hindsight, what eighteen-year-old wouldn't be? Your words said no, but your eyes begged to go home. Your eyes begged to be spared from life as a Guardian. Some days, most days, I wish I did. I wish for things...that will never come to pass. Serenna, you are the closest thing to a daughter I have ever known. Lie to yourself if you must, but not me." He walked away and left Serenna standing there, dizzy, sweat dripping down her forehead.

I love you, David, she thought, but couldn't say out loud. The anxiety of being loved was worse than anything Nyfe could do. Daughter? *Daughter?* Of course she would've done it. She would have launched that spike right through his heart. "Well fought, Guardians," she said, brushing the hair and sweat from her face. Not the most original of words, but anything to break the silence. "Resume formation until we reach the citadel. David will enter first, with myself and Five following last. I will not lie to you. I have no idea what to expect once we enter that fortress. Harbingers of Death are terrible, *terrible* adversaries. Do not rely on my shields for survival. Awareness is a Guardian's greatest protector." *I should end with an inspirational quote. Something… um…what to say?* Nothing came. Nothing had always been the default response to problems without answers.

"A peculiar speech. Perhaps I misjudged you, crystal girl. You lead with a cold tenacity I cannot help but admire."

Great. Silence would have to do. Serenna could keep them alive, but perhaps every man is responsible for their own inspiration.

CHAPTER 41

A SHADOW OF SOMETHING BEAUTIFUL

een took a deep breath before entering the Vaynex citadel. He had been here frequently in the past few weeks, but as he stepped over the body of a dead zephum, it was like entering a nightmare for the first time. A few of the candles were lit, while a dark glow from the throne illuminated the entire hall. All the things he never wanted to see were in perfect view. Fallen bodies, crawlers skittering on the painted ceilings, and...*that* demon. Rinso the Blue. Nyfe was here too—somehow, as a Guardian.

Serenna met his eyes and refreshed his crystal shield. She didn't smile, and neither did he. Not much to smile about these days, though he would've leapt for joy if Serenna had launched that spike through Nyfe's head. The fact that she had even considered it was the only thing keeping him from a panic attack.

"Welcome, to the eye of the storm," a voice called out from the back of the citadel. It wasn't a yell, but the force vibrated through the halls, echoing over and over. Tempest's voice. The tone and professional demeanor was there if you listened, but it was barely a whisper compared to the layers of hatred drowning out everything peaceful. *"Gaze upon the remnants of my empire. Isn't it glorious?"*

Rinso demons and crawlers surrounded the team as they drifted forward, illuminated by Serenna's faint platinum glow. *"Why the rush? Take a moment to appreciate the true glory of my people. All these zephum painted upon the walls, immortalized for their contributions to violence. Care to guess who isn't represented? Try Yorga Womptor, Matriarch of the Womptor clan. Her contributions to medicine was one of the only reasons mixing the clans did not lead to disease and famine. Yet, no painting, no statue. The worship of honor delegates their entire purpose obsolete. Or, in some cases, in my case... irrelevant."*

"Surely, I was never so insufferable," Nyfe said. His voice sounded more like his Terrangus days as general and less like the weird, monotone Vanguard people. Why was he here? Sure the Harbinger had arrived with no warning, but couldn't Serenna have recruited someone else? *Anyone* else? What had she even done while Zeen recovered...

Stop it. She read and watched over me every day. In reality, our situation is my fault. It's like her father said, if I just went ahead and died, none of this would be an issue. There would be an unstoppable Guardian team, led by the perfect woman with nothing holding her back. There wouldn't be a Harbinger Tempest. "Shut the fuck up," Zeen said, glaring at Nyfe—

One of the crawlers dove at Zeen. Before he could plant his foot to swing Hope, Nyfe rushed upfront and stabbed the crawler through the chest. *Damn, he's fast.* "Nyfe, what are you even doing here?"

Nyfe didn't look in his direction. He kept his blade forward and scanned the citadel for more enemies. "I already told you. Nyfe is no more. The entity before you is Vanguard Omega."

"So that's it?" Zeen said, stepping up to him. "Your name changes and all is forgiven? You killed me. Get that through your fucking skull. You *killed* me—"

David grabbed Zeen and pulled him back. "Now is not the

time." And that was all it took. Something about those eyes. For all of Zeen's pain, David had suffered through a loss that would always go unspoken.

"Fine," Zeen said, nudging David's hand away.

Harbinger Tempest rose and stepped forward. He was much taller than Zeen remembered, or perhaps the ethereal wings that sprouted from his shoulders gave him more of a presence. His giant sword looked familiar… Ah. It was Sardonyx's blade. Tempest held it forward with one hand like it was weightless. "I must admit, power has given me clarity. I spent all those years trying to improve the existence of a people better left forgotten. It's all irrelevant now. Humans, zephum, gods, *all of it!* Time must cease to exist. The flow of eternity evaporating into the tranquil haze of nonexistence. My final contribution to the realm."

"Stand down!" Zeen yelled. He immediately regretted it, but…this was Tempest. His friend. How did they ever get to this point? "Tempest, I mean, come on. There must be a way to fix all this. Um, look at Nyfe! If he changed back so could you. It…doesn't have to end this way." Zeen felt Serenna's melting glare but refused to meet it.

Tempest erupted in a surge or dark energy, his blade glowing with an ebony force pulsing from the steel. Everyone shivered; the summer heat was no match for the chill of death. "I was born to be a storm. You say it doesn't have to end this way. And yet, here we are. I will grant you a quick death. A pity you will never see a realm without Time. I think…you would enjoy it more than anyone."

Serenna erupted in platinum energy before Zeen could respond. "Stop speaking to him. No demon has ever been slain by words. David, Bloom, you two are on Tempest. Zeen, Nyfe, defend me and Five from the demons. Go."

With Nyfe? Was she nuts? "Put me on Tempest. I know him better than anyone else here. Perhaps I can—"

"That is precisely why you are on demons. Do not question me, Zeen. If you have any respect for me at all, follow your orders and keep me alive."

Fine. What an unfair response, as if he could refuse. He charged a crawler instead of letting it come to him. Let Nyfe handle the Rinso demons. Zeen was stressed enough without having to kill the friend he had never met. A sloppy swing tore a crawler in two, but opened Zeen up to a counter on his left side. His crystal absorbed the brunt of the claws, illuminating his view with a large crack before going lucid. *Relax, take a deep breath. Rage is the quickest path to the grave.*

He took a deep breath and swiped at the closest crawler, ensuring not to tense as the blade pierced its armored skin. Act like water. The expected counter came from his right side; he ducked with a grin before slashing Hope through its chest. Zeen resisted the urge to check how his team was faring against Tempest. Between David and Bloom, they would hold their own—

Zeen shifted his feet to parry a sword swing. All the relaxation and confidence shattered as Rinso pressed his blade and stared into Zeen. Its expression was pure…emptiness. No thrill of battle, no fear of meeting the end. This wasn't the man who had defeated Rensen the Red, defeated Warlord Vehemence, and finally won the heart of Olivia.

You aren't Rinso. Rinso lives in my heart, alongside the zephum who created him. Goodbye, old friend. Hope pierced its chest, and the demon fell to the ground without a change in its expression. Not even its eyes closed—

A shrieking Nyfe flew above Zeen's head and broke his focus. Damn. Despite how much he hated the man, that unfortunately meant the colossal was now Zeen's responsibility.

Nyfe crashed to the ground with a loud groan, then eased himself up. "Stay behind me," Zeen said. *Did I really just say that?* "Take a minute to compose yourself while I distract the colossal. I trust you can handle the other demons in the meantime?" Hopefully, Nyfe's groan meant 'yes.'

Each step towards the colossal brought a sliver of doubt. Zeen had never fared well against these things though, to be fair, most people don't. *Distract and dodge.* He did a quick slice at its leg, keeping his distance to maintain enough room to dodge the upcoming counter. As usual, the stupid beast slammed its fist down from above. A mixed bag with those attacks: they were relatively easy to dodge, but one mistake would leave a splattered Zeen on the citadel ground—

A blast of void energy from Tempest's blade shattered Zeen's crystal and set him off-balance. An awkward misstep tripped him up; he started to fall at the same time the colossal's other fist came down. Nyfe tackled him from the opposite direction, avoiding the blow, but giving them a rocky tumble next to a dead zephum. The shock of it made Zeen force himself up, followed by pure agony in his right ankle.

"Just like the old days, right Zeen?" Nyfe said, staggering for a moment before regaining his battle stance. "I guess now instead of butchering Mylor soldiers, it's demons. Honestly, they all look the same to me."

Zeen glared at him, clutching Hope. "So you're back? This whole Vanguard thing was a lie?"

"No lies unfortunately, just delusions layered upon delusions by a god somehow more unhinged than Death. The more of a beating I take, the less I feel his control. With the way Serenna delays my shields, I'll be busted up in no time." Nyfe snickered as a new crystal shield surrounded him. "Oh, I spoke too soon. Let's go." He rushed in without clarifying how exactly they were to 'go.'

It was nearly tragic how well Zeen and Nyfe could work together. A small part of him—a part he hated—was thrilled to battle alongside his former general. Nyfe and Zeen had killed countless soldiers all over the realm. They had been called heroes, but one kingdom's savior is another's butcher.

"Zeen!" Serenna yelled. "You're on Tempest. Now!" Crawlers jabbed at her platinum barrier while she shielded David again. Trickles of blood poured from her eyes as she fell to her knees. To be honest, Zeen never understood how crystal magic worked, but it didn't take a sorcerer to know blood flowing from the eyes was a bad sign.

Orders be damned, Zeen rushed the crawlers by her barrier first. They were too slow to react; no demon in the realm would keep him from protecting his lover. He cut through them like they were nothing.

An exhausted Serenna met his eyes. "Zeen... Thank you... Now, please go," she whispered, rising and refreshing his crystal shield. Perhaps she understood. Love was the most powerful force in the realm. It outranked orders, judgment...everything. It was distracting of course, but only in the way that its sheer wonder meant nothing else could compare.

The distraction faded as David lay on the ground, clutching his shield and the odd-looking sword. He was panting in the way men did when a lack of air was the least of their worries. "Bloom requires aid," David said. "Everything is...falling apart."

Zeen grabbed his hand. It felt so light, despite the steel armor. "Leave it to me. I'll make you proud."

"I'm too old for pride," David said, pulling him in before he could leave. "Slay the Harbinger. Succeed where I have failed. You and Serenna...even Francis and Mary. It's the only thing that matters..." Zeen nodded, though he had no idea what David meant. He must have taken a hard fall.

When both Serenna and David give a command, it must

be obeyed. Zeen gripped Hope, approaching Tempest, taking a deep breath. It was like the final act of a dream that wouldn't end, similar to when Rinso had approached his brother Rensen for the final blow. A shame to battle inside a fortress. None of the rain and gusty winds, none of the stormy clouds to emphasize the doubt smothering from within. The paintings were epic, but no art could ever rival the beauty of a natural rain—

"Do something you fuck!" Bloom yelled, throwing a fire detonator to knock Tempest back. Blood flowed down her snout, with her left arm shaking awkwardly.

How long did I stall? Probably too long, so he rushed Tempest's side and did a quick swing. Surprisingly, Hope went unblocked, getting a clean slash across Tempest's upper shoulder. *Did I really just wound Tempest?* There was an opportunity to bring his blade down for a cross slash, but Zeen hesitated. *Harbinger or not, this is my friend. I swore to the God of Strength I would watch over him. I was given a chance to return to the realm, to make everything right…*

And it's never been worse.

"Boss, he's just standing there. By Strength's balls make him do something!"

Fine. Zeen closed his eyes and swung down, a tactic that had never worked in his days at war. The heart doesn't require vision to acknowledge a dreadful truth. He opened his eyes as a sharp pain shot through his hands. Tempest parried the strike, then swung his blade right at Zeen's head.

Zeen ducked under the near-fatal blow and stepped back; he gripped Hope and took a deep breath. *Tempest would kill me. Just like that, no hesitation or warning.* "You must fight this, Tempest! What would Rinso say if he could see you now?"

To his surprise, Tempest sighed. "Creativity must yield to destruction. I don't hear his voice any longer. I don't feel his struggles or comprehend his pain. Rinso was merely a shadow of something beautiful. I was born to be a storm. All that matters now is removing Time from our realm. You could join me, Zeen. Take out Serenna, and the rest will fall."

The Tempest he knew was gone. Truly gone. "Sorry, old friend. If any part of you still remains, please know I take no joy in this." After a fire detonator took Tempest off balance, Zeen rushed in and got a quick swipe through his neck. The blow would have ended anything mortal, but just as with Harbinger Nyfe, dark streams flowed into the wound, mending it in an instant. Zeen and Bloom rushed in with an unspoken synergy; they swung their weapons—

Tempest roared and unleashed a nova of void energy. It shattered both their shields and launched them to the ground. Zeen took a bad landing on his head; a high-pitched ringing drowned out all sounds while his vision shifted everything back into place, revealing Tempest manifesting a blast of void power.

It should have been easier to get up and dodge, but everything was so weak. He eased himself up as the blast soared in his direction. His wounded ankle gave up after putting too much weight on it; he fell to one knee and glanced at Serenna, silently hoping for a last second shield. That seemed unlikely as a pair of Rinsos broke through her barrier, rushing to take jabs at her crystal sphere. Nyfe and Five were taking the crawlers closest to themselves, while Serenna swiftly crafted tiny crystal spikes and launched them through her attackers.

David stepped in front of Zeen, taking the void blast with the center of his shield. The shield exploded in a flash of platinum energy after the block, then David muttered what sounded like an expletive and drew his sword. "Bloom," he said, "prevent Serenna from getting overrun. Zeen and I will handle this one."

I hope we can, Zeen thought, easing forward with Hope drawn. "What's the plan?"

"Plan? If you continue to hold back, Serenna will die. If that's not enough…then you are not the man I thought you were." David rushed in and swung wildly. He moved much slower than Zeen remembered, with none of the skill or patience of the man who had out-dueled him in Terrangus.

I'm not holding back. Am I? Hmm. If I even have to ask, I have my answer. Zeen rushed in beside David and…well, swung wildly. Tempest wielded the wrath of a Harbinger, but the zephum had never been much of a swordsman.

Tempest parried David and pushed him back to the ground, allowing Zeen to get a brutal slash all the way from his upper leg through his face. *No hesitation,* Zeen thought, coming down the opposite way, cringing as his blade ripped into scaly flesh. *No hesitation.* He spun and swung his sword, tearing open Tempest's throat. Seething void energy entered the wound, a bright ebony glow that obscured Zeen's vision.

It didn't matter. Instincts from facing demons and zephum guided his hands to blow after blow. Tempest erupted again into a blast of void energy. Zeen planted both feet, ignoring the pain in his wounded ankle. Physical pain is temporary. The pain of dying in Serenna's arms, of failing to uphold a god's sacrifice, was true pain.

I don't want this pain anymore.

The Harbinger swung his glowing sword, again at the head. Zeen dodged and stepped forward, slashing his blade into the zephum's leg to break his balance. Zephum warriors had always been large, strong—and laughably predictable. As expected, with his leg wounded, Tempest swung his sword in a desperate swing that missed.

I just want to be happy.

Zeen had killed nearly a hundred of these things in the Koulva mines. What was one more? With the zephum off-balance, Zeen thrust his sword through its neck. It cried out, with less energy coming to mend the cut. All the void energy in the realm wouldn't save this monster. Zeen slashed by the elbow, down by the knees, all the spots considered 'dishonorable' by people who spoke of war but had never seen one.

Bloodlust invaded his vision and he welcomed it. It was the only way to survive. He thrust his sword through the demon's chest and pushed down, using rage to force his sword through. Why was this thing still alive? Tearing into the heart would silence it...

Tempest gasped from the ground, with the void energy dissipating off his body. He gazed at Zeen not in hatred, nor fear but...in gratitude? "I suppose...I was never much of a storm," Tempest said with a weak chuckle. "I'm glad it's you. Watch over my people, Zeen. Give them the dream, not the maelstrom."

Zeen's rage faded, leaving him alone with the truth. He had become a monster, a fragment of a past best forgotten. "Tempest... Why? It was never supposed to be this way."

"And yet, here we are. Finish it, Zeen. You have my blessing to send me to whatever life comes after this nightmare."

"No." He let go of his sword and reached out his hand. There was good somewhere in Tempest. If Nyfe could be saved, it would be terrible not to—

Zeen staggered back as two crystal spikes pierced Tempest's neck. Then another. Then one more. "*Stop!*" he yelled, but it was too late. Tempest could barely groan before he closed his eyes one last time.

Serenna limped over with fatigue and blood filling her face. "It is done," she said, then drove the Wings of Mylor into the ground and leaned against it. "The realm lives to see another day. We won..."

Zeen could barely breathe. His friend lay there motionless, a final testament to the God of Strength, gone forever. *I swore to you. I swore to you!* He rose and approached Serenna. She had a faint smile, but the sentiment would not be returned. "How dare you? We could've saved him. All you had to do was trust me. You never trust me."

Serenna's smile had long faded. "Are you mad? Have you learned nothing from last time?"

"I swore to the God of Strength I would watch over Tempest. My word means nothing now. I didn't even get a chance to try…"

"You're a fucking idiot," Bloom said, spitting out blood. "No wonder Sardonyx favored you. Let's get out of here. This place is gonna be pure anarchy once they realize the Harbinger is slain."

Zeen's trembling hand gripped Hope. The name felt like a mockery. "No one leaves until we bring his body to the Valley of Remembrance. It's the least…the only thing we can do. Serenna, I can't do this alone."

"You can't do it *at all*. It's pure mayhem out there. We need to get back and mend our wounds. I… Enough words. We leave *now*. If you choose not to follow, you are no longer a Guardian."

What would Rinso do? I suppose it doesn't matter anymore. Maybe it never did. Zeen turned to the empty spot behind the throne where Strength had used to stand. Honor is a difficult emotion to describe, but the shame of its absence holds an overwhelming dread. "Whatever. You win."

Serenna didn't bother to respond. Did she truly care so little for him? After everything they had shared—

Wisdom appeared in the middle of the citadel. He waved a spectral hand, then Nyfe and Five collapsed to the ground, shaking. "I have come to reclaim my toys! You have my gratitude for watching over them so admirably. Pardon me for a hasty exit, but it seems my goddess colleagues are here as well. Too many grouchy, immortal women in the same fortress does not bode well for anyone... Particularly *me*." He created a platinum-tinted portal. "Say farewell, Omega!"

"Help me," Nyfe said. All the cracks and missing pieces of his helmet revealed a genuine frown. "I'm trying to do better. I did my part and saved the realm. Please, someone help me."

"You are beyond redemption," Serenna said. She glanced at Wisdom and gripped her staff, but David eased a hand to her shoulder and whispered something that made her retreat. She sighed and turned to Five in pure exhaustion. "As for you, Robert, you will always hold my respect. Our paths will cross again. Hopefully, on the same side."

Five's dissociated expression didn't even flinch. He walked into the portal without words, followed by a screaming Nyfe. Wisdom chuckled before the portal faded.

The rest staggered over to the Guardian room portal, accompanied by an awkward silence. There are few things worse than a hollow victory. Serenna sent everyone through to Mylor until it was just the two of them remaining. The pale glow of the portal's energy seemed so unwelcoming.

"What are you waiting for?" Serenna asked.

"Send me home."

"It's already triggered to Mylor. I'll meet you right after."

"I said home."

There was an agonizing pause as she let the portal drop, leaving the two of them with nothing but the crackling of forgotten torches. *I love you, but I need some time alone to process today.*

The portal erupted into an ebony glow. Zeen glanced at her, unable to decipher the blank expression on her face. Maybe she had an inner conflict of her own, but it was impossible to tell. There are moments where we can literally feel the regret manifesting itself for later.

Zeen stepped into the portal, knowing this was one of them.

CHAPTER 42

BORN TO BE A STORM

A faint gust of wind blew across Tempest's snout. His eyes opened, gazing towards an orange-tinted sky. Tall blades of grass surrounded him on all sides. He attempted to wiggle his arms, legs, tail, anything really, but nothing responded. A unicorn galloped up to him, then leaned down and licked his face. Warm, sticky saliva quickly replaced the numbness. Ah, the Great Plains in the Sky. He had ventured to this realm several times with Father and Pyith, always enamored by how the god of a warful people favored such a peaceful setting.

Rather strange to be here; he had assumed the end of Strength meant the end of the Plains. Feelings gradually returned as the sun beat down. Normally, it would have been uncomfortable, but any feeling unrelated to Death was a blessing. Tempest was again Tempest. Whatever that meant. A failed warlord's son, a failed scholar, a failure in all things. Still, it was a familiar failure, and for that, he was grateful. He forced himself up and hugged the unicorn. The majestic being looked familiar, but he couldn't place it—

A zephum in a rocking chair was in the far distance. Odd, it looked nothing like the fallen god. "Strength...you live? Is that truly you?" The wonder of it all took his weakness away as he limped forward.

"Guess again, my son. I must concede, these chairs are rather comfortable. Perhaps honor and luxury can coexist. Sometimes."

"Dad? I…I dare not beg for unwarranted forgiveness, but I am sorry. Oh, I am sorry, Father. Please…"

Tempest's unicorn and two others approached Sardonyx and neighed in anger. They stood on their hind legs and hounded the once-warlord. "Blasted beasts! Stop your nonsense!" he said, waving them off to gallop away. "The unicorns do not favor me! I suspect their reasoning, but they should maintain honor in the presence of a *god*."

Clarity faded from Tempest. He stood within the Plains, feeling like someone had bashed him in the head. "A god? Are you the next God of Strength?"

"Ha! The Time Wizard offered me the role, though I refused. You would have enjoyed him. He spoke in riddles, using complex words where a simple one would suffice. No, my son. I demanded my ascension based on one criteria alone. The aspect I favor among all else. The God…of *Tradition!*" Sardonyx waved a hand, creating a second rocking chair next to him.

"I suppose the title suits you," Tempest said, taking the empty chair. It was exactly the same as the one from his study. "Dad, there are no descriptions, complex or simple, that describe…you know. The words have always eluded me, but I love—"

"Shh. We are not here for that. Farewells are done with glory and honor! Now tell me: you ended *Rinso - Volume Three* on a rather bizarre note. What does volume four have in store for our human?"

Ah, farewells. There is no coming back for me. Bless him for not offering. "I have an idea but, I'm conflicted on the ending. I wanted Rinso and Olivia to die in each other's arms, standing in defiance against the God of Death. In the end, they didn't win. They couldn't win, and that was the beauty of it! To stand against the inevitable and just…fight! To die with honor!" He nearly laughed at the absurdity. To defy zephum culture all his life just to force it upon his creations. We become our family. The trauma, the fury…the *glory*. We never escape, though, after a while, that becomes more of a blessing than a curse.

Except of course, when it's far too late.

"Absolutely not!" Sardonyx yelled, slamming his fist on the armrest. "You must give your audience a happy ending."

"But, Father, they don't often exist."

Sardonyx smiled, rocking back in his chair. "That is precisely why. The artist must bare their story like a blade, creating hope where it cannot exist, creating strength for those who cannot wield it."

Where had this zephum been all his life? A terrible silence followed his father's words. They both rocked in their chairs, gazing out towards hazy fields of regret. "Warlord…Dad, I really am sorry. Everything happened too quickly. I wish I could go back and just—"

Tradition did not budge. Did not falter. "Tell me about Rinso and Olivia. Describe to me how they defeat Death. Spare no details! I want to know every sword thrust, every pang, every drop of sweat and blood. Even the dishonorable crystal shields! A pity you chose a sorceress for his mate. Rinso needed a powerful shield woman with honor in her blood! One who… Tell me how it ends. From the beginning."

Tempest paused. For all his time with Rinso, he had never imagined a happy ending. "Well, I suppose if they were to battle Death, they would enlist the aid of Warlord Hyphermlo. The Gods know he owes them a favor after book two. Maybe I could find a way to bring Cympha back, or better yet, I wouldn't kill her at all. She deserves to live on…"

He flinched as his vision blurred. It wasn't that his body was tired, but it begged for a different sort of rest. "So, the four of them step into the void. I would spend about three pages describing how dark the darkness was, then make Rinso explain the temperature, to ensure the reader understood he was cold. It only makes sense if he's cold. A shiver, a quiver, a vibration even. I always found it interesting that we associate fear with cold. I wonder if that's related to Boulom? Well, as I was saying, our heroes would enter the void. Rinso would shiver from the cold. I would ensure to really emphasize just how cold it was…"

Tempest went numb as he continued speaking. If the wind was still blowing, it made no sound or chill. Darkness encroached his vision as he forced the words out. They stopped making sense, but speaking was the only way to ensure he still existed. Ah, it would all be over soon. Tempest's end may not have been honorable or glorious, but the embrace of Sardonyx's unspoken love brought him the tranquility he had always yearned for. *I was born to be a storm. How I wish it never came to pass.*

May you find me, Pyith, wherever storms go when the sun returns and the clouds fade.

CHAPTER 43

MOUNTAINS

David took a deep breath after entering the portal to Mylor. His body was barely holding it together, but clinging to the lie of composure would uphold the illusion that he still deserved to be a Guardian. Perhaps he did mentally, but physically, those days were over. His legs seethed with each step; the thrill of victory was no match for the soreness in his lower back. Forcing heavy armor on the old man had not been a wise idea. *Wherever you are, Melissa, I hope you're laughing.*

Serenna materialized, with a mixture of blood and sweat dripping from her hair. The classic signs of fatigue were all visible: dark circles under the eyes, hunched composure, walking like a drunk, but there was something else... Anger or fear? Ah, defeat. It would surely explain why Zeen hadn't followed. Stupid, stupid, boy. All those lessons only to learn nothing. At least no one was foolish enough to ask the obvious question—

"Zeen's not coming?" asked Bloom.

After an awkward pause, Serenna sighed and said, "Payment will be delayed until a new warlord is crowned. Even then, I cannot guarantee their cooperation. You are both dismissed, but if you wish to stay in Mylor, my kingdom welcomes you."

Any sane person would've taken the hint and shut up but, of course, Bloom snickered and said, "Ah, that's too bad. It's always best to fuck right after a battle. On that note: I don't suppose there are any other zephum here?"

"Bloom. Walk with me," David said, meeting Serenna's glance for an instant. Her words were silent as usual, but her eyes whispered, *Thank you.*

"Where are we going? If you have a stash of zephum ale send it my way. Everything here tastes like piss."

"Be that as it may, it's still better than anything from Terrangus. I always wondered: do your people actually enjoy zephum ale?"

"We enjoy what it does to our senses." They paused as they entered the Mylor banquet hall. A group of people cheered at their arrival. Senator Morgan stood with a laugh, finished his entire chalice of wine, then fell face-first into the table. What a useless senator. His last name was more powerful than any shield Serenna could ever cast.

"These moments aren't for me," David said. "I'll be in the gardens if you grow bored of humans telling you how great you are."

"Fuck 'em. Lead the way."

David nodded, then approached Morgan's table. So many words, so many voices, questions, statements, a cacophony of empty thanks from every direction. Apparently, his time as the champion of Fear was forgiven. People tend to ignore the past when the future needs fixing. He grabbed a full decanter of wine and walked away, ignoring them all.

"Reminds me of the first Harbinger I saw in Vaynex," Bloom said, following David through the corridors. She peered at the paintings on the pale walls, seemingly amused by the exaggerations. "It just pissed me off so much. My people always spoke about honor and glory, but I saw them run when the demons came. When I say run, I mean they fucking bolted. Now, I won't tell you honor is a lie, but I will say they stick the word in their sheath and make believe it's a sword."

David snickered as they entered the gardens... Damn. Serenna was already there, leaning over the balcony while she gazed upon the mountains. To his surprise, Serenna smiled as they approached, then she walked away without a word. *We are invading her peace...*

"... So I mean, yeah, it never made sense after that. At least I was born a mechanist. Imagine if a fucker like Dubnok could throw detonators? One of these days, I'll manage to trigger them with just thoughts like your mate could. Nearly blew my snout off practicing."

By Fear's mercy, she just keeps talking. "Tell me what you see," David said, leaning against the balcony.

"Huh? Oh great. You're going Sardonyx on me. Just mountains, Boss. No matter how badly we yearn to see something else, it's just a pile of rocks. Go ahead and tell me I'm wrong."

David smiled, then handed Bloom the decanter of wine. "You're not. That's the beauty of perspective. Serenna spent her whole life in this kingdom. Those mountains represent consistency. Her life changed when I invited her to the Guardians. Her life changed when Terrangus invaded her home. Her life changed today...and will continue to do so. But not those mountains. No matter how hard the realm drags her down, there will always be peace in that view. It will outlive us all."

Bloom took a deep chug and wiped her snout. "I just don't see it. If it makes you feel better, I can lie and call them honorable piles of stone, gifted from the God of Strength himself. You don't really buy this stuff do you? As far as I remember, Terrangus has no mountains."

"My mountains were a woman. My mountains now are the memories of that woman. No matter how far I fell, I was just David to her, free of all the flaws I wore like armor. She walked my entire journey with me, from a young man, to a bold man, to a tired one. It's cruel that I remain... And yet, I must. I will not leave this realm until I am worthy of the mountain she saw in me."

A few moments passed as David sighed. Bloom held the decanter out. "Care for a swig?"

"Tempting, but a pain that is constantly numbed is a pain that will never heal." The sword from Fear radiated inside his sheath with a comforting energy. It was about as close to a hug as he could hope for.

CHAPTER 44

PAIN IS STRONG, BUT NOT INVINCIBLE

 groggy Zeen held the bottle to his mouth in his old Terrangus barracks, forcing out the last remnants of wine. It had been two weeks since the defeat of Harbinger Tempest. Two weeks of squalor and regret. Serenna had never come, but this shame wasn't hers. She had never accepted a god's promise, only to fail so badly Tempest became a monster…a Harbinger.

Maybe Serenna finally realized she could do better. The more he drank, the more that thought made sense. No wonder David drank so much. Now, there was a man who understood the realm. Pain is strong, but not invincible. Just keep numbing it. Numb everything—

A knock at the door? No one had visited in quite a while. Vanguard after Vanguard had come the first two or three days to check on him, but after Zeen had drunkenly insulted one of their mothers, they left him alone.

As did everyone else.

Zeen staggered over to the door. He had no idea what time it was, but it was definitely too early or late. Standing outside the open door was something that should not have existed. Maybe it was time to stop drinking. Maybe tomorrow.

"Rinso?" Zeen asked, his mouth stuck open.

"Indeed, it is I!" Rinso said. It was clearly Sardonyx's voice, but he faked an accent, which sounded like someone who had never been to Terrangus before. "I have come to help my fellow human! May I enter?"

"Um…sure. Let me just, um, move some bottles around."

Rinso stormed in and rubbed his chin, nodding his head in clear disapproval. He dropped the accent entirely when he said, "There is no honor in this! How could you ever defeat Warlord Vehemence in such a pitiful state?"

Whew, Zeen had a lot of questions. He had never believed in ghosts, but one stood in his chambers, berating him in the voice of a fallen friend. "But I'm not Rinso. I am unworthy of the name."

"That changes *now*." Rinso or whatever it was threw a pile of papers on his table. He knocked the empty bottles to the ground and placed a quill pen and ink on the cleared spot. "You have my blessing to give him a glorious end."

Zeen couldn't stop himself from laughing. "Are you mad? I don't even know where to begin. I am a terrible storyteller."

"Hmm! That never stopped my son."

"Sardonyx, what is going on here? What are you?"

A bright red flash filled the room as Rinso changed into Sardonyx. "A friend. Take a bath and find some honorable clothes. It is long overdue that Rinso embraces Olivia."

"No." The word rushed out before Zeen could think of anything else. Serenna couldn't see him like this. Maybe she believed he was doing great and not…whatever the opposite of great was.

"I never asked when I was warlord, and I do not intend to ask as a god. Bathe! Wash away your shame and dishonor!"

"Fine. Give me um…an hour or so and I'll be ready."

"I'm not leaving until you are clean," he said, waving a

hand and filling the empty bath with water. There were very few things Zeen could think of more scary than Sardonyx with magic. Hmm. There was no steam coming from the water.

Zeen gasped as he put his hand in. "By the gods! Can you at least make it warm?"

"You must earn the warmth! Freeze, and consider why am I here today."

Zeen took off his shirt and waited for Sardonyx to turn away. When he didn't, Zeen stripped and entered the water. He held back a scream as the freezing water consumed him. Actually, it was almost pleasant to feel something again.

Almost.

After the bath, he scanned his mess of a room for clothes. Everything was strung out and wrinkled, and now that he was clean, the unfortunate odors of his room made themselves known. *None of this will do…*

"Here," Sardonyx said, handing him a brand-new pair of black leather pants and armor. "I even added the *flying rat* on the shoulder. Your mate will be pleased."

I sure hope so. "Thank you, Warlord—"

"*God.*"

"Yes, sorry. God…are you not angry with me? I mean, I failed Strength and Tempest completely."

Sardonyx scoffed, turning away with his hands behind his back. "You recall the mantra: Strength without honor—is chaos. I spoke the words my entire life, never bothering to wonder what they meant. My chaos was shrouded in anger, an anger that cost me everything. Finish volume four…for me, if no one else. Make it a glorious ending."

I think it's time to escape my own chaos. "You have my word."

"I know. I love you, Zeen. You are just *awful* at saving people, but by Strength's name, never stop trying. Meet me outside the barracks when you are prepared. Do not linger."

I love you too. Zeen nodded at the fading Sardonyx. Odd, he expected the new god to open a portal or something the way Wisdom could.

*

Whew, it felt good to step outside. The sun was nearly all the way down, giving way to the gentle chill from the Terrangus breeze. Too bad there wasn't any rain. It would have felt nice to tilt his head back and let it tap on his face—

Sardonyx rode a giant unicorn from the skies. It had white hair, a platinum horn, and enormous crimson wings that made a loud whoosh as they flapped. Terrangus city folk fled for their lives screaming, allowing Sardonyx to land in front of Zeen and let out a mighty guffaw.

"Behold! A mighty steed worthy of a god!" He reached out his hand and pulled Zeen onto the unicorn behind him. "Hold on tight, Human Warlord. We ride to Mylor!"

Zeen had always dreamed of riding a unicorn out into the Terrangus storm break, but this was not what he had in mind.

CHAPTER 45

SWORDS AND EYES

ou have it ready?" Serenna asked her father in a hushed voice. "I haven't felt Valor's presence since the Harbinger, but I do believe she is still within Mylor. It would be simply wonderful if we could pull this off without her knowledge."

"Yes, dear," Charles said. "As we speak, my men are placing it on the wall opposite your bedroom. I always wondered why that spot was so empty. Figured my predecessor pawned whatever was there to pay off a mistress or something."

"Hush!" she said, giving him a gentle smack. "Landon's here. Wait for me in your office."

Landon entered the gardens; he bowed to Charles, then hugged Serenna. "My lord. Guardian Serenna."

"Please don't call him that," Serenna said, then turned to Father. That was his cue to leave, which he took. "How is he?"

Landon paused. Each moment of silence answered her question. "The Vanguards have ignored him for now, but I worry they will act once the riots stop. Only time I see him leave the room is to pick up more booze. I know you hate hearing this but...go to him. Every man has a point of no return."

Damn you, Zeen. Damn you. "Your concern is noted."

"Right. Same time tomorrow then?"

"Yes, but while you're here, why not stay a while? I have someone I would love for you to meet."

"Girl, I'll stick around, but don't expect me to marry some Mylor floozy. You young ones have no respect for commitment."

Serenna sighed. "Not that sort of meeting. Oh, Landon. I am certain you will be pleased. I cannot wait!"

*

An hour passed. It felt longer, but Landon had reminded Serenna many times he wasted an hour standing in the gardens. "I must get home. Isabella is cooking tonight and she's the only granddaughter who can make something other than beef stew."

"Wait," Serenna said, grabbing him by the arm. "Enough time has passed! Smile, Landon. Scowls are not the protocol of Valor." She dragged him through the corridors, ignoring his whining. They stopped outside her door, gazing at the portrait shrouded in a giant cloth.

Landon probably wouldn't recognize Valor. He knew Everleigh the mortal, and not the platinum-haired angel wielding a scythe. Still, how often do we meet our heroes? "Art? You brought me here for art? Listen, girl, if I miss dinner for this, you will rue the day!"

"Valor!" Serenna yelled, erupting in her platinum form. Most of the onlookers cheered in awe, but Landon just sighed. She loved him all the more for his indifference.

"Not bad, Guardian," Landon said, "but your aura will never match the intensity of—"

Everleigh, the Goddess of Valor, appeared in the room, wielding her scythe, drowning the room in pale energy. She gazed upon them, judging them all, then stopped at the shrouded portrait. With a wave of her hands the shroud vanished, revealing Guardian Everleigh's portrait. Similar to Serenna's, it revealed her in *very* tight leather armor. But this was worse. Far worse. The armor only covered her intimate areas, leaving the vast majority of her skin exposed to swords and eyes. No dignified warrior would ever wear such nonsense.

"Impossible... Everleigh? *The* Everleigh?" asked Landon, cautiously stepping forward. "Mom?"

Valor turned away from the portrait, and to Landon. "I...was too afraid to check. By Noelami's grace, is that you, Little Landy? My goodness! You have grown into an old man!"

To Serenna's shock, Landon fell to his knees. The old man gazed upon Valor as if she were the most precious thing in the realm. "Mother? You're a goddess! I always knew you couldn't die! You were too damned angry to ever give death the time of day. I have little ones now, with little ones of their own. The Bennet line has persevered."

Everleigh and Landon embraced, to cheers from the soldiers surrounding the portrait that apparently no one cared about. *Mom? No wonder he loved her so much. I suppose the realm makes...just a little more sense now.* No need to interrupt a happy moment. Serenna began to walk towards the corridors...

"Go to the gardens, crystal child," Valor said, giving her a quick glance. "You will never wield my scythe but you will always wield my gratitude... And respect. Your happiness is en route, escorted by a lizard-god and a flying horse."

That was about the strangest thing Serenna had ever heard. She nodded, then left the room. To her relief, no one followed, apparently enamored by the giant angel hugging an old man. Ah, to be forgotten. Ignored, even. *Should I visit Zeen? He clearly needs me but...I don't want to discuss Vaynex. It was not worth the risk with all the chaos. Somewhere, deep down, he must know that...*

Unless I'm wrong.

She sighed as she entered the gardens. There was an odd…something in the far distance but her mountains remained, as they always did. She couldn't explain why, but the view brought her peace. The mountains had become the friend she always needed. Never judged her like David and Valor. Never made naive demands like Zeen. The mountains stood far away, offering their silent thanks in place of a realm that never loved her.

Hmm? The distant object was moving closer. A demon? She grabbed her staff and stared it down. Whatever it was had wings and a glowing red aura. A coward's tactic, to invade during an intimate moment. Let her people celebrate. This demon would be slain before any of them ever knew it existed.

She paused, squinting. A unicorn? A *flying* unicorn? That couldn't be right. More bizarre was the fact two riders were on the steed, one zephum, and a human…

Zeen? My love, what have you done?

The unicorn landed in the gardens, crushing her lilies. It neighed gloriously and rose on two feet, sending both riders to the ground.

"Sardonyx, you're alive? What sorcery is this?"

"Not sorcery…but *tradition!*" Something was different about the warlord. He had an aura of sorts, a red haze that followed as he stepped on *more* of her lilies.

Hmm. A lizard-god and a flying horse. That means… "You're a god now?"

Sardonyx smiled as he climbed back onto his unicorn. He winked, then rode off into the Mylor dusk without a word. Apparently, that meant 'yes.'

"Hey," Zeen said, easing himself off the ground. Dark circles hung below his tired eyes, but a pleasant lavender scent clung to him.

"Hey." All the anger and regret faded as they met eyes. A

year ago, she would've killed for this moment. A year had come, and the only thing dead was her ability to resist. *Is saving face really worth it? Should I just apologize?*

"Do you still love me?" Zeen asked, taking light steps forward.

She grabbed him and pulled him in. It was more of a stranglehold than an embrace. She held back a scream as his arms wrapped around her. She said nothing. Foolish questions do not require answers.

Tears are not the protocol of Valor, but streams of joy flowed from her eyes.

EPILOGUE

HEAVEN

tanding within his private chambers—which, right now, were *very* un-private—Francis forced himself to breathe. Let it be known that medical textbooks fail to adequately describe the horrors of childbirth. Perhaps 'horrors' was not the correct word, but the act had provided images that would forever haunt his nightmares. By Wisdom's glory…whew. Just whew.

"My lord," one of his Vanguards said from behind. "It would appear Eltune Dubnok has indeed secured the Vaynex throne as warlord. Our first pair of ambassadors were slain before they managed to reach the citadel entrance. What are your orders?"

"Go away." Francis waved him off, easing towards Mary and their child, as slowly as possible. These could be his final moments alone. Would his mind rot without solitude? Would he…

Baby Calvin, a little bundle of perfection, screamed in her arms. It sounded like pain. Why was his son in pain? If the healing mages had made any errors, their entire families would burn until their screams tore open the sky.

No one will ever harm this child. My son will laugh and frolic within the fields of Serenity, never knowing anxiety, pain, regret…anything.

"Congratulations!" one of the mages yelled, slapping him on the back. A chorus of cheers followed, nearly sending Francis to his knees from the wall of sound closing in on him.

Why congratulate me? All I did was help create the child which, to be honest, was rather pleasant. Look at her… She's a mother. An empress. I have stalled long enough. We will marry as soon as possible and solidify the Haide family.

"Silence!" Francis yelled. "Your off-pitch cacophony is distressing the child. It's time for peace. Leave us. And…thank you." Too many people, too many emotions. Normally, one would rise up and dominate them all—usually anger or fear—but everything rushed to his mind at once. Noise. Distraction. Chaos. Love. A child should be raised in silence. That was how Francis had been raised, and he turned out perfectly fine.

They left, leaving the two…three of them. "Emperor, do you wish to see your son?" asked Mary, rocking little Calvin.

"Please don't call me that. Not today. Let me just be Francis."

"How about Father?"

"Daddy," Francis said, easing forward. It was like walking towards the void. "I called mine Daddy. He loved me. He hated everything else but I swear he loved me. I think…other than you…he was the only one. Perhaps I wouldn't have been me if…me was…I was…you know."

Mary smiled. "You're perfect just the way you are. Would you like to hold him?"

Calvin kept screaming. He screamed and screamed, clearly out of abhorrence for his broken father. He *knew*. Children and dogs can always tell when their owner is a fraud. They lack the elegance of words to explain why, but they always know.

"May I?"

"Of course." Mary lifted the child to Francis, who picked him up.

Back in the days of Boulom, the presence of gods was still uncertain. People had no choice but to cling to faith, creating abstract beliefs such as heaven and hell to justify praying to the skies. Hell always made sense. Pain was easy to describe, easy to use as a threat for good behavior. But heaven? *Heaven?* What mind could conceive such a concept? Every man's paradise is a unique and intimate dream. One that never comes true.

But as Francis held Calvin in his arms, he understood the inspiration of heaven. His son stopped screaming, smiling at his father, unknowing or uncaring of all his flaws.

"*What a precious little boy,*" Wisdom's voice said through his thoughts. "*Remember this moment. Remember that smile every time you falter, every time you mistake mercy with ignorance. Give him paradise. Give him Serenity. The alternative? Well, you're an intelligent man.*

"*Use your imagination.*"

For as long as Francis could remember, he had always wondered how much a person could be damaged before they were considered broken. The cracks had seemed to widen since wielding his staff but, perhaps broken was his role now. Some of the most beautiful things to exist only do so with the protection of monstrosities.

As long as he provided Serenity for his son, let him break.

MEET THE AUTHOR

Timothy Wolff lives in Long Island, New York, and holds a master's degree in economics and a career in finance. Such a life has taught him the price of everything but the value of nothing. He enjoys pizza bagels, scotch, karaoke, oxford commas, and spending the day with family and friends. The obvious culmination of the past 36 years was to write a 400+ page fantasy novel where a drunk teams up with a swordsman, two mages, and lizard-people to oppose god. Why do we write these in the third person?

Strength without honor—is chaos!

He can be reached at:

@TimWolffAuthor on Twitter, X, or whatever the hell the site is called by the time this book is published.

Timwolffauthor on Instagram/Threads

timwolffauthor@gmail.com

THANKS AND ACKNOWLEDGEMENTS

First and foremost: to anyone still reading at this point, I thank you beyond words. The first draft for the final book, Age of Arrogance is nearly complete. I'm aiming for a July/August 2024 release depending on availabilities.

First thanks have to go to my immediate family. Both of my parents have been extremely supportive, despite not being fantasy fans in the slightest. My brother though, when I handed him Platinum Tinted Darkness, looked at it and said, "Four hundred pages? I'm not reading this shit." True to his word, he did not read that shit.

I severely underestimated how much I would enjoy social media. I won't name names, since I absolutely dread missing someone and being a jerk, but the entire Fantasy Indie community is amazing. Additional thanks to my beta readers, Amber Lilyquist and J. Flowers-Olnowich. Jonathan Oliver is my editor, and I fully recommend him to anyone considering writing. It's always a joy to hop on a zoom call with an industry professional, who politely nudges you out of terrible mistakes.

An enormous thanks to my cover artist Alejandro Colucci for bringing the image of Tempest Claw to life. I really can't get over how well he takes my wacky descriptions and turns them into something amazing.

Milton Keynes UK
Ingram Content Group UK Ltd.
UKHW010900081223
434021UK00001B/31